The Fur, Fish, Flea and Beagle Club

R. M. Byrd

This is a work of fiction. Names, characters, places, and
incidents either are products of the author's imagination
or are used fictitiously. Any resemblance to actual events,
business establishments, locales or persons, living or
dead, is purely coincidental.

Front cover photo by the author

Back cover photo by Catherine Littrell

Though John Adams said 'the scholar is always made alone', no book is written in a vacuum. I owe great debt to a great many people, most of whom out of space constraints must remain unnamed, but I must thank my mother Joanne Byrd from whom I got my love of books and literature, my dear friends at the Geneva Writers' Group of Geneva, Switzerland (particularly the genius of Susan Tiberghien) in whose company I first thought of myself as a writer, and last but not least I must thank my wife Kate, without whose love and support this book would never have happened.

Contents

Chapter 1

The Arrival

The boy was fourteen and his life hung on the twilight edge between the anxious ignorance of childhood and a manhood that wished part of what it knew could somehow not be true.

Jamie sweltered on the front screen porch of his home, stretched out in overalls across a double chair swing. One foot dangled to touch the floorboards for an occasional push. His fingers scratched the ears of his dog Toby, who panted beneath soaking cool from the floorboards. He held 'The Adventures of Robinson Crusoe' upright on his stomach.

Normally after Sunday dinner his father slept on the porch glider, newspaper spread forgotten across his lap, faithfully keeping the Lord's commandment about holy rest. That meant Jamie could read without interruption.

But today Jamie's eyes could not settle on the words, distracted by a pickup's dust cloud churning up the long lane leading to the family farm.

Nor was his father stretched out on the glider. Grant Garrath stood in the shade under the oak and maple trees in front of the house and watched the same as his son. He gripped his hands behind his back and rearranged the dirt under his feet.

The approaching dust cloud was the pickup truck of Gil Custis, who ran the hardware store in town. Gil was delivering a package. The package was Ned, his own only son.

"Jamie! Jamie Garrath!" His father's no-nonsense voice.

Jamie closed his book, laid it on the floor and looked at Toby. Toby jumped up, his tongue dripping out of the side of his mouth.

1

"It's time, huh?" The split oak seat creaked as Jamie pushed up and off the swing. "Time to meet the mischief, as Daddy says."

Toby trotted over to the screen door, nails clicking on the gray painted wood.

His father called out again.

"Comin'!" Jamie yelled back, both to his father and to Toby, who wagged his entire body. "You're a lot more enthusiastic than you oughta be, y'know." He pushed open the wooden screen door against the squeal of the rusty spring and Toby leapt out.

The dusty rooster tail coming up the lane grew until Jamie could pick out the bright green of the pickup with low varnished sideboards and hear the grind of gears Mr. Custis never seemed able to find.

As Jamie walked up his father glanced backwards at him, shifted his felt fedora brim even with his eyes and flexed his fists behind his back. Jamie stood a little behind and gripped his hands the same.

The pickup truck slid to a stop and the dust cloud blew right on past. The deep-throbbing engine died.

His father raised one open hand in greeting. "Hello, Gil."

The truck door cried a tight creak as Mr. Custis pushed it open. It struck Jamie as odd the door should creak. The truck was only four years old, a '32 Ford Model B with 'Custis Hardware' freshly painted on the side.

"What say, Grant." Mr. Custis looked in the back of the truck. "Come on down, boy."

Jamie spotted Ned sitting in the back of the pickup peering over the edge of the sideboards. He knew Ned from school but had never talked with him much because Ned was a little different and tended to keep to himself.

Ned climbed out of the back of the pickup and pulled his flat newsboy cap off his head. The boy's black hair stood straight up like a scrub brush. He slapped at the dust on his clothes with his cap, then walked up behind Mr. Custis, eyes down. His hands stuffed deep into his pockets and stretched his braces tight. Jamie blinked. Only grown men wore braces. Beneath the dust, Ned's jeans were new deep blue with a three inch wide light blue roll up at the bottom. His shoes were polished shiny brown. His shirt buttoned up to the top despite the heat and he stood there still as a stump with his eyes on the dirt.

"Ned, stand up straight." Jamie watched Mr. Custis grip Ned's shoulder. "Like you been raised right, so folks will know you're somebody." Mr. Custis looked up at Jamie's father. "We 'preciate you doin' this, Grant. We sure do."

Jamie could not take his eyes off of Ned and his shiny shoes while his father and Mr. Custis talked over their heads.

"Jamie? Wake up, boy, I'm talking to you."

"Sir?" Jamie jerked out of staring.

"Take Ned and show him around the place while Gil and I have a talk. We'll carry his things inside."

Jamie squinted up at his father and then back at Ned, whose black eyes had lifted to look back. "Yessir."

His father and Mr. Custis moved off. "Now Grant, I'm just sure this'll be good for the boy. It'll be good for both boys, I know it will …"

Mr. Custis' jaw-flapping faded from earshot and was cut off by the screen door slam and left Jamie standing in the dust with Ned. Toby came up behind Jamie and leaned his neck against Jamie's leg.

Ned stood quiet, stillness in his eyes like a Doberman puppy Jamie had seen one time. Puppies are supposed to jump around or slobber smiles and want to play. That dog had just laid there with its muzzle down on crossed front paws watching and looking around at everybody like they were meat, right in the eye. That just wasn't natural. For a dog or a boy.

"Hi."

"Hey."

Toby quit leaning on Jamie, lazy-walked over to Ned and shoved his nose up under Ned's hand. That got a smile.

"Nice fella." Ned rubbed Toby's head and scratched behind his ears. "What's his name?"

"Toby." Jamie looked at Ned's hand on Toby's head. "He's mine."

The smile faded. Ned lifted his hand from Toby's head and folded both hands under his arms. "All right."

"Aw, dammit. You can pet him. He likes you; that must mean you're okay. He can sniff out an asshole quicker than spit flyin' in a windstorm."

Jamie saw Ned's eyebrows push down.

"You want to help with the milking?"

"You got cows?"

"No, we milk dung-beetles, whaddya think?"

No response.

" 'Course we got cows. Well, one milk cow. She's a good ol' gal. Gives more milk than we can drink."

The slap bang of the screen door caught Jamie's ear and he turned and watched his mother pace over toward them. Her arms were crossed.

Jamie had long since documented his mother's pattern of warning signs leading up to the point of peril as a matter of self-preservation. Crossed arms meant she was not to be challenged, no matter how gentle the tone. If one was so unwise as to ignore the first sign, she uncrossed her arms, put hands on hips and leaned her head a little to the side. If one extended their lack of wisdom to pure foolishness, the third and final signal was her hands on her hips shifted into fists, coupled with a slight lift of her chin and shoulders.

She stopped beside them and smiled at Jamie. "Why don't you get Ned to help you with the milking?" She looked over toward Ned. "It's about that time."

Toby leapt to his feet and bounded off toward the milking shed.

Jamie knew all right. Milking had been his job ever since he had been old enough to get his hand around a teat. He also knew milking one cow was a one-man job.

"All right." Jamie jerked his head. "Come on."

4

The boy followed him without a word around to the back porch and into the kitchen to get the clean milk bucket with its close fitting lid. Jamie half filled the bucket with warm water from the reservoir in the side of the cook stove, grabbed the small milking pot, and then headed back out the back door with Ned in tow.

"Watch you don't let the screen door slam. Momma and Daddy hate it." Jamie let the door fly back as Ned came through.

Jamie glanced backwards over his shoulder as he trotted toward the milking shed. Ned followed behind, still looking down at the dirt, this time with hands shoved so far down into his pants that his elbows were straight.

"If you don't watch it, you're gonna shove your pants off."

The little Jersey cow was already slowly walking spraddle-legged across the pasture toward the milking stall for her evening feed and pressure relief. Toby drove her along, prancing, head up; all slobber smiles and tail swishing straight up in the air.

"Your cow got a name?"

"Yeah." Jamie winced. "Elspeth."

"You're kidding."

"I wish I wasn't. My little sister Gloria named her. She can't even say it without shooting spit like a scattergun since she lost her front teeth. 'Course she calls the screen door the 'scream' door too, so it's not like she's walkin' around with a good grip."

Jamie stepped inside the shed and set the milking bucket down on the floor. When he turned to let the little jersey in he saw Ned standing next to the gate in a staring contest with the cow.

"What?"

Ned looked over at Jamie, back to Elspeth, then blinked back to Jamie. He quirked a smile. "She looks a lot like my grandmother."

Jamie burst out laughing.

Ned did not smile back. "Honest to God. Don't' tell anybody I said so." Ned looked back at the cow. "Gramma's even a redhead."

Sure enough, the cow's topknot was dark auburn.

5

"You know, I've been wanting another name for her." Jamie faced the cow. "Elspeth, I hereby absolve you of the burden of your name." He made a cross in the air in front of her face. "I hereby dub thee 'Gramma', a name more fitting with your character and station in life."

The newly re-dubbed 'Gramma' flicked her ears and flapped her tail across her rump at buzzing horseflies in complete indifference to her increased status. She mooed her impatience to get into the milking stall.

"She don't look too impressed, Ned."

Ned nodded. "It's what Grandmother's best at."

"What's that?"

"Not being impressed."

Jamie opened the gate to the stall. "Come on, Gramma. Let's relieve your hunger and suffering."

He dumped grain into the feed bin at the end of the milking stall, slid a wooden bar behind Gramma to hold her in, then sat on the milking stool and washed her heavy bag with the warm water. He looked back over his shoulder at Ned, who leaned up against the shed wall and brushed dirt off of his new dark blue jeans. He followed the creases with his fingers.

"You wanna try?"

Ned looked up at Jamie and then at Gramma's bag. "Okay, sure."

"Grab the other stool." Jamie shifted a little to one side. "See first you gotta wrap your thumb and first finger around the top of the teat, see? That shuts off the flow of milk back up into the bag. Then you squeeze down with your other fingers like this." As Jamie demonstrated a strong stream of milk squirted out and hit the side of the milking pot. "When the little pot is full you dump it into the pail."

"That's all there is to it?"

"Just keep doing it with both hands 'til there ain't no more milk."

The first couple of tries went awry; one even squirted onto Ned's shiny shoes, but to Jamie's surprise, the town boy showed a remarkable talent for milking. Once he got the hang of it he filled the small pot with milk and dumped it into the bucket with surprising regularity.

"Hey, I kinda like this."

"No accounting for taste. The novelty will soon pall, I guarantee."

At that moment a train whistle blew. Gramma lifted her head out of the trough and moaned a little moo.

"There a train landing near here?"

"There's a crossing." He watched Toby push his nose up against Ned's face. "There's one comes by mid morning too. The train's got to slow down to a crawl through here because of the steep grade, but ever since somebody got hit a year or so ago they've gotta give a blast to make sure nobody wanders out on the track. Farmers been complaining about the noise for a coon's age but it ain't done any good."

"Who was it?"

"There wasn't enough left of him to tell, but they think it was just a tramp."

The streams hitting the side of milking pot stopped for a minute. "I wonder if his family knows what happened to him."

"The only thing he had on him was a watch with 'HH' engraved on the inside. Not a lot to go on."

"They might be hunting for him."

"Likely he didn't have much family, if any. Or they didn't care much about him."

Jamie watched Ned shake his head as the streams started again. "No. His family's looking for him."

Toby ambled to the corner of the shed. He plumped down on the straw and panted a little moaning woof up at Jamie.

"How long do you keep this up?"

"Until the milk gives out. Your hands gettin' tired? I can take over if they are."

"I'm all right. I was just wondering."

Jamie shifted his stool and leaned against the wall. "I don't mean to be nosy, well maybe I do, but what are you here for, exactly? I mean other than to work at Daddy's sawmill?"

Ned lifted his shoulders and let them fall again, his eyes fixed on what he was doing. "Don't know. Pop said I needed to work at something different for a while."

"Different from what?"

Again the shoulder lift.

Jamie sniffed and rubbed his nose on his sleeve. There'd be time.

"I think she's done."

Jamie pushed his way forward. "Here, let me at her for a minute."

They switched places and Jamie felt Ned's eyes on him as he pinched each teat between his thumb and index finger and stripped the last little bit of milk. Then Jamie stood up, cleared out the milking pot and the bucket and released the bar that kept Gramma in the stall. Gramma didn't move.

"What's wrong with her?"

"Nothin'. She's just asleep. She does that sometimes."

Now Jamie felt Ned's eyes boring at him for real.

"Look, just 'cause I didn't grow up in the country is no reason for you to make fun of me."

"What are you talking about?"

"She can't be asleep. She's standing up."

"Oh yeah, she can. Cows sleep that way."

"Come on."

"Pass your hand in front of her face."

Ned stepped forward and waved his hand right in front of her eyes. "Damn. She's dead asleep."

Jamie laughed air out of his nose. "You must have the magic touch. Come on, Gramma." Jamie slapped the little Jersey on her rump. "Let's go." She started and backed out of the stall, a lot calmer than when she walked in.

Jamie heard a clank, a curse and a splash behind him. He turned and saw Ned with the bucket in his hand and terror on his face. Fully half the milk from the bucket soaked into the dirt floor. The other half soaked the legs of Ned's brand new jeans deep blue and reflected white on the toes of both of his shiny black shoes.

"You must not'a held your mouth right."

Ned waved his free hand in the air and stared down at himself. "What am I gonna do?"

"It's not like we need the milk, we usually got to give some away, but Momma's gonna have a hoppin' hissy fit with a tail on it when finds out she's gotta wash clothes tonight."

"Tonight?"

"Sure. Matter of fact, it's gotta be done right now. If it's not th' milk'll sour in the cloth and you'll never get the smell out."

Jamie was rewarded by pure dread on Ned's face.

"Come on."

As he led Ned back to the house, Jamie listened to heavy depressed thumping steps behind him and grinned in the gathering twilight.

Chapter 2

A Nodding Acquaintance

Jamie's eyes jolted open. Outside the open window, the starter in his father's pickup ground and bullied the engine to life. He pushed up to look out the window and saw the back of the battered square cab turn away out of the yard and out of view as its tires rasped on the hard-pack sand.

Throwing back his sheet, Jamie shoved out of bed, slapped his feet to the floor and immediately turned under a toe. He bit his lip to force back the forbidden four-letter curse until the pain faded, then deliberately hiss-whispered the word anyway. He grabbed and stepped into his overalls, heaved them on and promptly got one foot jammed in the leg. He hopped, jerked harder, tottered against the bedpost and almost fell before his foot finally came free. He elbowed the straps on over his bare shoulders, spit further forbidden words under his breath and limped barefoot to the kitchen.

His mother glanced up from sliding a piece of split oak into the stove when he appeared at the kitchen door. "Decide to get up, did you?"

Jamie leaned in the doorway and rubbed his foot. "It seemed like a good idea at the time." He yawned.

"Cover your mouth when you do that." His mother warped a smile. "Why don't you pour yourself a glass of milk?" The cast iron frying pan scraped the black stovetop as she slid it into place. She laid down strips of streaky lean bacon.

Jamie grabbed a glass from the cupboard shelf and opened the icebox. "Where'd Daddy go?"

"Just to Silerville to get a few things. Don't worry, he won't leave you behind. He needs you at the mill."

Jamie studied the bottom of his glass then hefted the white enamel milk pitcher and poured. "Does he need Ned too?"

Bacon sputtered in the pan and his mother scraped at it with a wooden spatula. "Now, that's a good question, Jamie. I think the answer is yes." She pursed her lips. "But I think a better question might be 'Does Ned need the mill?' "

Jamie looked up.

His mother raised her eyebrows. "Um-hmm. I think the answer is yes, but I couldn't put my finger as to exactly why. The Lord just works … "

Jamie gulped his milk and nodded. " … in mysterious ways. Yes Momma, I know."

"It's true. And don't slurp and close that icebox."

He pushed the thick door on the icebox closed until it clicked. "I just wish somebody would figure out a different way to say it. I've heard that one to death."

His mother put one hand on her hip and pointed the spatula at him. "For that, young man, and for letting Ned spill milk all over, you just put that down and go get some more from Elspeth."

"Aw, Momma. It's not like I told him to. It was an accident. Not my fault his daddy read him the riot act."

"If we hadn't been there he'd probably have gotten the belt, you know that, don't you?"

Jamie stared at the floor.

"Go on now."

"Yes ma'am." Jamie hitched his thumbs in his overall straps, slumped onto the porch and slid into his boots. He grabbed the milk bucket and banged through the screen door. Toby bounded up, bounced against his hand for a quick rub and twisted away again, flying in his dancing run. "That's right, boy. Go get her; go get Elspeth." Jamie swung the bucket around stiff-armed in a circle as he walked. He thought of yanking on his little sister's short leash about the name change and his face tightened into a grin as he stepped up to the milking shed. " 'Gramma' it is."

The grin lasted till he got back and saw Ned at the table, collar buttoned up tight, shoveling eggs into his face like there was no tomorrow.

Jamie lifted the milk bucket on the counter with both hands and made a bee line straight for the bacon on his plate.

"Jamie?" His mother's gaze dipped to his hands and back up to his face.

"Yes ma'am." Jamie rolled his eyes and head and stepped back out onto the porch to wash up. He took the Mason jar of water that sat to the side and poured it down the top of the pitcher pump to prime it while he pumped on the handle. Cold, cold water splashed into the basin underneath. He pumped the jar full of water again, set it back to its place beside the pump, then dipped his hands into the basin and splashed his face. He wiped his hands on his overalls.

As Jamie came back inside he saw his mother spoon scrambled eggs on top of the bacon on his plate. Ned leaned back and gulped the last of his milk.

Jamie drew back his chair, landed in his seat and crammed food into his mouth. The thick bacon was strong salt on his tongue.

By the time he looked up his mother's hands were buried in soapy water in the dish pan. "Why don't you two get fishing poles and go get us a mess of fish for dinner?"

"What about getting in the eggs?"

Jamie watched his mother smile down, then glance over her shoulder at him. "I'll get Gloria to do that. You two just go on now."

Jamie pushed back from the table and took a single step toward the door. "You sure I can't stay and watch when you tell her she's actually gotta work?" His little sister was not a person who liked doing anything that got her anywhere close to a farm animal, particularly chickens and their associated ick.

His mother straightened and her voice dropped half an octave. "Go. Right now." She pointed one soapy hand at Ned. "You too. Go on, get out from under my skirts; I got things to do. And don't let the screen door slam on your way out."

Jamie only paused to lean and whisper in Ned's ear. "Come on while we got the chance." He grabbed his straw hat off the back porch nail and was out the screen door before his mother could change her mind. He heard Ned's boots clump and the screen door slam behind him. Toby danced to greet them then ran straight to Ned.

"Hold up a minute." Jamie stepped inside the backyard shed, his boots scraping on the worn wooden floor. He reached up to the hooks on the low rafters for two fishing poles, but his hand paused and he took down only one. He grabbed the bait can from the high shelf, the little trench spade from the corner and dashed back outside.

Jamie led out of the yard, through the garden and toward the cow pasture at a trot. Toby leapt forward and wormed his way under the gate. Jamie stopped to open it and held it for Ned.

"Close it behind you, we don't want Gramma to get out."

He glanced back once over his shoulder to make sure Ned dropped the latch then trotted down the narrow brown path that curved down the hill toward the woods across morning-wet grass. He stopped where Toby lay panting, waiting for them at a spreading mulberry tree in the pasture just short of the woods.

Ned followed, gasping a little. "Where are we going? What's here?" Ned leaned on his knees and his braces bit into his shoulders. He stood back up and pushed his newsboy cap back off his forehead. "What are we stopping for?"

Jamie glanced at Ned's work boots. They gleamed fresh polished brown. Jamie shook his head, laid his pole down and drove the little spade with the cross t-handle into the cool bare earth under the tree. He felt Ned's eyes push on him as he lifted little spade-fulls and gently pawed through the dark dirt for worms. "This the best place in three counties for bait. Not only for night crawlers," he held up one dangling squirming worm longer than his hand and dropped it in the can, "but these too." He dug a little deeper then held out his palm to show Ned three little gray-white balls rolled up trying to hide. "Grubs."

"Fish like those, do they?"

"The night crawlers are the best for perch but when a bass decides to hit a grub … you've just never felt anything like it."

Ned nodded.

When Jamie had a dozen or so he scooped a little fresh dirt in the can and covered the dirt with a big handful of grass. He scraped the dirt pile back into the hole with the little spade then pressed it back down with his foot. He stuck the little spade in the earth. "Don't let me forget to pick up the shovel on the way back. Daddy'll have my hide if I forget it."

"I've never seen one like it."

"It's a trench shovel. Daddy traded a vet a bushel of sweet corn for it."

"Was it used in the war?"

"I guess. He never said."

Their expedition fortified, they climbed the wooden fence ladder over the barb wire fence next to the woods while Toby again squirmed underneath. Jamie led Ned down the path through the trees toward his favorite fishing hole, the old grist mill pond that everybody called Little Lake.

Jamie tramped along the path just on the back edge of a trot, focused on the dappled light that flowed down through the pines to the path beneath his feet. If they didn't get to the water before the air heated up, the fish would drive to the bottom and refuse to bite.

They approached a long turn in the path where it broke from the woods and crossed the dirt road that led to the saw mill. Across the road they could see the Widow Morrison's house in its little copse of Chinaberry trees and carefully manicured Cape Jasmine bushes. Jamie was watching the ground for trip roots when he felt a tug on the back of his shirt. "Hey, hold up a minute."

Jamie turned to see Toby push against Ned's legs. "What? You can't be tired already."

Ned reached down to stroke Toby's neck and shook his head. "No." He nodded toward the Widow's house. "What's he doin'?"

"Who?" Jamie looked around.

"Him." Ned lifted two fingers in the direction of the Widow's house. "The way he's leaning on her mailbox. Is he drunk or something?"

Jamie's eyes followed Ned's fingers to see the mailman standing beside his truck and leaning on one elbow on the Widow Morrison's mailbox.

Nathan Ichabod Hindmarsh Norris loved being the mailman. His public nickname was Nod, due to his habit of bouncing his head up and down when on the receiving end of gossip. He was tall and thin with a narrow head and a nose so large his head looked like a triangular stone hatchet. When gossip was particularly juicy, Nod got to going like a woodpecker. Jamie had thought it highly likely more than once that Nod was going to bounce the boogers right out of his nose. His daily appointed rounds were his perfect excuse to wander all over town wedging that nose into everybody's business but his own. That peculiar brand of personal drive in a town as small as Miller's Landing is always unpleasant, but to make matters worse, Nod was not overly particular about what information he chose to collect and subsequently disseminate. Quantity, not quality was his measure and primary stock in trade. There is a saying that the vast majority of everything known is trash. Another saying states that a man is the sum total of all he knows. One time Jamie's father told him that to squeeze those two sayings together went a long way toward understanding Nod Norris. Jamie never found out what his mother thought. She had been too busy coughing behind her hand while his father deliberately took a slow puff on one of his infrequent cigars.

Nod also made it his special responsibility to squeal on any boy doing anything remotely nefarious within reach of his black ball-bearing eyes and wing-nut ears. What was not known was conjectured and reported as fact. Jamie himself had his hide tanned for snitching watermelons from Mr. Thomas' garden though he had no hand in it. No matter that he had gotten away with putting banana peels in mailboxes the week before, a single miscarriage of justice was more than enough for Norris to be seen as malevolent enemy.

15

"He don't look drunk." Jamie watched the man ease letters one by one out of the Widow Morrison's open mailbox as he leaned his elbow on it. Nod's hatchet face was not pointing down at the box where his business was supposed to be, but weaved back and forth toward the sheer linen curtains in the widow's upstairs windows.

Ned whispered behind his ear. "Damn if he ain't doin' a 'Peeping Tom'. Big as all daylights, right in front of God and everybody."

"Come on, we gotta move." Jamie tugged at Ned's sleeve. "If he sees us stopped right here he'll know we're lookin' at him."

Their boots padded on pine straw then ground on dirt as they crossed the road toward the path to Little Lake.

Out of the corner of his eye Jamie saw Norris' nose jerk swivel and a flutter of letters to the ground. The man stooped to pick them up, straightened, stretched his long neck, hitched his bag on his shoulder and stepped back to his mail truck.

Jamie stopped behind the first tree after they crossed the road and peered back. "He looks about smart as dirt and half as graceful." Nod lifted the widow's letters to his nose. "Did you see that?"

"Yeah, well. Maybe he likes the smell of paper. Why else would you be a mailman?"

Jamie shook his head. "He ought not to be doin' that."

Ned chuckled. "I don't see why you're so bothered. It's not like it's something we wouldn't do if we ever got the chance. 'C'ept the sniffing part. That's just peculiar."

Jamie turned, started down the path again and looked to the ground as he walked. "Maybe, but it ain't right Nod doin' it. This is my patch of dirt. He ain't supposed to be here, so if there's peekin' to be done ..."

Jamie no longer heard footsteps behind him so he stopped and turned around. Ned stood still in the middle of the path. Toby sat on the path beside Ned, looking up at him.

"What?"

"Why don't we play a trick on him?"

Jamie sidled back up the path. "What kind of trick?"

"You know, like rocks in his hubcaps or something."

"How about a couple of dead perch on his engine block? Or we could put Wandering Tom in the mailbox."

"Wandering Tim?"

"No, Wanderin' Tom. Meanest, nastiest tom cat around. He's been yelled at, shot at and chased with dogs. Some even tried poison."

"Oh yeah?" Ned smiled. "Oh, yeah."

Jamie ram-rodded his finger straight at Ned. "Whoa, hold on there, that was a joke. I don't want to tangle with Old Tom either."

"Could we catch him?"

"I ... I don't know. He's always looking for food. The widow probably feeds him; she's soft in the head that way. A rabbit box trap mebbe, but I don't know how to make one."

Ned lifted his shoulders once. "It just sounded like something we could do." He pushed past Jamie and started down the trail.

Now it was Jamie that stood still. The idea grabbed him like a cat clinging to a branch over a barking dog and he felt a slow grin gradually grow on his face. "Once we built the thing," he twisted around toward Ned's receding back, "how could we tell if it was Tom in there or a rabbit or an honest-to-god-stink-up-the-world skunk? 'Cause I don't want no part of no polecat."

Ned stopped and swiveled back around.

Jamie stared at nothing, talking to himself. "We could put a little window in it ... make it out of screen wire. The other problem is ... we just lower the lid down on the widow's mailbox, set the rabbit box up on the open lid, slide up the box gate, shake it a little and he's in there."

"Jamie, for a church boy you've got some ideas." Ned grinned. "Let's build ourselves a rabbit box."

"I don't know how. Never did anything like that before."

"We can learn."

By the time they got to the lake the morning mist had already burned away, the last tiny tendril wisps of vapor slow spiraled upward and vanished.

"You wanna have the first go?" Jamie held out the fishing pole to Ned.

"That's all right, you go ahead." Ned wandered off to the end of the faded gray wooden dock, sat down, leaned back against one of the pilings and pulled his flat cap down over his eyes. "I don't get to do nothin' very often."

"Suit yourself, but you're missin' a whole lot of fun."

Famous last words, for in spite of the best fishing worms in three counties, every fish slept steadfast on the bottom. Jamie tried everything he knew, putting the bait deep, keeping it shallow, fresh worms to keep 'em active, moving all around the dock, under, up and down. He even tried fishing off the path around the lake, something he didn't like because it was so hard to work the line through the trees and bushes. All for nothing. At the end he sat down on the dock and frowned at his lonely bobber.

Ned lifted his cap to look at Jamie. "That's your 'whole lot of fun'?"

"Oh, funny, you're real funny." Jamie lifted his line from the water, ripped the last worm from his hook, tossed it in the water and watched it twist slowly out of sight. He turned his cane pole in his hand to wrap the line around it and stuck the hook in the cork bobber. "We just got here too late, that's all. It's too hot. All I been doin' is drowning worms."

"What's that over there?" Ned pointed toward a little shed nestled deep in trees on the far side of the lake.

"That's 'Gunshot Cabin'." Jamie looked at Ned out of the sides of his eyes. "Fella by the name of Burse Coughman decided to leave his wife and just fish for the rest of his life."

"Burse?"

"It was supposed to be 'Bruce', but his momma was too tired to spell it on the birth certificate after she'd had him, but the point is he built it to get away from his wife. And she weren't too terribly happy about it."

"So what happened?"

Jamie pushed his straw hat back on his head. "Well, that's a matter of some debate. We heard gunshots early one Sunday morning. Daddy got his shotgun and came down to take a look, but by the time he got here, there was only bullet holes and a bloodstain on the floor. Nobody's seen Burse or his wife since." He leaned toward Ned. "Some say Burse and his wife killed each other in a suicide pact and threw themselves in this very lake and one day they're gonna come bobbin' to the top, all pale and covered with slime and white eyes starin' at the full moon." Jamie watched Ned for signs of spook. "You wanna go have a look?"

"Okay, sure."

They padded through the pines along the edge of the lake until they came to the cabin. It was a plain rough pine cabin with a single pitch roof and a covered porch that extended a few feet out over the water. Toby got there before them, jumped up on the porch, sniffed all over the floor boards then jumped right back off the other side, nose to the ground.

"He a hunting dog?"

Jamie watched Ned move into the cabin. "He loves to sniff things, but we've never taken him hunting. Daddy thinks there's too many fools down from Raleigh as it is, peppering the woods with buckshot."

"Well somebody around here hunts." Ned handed Jamie a little red pin-on button. "And your dad might be right. Some fool has more money than they have sense."

Jamie looked at the button. It had 'Combination Hunting and Fishing License - $3.10' printed on it. "Geez. That's a lot of money just to stomp around in the woods."

He stepped inside. The only remnants of habitation were cigarette butts, a ball of tangled fishing line and a beer bottle.

And a bullet hole in the window.

Chapter 3

A Near Thing

By the time Jamie and Ned returned the sky rippled swirls of violet gold and charcoal shadows. The aroma of oily meatloaf mixed with smooth fresh baked bread greeted them as they came in through the back porch screen door. They splashed through washing up at the porch pump, ran wet fingers through their hair and hurried inside to the supper table.

Jamie's father looked up as they slid into their chairs. He had his newspaper spread out beside his plate. "Any luck? About time you fellas got here."

"No sir, they just weren't biting. Tried everything."

"Probably weren't holding your mouth right."

"Daddy, you don't let us read at the table." Gloria bounced beside her mother's chair. She pinched her face together and shoved her lower lip out at Jamie and Ned. "And they slammed the scream door again."

"Stick your boose back in your face, young lady. And don't do as I do, do like I say do." He looked up long enough to scoop one more spoon of mashed potatoes onto his plate. "I have work tonight after supper and I need to read the paper." He set the serving dish down and picked up the paper. "Yankees won."

"Who against?" Jamie's mother looked at Gloria. "You want some more, Honey?" Gloria's curls swung as she shook her head.

"Indians. It was closer than the last one, five to four, but it says here that it was the longest game in history without a strikeout. Sixteen innings, imagine that."

"That's a better game than that one with the A's, though. What was it, twenty something to two?"

"Tnnyviv." Ned mumbled upward through his mashed potatoes.

"What?" Jamie paused, fork in mid-air and cocked his head at Ned. "I didn't quite catch that."

Ned swallowed hard. "Twenty-five. It was twenty-five to two."

"Do you follow baseball, Ned?" Jamie's mother delicately cut her meatloaf. "And don't talk with your mouth full."

"Yes ma'am." Ned reached for the basket of rolls, took one and held it up to his nose.

Gloria giggled beside her mother and smirked at Ned. "Don't talk with your mouth full, don't talk with ..."

"You hush." Jamie's mother frowned at Gloria then extended the platter of meatloaf to Ned. "Does your father follow baseball?"

"Thank you, Ma'am." Ned stabbed a slab of meatloaf onto his plate then set the platter down. "No ma'am. He thinks it's stupid." He scooped at his mashed potatoes. "But Doctor Voyce can't get enough of it. Pop memorizes the scores so he'll have something to talk about with him."

Jamie caught a glimpse of his father's raised eyebrows as he pressed and scraped the last potatoes off his plate.

His father dropped the paper. "'The Thin Man' is on the radio tonight. I want to give it a listen, so I need to get some work done before it comes on." He rose from the table and dropped his napkin by his empty plate. "You children help your mother out now." He clicked his pocket watch open and closed again. "It starts in an hour. Quiet till then."

"And you, young lady, are upstairs for your bath." Jamie's mother reached out to gather dishes.

Gloria slipped off her stool, eyes fixed on Ned and leaned into her mother and whispered in her ear.

Jamie's mother shook her head. "No, you can't. No one likes to be stared at. Now you go upstairs to the bathroom and get your clothes off. I'll be up with hot water in a minute. Go on."

"Aw, Momma." Gloria shoved her lower lip out of her face, balled up her little fists and thump-stomped up the stairs.

After the supper dishes were washed, dried and put away Jamie lay on his back on the couch in the living room, a pillow stuffed behind his head and Robinson Crusoe balanced on his stomach. Ned sat in the wicker rocking chair by the window, his head leaned back and his eyes closed.

His mother called out from the kitchen. "Jamie honey? Time to fill up the Delco. These lamps just aren't enough for what I'm doin'. And why don't you take Ned with you and show him how to do it?"

Like mowing hay brings on rain, sitting down to read always seemed to bring more work to do. Jamie let his book drop on his lap and yelled at the ceiling. "Do I have to? It's not a radio night."

" 'The Thin Man', remember?"

"Oh, yeah."

His father sat at his desk in the corner of the living room and sifted through papers. He lifted his eyes to look at Jamie over the top of his reading glasses and spoke in his brook-no-opposition voice, low and soft. "Go do what your momma says, boy." He looked back down at his papers. "And fill up the wood box while you're at it."

"Yes-sir." Jamie slammed his book closed and pushed up.

Ned got to his feet.

Jamie trudged out onto the front screen porch. The evening light was fading dark and he had to watch where he put his feet. He was about give the screen door a little extra push to make it slam behind him, but when he turned around Ned was close on his heels.

So he jumped off the porch, trotted over to the woodpile and started loading his left arm with wood.

When he looked up he saw Ned loading his own arm. "Thanks. The box ain't that big. We'll be done in a minute."

Ned shrugged at him as much as he could with an armload of wood. "That's ok, I'm used to it. This is easy. I don't get help at home."

"Yeah, me too."

They trudged around to the back of the house and up on the back porch. With Ned's help the job didn't take but one trip. As Jamie finished placing the wood from his arms into the wood box he looked in through the kitchen window. By the steady yellow light of the kerosene lamp he could see his father in the kitchen, leaning against the counter with arms folded, looking at the floor. His mother rested her elbows on the table and studiously peeled apples. Both their mouths were set in a line. There was no sign of Gloria. Jamie guessed she was upstairs, lost to the world playing in one of the eternal baths she always complained about.

Jamie pushed open the screen door and spoke to be heard. "Now we fill up the Delco." He stepped out into the deepening darkness and held the door open for Ned. As Ned passed dusting dirt off his shirtsleeve Jaime let the back door slam to. He grabbed onto Ned's arm and held him there.

Jamie saw Ned's mouth form 'What?' He put his finger to his lips for quiet, tapped his ear for Ned to listen then pointed through the window. He leaned over a little so he could still see inside. They didn't have long to wait.

"Now Grant, I'm just not happy at Jamie being around all those men at the mill. He's only fourteen. I just don't know you can expect … I just don't know."

Jamie held his breath. The dance between his mother and father was intricate in traces of subtlety and innuendo he could glimpse but not understand. It was like watching the lowered curtain at a school play billow and sway between acts. You tracked the shifting folds to try to figure out what was going on behind, but when the curtain finally lifted you were still surprised at the result.

24

"Yes, I know he's fourteen. Hannah, he's … he's like a corn plant that's already broken up through the sand crust into the sun. Eventually he's got to see some rain and a little wind or he'll grow up spindly and weak with no spine."

Jamie's mother stopped peeling and laid down her hands down in her lap. She coughed a single laugh. "Our boy is not spineless, Grant. If anything he's got a little bit too much dander in him."

"I know it might seem that way, honey. But he has to go to work sometime. He ain't Huck Finn."

"Isn't Huck Finn."

Several slow beats passed until his father responded. When he did the words were slow and clear. "He needs … to go … to work."

"But Grant …"

"But nothing, Honey. I'm not making him do it. I know men who hafta take a switch to their boys to get them to hit a lick at a snake. Jamie asked if he could work at the mill. Hannah, he *asked*. Don't you see? If I don't let him it'll damage his spirit."

"He's still a boy, Grant." She stared down at her hands in her lap. "They both are."

Jamie's ears rang in the silence.

"All right." His father rubbed his forehead and ran his hand through his hair. "I hear you. And yes, he is still a boy." He took breath and released it slowly. "Tell you what. I'll let him and Ned work till the afternoon break at two, every day. They won't have to work during the heat of the day and it'll give 'em a little time to fish and be boys. And I'll let them off at noon on Saturdays. How's that?"

Jamie squeezed the edge of the step railing. He felt the final see-saw moment in the balance. This was the very understanding he and his father had already come to because his father was afraid he'd get heat stroke.

He heard a chair scrape against the floor then heard his mother's long sigh. His heart leapt, for that was her signal of capitulation. She had accepted the offered compromise.

"Well, all right. But if and only if you promise to keep them away from log handling and for God's sake keep him away from that saw. Grant, the idea of him losing a hand or a leg to that thing just scares me half to death."

"I know, darlin', I know. He'll be safe, I promise. They won't be anywhere near the saw. All right?"

His mother stood up and his parents came together with quiet and indistinct murmurs Jamie wished he could hear, especially when a low giggle from his mother danced an echo clear out past the screens to where he and Ned stood. But if the Delco didn't crank and start lighting up the house real soon his mother would want to know why. He tugged on Ned's shirtsleeve and tiptoed out across the grass to the tool shed as quick as he quietly could and grabbed the gas can to fill the Delco.

Ned was right by him and Jamie saw him twisting back to look at the house with his hands in his pockets.

Light was fading fast. Ned's voice reached to Jamie as he fitted the gas can spout to the little low-slung tank by feel. "Got any idea what we'll be doing tomorrow?"

Jamie set down the can, screwed the tank cap back on and grabbed for the hand crank. "No idea, never been inside the place."

"So you've never seen this saw they were talking about?" Ned rubbed his wrist.

Jamie fitted the hand crank to the flywheel. "Nuh-uh. But it oughta be fun, huh?" He grinned at Ned, leaned on the handle to spin the flywheel and the little engine coughed and putted to life.

Chapter 4

What Cannot Be Avoided

Jamie blinked as slow morning light etched the world. A glance showed that Ned slept on, buried face-down under twisted sheets except for a patch of black hair poking up and one protruding foot. Quiet clatter echoed from the kitchen. No voices called to him so he slid his book from the bedside table. He pulled the pages apart at the cardboard marker. As he waited for light to ripen the words on the page into meaning he thought maybe he could bring the book with him today in case of stubborn fish. Robinson Crusoe breathed and walked upon the sand of his island until his mother's two-tone morning song, 'Ja – mie' and the smell of bacon reached out to him. He got up, slid into his overalls and padded into the kitchen.

Jamie looked around. "Daddy left for the mill already?"

His mother smiled as she laid bacon and oatmeal on the table. "Left way before light. Went to Silerville to get something he forgot yesterday, but never fear. You have plenty of time for breakfast and get a few things done for me before he gets back."

He jumped a foot when Ned spoke behind his ear. "Morning, Miz Garrath."

He turned around to Ned and spoke through clenched teeth. "Don't do that."

"Sorry." Ned was already dressed, hair combed and shirt collar buttoned up tight.

Jamie sat down at the table and stared at Ned's top button. "You're know that collar's gonna choke off the blood from your brains, don't cha?"

Ned didn't respond.

His mother set cold milk in front of both of them. "Don't dawdle; there's things to do."

There certainly were. Between milking, trimming and filling the kero lamps, getting in the eggs and a hundred other things his mother had for a body to do, there was no room to slide fishing or reading in edgeways.

The final hopes for reading Crusoe to pigheaded fish died when his mother set them to hoeing in the garden.

"The weeds in there are ankle deep, so get to it. Watch you don't chop off any more stalks of sweet corn or I won't have enough to put up come canning time."

"Yes Ma'am."

The ground of the garden beneath their feet was sandy, dry dimpled from the last rain. They slid their hoes just beneath the surface crust to slice off grass and weedy intruders. As he churned at the ground, Jamie's mind ached, starved for something to think about and reached back for Crusoe to fight off the weight of creeping dull anger, burning feet and aching back. He didn't know if Crusoe even had a hoe on his island paradise, but imagined himself under palm tree fronds waving to the trade winds and cannibals invisible in the woods beyond, just waiting for him to make a mistake. Ned wasn't exactly Man Friday, but when Jamie looked up at him, he sure seemed to work like it, bent over and hard focused on his hoe, one shirt sleeve waving unrolled. Up the rows and down, up and down, until finally even Robinson Crusoe had had enough, and Jamie straightened and stretched the knot in his back.

The train whistle blew in the distance. "Well, holy hell and hallelujah." Jamie pushed his hoe into the sand and leaned his face on the end of the handle. "Hey, Ned." Ned continued chopping, so he spoke a little louder. "Ned."

"Yeah, what?"

Jamie lifted his hoe to his shoulder. "Quittin' time. That's the noon train from Silerville at the crossing. Time to eat."

Ned straightened. "Suits me."

They plodded from the garden, fine gray dust coating their boots and the bottoms of their trouser legs. The hoes clattered into the corner of the tool shed as they dropped them off. Jamie spoke to the fishing poles that beckoned to him from the rafters. "Sorry fellas. Maybe later." He slid his hands flat into his back pockets and turned away.

As he walked up toward the house, he saw his father's square cab pickup in the yard and Ned leaning over the tailgate looking into the back. Jamie stopped beside him. There were four cardboard boxes along with a half dozen hanks of plow line, three cans of Pittsburgh Paint, a pile of thick link log chain, several rolls of flat leather drive belts of various sizes, a small can of kerosene and a large can of gasoline.

Ned leaned his elbows against the side of the pickup and pushed his flat cap back on his head. "Today?"

Jamie nodded. "It's a pure possibility."

Up at the house they swept the dust from their boots and pants with the outside broom, then clumped onto the back screen porch to pump water over their hands and faces. They dried off with the flour sack towel, then stepped into the kitchen.

Jamie's father sat at the head of the table. One hand held his newspaper down flat while the other paused in the air with a serving spoon full of potato salad. He peered through low-slung reading glasses at the public notices. Gloria sat beside him with both hands pressed to her lap and swiveled her head around, mouth open, like a baby sparrow beggin' for bait.

His mother lifted a plate of fried chicken to the table. In addition to the chicken and potato salad there was fresh bread and sweet green tomato pickles on the side. This was topped off with dripping glasses of deep golden sweet iced tea. Jamie and Ned both reached for their glasses and slurped before they scraped their chairs away from the table and sat down. They both reached for the bowls and plates of food.

"Heads down." His father's voice froze Jamie's hand in mid-reach. He tried to keep the twist out of his mouth, put his hands down into his lap and bowed his head. He stole a glance up at Ned, who followed his lead and did the same.

"Lord, help us in work, help us in faith, help us to love. We thank thee for thy bounty and all thy many blessings, Amen."

'Amen' was the starting gun for putting on the feedbag. The next few moments passed in silence punctuated with the rustle of his father's newspaper and serving spoons rattling on plain white plates.

Jamie heard his mother. "Grant? Leave some for somebody else."

He looked up and saw his father stopped with serving spoon in the air, a small mountain of potato salad on his father's plate.

"What about me, Daddy? I want some too!" Gloria was not about to be left out when there was complaining to be done.

"All right, darlin', all right, hereyago." His father spooned sticky cream potato salad from his own plate onto Gloria's.

"Daddy, those are yours; I want mine off the big plate."

His father's voice dropped half a tone. "You'll eat these or nothin', young lady."

Gloria dipped her head and pushed out her lip.

His father finished tapping the salad onto her plate and set the dish back down. "This afternoon I'm gonna pick up Snow down at Fred and Adam's then go on down to open up the mill, see what kind of shape it's in. You boys want to tag along?"

Snow was his father's foreman at the mill. "Right after dinner?"

His father nodded. "Soon as we finish eating."

"Jamie, don't cram your food in that way." His mother's voice in his ear. "You'll ruin your digestion. There's plenty of time."

Fork still in his mouth, Jamie looked up and watched his father glance up at his mother, then back down at his paper.

"Your momma's right, Jamie." His father picked up his knife and slowly cut up the green tomato pickles on his plate. "Now that I think about it, I've gotta get some papers together before we go down there anyway. So slow down and eat like you're supposed to." He set down the knife on the edge of his plate and picked up his fork.

Jamie mumbled as close as he could get to 'yessir' with a mouthful of potatoes.

Gloria shook her fork in the air at him. "Don't talk with your mouth full."

Jamie tried to press the smile from his face as she was silenced with a quiet hiss and a pointed finger from his mother.

His father turned his paper over. "You know that hobo we found down at the crossing a while back? The one with the watch? They found out who he was."

"Really?" Jamie's mother lifted the iced tea pitcher from the table, stood up and stepped over to the icebox. "Who was he?"

"Howard Hawks from Silerville. It says here he went missing when his wife and daughter died from the flu. Apparently he just wandered off. His family's been hunting for him ever since."

Jamie looked up at Ned. "How'd you know?" he whispered.

Ned shrugged and went back to stabbing at his food.

Jamie's father shifted pages. "Joe Louis and Max Schmeling are gearing up for their fight."

"Reading at the table again, honey?" Jamie's mother dropped ice chunks into the tea pitcher.

His father did not look up. "Only time I have to do it."

"It's barbaric."

His father looked up at her over his reading glasses. "Reading at the table? It may not be strictly polite, but 'barbaric' is carrying that a little far, don't you think?"

"No." Jamie's mother placed the pitcher on the table, sat back down and forked a chicken thigh onto her plate. "Louis and Schmeling. It's the Romans and their gladiators all over again."

"That's as may be, but I still hope Louis pounds him into the canvas like he did Baer." Jamie's father rattled the paper, folded it and placed it back down. "Maybe that'll shut up this Hitler fella for a day or two."

"Isn't there something a little more pleasant to share in there?"

"Well, let's see." Jamie's father picked the paper up and turned to the next page. "There's a beauty contest."

"That's no better." Jamie's mother dropped her wrists to the table, fork and knife upright. "They parade those girls in those swim suits like a cattle drive of boiled chickens. It's shameful, that's what it is." She sawed at her tomatoes, scraping her plate.

His father lifted the paper to peer closely at it. His voice reached out from behind the gray newsprint. "Well, I hate to tell you honey, but these gals aren't wearing any suits at all."

"What?" Jamie almost spit potatoes. When he looked up he saw Ned's wide eyes blinking at his. "Can I see?"

Jamie heard his mother's knife clatter onto her plate. "You hush, young man. They wouldn't put a picture like that in the paper."

His father's voice quivered a little bit behind the rattling paper. "They're a bunch of cows, is what they are."

"Grant! I've never heard you talk such a way. They may not act like they've got good sense or any raisin', but that's no reason for you to talk like that. What ever makes you say such a thing?"

Jamie's father peered around the edge of the paper. "It's a beauty contest for cows, Honey. Angus and Shorthorn, mainly. Lipstick, dresses and all." He ducked back behind the paper. "They've even got a little crown. Maybe we could enter Elspeth if we live close enough. I wonder what they do for the talent competition?"

His mother's chair scraped back. She got up, walked around the table, whacked her husband twice on the head with a folded towel, completed her circumnavigation and sat back down.

"Where is it at, Daddy?"

Jamie watched his father rub his chin. "Ahhh ... let's see ... Kansas. Too bad."

"I wonder if we could do that here?"

"Ohh." His mother tossed her napkin onto her plate and started clearing the dishes. "Never heard of such a fool thing."

With his mother putting food away and his father settled at his desk, Jamie eased his escape out onto the front screen porch to read. Ned followed, lay down on the glider and closed his eyes. Jamie had just sunk down into the part where Crusoe was building up his cave for defense against savage natives when his father came out of nowhere.

"Whatcha reading?"

Jamie was yanked out of his escape to paradise. "Uhh ... Robinson Crusoe."

"Again?"

"It's a good book, I like it."

"Not much point in reading a book again once it's been read good and proper, don't you think?"

"Folks go to see movies over and over don't they?"

His father stood over him, hands clasped behind his back. "Come on, let's go to the mill. Let's go do something."

Chapter 5
The Mill

Jamie and Ned climbed into the back of the pickup and settled in between the boxes and gear, up against the painted wooden sideboards. Toby jumped up after, wormed his way between them and leaned against Ned. That got a hard look from Jamie's father.

"I'm not sure Toby coming along is a good idea, son. A saw mill is not a place for play."

"I'd really like to bring him, Daddy."

"Well, all right. But if he gets in the way, you'll have to walk him home through the woods. Understand?"

"Yessir.'

"And take off your hats while we're drivin', don't want 'em to blow off in the wind."

"Yessir."

Jamie watched his father climb into the cab of the pickup truck and pull the door closed behind him with a quiet click. The engine coughed to a smooth rumble. He held onto the sideboard with one hand and onto Toby's collar with the other. When they pulled out onto the main road he watched the wind flatten Ned's hair against the back of his head in the wind.

When their pickup stopped at the gas pump in front of 'Fred & Adams' store, Jamie saw Snow sitting on one of the benches under the lean-to shelter, opening a small can of beans with his knife. He was a black man with old eyes, smile creases around his mouth and a thin Caesar's wreath of white hair crowning his head. His rangy bones set folds in his faded overalls to sharp angles.

Fred Black stepped down out of the store as they pulled up, belly straining his belt, all white shirt smiles and Brylcreem slick. "How much today, Mr. Garrath?"

"Just a couple of gallons, Fred. You goin' away from Gulf like you were talkin' about the other day?"

Fred walked over to the pump tower and began rocking the long handle back and forth to drive gas up into the glass cylinder on top. To Jamie gas pumps always looked like lighthouses sticking up out of the dirt.

"Not yet, Shell still wants too much for their gas." He stretched his smile wider. "I'd have to go raise prices and you know how I'd hate to do that."

"Uh-huh." As Fred laughed Jamie's father turned to Snow, who now calmly spooned baked beans from the small can into his mouth. "Beans for dinner?"

Snow nodded at Jamie's father, smiled wide with his mouth closed then chewed and swallowed. "Yes sir, Mr. Garrath. Just workin' on my popularity. S'afternoon I should be able to hire m'self out for crop dustin'." Snow smiled at his own joke. "I'm on my own bach'in it for a couple'a days. Flora's sister is sick so she's over there takin' care of the children."

"Nothing serious, I hope."

"Nah. Just some woman complaint." Snow scraped the last of the beans into his mouth, stood up and tossed the empty can into the battered fifty-five gallon trash drum. "Glad you openin' up the mill, Mr. Garrath. Good to have good work."

"No more than I am. There's nothing better'n the smell of fresh cut wood and sawdust."

Snow pointed with two stiff wrinkled fingers. "My daddy used to say somethin' like that 'bout farmin'. Whenever first good spring day come 'round my daddy he'd say 'Lord, it's the kind of day that just makes you wanna go plow some ground.' And he was right, yessir."

As the men talked Ned leaned over to Jamie. "Who's that?"

"That's Snow. Daddy's foreman."

"He's the foreman? Why does he point that way? Something wrong with his fingers?"

"His middle finger's froze from being busted or something. When the mill closed before he started workin' for us plowing corn, stuff like that. He's a nice fella, but don't fool with him 'cause he's smart as they come and tough as a pine knot."

"You folks got enough money to pay somebody?"

"In vegetables and milk, we got more than we can use. And Daddy writes him a check when a crop comes in."

Fred clattered the gasoline nozzle out of the fill pipe and hung it back up on the pump tower. "That'll be a quarter, Mr. Garrath."

"You sure, Fred? I just asked for a couple of gallons. I should be getting back a nickel."

"Well I got to listening to you and Snow and put in a little extra by mistake. You know how it is."

"Uh-huh, yeah." Jamie's father leveled his eyes at Fred's slick smile. "See you later, Fred." He dropped the quarter into the man's outstretched hand and turned toward the truck. "Come on fellas, let's get to it. Snow, you come on and sit up here with me, we got a couple of things to talk about. First thing is that saw blade. If I remember right, it was running hot, so we're gonna have to baby it till I can get it hammered or the teeth re-swaged and sharpened ..."

Jamie watched Fred Black's face shift from wide smile to hard dimpled frown as the man's eyes glittered at Snow sliding onto the front seat of the pickup. The man's face shifted right back when he saw Jamie looking at him and waved as they pulled away.

The truck slowed to a crawl at the bend in the road where the Widow Morrison lived close to Little Lake. Jamie both heard and felt his father's smooth downshift before they bumped through the turn onto the road to the mill. He twisted around over the sideboard to see the sign hanging from a tall dead tree by the side of the road, 'Garreth Lumber and Sawmill.'

The hard rippled road dead-ended in a solid wooden fence about eight feet high that cut into the woods both to the left and right. The mill gate was solid like the fence, two doors of rough cut planks weathered gray, held shut by a chain threaded through two holes drilled in each edge plank. The chain was neither enough to keep out a determined man with a hacksaw nor a man who could climb, but like his father said, a lock was just to keep an honest man honest anyway.

Both boys stood up in the truck while Snow got out and walked up to unlock the gate. They heard the dull staccato of chain pulled through the holes then rusty corduroy creaks as Snow dragged one door open through the dust, then the other. Snow stepped up onto the truck running board and his father drove through and inside.

Jamie hung on as the truck bounced up the short drive and stopped to the side of a small clapboard cabin. His father stepped out then reached into the back of the truck and grabbed a broom.

Jamie jumped down out of the back of the pickup and followed his father up to the screen door. Ned stayed in the back of the truck, looking around. Toby panted beside Ned, his paws on the top of the truck cab. "It looks like somebody's house, Mr. Garrath."

His father fished in his pocket for the key and responded to Ned over his shoulder. "That's 'cause it used to be somebody's house, Ned. A fella by the name of Joe Carter came out here a few years ago to make a go of bein' a farmer. Trouble was he had more money that he had sense and didn't know a damn thing about farmin'. On top of that," Jamie's father unlocked the screen door and stepped up onto the porch, "he was too much of a damn fool to take anybody's help. He did build a pretty fair little house though."

It was a pretty fair little house. A small whitewashed clapboard cabin set on brick pilings, it had a tin roof and a large screened porch that stretched all the way across the front and down the near side. A tall red oak stood close by and spread its limbs over the screen porch and a well just beyond. The well was covered with a small pole shelter and the concrete cylinder was capped with a pine board disk and a black iron pitcher pump.

Further beyond, to the right, in a clearing amongst the trees, Jamie saw a long pole shelter with machinery underneath, and the great circular saw blade gleamed at him.

His father caught Jamie looking. "We'll get over there soon enough. Come on, there's work to do."

Jamie mounted the steps onto the wide screen porch with Ned now close behind. His father unlocked the cabin door then raised and spun the broom in the air in front of him to wind down spider webs as he stepped inside. When Jamie followed he saw the front room went all the way across the house. There was one back room beyond. Toby squeezed by him and thumped his tail against Jamie's leg.

"Just two rooms?"

"Yep." His father handed him the broom and a dustpan. "And it's your first job to clean it out. Ned, you go open up that back door and sweep in the back. Jamie, you start in here. Sweep the whole place, front and back, and clean what you can. That means the porch too and get your dog out of my office." He gathered a few tools in his hands from shelves in the back room and stepped back outside onto the porch. "Snow? Let's see if we can get that pitcher pump workin'." Jaime's father stepped outside and he and Snow headed off toward the well.

The inside of the house was smaller than it looked from the outside. The back room had mostly empty shelves lining the walls and piles of bits of paper and cardboard where mice had munched on files and boxes in search of nesting material.

The front room was more interesting. What walls were not windows were laid with surveyor's plots of timber tracts and up behind the desk was a plat of the mill overlaid with glass. Jamie touched a grease pencil that hung from a piece of thick string. There were grease pencil hieroglyphics on the glass, codes of what wood was stacked where and how long. Low wooden filing cabinets lined one wall underneath the windows and a small potbelly wood heater perched in the corner with splayed legs. A blue enamel coffeepot waited on top. Most of the room was taken up by a simple desk and a large rough work table in the center with a wooden swivel chair in between.

Jamie took Toby by the collar and led him outside. "Sorry boy. You gotta stay out. We'll be with you in a little while."

He and Ned took the brooms and started sweeping. It was hard, digging at the dust caked on the floor. No sooner had they began than gray clouds filled the air and both of them started to sneeze.

Jamie's father stepped back in and waved his hand in front of his face. "You boys might want to sweep more and flail around a little less. Keep the dirt on the floor where it belongs." He coughed and waved his hand in front of his face. "And you might want to open the windows before you suffocate. Just a thought." He grabbed a thin spout oil can from the back room shelf and went back outside.

The inside of the house was not finished; it wasn't even painted. It was dark natural wood and when Jamie leaned to it and sniffed it smelled of dry oil.

There was a candlestick telephone sitting on the desk. Jamie spoke just loud enough for Ned to hear. "We don't even have a phone in our house."

Ned's voice returned to him from the back room. "It's a business. Pop's got one too. You'd be surprised how much they talk when there's money in it."

It wasn't long before Jamie's father called from outside. "Put down the brooms, I got something else for you. You can come back to that."

They dropped the brooms, went outside and followed Jamie's father around to the back of the house. Piled up in the back inside ell corner of the cabin there was a big pile of boards, cans, bottles, sheets of tin and general junk.

"We need to get this cleaned up. Sort out the pile first. Make a neat stack of the wood that ain't rotten over on the side of the house, but not up against it and make a pile of the other junk out front where we can load onto the truck to haul it away. And," he leaned down and pointed underneath the house, "clean out all that junk from under there." He handed them both gloves and hoes. "Be careful of snakes and black widows. Use the hoes to drag stuff out from under the house. Don't want you bit by a copperhead first day. Understand?"

Both boys nodded.

"Okay. The pitcher pump is working now, so if you get thirsty there it is. I'll be back to check on you in a little while."

"Yessir."

They watched Jamie's father walk off with Snow toward the large shelter beyond the trees. He was talking and gesturing to Snow with his hands and Snow was nodding back.

Jamie heard Ned from behind him. "Ain't this romantic, though?"

He glanced over at Ned and then back at his father's back walking away from him. Ned was right. He wasn't sure what he had expected, but this wasn't it. He sneezed dust from his nose. This certainly was not it.

They split up the chores. Jamie attacked the pile; Ned yanked stuff out from under the house. In a little while Jamie had an education about Ned. Mr. Edward Seth Custis could cuss like nobody Jamie had ever heard. It wasn't constant and it was all quiet under his breath, but Ned could cuss long and naturally and more inventively than anyone Jamie had ever heard. It was like music and Jamie listened with the joy of learning and hoped he could imitate part of it in the future. He then heard silence behind him and turned to see Ned reaching up to unbutton his collar and looking at a tall rectangular box he had apparently just pulled out from under the house and set upright. Toby sniffed at the box.

"What's that? What's in it?"

Ned shook his head. "Some kind of box. Wonder what it's for?"

Jamie dropped the board he had been heaving on. A big gray cloud rose up and he coughed, spit and went over to look.

The box was tall and narrow, about the size of a largish book on top and came up to their waists. It was wooden, weathered gray and nailed together. There was a sliding door on the top.

Ned slid the door back and forth. "It's a queer sort of box, ain't it? I can't make out what would have been stored in here."

"Something tall and skinny, I guess."

"Let's not break it up 'til we figure it out."

Snow's voice echoed from behind them. "You boys lollygagging already?"

They both turned to Snow, who smiled at them from around the corner of the cabin in spite of his words. "Mr. Garrath said you might want to split up the wood into two piles, one for wood we might be able to use, the other to be cut up into firewood." He grinned, clapped his hands, said "Hot damn!" and walked off with a spring in his step carrying a great smile on his face a mile wide and twice as shiny.

Jamie looked over at Ned. "You get a sneaking suspicion he's happy to be here?"

Ned gave one laugh snort. "Oh yeah. But what does that mean?"

"More work for us, more'd likely."

Chapter 6

The New World

Jamie could not understand why he was awake. A deep body shiver answered and he groped for his sheet, tried to pull it back up over his shoulders to re-establish his warm cocoon and found himself in a tug-of-war. He strained his head up in the darkness and saw the dim outline of a round furry head. "Toby? What the hell are you doin'?"

He heard tendrils voices, the faint clatter of dishes and heavy clank of the cast iron stove door.

Oh, yeah. Work. Jamie pushed upright and ached across his shoulders. He felt for matches on his bedside table, closed his eyes against the eye-stabbing blaze, and then held the match to the candle wick. He swung his legs over, placed his bare feet on the wooden floor and yawned a quiet curse.

"Yeah." Ned groaned from the shadows.

Jamie squinted past the flickering candle glare at Ned. "You too? You awake long?"

"Since I heard your mom bang her frying pan on the stove. Then he trotted in and bit the covers off your bed. The tug-a-war was a show. You wake up slow, don't you?"

A yawn took over Jamie's mouth so he just nodded 'Uh-huh'.

His father's head appeared in the doorway and nodded in approval. "Hmm, good. You're already awake."

Jamie yawned again and shivered. "Don't blame me; it's Toby's doin'."

His father looked down at Toby sitting on the floor by Ned's cot with the sheet swirled around him. Toby thumped his tail on the floor, bright eyed and laughing.

His father addressed the dog. "Not gonna be too much fun today, boy. The mill is a place for work, y'know."

Toby closed his mouth, nodded at Jamie's father, and then raised his ears back over to Jamie.

His father narrowed one eye at Toby, and then looked back at Jamie. "Come on, boys." He clapped hands just once. "Up and at 'em, time's a wastin', no time like the present, don't sleep your life away."

Jamie yawned so wide he had to cough himself out of it. Knowing his father loved to overuse sayings to emphasize how stupid they were did not make them any less painful to hear.

But his father knew that. "You up?"

Jamie nodded and scratched his head.

"Good, 'cause it's time for breakfast." He clapped his hands together. "Boots on, remember." His father's head disappeared from the doorway. "With socks."

Jamie reached for his clothes. Only then did the tendril scent of bacon and toast reach his nose. He hoped his mother would let him have coffee this morning like his father. It wouldn't hurt to ask.

No such luck. Breakfast was quiet, little talk, less dawdling and no coffee. Jamie brushed his teeth, pulled on his denim work coat and followed his dad out the door into the moist scent of dew on the grass. The charcoal night gave way to the sun, much as Jamie gave ground to wakefulness, fatigue fighting a rearguard action against the inevitable.

Jamie clambered into the back of the open truck and slumped down with his back against the cab and propped his elbow up on the side. Toby scrambled up too and sat right beside him. He watched Ned vault over the side of the truck to plop down beside him and slide his cap off and stuff it into his coat pocket. He closed his eyes to Ned's grin. "Where'd you get so all-fired full of piss and vinegar?"

His father's voice rose from the driver's side window. "I heard that, young man. You watch your language." The truck engine rumbled to life. "And take off that hat if you don't want it to blow away."

Jamie pulled off his straw hat and shoved it under one leg.

The truck dipped, pitched and rolled out of the long driveway over dusty mud holes and bumped out onto the main road. As the truck gained speed on the smoother track Jamie felt damp morning air blowing around his neck. He pulled his collar close and held his arm around Toby for warmth. The wind pounded the sides of his head and ears. He shut his eyes to it until he felt the truck brake for the turn down to the mill.

Jamie heard Ned's voice in his ear. "Ya think Nosy'll be at it again?"

He squinted his eyes open. "I don't know. Let's take a look when we go by."

But as the truck rattled and ground onto the second-gear washboard dirt road that led to the mill he looked right past the widow's house over toward Little Lake across the road. Jamie was drawn to water. Every time he saw a lake or a stream he felt he needed to stop and stare, needed to let the sight soak in through his eyeballs if he couldn't dive in or fish in it.

The lake was glass. A dim ghost of fog hovered above the surface, making the trees look like ladies lifting bustle skirts to step over mud, but not so much that their reflections were dimmed in the slick mirror of the dark water.

His eyes caught movement across the surface. Then it came again, a long switch flicking against the sky, this time with a dark trailing hair of line attached. He lifted up on his hands and craned his neck just a bit higher and saw a faded dark brown fedora pushed back onto the crown of a thin man's head before the truck rattled around a bend and the lake was blocked from sight by the pines. He sifted his memory for an image to connect with but came up empty.

He filed it away with all the other things he did not understand to think about later and opened his eyes to the sawmill.

A small group of men were gathered at the gate, waiting.

The pickup rattled to a stop in front of them and Jamie's father handed Jamie the key to the gate out of the truck window. Jamie reached for it and hopped out. Toby followed.

They made way as he walked up through them, unlocked the gate and pulled the chain from the worn hole in the vertical wooden board in two corduroy pulls. He swung both doors wide and stood by one with the chain in his hand.

As his father drove through, he spoke to Jamie through the truck window. "Close one gate, but leave the other one open for them to come on in."

Jamie said 'Yessir' to the side of the truck as it passed. Jamie closed the stationary gate, shoving the vertical lock bar down into a pipe driven down flush with the surface of the ground. He fastened the other gate back with the chain looped around the stop post.

When the men saw the gate was to remain open they moved as a group past Jamie through the gate. He followed their footprints in the dusty sand earth up to the cabin office.

Men at the back of the group elbowed each other in conversation. Only one had he seen before. 'Dancin' Charlie' was small, red-headed, bow-legged in baggy overalls and always in motion. Charlie chattered with a huge black man who nodded back down at him, calm hands in his pockets.

Jamie's eyes were drawn to a very thin, very still, very quiet Indian who wore a broad brimmed army campaign hat and carried a woven bag slung crossways across his back. The man walked a little apart from the others, stepping lightly on the balls of his feet.

By the time Jamie reached the cabin his father had gotten out of the pickup. Snow stood beside him, talking with a slender black man who limped as he shuffled his feet in place, unable to keep still. Ned stood behind and watched.

His father half-turned toward Jamie. "Why don't you and Ned go fire up the wood stove? I don't know about these folks, but I could use some coffee." He turned to the men. "How 'bout it?"

"Sure could."

"Would be nice."

"All right." Jamie's father nodded and held out a paper bag to Jamie. "Take this, get the fire going in the stove and put on the big pot from the back room. There's tin cups in the back room and water in the well. Go on."

Jamie climbed the stairs onto the porch and went inside to get the fire started while Ned went to the well. He slid big splinters of fat lighter wood into the stove and held a match to it. Ned came in with a bucket of water then charged the coffee pot.

While the coffee cooked they walked back out onto the porch and watched Jamie's father through the screens as he moved among the men.

Jamie's father looked over the group. He reached out and shook hands with a couple of them, then climbed up into the back of the pickup bed and clasped his hands behind his back. His voice was no louder than usual but carried clear like Jamie had never heard it.

"Good morning gentlemen. Glad you could make it. For you folks who have worked here before this is old hat, but for those who haven't, I need to say a couple of things." He slid his gray fedora back on his head. "First, this can be a hazardous place to work, so there will be no drinking on the job or showing up with a couple under your belt. Now don't go thinking I'm a prohibitionist. What you drink or don't drink on your own time is none of my business; I really don't give a damn. But I do give a damn what happens inside these gates and things are a whole lot safer when everybody's sober. For the same reason there is no horseplay. You fellas who have worked here before have seen it same as me, so you know what I'm talking about. A loose log can crush a leg, the kiln gets hot enough to burn you right down to the bone, and that saw over there will take a hand or an arm and never even know you were there."

Jamie saw the slender black man beside Snow shift his weight and look down at his feet.

His father rubbed the back of his neck. "We'll get you gloves for the logging crews and such, but no gloves, long sleeve shirts or anything that dangles will be worn anywhere close to the engine, the saw or the planer. That's 'cause if anything loose attached to you gets caught up, the machinery is too stupid to stop, and nobody on this earth will be quick enough to save you." Jamie's father turned his head to the side and Jamie caught just a glimpse of a smile. "That's in case somebody might be so much of a dandy to wear a tie."

There was a gentle chuckle from the group. Jamie noticed though some had their collars buttoned all the way up like Ned, not a single man had a tie around his neck.

His father paused, pressed his lips together and scanned the faces looking up at him, steady in the eyes. "One last thing. This year, as the senior men, Snow is my foreman and lead sawyer and James Carson is lead on the kiln. They know those things inside out, I trust them and pretty much what they say goes. Any man got a problem with that; there's the gate right behind you. Fellas, raise your hands so everybody'll know who I'm talking about."

His father pointed at Snow and the slender black man with the limp. They leaned against the side of the cabin, their hands lifted in the air. James Carson was young, his face almost girlish, but he held his head up straight and held back whatever smile may have been in him. He shifted his weight.

Snow looked bored, but his eyes moved over the group. Snow looked much older to Jamie now that he was standing next to Carson, what little hair he had ringed round his head as white as his name.

Three men in the middle of the group frowned hard, shook their heads, then turned and shouldered their way through the others and stalked out the gate. No one else moved.

Jamie's father waited until they were gone then pulled on his braces and let them go with a snap. He took a deep breath. "All right, good. Oh, and by the way, pay is a quarter a day more than last time. That takes it up to eighteen bucks a week for labor, a couple more for the foremen."

An appreciative murmur rippled across the group. Jamie's father talked right across the top of it. "But don't go to thinking that's 'because I'm getting soft in my old age. You'll earn every cent. I'm happy to tell you that between Army contracts for pine and the hardwood contracts with the furniture folks, we should stay busy, maybe even into cold weather. And we've been talking with some boat-builders down on the coast that want quarter-sawn and some special clear pine for masts and spars, especially if we can do a little draw knife work to save them some time. So things looks pretty good." He clapped his hands together. "Now, let's get some coffee and start cleaning up the place. See Snow so we can get all your names down and shake out what everybody's work is. Thanks for coming."

Jamie watched his father step down and motion Snow and James over to him. He spoke to them quietly, one hand light on James Carson's shoulder. He'd never seen his father touch another man like that. His father looked up at Jamie as if he sensed he was being watched and motioned both of them back out to speak to them.

"When the coffee's done set up the cups and big pot out here on the tailgate of the pickup and keep pouring til it's gone. This is just for this morning. Your every-day chores are to clean out the ashes in the stove if they've been left from the night before, light a new fire, put on the small pot for us, and then fill up the wood box and keep it filled. Fill up the water cask by the well and keep it filled. I don't need these men falling out in the heat because they didn't get enough water. I know it doesn't sound very important, but when you see how thirsty these men can get you'll understand. Heat stroke is not fun. When you get that done, finish sweeping out the cabin. I'm sorry, but I'll not have a whole lot of time to spend with you today. Okay, let's get to it." Jamie's father clapped his hands together, and then turned to walk over towards the saw where it loomed low in its long pole shelter behind sparse trees.

As they set up the coffee pot and cups on the tailgate of the pickup Jamie got a closer look at the men who had come to work. He knew Snow and he'd seen Dancin' Charlie at the Post Office a few times. The rest were new to him.

Standing next to Charlie was the large black man. Now that he was up close Jamie saw he was a full head and a shoulder taller than Charlie, bigger than the strong man at the State Fair when Jamie sneaked a peek through the canvas Midway tent. When the two of them came up for their coffee Charlie was jabbering, as usual.

"Bwana, I'm tellin' ya it can't miss. Ya gotta go in with me on this one." Charlie laughed, slapped one hand against another then adjusted his short brimmed fedora.

The huge black man just half smiled and shook his head. "Like that thing you tried to set me up selling hand cream? That stuff was just lard with food coloring. And why did you have to use that yellow-brown? It looked like mason jars of baby shit."

"Now Marshall, my good buddy, Bwana, you gotta know I learned my lesson on that one. How could you think I'd steer you if I didn't have a really great feeling about this one, hmm? Here, have some coffee. Jamie, this is Marshall. You met Jamie? Mr. Garrath's his daddy, ain't that right, Jamie?"

Jamie opened his mouth to say hello, but Charlie had no intention of letting Jamie get a word in edgewise and pulled Marshall away by the elbow, chattering about his grand plan.

Ned set more tin coffee cups on the truck tailgate and snickered under his breath. "That man's got more wind than a bag of assholes."

Jamie snorted. "Got enough tongue for ten sets of teeth."

Snow came up. "Give me two cups, if you would. I need one for Little Foot." Jamie poured. Snow stepped away and handed the second cup to James Carson.

The rest of them came in a group. Stepping up after Snow was a thick-set man with a beard Jamie thought could be a dead ringer for Paul Bunyan, a lightly built dark haired young man who kept combing his slicked back hair, a tall blond man who looked like a Viking, and then a little man with a parchment skin and a high voice who cupped his hand over his ear.

Last was the Indian, who leaned on one hip a little apart from the others and waited with one hand grasping the opposite elbow behind his back. When he came forward he reached for his cup with long slender hands. Close up Jamie could see deep scars on his face. The man nodded silent thanks and moved on.

Ned spoke behind his ear. "I can't say I like the feel of that one."

"Me neither." Jamie picked up the coffee pot and looked at Ned. "Come on, lets' get the chores done so we can take a look around."

After their chores they set out. Some of the older men cleaned up and worked in and around the saw. Others swung the heavy curved bush axes and sling blades to clear off weeds and brush in the wood storage yard. Still others sharpened axes and the steel points on cant hooks.

"Jamie! Ned!"

Jamie nearly jumped a foot when his father's voice found him. He and Ned had been watching the Viking sharpen a cross cut saw.

"You finished with what I told you to do?"

Both Jamie and Ned nodded.

"All right, then finish cleaning up the corner behind the cabin. Get to work now. And keep Toby out of the way." Jamie's father turned away, looking down at papers in his hand.

Jamie heard Ned cough behind him. "He's busier than a rooster in a two story chicken house."

Jamie watched his father's back. "Yeah."

"Let's see if we can finish this up today, all right?"

Jamie and Ned were behind the cabin in the inside corner, cleaning up the trash pile and under the cabin. Jamie spit dust, turned around and stared at Ned. "What did you say?"

"I said let's see if we can …"

Jamie cursed. "I heard you, I just can't believe you said it."

"I'm just tired of working in this little hole, is all. The only thing interesting is that box I ain't figured out yet."

"That ain't the only thing you ain't figured out. Why're you sticking your hand down there underneath? You should be pulling that stuff out with the hoe."

"I'm just trying to hurry."

"You're going to hurry yourself right into a bite from a copperhead. They love holes like that and their bite ain't very forgiving."

"Copperheads?" Ned froze. "You mean snakes? What do they look like?"

"I don't mean pennies. You never seen a copperhead?"

Ned shook his head.

Jamie warmed to telling Ned something. "They're fat in the middle, fairly short and real strong. You usually don't see them until it's too late 'cause they blend in with the ground."

"So why do you call them copperheads?"

"They're kinda copper colored like dead leaves and their head is real triangular, like this." Jamie put the tips of his thumbs and first fingers together with his thumbs lined up straight. "'Cept of course their heads ain't quite that big."

"And they're dangerous?"

"Oh, yeah. If you're weak like a girl you might even die, but you'll get sick for sure. Come on, let's throw that box on the trash pile, it's mostly rotten anyway."

"I think it might come in handy, but okay." Ned picked up one end of the box. "You ever seen a copperhead around here?"

"Oh yeah." Jamie picked up the other end of the box and the two of them carried it around to the front of the cabin to the trash pile. "Snow told me one time that the only way to cure snakebite is to tie a toad to the snake bite wound. If the toad dies, get a fresh one and tie it on. You just keep doin' that till the toad lives and you should be cured."

Jamie watched Ned's face draw up. "You pullin' my leg."

"Not a bit of it. Ask him." Jamie pointed to Snow walking up behind Ned. Ned glanced over his shoulder and shook his head.

"Why you boys throwin' away a perfectly good rabbit box?"

Jamie watched Ned's head lift like a hound on a scent. "Rabbit box?"

Snow nodded to the box between them. "Yeah. It's a pretty old one by the looks of it, but it looks alright."

Jamie looked at the box. "Is that what it is? How does it work?"

"Put it down and I'll show ya." Snow guided the box down on the ground, laid it on its side then lifted the slide door and let it slide back down. "You hook a string to the top of this door, run it back to the back of the box to a trip stick and when the rabbit come inside the box he hits the stick. The door slides down and you got yoursef' a rabbit."

Jamie saw Ned screw up his face. "Why do you catch rabbits, anyway?"

"Free meat, and that's a thing worth doing. But you boys be careful now. There's lots of things that get caught in a box trap besides rabbits and some of 'em ain't so kind."

Chapter 7

Just An Idea

Ned liked the early morning ride to work. The wind in his hair felt like freedom and when they passed by Little Lake he smelled mist clinging to the air around the water.

As they passed the Widow Morrison's house, Ned caught a whiff of polecat just at the moment he looked at the widow's mailbox. The thought that slid into his brain lifted his eyebrows and bubbled out into a laugh. He leaned over to tell Jamie.

But there was no time. As soon as the truck pulled up to the cabin Snow called out for them to climb down and pulled Jamie off toward the saw. Ned watched them go then looked down and was glad to see Toby sitting at his feet.

Jamie's father called, and as Ned turned he saw the Indian standing beside him.

"Ned, this is Cyrus Conner. Everybody calls him 'CC'. You're working with him today clearing out tall grass and scrub bushes inside the fence. You're going to start out by the back gate where the logs are stacked and work your way up to the front. You know what poison ivy looks like? You allergic?"

Ned's brain balked for a bit as he tried to swallow both questions at once. "Uhh, yessir and not that I know of."

"Keep an eye out for it. Here's your sling blade." Jamie's father handed him the tool. "You hack down the tall grass while CC gets the big stuff with the bush axe. Don't chop your toes off." Jamie's father turned and walked toward the saw shed.

Ned gripped the handle of the sling blade and looked up at the Indian. He was tall, rangy and muscular. The heavy blade of the bush axe hung loosely in his hand.

"Ready?" The Indian's voice was husky and low.

Ned nodded.

"You go first. I'll come after you with the axe. We'll drag the brush over to the trash wood pile out of the way after we get an area done. Sound about right to you?

"I guess." Ned nodded again and headed toward the back gate. His back crawled as he heard the footsteps of the tall man crunch behind him and thought of the broad curved tip bush axe. When he tried Ned could usually read people, read their emotions if not their thoughts. Not this man. On the Indian Ned drew blank. He glanced over his shoulder at him, then lifted the sling blade and swung at the tall grass. Toby trotted out the back gate and into the woods beyond. Ned wished he were going with him.

They worked hard, hacking and sweating, till the mid-morning train whistle, Ned glancing over his shoulder every now and again to check where the Indian was. When the whistle blew, Toby bounded back in the gate and jumped up on Ned. "Hey, fella. Am I glad to see you."

The Indian set down his axe and held out his own hands palms up. "Let me see your hands."

Ned didn't want to be foolish, but he didn't want to be chicken either. "What for?"

"Let's see your hands."

Ned placed his hands into the Indian's palms down. The Indian turned them over and looked at them. "Humph." He dropped Ned's hands and turned and walked toward the well. Only then did Ned look. His palms were red raw with tiny bright wrinkles that threatened blisters, particularly around the base of his thumb.

Ned followed him toward the well, looking for Jamie. The men crowded around the well and the water cask, filling their mason jars. Ned had to wait until they cleared out to fill his own. Toby pawed at his leg.

"We need to get you some water, don't we boy?" Ned retrieved an old tin plate from the trash pile by the cabin and set it down on the ground. He poured water into it from his water jar.

Toby slopped at it with his tongue. Ned sank down by the cabin wall and drank deep. None of the men talked much except for Crazy Charlie, who never seemed to stop. Jamie was nowhere to be seen.

After the break Ned changed his grip on the sling blade and spent a little more time clearing out the brush branches they'd already cut out away from the fence. He again glanced over his shoulder at the Indian from time to time, but the man seemed oblivious. Ned took less and less notice while his shirt became more and more sweat-soaked as the sun climbed high.

At the noon train whistle Ned dropped the sling blade and plodded straight to the well to fill up his jar before he ate. Toby trotted beside him.

He tried to beat the gray dirt and green streaks from the bottom of his pant legs but couldn't bring back the new dark blue. He poured out more water for Toby and had no more gotten his lunch and sat down, leaned his head against a tree in the shade and closed his eyes before he heard the grind of boots on hard sand. He squinted up and saw Jamie, who was covered with grease. He looked Jamie up and down. "What have you been doing?"

Jamie grinned back. A glistening steak of black grease was smeared across one of his cheeks. "Helping Snow work on the saw and the planer. You never seen nothing like it."

"Yeah well. Haven't much chance, now have I?" Ned closed his eyes and took a bite from his chicken sandwich.

"Hell, who rained on your parade?" He felt Jamie plop down beside him and turned his head to watch him dig into his sack and gulp water out of his mason jar. Jamie mumbled through his mouthful of food. "Oh, what was it you were laughing about this morning? We got pulled apart before I could ask you."

Ned laughed as he remembered. "I just thought how surprised old Nosy would be if he found a polecat in the mailbox while he was starin' into the widow's window."

Jamie's snort almost blew the bite he was chewing right out of his mouth. "'Specially if he caught it hind end first."

"We do have that rabbit trap." Ned slid his eyes toward Jamie.

"Oh ho, no way, no how. I'm not dealing with no skunk and that's final. I've had my bath in tomato juice. It ain't no fun. Momma and Daddy both would skin my tail."

"But wouldn't it be something, though? There's just no way he'd ever mess with the widow again. What do skunks eat?"

"I told you, I ain't doin' it."

"I'm just wonderin'."

He watched Jamie take a bite out of his apple. "Most any kind of human food." He held up the apple. "Apple cores, table scraps, anything. Momma's always telling me to be careful when I go down to the woods to throw out slops to watch out for them. They're not much afraid of people."

"Mmm, that so?" Ned leaned back against the tree, his head taken with the image of Nosy Norris twisting in scented agony.

"I told you, no way, no how."

"Mm-hmm, yeah."

Chapter 8
Whispering Waters

"Honey, you are not going to believe this." Grant Garrath banged through the screen door just ahead of Jamie and Ned. He tossed his hat on the rack and flopped down in his chair at the dinner table.

Hannah called out to the quickly retreating boys. "You two go wash your hands and get ready for supper." She placed another clear green glass plate on top of the checkered table cloth and stopped with the stack of plates under her arm. "What?"

Grant clapped his hands once. "The grand metropolis of Miller's Landing now has a hunting and fishing club."

Hannah rattled the next plate down on the table. "Grant, you are not going to join one of those clubs."

He pressed his face tight with the heels of his hands. "Darlin', I don't even hunt. The shotgun's for ..." He stopped to take the hard edge out of his voice. "I just overheard Dancin' Charlie during the afternoon break. He's convinced his bunch of boys to start one."

"Charlie? Not one of them has the sense God gave a ... do any of them ...?"

"Own a gun?" Grant shook his head. "Not one."

"Then why on earth ... ?"

"Per-zactly. It makes about as much sense as a steering wheel on a mule, but they're gonna start having meetings down at the old Anders place. To do what, I have no idea." Grant held one hand up. "And hold on, I want to get this right. They couldn't agree on a name so they shoved two names together ... they want to call it ... 'The Gentlemen Colonels of Whispering Waters.'"

"Oh, land." Hannah giggled just once, straightened her face and reached for the pile of napkins. "Who owns that place now, anyway?"

"I expect the Anders still do. Nobody's done a thing with it since the day they left, but I've never seen a 'For Sale' sign on it either."

"They'll be lucky not to fall through the floor. That place has been vacant for how many years is it?" Hannah began placing knives and forks. "I'd bet you anything Fred Black is behind it. It sounds about like him."

"You think Fred might be lookin' for a little help to his backroom sales since he had to shut down his moonshine bell tree?"

Hannah shrugged and paused by his chair with her hands on her hips. "It wouldn't be the first time that bootlegger has swayed somebody just to get their money." She placed her hand on Grant's shoulder for a moment.

He rested his hand on hers and looked up at her. "I like your hair up like that."

She dipped her eyes and smiled back with only her dimples, then called out to Jamie and Ned. "Boys! Wash up now, it's time for supper."

For the 'Gentlemen Colonels' in question, going to the hunt club more often than not consisted of sitting around on hand-me-down chairs and bang-together benches by a low fire in the Ander's place while they grimaced down rough-cut moonshine from Dancin' Charlie's blind hole. Rarely did their talk refer to killing anything. In fact, their total death tally was one deer by automobile, two raccoons from a felled firewood tree and Mrs. Isabella Johnson's miniature poodle 'Minny-Poo' via a forgotten bowl of brandy soaked prunes.

Their moonshine mumblings did however give birth to hare-brained schemes of grand scale. Trouble was, once the bunch was three sheets to the wind, that the needed common sense to reel themselves back in was in short supply. Learning tends to be a function of memory. Charlie's boys were just too forgetful to avoid repeat.

The original purpose of gathering this night was to celebrate employment. Afterwards not one of 'The Gentlemen' could reliably recall whether it was Charlie or Lowell Lowry that made the original suggestion of walking to the beach. No matter that it was over a hundred miles away. They did recollect Charlie and Lowell leaning conversation at one another.

"We'll get there by midnight, dive in, take a swim, taste a little saltwater. We'll be back 'fore breakfast and then go to church. Whaddyasay?' Charlie unscrewed the lid on a fresh mason jar, took as deep a sip as he dared, wheezed and held it out to Lowell.

Heads nodded all around at the idea and a short chorus of affirmations echoed.

Lowell belched as he took the proffered jar, smacked his teeth and clacked his false teeth. "That's right; a body should go to church." He lifted it to his lips and drew in the pungent clear liquid.

"So it's a plan?"

"What's a plan?"

"To go to the beach and take a swim in the surf."

"In the what?"

"The surf. Th' place at the beach where the ocean and the sand get together. Don't you know nuthin'?"

"I know the room's spinnin'. And in the wrong direction, if I may say. If it were spinnin' the other way it would be all right, but this way is makin' me dizzy." Lowell sniffed. "And I know I'm going to church tomorrow and pray for mother."

Charlie crushed his hat off his head and held it tight to his chest. "Why? Is she gone?"

A slow nod. "Yeah. She left early spring when the daffodils were just beginnin' to bud." Lowell drew his red bandana from his pocket and pinched it around his nose. He blew hard and honked like a tuba. "She loves daffodils. I do miss her. She is the best damn mama a man could have."

Charlie backed up unsteadily, felt for his chair by waving his hand in the air behind him, found it and slowly lowered until he was sitting solidly on the tortured cane seat. Splashy tears left shiny trails down his face. "A man oughta have a good mama. You been lucky that way, then?"

A weaving unsteady nod. "Oh yeah." Sniff. "And now she's gone."

Charlie launched out of his chair and landed with a thump on the bench beside Lowell. He slung his arm about Lowell's shoulders. "That's so sad she left ya. Was she a church-goer?"

Lowell reached up, slid his false teeth out of his mouth and yawned. He dug at the back of his gums with one finger. "While she was here, yeah. Now I dunno. Pro'bly."

"No proba-bubly about it. There's plenty of chance for talking to God where she's gone."

Lowell nodded. "Lot of nice people too. She loves it there."

"Who … wouldn't? They say it's a nice place. I'd like to go there. Knowin' me, I won't, but I'd like to."

"Me too. Maybe someday." Lowell rubbed his sleeve across his nose. "Aunt Rachel is there. Mama likes talking with her."

Charlie hugged Lowell about the shoulders, slid his hat back on his head and took the jar from Lowell's hand. He tilted it to his lips again, swallowed, wheezed a sigh, then coughed and leaned back against the hard wood wall and patted Lowell on the back. "Lowell?"

"Yeah?"

"What'd she die of?"

"Who?"

"Your mama, that's who."

"What about her?"

"What'd she die of?"

"Who?"

"Your mama, the one what borned ya."

60

"What about her?"

Charlie handed Lowell the mason jar and leaned back against the wall. He pressed one palm against his forehead. "Lowell?"

"Yeah?"

"What ... did ... your ... mama ... die ... from?"

"Mama's dead? Who said?"

"You said she left."

"Oh, yeah. I did say that."

"So, what'd she die of?"

Lowell weaved his gaze at Charlie then slung his head back and wheezed a single soundless laugh through his empty mouth. The laugh was short-lived because he slammed his head into the wall boards with a thump. "Ow." He rubbed his head then looked at Charlie and laughed again.

Charlie squeezed his eyes shut, slapped his palms on his knees and did his best to focus on Lowell. "I don't see that death is all that funny, Low'. I mean she were your mama and all. If I were her I don't think I'd take it at all kindly that you laughed at me after I was in the ... cold ground."

Lowell hissed his laugh again and pounded his feet on the floor in a pretty good imitation of Charlie's laughing dance. "Mama ain't dead, Charlie." He leaned in close. "She's just gone to visit Aunt ... Rachel."

Cackles and hoots burst from the men sitting on the floor around the room. "Git that, willya?" One fell over holding his stomach. "Git 'em, Charlie."

Charlie swiveled his face around at the hoots and catcalls, then swung his eyes back around to Lowell. "Wha? You told me she was dead."

"No, I didn'."

"Yes, you did." Charlie yanked his hat off and smacked Lowell on top of the head with it. "You ... you-you tol' me she was dead. Say you did or I'm gonna smack you into next week. That ain't no good thing 'cause you be missing a paycheck."

"No, I didn'."

61

Charlie lifted his hat and smacked Lowell's head with each word. "Yes ... you ... did ... and ... I'm ... gonna ... make ... you ... say so."

Lowell crammed his false teeth back into his mouth, stood up and balled his fists by his hips. "No, I didn', and stop slapping me wid that great dirty head lid of yours."

"Oh, a great dirty head lid, is it?" Charlie slapped his hands to the bench and pushed himself up. "Boy, you and me gonna have a little word of prayer ...."

Whosoever was within reach scrambled to scatter as Charlie reared back for a great roundhouse swing at Lowell, but by the time his swing winged back forward Lowell had bent down to delicately place the Mason jar on the bench. Charlie's staggering momentum took him over his own chair. Lowell ducked at the end of the swing then charged toward Charlie's falling figure, fists flailing in wide alternate swings. By the time he got there Charlie had slammed to the floor and was moaning. Lowell tripped over Charlie's feet, keeled over like a tall pine and dead-weight bounced when he hit, much the same as a tree.

They both rolled over, elbowed up from the floor, breathed hard and wondered how they had gotten there.

Charlie's voice returned first. "What'd I ever do to you?"

"What'd you ever do to me? What'd I ever do to you?"

They wavered stares at one another then slumped back, sprawled flat on the floor.

Neither question was ever answered, exhausted sleep being the great equalizer of inebriate men. The beach, mothers and hunting were all forgotten in the alcoholic fog. So ended the first great adventure of The Gentlemen Colonels of Whispering Waters. It was not to be their last.

Chapter 9

Birth of the Fishing Beast

Ned felt pain in his hands as dumped his armload of firewood in the box on the office cabin porch. He straightened, looked closely at his red palms and then up at Jamie's father. "Mr. Garrath, could I get a pair of gloves?"

"Good idea. Tell you what, go get a couple of pair for the both of you. They're in the back room in a blue cardboard box on the shelf against the back wall."

After he found the blue cardboard box that turned out to be a green cardboard box, Ned saw two fishing poles leaned in the corner, along with the little trench shovel. He hadn't seen Jamie's father get either of them. He looked at the gloves in his hand and back up at the poles, his mouth tight.

Ned strode back outside, gloves in hand. He heard Jamie's father talk about sorting through wood piles and stacking as to length and size.

Jamie groaned. "Untangling piles of dirty boards, will the excitement never cease?" He held out his hand to Ned for one of the pairs of gloves. "Gotta be experts at something, I guess."

"Don't you get smart with me, Mr. James." Neither Jamie's father's face nor his voice was smiling. "You get to it."

"Yes sir."

By afternoon Ned had lost all remnants of enthusiasm. He heaved a rotten grime laden board toward the trash pile. The board missed by several feet, landed flat and sent up a cloud of dirt. He spit in the dust and looked at Jamie, who was reaching to grab another buried plank. "Thought you'd never have so much fun, hey?"

"Huh? What?" Jamie tugged at the plank.

"What's on your mind?"

"Well," Jamie grunted as he leaned his weight back hard against the plank, "how we're going to get that rabbit box ..." he slipped as the plank came free and hit one knee on the hard ground, " ... ow ... to work."

"Can't be too hard, can it?" Ned pulled off one glove and tried to rub the grit from his eyes. When he opened them again he noticed Jamie's father, Snow and Cyrus beside the pickup. "Lots of people do it, some 'bout as smart as a bag of hammers." He watched Jamie's father talk directly to Snow. Snow nodded and walked off toward the saw shelter. Jamie's father and Cyrus climbed into the pickup and pulled out through the mill gates. He bent down to pull another board out of the pile. "We could always ask somebody."

"Nah. We'll figure it." The afternoon train whistle blew and Jamie dropped the board in his hand straight down into the dirt. "Tell you what, you go fill up our water jars and meet me at the hideout. We'll go figure it out right now."

"Hideout?"

"Yeah, the corner in the back of the cabin."

"Oh."

When Ned got back he saw Jamie sitting by the old rabbit box, turning and looking at it and pushing on it with his hands. He handed one of the jars to Jamie. "Where do you think they were going?"

Jamie took the jar and unscrewed the lid. He shook his head, eyes on the box. "Daddy and the Indian? No idea. Maybe looking at timber stands."

Somehow Jamie referring to Cyrus as 'the Indian' didn't sit quite right with Ned. He took a deep drink. "His name is Cyrus. Your pop said people call him 'CC'."

"Who?"

"The Indian."

"Oh, okay." Ned watched Jamie scratch dirt onto his nose. "You know this thing is rotten? Any self-respecting rabbit could break out of it quicker than a pig pushin' up to a trough. Here, watch this." Jamie pushed one finger right through a patch of black wood. "See?"

He knelt down by Jamie and looked closely at the box. It was true. And the rotten spot Jamie had pushed his finger through was not the only one.

Ned watched Jamie push the box back over on the ground. "Only one thing for it."

"What's that?"

"Build another one."

"You think we can?"

"Oh, you bet. You get some wood out of the scrap pile and I'll get the tools."

Ned scrounged around the trash wood piles for boards about the right size and carried them back to the hideout. He watched Jamie work, lent a hand here and there when a board needed to be steadied as Jamie sawed and handed him nails when needed. When it was finished the new one looked pretty much like the old one, but for the life of him, Ned could not understand how it worked, how that sliding door on one end was held up and tripped to let down.

Jamie stopped, the hand gripping the hammer stuck on his hip and just stared at it. "I can't figure it yet. I'm stuck."

"Yeah?" Ned sipped at his water.

"Only one thing to do." Ned watched Jamie scratch his nose again. "When I'm stuck like this I always try the same thing to get my brain blood moving to make me think right."

"And what's that?"

Jamie's mouth widened and showed white teeth. "Fishing. You want to go? And you wanna fish this time?"

At the word 'fishing' Ned saw Toby jump up, wag his body and start to laugh. The only time Ned had ever seen fishing was when Jamie had taken him. "I don't know. I've never done much of it."

"How much?"

"Well … none." Ned looked down and shoved his fists in his pockets.

Jamie pulled his hat from his head and slapped it against his knee. "You mean to tell me you've never had a fishing pole in your hand? Never, ever?"

"That's right, never ever." Ned shoved his face out at Jamie. "I grew up in town working a store all the time and Pop don't fish. You got somethin' to say about it?"

"Whoa, whoa, whoa, come on. It's fun once you try. Daddy even got the poles for us, they're right there in the back of the cabin."

Ned made his hands relax. "Yeah, well."

The path from the mill to the lake was more closed in than the path from the house because it wasn't used as much. Branches and briars ripped at Ned's ankles and he almost ran smack into Jamie's back when Jamie slowed to look around. Jamie then stepped off the path entirely and circled the black soft loam at the base of a big persimmon tree.

"What are you doin'?" Ned watched Jamie place his straw hat on the ground and start to scrape the leaves from between two roots.

"Worms. This tree has the best night crawlers I ever saw." Jamie grinned up at Ned and held up his finger to his mouth. "Don't tell nobody. Found it myself last year; it's a secret."

"You said the mulberry tree had the best night crawlers in three states."

"It does. This one's better. Swear on your mother's grave."

"She ain't dead."

"Swear."

"Yeah, well all right. I swear."

"Why do you wear suspenders?" Jamie did not look up, just kept digging. "I've never anybody but grown-ups do that."

"I just … I don't like the way belts feel." Ned swallowed and watched Jamie scrape away the layers of loam. "Braces are

66

just more comfortable." He saw a small shrug in Jamie's shoulders, but it didn't matter. It was none of nobody's business but his. Toby came up and pushed against Ned's leg. "Why are you so all fired up for working at the mill, anyway?"

"To be with Daddy." Jamie lifted a spade full off to the side and pawed through it. "Sometimes it feels like there's this stranger coming in and out of the house. Comes in, sits down, eats, listens to the radio for a little while Momma clears the supper dishes off the table then spreads his books out."

"Yeah, well. Don't let it worry you. I'm not sure which is worse, not being with your dad or being with him all the time."

"What makes you say that?" Jamie pulled huge night crawlers out of the deep black loam and laid them into his hat.

Ned stuffed his hands in his pockets. "'Cause Pop's the same, c'ept I'm there all the time. He's either got his nose buried in his big account books or goin' to do church stuff so he'll look all spanking clean."

"Daddy does that too, 'cept he don't wear church on his sleeve." Jamie spaded the hole in again. "Don't tell him I told you, but he don't get on with the preacher."

"Pop calls the preacher Ol' Crap-horn."

Ned watched Jamie laugh as he lifted his hat carefully, since it was half full of dirt and worms. "Is that like a horn-of-plenty except full of …."

"Yeah well, pretty much. I hear a bunch of stuff but I'm not sure of what all of it means. Ever-body complains, but nothin's changin.'" Ned twisted a smile. "I don't think my pop likes him very much either."

"I sure don't. It's not so much that he shouts all the time and waves that walking stick of his around, but it sure don't feel very good to be told you're gonna go to hell no matter how hard you try." Jamie scraped the hole full again, stood up and leveled clear eyes at Ned. "It's like you're supposed to hate yourself all the time. They tell a body what not to do, but if it don't do any good what's the difference?" Jamie stepped back onto the path.

Ned crunched along silently behind Jamie. Toby pushed his way past Ned's legs to run ahead to Little Lake. They ducked under branches, carried the cane poles backwards to keep the lines untangled from the branches and brush.

When they arrived at the lake Ned tried to answer the question. "I'm not sure what the whole point of church is. It just takes the wind out of my sails to want to do things. It's not that I want to brag, but sometimes I'd just kinda like to enjoy something I've done for a minute. Seems every time I get to there Ol' Craphorn just say we're all black sinners through and through no matter what we do."

"Look, can we just fish? You're taking all the fun out of life here. I feel like all the joy in the world is just peeing out of me like Gramma when I'm trying to milk her."

"Oh yuck. Awright, you win. Let's fish."

Ned took a deep breath of pine air. Shadows from the trees cast across the water swayed back and forth as a small breeze rippled the world. But Ned saw that Jamie had things other than beauty on his mind. This time he watched Jamie closely as Jamie took the slender cane pole and unspiraled the slim braid line from around it. The line had a single small hook on the end, a small lead bead attached to the line just a little above and what looked like a half of a cork from a wine bottle just up from that. He watched Jamie dig in his hat for a worm and thread the hook back and forth through the worm's wiggling body. Jamie winked at Ned. "The lead keeps the worm down and the cork holds the worm up off the bottom. You watch the cork and when a fish bites the worm you see the cork wiggle. Then you pull it in. Simple."

"What do you do when they bite?"

"Heave 'em in. Then we put them on a stringer, take 'em home, dress 'em out and fry them up in Crisco." Jamie smacked his lips. "Food from the gods, that's what it is. 'Specially the tail when they fry up all crunchy."

"I'll take your word for it."

"Here, you take this one; I'll string up yours. See if you can lay that worm right down next to that stump, but not too close."

The water was smooth in the spot and smelled of algae baking in the sun on the mud flat beside the pier where thin stalks of water grass curved up out of bubbling holes in the muck. Ned swung the worm out over the spot and lowered it into the water.

"Might be good to use a cricket. You can hear them, can't you?"

Ned could indeed hear the quiet, then not so quiet, crickets ripping their evening song. "Hey, how did you know when you got a ... " A quivering jolt shocked his hands, shot right up to the top of his head and popped like a firecracker, except it didn't because then it was gone. Then his memory heard Jamie's voice in his ear to pull him in, set the hook, pull him in, aw he's gone.

"What ... was that?"

"That, my friend, was a fish."

Ned turned toward Jamie and saw his hazel eyes blink tight and dimples play across his cheeks.

"But ya gotta be just a lit-tle bit quicker."

"Yeah?" Ned turned back to the water. He wanted to feel that again, right now. "Yeah. Well, how 'bout that?" He tossed the line back in the water again.

"Hold up there a sec. Let's freshen that worm. If ya don't got a fresh worm, they'll never come callin.' "

Ned chewed on his tongue open mouthed as Jamie gripped another squirming worm and drove the hook barb through it back and forth. He watched Jamie wipe the blood and fluid on his overalls as he tossed it back in again.

Truth be told, Ned was more hooked than the fish. He held himself still so he would not have to admit it. He had never felt anything like that. Ned Custis, neophyte angler, waited, watched and wanted more.

But that was the only bite that day. The air grew open and still, not a mouse breath moved and the electricity faded in his arms. He leaned back against one of the wooden pilings. He blinked one slow time and the sun was gone, replaced by shadow and cackling crickets he could not see. He looked around and saw Jamie in the same condition, head lolling to the side. Jamie's hat was kicked over, the dirt dried and forgotten, the worms having crawled away to escape, only to drop off the dock to a watery grave. The air and his mind were still, not thinking, just watching.

Despite his best effort to stay that way, his mind betrayed him and churned once more.

Ned knew it was time to go or Jamie's mother would worry. Dammit. It was nice, just sitting and taking in whatever came to eye and ear. Ned heard Jamie's boot shift and slide across the wooden planks, then Jamie's drawl. "We gotta get home 'fore dark."

Ned yawned through his words. "Yeah, well. Time to go, huh?"

Jamie nodded and turned back to the water. "But I gotta admit, Daddy is right about one thing."

"What's that?"

"He says 'You cannot tell me there's more God in church than there is right here.' I do believe he might have something there.

Chapter 10

Cramphorne

"Somehow I never thought about goin' to church when I got sent here."

"You got your Sunday-go-to-meeting clothes, don't you? Something more than a Carolina tuxedo?"

Ned's face screwed up like a question mark.

Jamie laughed. "I'm sorry, that's a joke of Dancin' Charlie's. It's just a clean pair of overalls with the hammer loop ironed down flat. Anyway, you got Sunday duds?"

"Yeah, I'm sure Mom packed 'em; I just gotta find 'em." Ned lifted the lid of his suitcase and started lifting and digging through clothes.

"No rest for the wicked then." Jamie laid out his pants and shirt on the bed.

"What does that mean?"

"It's just something Daddy says when he doesn't want to do something."

"I guess I better say it today." Ned lifted his wrinkled Sunday jacket from the suitcase. "'Cause I sure don't want to do this."

Jamie's mother stuck her head in the door. "Hurry up to breakfast, we're running a little ... Ned Custis, is that your Sunday suit?"

Jamie watched Ned turn with a tight smile and mother-fear eyes, then freeze while Jamie's mother thumped into the room and took the hanger from his hand.

"Oh, give me that. I'll have to put an iron on the stove and see if there's enough time to ... Oh, what's your momma going to think … " She passed out of the room hissing whispers Jamie preferred not to hear.

Jamie did not mind Sundays per se. He was in complete agreement with God insofar as God designated Sunday as a day of rest. Jamie liked resting, was solidly in favor of it and indulged whenever he could. What Jamie did not understand was why Sundays were thought to be restful, particularly if spent in church clothes. Sunday-go-to-meeting clothes were hot, starched shirt collars were just plain itchy and the shoes hurt.

Most of the folks Jamie knew looked a little out of place in church. Women wore stiff hats, walked upright and careful in high heels, and carried thin slab-sided purses in gloved hands. The men looked as uncomfortable as he felt, faces tanned from mid-forehead below their hat line to their collar and rough-callused hands emerged from the sleeves of their brushed suit coats.

Only the minister was in his element.

The Right Reverend Costigan Analicious Cramphorne was a broad, bluff-bellied bulldozer of a man whose ego was sufficiently blind as to believe he was both humble and great. His greatest ability, as opposed to virtue, was the talent of complaint. This is not to say his complaints were effective or well-received. They most decidedly were not. But they flowed in a constant stream, varnished at the temporary pauses with 'Somebody ought to do something'. The idea that the 'somebody' could or should be him never entered his mind. This was the primary friction between himself and the self-sufficient parishioners he served. Being self-made, hard-working and independent to a fault, they did not take kindly to the idea of being somebody's mule. Toil they did and were glad of the chance to pound a living from God's good earth, but their toil was for themselves and their loved ones, not some outsider suffused with overblown delusions of self-importance. Thus the lines were drawn and dug in.

Jamie heard the opening verbal artillery barrage booming even before his father parked the car into the gray sand beneath the pines that surrounded the white clapboard structure known as the Miller's Landing First Presbyterian Church. In matter of fact it was

72

the only Presbyterian Church, but that didn't seem to bother anybody but Jamie.

Jamie saw the oh-so-brief glance and head shake that passed between his father and mother as they sat in the car with the engine running.

Gloria piped up between Jamie and Ned in the back seat. "Are we going in?"

His mother's mouth tightened in a smirk. His father said, "In a minute, honey. Just need to let the engine cool off a little."

Jamie heard more artillery over the sound of the engine and lifted his head to look through the front windshield. He saw the silver-headed, black-robed figure of the Reverend waving his arms at a rock-still man standing with crossed arms.

His mother turned the rear view mirror over toward herself and adjusted her hat. "Grant. It's time to go."

Jamie's father tilted his head to one side. "Just thought I'd sit a little bit to let the Right Reverend rage against the Philistines without interference."

"Now Grant," his mother said, "don't confuse the style with the message. Don't forget the third chance is a charm."

Jamie's mother did believe in giving folks more than two chances. This is not to say she left the door open to be taken advantage of. That just meant she gave folks a couple of chances to prove themselves contemptible before she wrote them off. "Ready?"

His father let out a heavy breath through his nose. "As I'll ever be." He switched off the car, swung his door open and stepped out into the white sunshine. Jamie followed and helped Gloria out of the car.

Ned tugged on Jamie's sleeve. "See you later, gotta go find my folks." Jamie watched Ned walk away, scanning the crowd for his mother and father.

Jamie's mother tugged on his other sleeve and pulled him towards the church. "Take your hands out of your pockets."

"There's no other place to put them."

"Clap them behind your back. It makes your clothes look better."

Jamie opened his mouth to say that whoever was in charge of the clothes shoulda made them look better with hands in, but thought better of it. He didn't mind so much. His father clasped his hands behind his back that way, usually when he was lost in thought.

The church bell rang one loud clear peal. The next excuse for a ring was a thin quivering tink. Mrs. Hera Cramphorne insisted with the fervent intensity of the faithful that the job of ringing the bell was hers despite the fact she had nowhere near enough strength or weight to pull on the rope and get the job done.

"When is Hera going to let somebody else ring that bell?"

"Grant, hush." Jamie's mother herded them together and up the slight hill to the church.

Jamie watched his father's face. It was always set hard before walking past the onslaught of Cramphorne's welcome at the church doors. It was an experience to make a body wince, a double barreled gauntlet between verbal blast and suffocating handshake. Every time he watched his father shake hands with Cramphorne he noticed that afterward his father quietly pulled out his handkerchief to wipe his palm and fingers.

Today Cramphorne rested one heavy hand on Jamie's shoulder and made a point of shaking his hand too. "This one's growing into a young man, Grant." The grip felt like his hand was swallowed in sweaty bread dough left too long out of the icebox.

Jamie's father clasped his hands behind his back. "Getting there, Reverend, getting there."

After they had passed the doorway his father silently handed Jamie his handkerchief. Jamie nodded thanks and tried to wipe the feeling from his hands. His father said "Yeah," put his hand on Jamie's shoulder and guided him to their pew.

The four of them sat down amongst the garden of fluttering funeral home fans beating the hot air around like giant butterflies laboring to fly free. Jamie and Gloria sat between their parents on the hard wooden pews smoothed slick by countless bottoms squirming under the weekly scrutiny of ministers staring

74

down from the pulpit, entreating their congregation to renew their resolution.

The great lumbering thunder of Cramphorne's voice obliterated any subtlety there may have been in the air.

"WE," he boomed to the sanctuary, "are all farmers. This time of summer, is the perfect time to reflect on the cultivation of our spirits as well as the noble earth we plow."

Jamie heard Ned's voice, low and quiet in the pew directly behind. "Ya think he's ever plowed ground?"

Jamie snorted and covered his mouth and tried to make it sound as if he was having a cough or a sneeze. Above his head he heard his father's low voice. "Shush." When he looked up he saw a tight frown dimple on his father's face he knew was a smile in disguise.

"WE must ensure the furrows we plow are straight ..." the Reverend pointed his hand straight ahead.

"We? You got a mouse in your pocket?" Behind him Jamie heard a quick pop, a quiet 'Ow' then a feminine whispered "Behave, young man. Where'd you learn such a smart mouth?"

Jamie bent his head, then took a breath and held it to keep from laughing.

"WE must tend our crops faithfully, weeding wherever we find the entangling vines of evil and sin and chop them out before they have the opportunity, before they have a ghost of a chance at winding themselves around our hearts and squeezing the righteousness from our souls. Because the Devil is a weed, my brethren, he is a weed. A weed that will never stop reaching toward the sweet deep root of righteousness."

Cramphorne raised his hand and clenched the air, his fist looking like a fat mottled mushroom poking out of the black sleeve of his robe.

"And like the choking weeds in our gardens that we know only too well, that devil will never stop coming for us, will never cease his wicked forays into our lives. WE must be ever vigilant, ever ready and more. WE must be ever on the alert for signs of encroachment into the gardens of our hearts. WE all know what that weed looks like. WE only have to look within our own hearts at that possession we covet, the shape of that bottle we feel we must have or any of a thousand other things that are the ghostly images of sin reeking, reaching to become real. Smite them! Recognize them for the wickedness they are and DRIVE them from your heart for they will melt like a snowfall in summertime under the bright heat of holy righteousness ...."

Not for the first time in church, Jamie's attention was beaten flat and sank into his own thoughts. He reached the point where he was past the bombast and simply watched the man wave his arms about like a great fat flapping black bird taking a sand bath in the back yard.

Jamie was startled out of his reverie by the clatter of tiny shoes on the hard wooden pew beside him. He turned and saw his sister Gloria jerk in a squirming fit. Jamie's mother stood and steadied Gloria by one arm. She tapped Jamie on the shoulder. "Come help me get her into the aisle."

Jamie held his face carefully still as he stood and lifted Gloria up and guided her out of the pew.

His mother took Gloria's arms from him. "I've got her now, Jamie. Thank you, sit back down now."

He watched his mother and Gloria move up the aisle to see if they needed any more help. The open double doors beyond them in the back of the sanctuary beckoned to him as an avenue of escape.

Jamie saw a tall thin man sitting in the last pew. Half the man's face was covered in scar like hard gray clay on a riverbank. Gloria stomped unsteadily in front of Jamie's mother, lower lip pushing the air when she looked up and saw him too. Her cry carried like a crow caw. "Mommy, look at that man! Mommy, what's wrong with his face?"

Jamie's mother bent down to her daughter, jerked on her arm. "You behave, young lady, you just hush right now. And leave that man alone." She looked up at the man as they passed him. "I am so sorry, Sabastian." The man nodded to her just once.

Jamie looked to his father, who shook his head and mouthed 'later', pointed at the pew seat and then back up toward the pulpit. Jamie followed his father's finger and looked up right into the red storm cloud of the Right Reverend Cramphorne's face.

Jamie felt his face go hot. He sat as quickly and as small as possible in the pew right next to the end.

The Right Reverend paused, glared around the sanctuary then grasped his hymnal from the edge of his podium. He sucked in a breath and boomed, "Let us all say 'Amen' to that feeling in our hearts and stand to sing number 464 in our hymn books. Let us raise our voices to the Lord for forgiveness of our sins ...."

Mrs. Cramphorne's fingers pounded the opening strains on the out-of-tune piano and Cramphorne's voice boomed through the sanctuary. The Reverend had caught even the choir by surprise and a great rustling of clothes and pages rose as everyone grabbed their hymnals and flipped to Hymn 464, Rock of Ages.

Jamie's seat by the aisle meant he could bolt once service was over and he took full advantage. As soon as he was through the double doors and into the sun he felt he could breathe again. He sat on the edge of the steps and looked for the man with the scarred face as he waited for his family to emerge in the quietly burbling throng that trickled out onto the lawn. His father sat down beside him.

He watched his father tap a cigarette out of his pack, stick it to his lip, flip open his lighter, apply the flame to the tip and draw the smoke in deeply.

"You all right, Daddy?"

His father nodded and exhaled smoke. "I will be in a minute."

"Grant! Grant Garrath!" A high male voice pitched at them from the throng.

"Or not." Jamie heard his father low mutter, then scanned the collection of small groups gathered on the grass.

He did not need to look very hard. Jeremiah Mason was clearly visible, steamrolling toward them, his skinny bow legs striding so fast they could hear the slap of pant cloth against his legs, his arms arched out from his body ending in stubby fists. Old Man Mason, as he was called, had very large hands for a man so small and wiry.

'Dammit Grant, dammit all to hell, he done it again! Sarah is just beside herself. She hates it when her choir gets caught out like that."

Jamie's father held up one hand. "I know, Jeremiah, I know."

"Not following the church service is just … I'm as religious as the next man, but I don't like surprises! I want God and his minister to be something I can count on, not some damn jackrabbit I gotta go off chasing ever time he gits a wild hair."

His father's hand came up quickly to cover his grin, but Old Man Mason wasn't finished.

"That ain't solid rock, now is it? No matter what the hymn says, no it ain't. I just don't like it, never have and never will!"

"We'll have to talk to him about it, I suppose."

"You, me and the Elders need to talk to the Reverend Flapjaw a little more'n that."

"Now, Mr. Mason. What's the trouble?"

"Don't you 'Mr. Mason' me, Grant Garrath. Lily Turner over at the county home tol' me that he done quit seeing the old folks and the shut-ins. That's a good part of a respectable minister's work seems to me, tending those who can't get to church on their own."

Jamie's father lowered his eyebrows at Mason. "He refused?"

"He just don't do it. Lily told me that when she asked him when he was going to visit, he just changed the subject. Gave her some platitude or 'tother about 'seeing what can be done.' You know what that means, don't you?"

"In another line of work, I'd say he'd picked out someone else he figured he could get to do it for him."

"What makes you think a minister's any different?"

"Well, he's supposed to be on a higher plane, isn't he? Leading his flock by example?"

Old Man Mason smiled wide, showing gaps behind his eye teeth. "My point per-zactly. What he's 'posed to do and what he's a'doin' are two different things. And you saw how he was thunderin' at Pete Alderman before services; I still don't know what that's about. Come the meeting, we've got to have a little word of prayer with that man."

Jamie's mother walked up with a red-faced Gloria in tow. Holding Gloria's other hand was Sarah Mason. Sarah, quiet and strong, came up behind her husband and took his arm. "You ready for some dinner? I need to get home and put on that roast."

Jamie watched Old Man Mason's shoulders relax. Whenever Mrs. Mason was around he was always quieter. It was as if Mason fought the raging sea and Sarah's presence smoothed the waters, her face his calm anchorage and ease from the storm.

Old Man Mason patted her hand on his arm. "All right." He tipped his hat to Jamie's mother. "Hannah." He looked at Jamie's father. "See you at the meeting, Grant. Good Sunday to you."

"Good Sunday to you too, Jeremiah."

Jamie and his father walked slowly back toward the car while his father finished his cigarette. "Who was that man in the back pew, Daddy? I don't think I've ever seen him before."

"That is Sabastian Wood. He's a quiet fella, keeps to himself a lot."

"What happened to his face?"

"He got burned in the war, but I don't know, exactly. He's never volunteered any information and I've never been rude enough to ask him."

"You never talked with him?"

Jamie's father shook his head. "Not to speak of. I've run into him at Gil's store a few times. We nod hello, but I've never sat down and talked with him, just never had occasion to. Why?"

"Momma seemed to know him."

"I think she knows him through his sister Clara, but don't you be getting all 'Nosy Norris' now, you hear me? That man has done harm to no one I know and he has a right to his privacy."

"Yessir. He ever been to church before?"

"He's there most Sundays."

"Why haven't I seen him? He's awful quiet, popped up like a ghost or something."

"Some call him that. He comes in after everybody else and leaves before the service is over. Like I said, he hurts no one and lives quiet. You can't ask for more from a man than that."

"What?" Jamie had heard of 'The Ghost' but had never laid eyes on him. "He's 'The Ghost'?"

His father stopped walking. "Mr. James, don't you ever let me hear you calling him that, especially to his face, you hear me?"

"But ..." Jamie's question froze stillborn. His father's face had turned to rock. "Yessir."

Jamie shoved his hands in his pockets and stayed put as his father took a deep drag on his cigarette and started back to the car.

Ned came up right beside him and whispered in his ear as soon as Jamie's father was out of earshot. "What happened with Gloria?"

"She's has little fits sometimes." Jamie looked at the ground.

Ned spoke quiet. "How 'bout that fella in the back pew?"

Jamie looked back up. "That's the Ghost. Can you believe it?"

"The who?"

"The Ghost. You've never heard of him?"

"No, but I've seen him though. He came in the store one time and bought the oddest bunch of stuff. I couldn't read him like I do other folks."

"What do you mean 'read him'? What did he buy?"

Ned looked at his feet. "Oh, linseed oil, some spar varnish, a tin of pumice and a can of talcum powder."

"What in the world ... ?"

"That what Pop asked him. He said he was getting his lines ready to go fishing."

"Fishing? That don't make any sense." But then it did. Jamie remembered the morning on the way to the mill when he had seen the long switch flicking against the sky and a fedora pushed back on a tall man's head. Going fishing took on a whole new meaning.

Chapter 11
Whitewash

Jamie stared into his bowl of oatmeal. He watched Ned pick up his spoon then rest his fist on the table, unwilling to break through the brown skin to the steaming oats beneath.

His father broke the silence. "Don't you like oatmeal, Ned?"

Jamie looked at his father's plate. "Why can't we have ham and eggs like you?"

"Because oatmeal's better for you. The ancient Greeks called it 'Ambrosia'. What are they teaching you in school anyway?"

"We haven't studied the Greeks. I just know they were before the Romans."

Jamie's father waved his fork. "Well, when you do, you'll find out the Greeks always quested for the vital substance of life, the one true foodstuff to give them health, strength and immortality. And they found it in the simple staple of the humble boiled oat. That's Ambrosia in front of you."

"But they didn't live forever, did they? I've never heard of any still alive."

His father leaned in his straight-backed chair. "Well, some say they did and some say they didn't. Others say they didn't give it enough of a try. And that's a tragedy. They were certainly strong. They pounded on the Persians pretty fierce a couple of times."

"Then why don't you eat it?"

"Because I'm a recalcitrant mule." He dabbed at his mouth with his napkin. "For you I had higher hopes."

Jamie looked toward his mother at the stove.

Her back was to him but she spoke anyway. "Would you boys like some raisins or brown sugar for your oatmeal?"

Ned lifted his bowl. "Please?"

His father pushed back from the table and lifted his coffee cup. "Tragedy, pure tragedy." He tilted it back to finish it. "Don't dawdle, now. Finish up, we gotta get moving." He gathered his papers, went over to Jamie's mother, kissed her cheek and stepped out the door.

In the back of the pickup Jamie held his head away from the cab for the bounce across the pot hole at the end of their lane. When they hit the hole he heard Ned's head bang then a curse. "Ow."

He turned and saw Ned's eyes clamped shut against the wind. "When we go down past the lake, I want you to look at something."

"All right. What am I 'sposed to be lookin' for?"

"Look over at the dock by the water before the pine trees shut off the view."

Both boys craned their necks and stared through the breaks between the pines.

"Now watch, watch." Jamie pointed to the thin reed ticking back and forth and the dark line flicking from the tip in curved graceful arcs. "There."

Jamie saw Ned's eyes grow a little wider under lowered eyebrows. "Who's fishing this time of morning on a Monday?"

"Is that what he's doing?"

"Yeah, fly fishing. Pop showed it to me in a magazine. He was all hot to learn how and have the stuff in the store 'cause it's how folks who got a lot of money fish." Ned leaned back against the truck cab. "Mom talked him out of it. Said it cost too much for something that probably wouldn't work."

"I bet it's the Ghost. You said he was goin' fishing." Jamie looked back toward the water. "Maybe he'd let us watch him. Maybe talk with him."

Ned shook his head. "Not me, uh-uh. No way in hell."

"Ain't you the least bit curious?"

"I ain't no cat."

"Daddy says he was in the war. That's what happened to his face."

Ned was silent. Jamie studied him while the truck bounced onto the washboard road to the mill. "You really don't like him, do you?"

Ned shook his head. "I don't know him well enough to not like him, there's just … it feels like he's broke inside."

"What are you talking about?"

"Every time I see him I get a shiver down my back like somebody jumped up and down on my grave with both feet and a fence post. Ever seen him up close?"

Jamie shook his head. "Just that one time in church, but not close, no."

"I did once, remember? He came in the store, got his stuff, laid it on the counter, paid for it and left. When Pop asked him about it he just croaked out the one word 'fishing'. It's the only time I ever heard Pop say he wished a customer would stay away."

"What do you figure really happened to him?"

"His face doesn't change, like it doesn't work anymore. He sets the creeps into me." Jamie saw Ned's face pinch up. "Whenever I look at him I kinda … hurt."

The pickup bounced on up to the mill gate. Before Jamie had a chance to move, Ned clambered over him, took the key from Jamie's father's outstretched hand and opened the gate. Ned made some people uncomfortable, so Jamie found it real interesting that he was spooked by the Ghost, a man so quiet that many had never even heard him speak.

Come the noon whistle, Jamie's mind had let go of the Ghost. He was tired of heaving boards and trash. Gritty sweat ran down his face and he smelled sun baked dirt beneath his feet. It felt

84

like the whole earth was one big crusty slab covered in hard sand that kicked up and choked his throat every chance it got.

Jamie and Ned retreated from the sun under the shade of the big oak trees by the office cabin. They took turns at the pitcher pump mounted in the well, the damp creak and gush of water a relief to their ears. They filled up their mason jars to overflowing, the cool water dripping down the sides, and then sat down on the bulging roots away from the bright dry heat. Toby plopped down beside them, panting.

Early that morning Charlie and Marshall had attached plow line to their lunch pails and lowered them down into the well where they would stay cool. Now they pulled them back up again and sat down on the ground. Little Foot stripped off his shirt, leaned against the tree trunk and fanned with his hat.

Chatter from under the next tree over drew Jamie's attention. He heard Dancin' Charlie's high cackle then the slow twang of the lightly built dark-haired man they called Rudolph. Rudolph seemed to Jamie to likely be the first man on earth to wear out a comb. The overalls leg pocket of most men at the mill held either a tool of some sort or a small cylindrical tin of powdered snuff. Rudolph kept a tin of pomade in his and used it frequently, dabbing little bits here and there to conquer strays in his slicked hair. Rudolph also smoked a lot. Jamie smirked at the idea of a grease fire.

Rudolph spoke loud enough for Jamie to hear.

"You think you know so much about it, well that just ain't so." Rudolph crushed his hat back on his head. "Maybe it's because you are so old, you just forgot what being in love is." He punched his finger in the air toward Charlie. "I bet that's it, you just don't remember, it's been so long."

Snow and Little Foot were sitting close to them and laughed, but Jamie noticed that Charlie's friend Marshall, the huge black man, did not. He just slowly rolled a cigarette. But large friend to back him up or not, Charlie was not about to let a challenge like that go untouched.

"Well, ain't you the fancy pants, Mr. Valen-tino? You just ain't been around long enough to know, is all. You just remember that after you been together for a few years and she gits a little wrinkle here and a little sag there and you get worn broke down from workin' and she throws you over for some young buck all full of piss and vinegar the way you used to be. Ain't that right, Marshall?" Charlie shook two fingers at Marshall as he lectured Rudolf. "He knows what I'm talkin' about, yes he does."

Rudolph dug in his shirt pocket for cigarettes. "I understan' Marshall's your friend and he'll back you up, but when ya git right down to it, you don't know, do you?. You don't know 'cause you ain't in it."

Marshall drew on his cigarette, let slow smoke out of his nose, then leaned his head back and pulled his broad-brimmed felt hat down over his eyes.

Rudolph tapped a cigarette out of the pack, then pointed at Charlie, the cigarette between his fingers. "And I'll tell you another thing, not that it's something you'd undastan'." He struck a match, touched it to the tip and lifted his chin toward Charlie. "I'm downright purty. Lots of gals told me so."

"Is that so?" Charlie hooted, a hard, high extended hack of a sound. Dancin' Charlie then earned his sobriquet. He picked up one foot and then the other as he laughed, then half-crouched on one leg and alternately pounded the other foot on the ground and slapped his knee in his own self-syncopated rhythm.

Even Marshall laughed at that, and Rudolph had to smile. "You just don't want to believe it, believe that I'm purty to the women." He took a half-step toward Charlie, then straightened up again. "Oh yeah, a woman'd have to be dumb as a stump to leave a man as purty as me."

Jamie snorted and almost spit the potato salad he had just spooned into his mouth. He put down the jar and reached in his flour sack for safer food, a drumstick wrapped in wax paper. "Good God almighty, would you look at Charlie dance?"

"Your momma sure knows how to make up a feed bag." Ned mumbled through a mouth stuffed full of chicken.

Jamie could not pretend any particular enthusiasm. He bounced the chicken drumstick in his hand. "Yeah, but I'm too hot to eat."

Ned mumbled at him.

"What?"

Ned swallowed quickly. "Strip the skin off. That gets rid of the grease."

Jamie did so and took a bite. It was better, much better. He laid the skin down on the tree root beside him for Toby. Toby lifted his nose to sniff it then turned away when a squall like a howling child rent the air.

"What was that?"

Ned looked up and shook his head. "I don't know. There can't be a baby out here."

Jamie shook his head too. "Not likely, but it sure did sound like one, didn't it?"

Their eyes searched for the sound. In the dim shadows underneath the cabin a striped orange mass with great green eyes stared at them. He yowled right at them again like they had just stepped on his tail.

Jamie said, "Would you look it, it's Wandering Tom."

"Who?"

"Wandering Tom, I told you about him. Old tom cat been hanging around since nevermind, but what's he crying at?"

"He wants your chicken skin. Hopin' you don't want it."

"He's right about that." Jamie lifted the skin and tossed it over right in front of the cat. Orange stripes flashed and both Wandering Tom and the chicken skin were gone and out of sight.

"Wow, that was quick."

They heard Snow's whistle to get back to work.

"Yeah well, so was lunch."

Ned followed Jamie as they rolled up their flour sacks and put them away in the pickup. He heard Snow call to them and turned to see Snow walking toward them carrying two five-gallon buckets. He handed each of them one. They were three-quarters full of a white watery fluid that slopped over the top as both boys heaved on the handles.

Ned staggered under the weight. "What is this stuff? It smells like fertilizer."

Jamie and Snow spoke in unison. "Whitewash."

Ned swiveled his eyes from one to the other. "Okay, what do we do with it?"

Snow looked at Jamie to keep his mouth shut then turned to Ned. "You're gonna paint the cabin. They's scrapers and brushes and a step ladder right over there in the tool shed. Thought this job was goin' to be a vacation, did you?"

Ned spoke directly to Snow without blinking. "Didn't know what to expect."

Snow frowned quick and nodded. "Fair enough. See if you can git the front of the cabin done by end of the day. Scrape it good so there's no loose peels and slop it on generous, use it all. When the bucket's is empty put 'em in the back of the pickup so Mr. Garrath can fill 'em up tonight from your gaslight generator. You done this before Jamie, I seen you do it at your daddy's. When you done, let me know." He pumped his thumb over his shoulder. "I'll be over there." Snow hitched his shoulders and walked over toward the engine shed, the legs of his overalls dragging the ground and puffing up little dusty clouds.

They put the buckets down. Toby sniffed at the white liquid and turned to lie down in the cool dirt underneath the cabin.

At the supply shed Ned grabbed normal paint brushes but Jamie waved him away. "Nope. Gotta use the big ones."

"These?" Ned held up two heavy brushes, coarse yellow bristles sticking out from wooden blocks with short wooden handles.

"That's them."

"How do you clean 'em?"

"Soap and water, but," Jamie grinned, "you gotta do it before the whitewash sets. Here, grab the other end of the ladder." Jamie pushed the step ladder over toward Ned and each taking an end, they carried it over to the cabin.

"Make sure you wear your gloves. And don't splash none in your face."

"Why?" Ned looked down at the watery mixture. "What's in this stuff?"

"Lime in water. But if you don't wear gloves it can eat on your hands a little bit."

"Lime?" Ned snorted. "Oh, Pop and I spread lime out in the garden with our hands, no problem." He stuffed the gloves in his back pocket.

"Nope, that's barn lime. Kind of a gray lookin' stuff?"

Ned nodded. "Yeah?"

"This is different. This is slake lime and it'll eat up your hands in a hurry. Not so much when it's mixed with water, but it's still a good idea to wear gloves. Tell you what, why don't one of us scrape and the other one slop on the whitewash. We can switch when we get tired."

"Okay."

They did just that until late in the day when Snow dropped by. The side of the building was scraped off as clean as you please and soaked with whitewash.

Ned said, "I'm sorry, Mr. Snow, but no matter how much we put on it just don't seem to get white. It just kinda soaks in and the board stays gray."

Snow laughed and rubbed his hands together. "That's all right, let it dry out some and it'll turn sure enough. Just look at your pants there."

Ned looked down and his heart sank. His clothes were covered with dry white.

"See? It'll dry up just like that 'cept a little whiter. Ain't no need to worry."

"I'm not worried about that, Mr. Snow."

"What's the matter then?"

"It's just that Mom's gonna kill me when she sees these pants and shirt. I know they're work clothes and all, but now they're ruined. And I don't have any more."

Snow glanced at Jamie. "You didn't tell him, did you?"

"Nope."

Ned turned to Jamie. "Tell me what?"

Jamie looked like he'd just swallowed the last bite of pie he was supposed to be saving for company.

Snow filled in the gap. "They's no problem with your clothes, boy. That stuff will wash right out, no problem."

Ned watched Jamie balance his brush down very carefully on the top of the nearest bucket. "I think I'll just lay this here until tomorrow … " Jamie had no chance to finish his sentence, because he had to dodge and duck a sloppy swipe of Ned's brush and run.

"You better give your soul to Jesus," Ned flung the paint brush right at Jamie's head " 'cause your butt is mine!"

Snow slapped his hands on his knees as he watched them gallop off down the path toward Little Lake. What he wouldn't give to be able to move like that again, lord oh lord, what he would not give. He picked up the brushes, closed up the empty five gallon cans and put them in the back of Grant Garrath's truck. He was still chuckling when he put up the ladder in the tool shed.

The boys sprinted hell-for-leather toward Little Lake. Usually Jamie could outrun Ned, but this time Ned was inspired. Down the path through the woods, Ned almost got close enough to grab Jamie's shirt when his toe hung up on a root. He windmilled his arms and recovered just as their boots pounded the planks of the dock.

Ned stretched and finally gripped into the back of Jamie's shirt. "Gotcha!"

When Jamie twisted around and grabbed his suspenders Ned figured out, all too late, that Jamie had no intention of stopping. Both of them flew off the end of the dock like hunting dogs after water birds and landed flat, lake water exploding into their mouths and noses in a shattered moment of white water and noise. Ned flailed in the water until he saw Jamie standing hip deep and realized he was not going to drown any time soon. He found his feet, water streaming off of him and watched Jamie holding his stomach in laughter. Ned looked down. White floated around him on the surface of the water. At that Ned felt the bands

90

of tension in his body shatter and fall away and he had to laugh too, loud and long. He grabbed Jamie by the front of the shirt and pushed him back into the water and then he didn't care if he was standing or not. He slipped down, laughing as hard as he ever had. If the water had been any deeper both of them would've downed.

A deep quiet voice rasped behind them. "I suppose that's all for fishing today."

Ned turned around and thought he was going to swallow his own head. The Ghost sat on the dock, his craggy countenance still as a stone, fishing rod laid across his knees.

"Oh ... we're ... uhh ..." Ned coughed.

The Ghost's face warped with what Ned thought might have been a smile. "It's all right." His voice ground the air. "They'd stopped biting." He hooked his fly on the cork handle, reeled in the line then unfolded his long legs to stand. His grabbed his canvas bag and an oval wicker bucket with one thin hand and waved at them with his rod in the other. "Have a nice swim." He turned down the dock boards. He didn't so much walk as he glided, all grace in every step and before they knew it he was lost aview in the pines.

Ned and Jamie dripped as they stood up in the water. Ned heard a rusty rasp then a hacking cough echo from the trees. "Is that him laughing?"

"Jesus H Roosevelt Christ."

Ned had to agree. As much as he was spooked by The Ghost, the relief at both his clothes and The Ghost finding them funny took the stand right out of his legs. "Goddamn." He sank back down into the water. "Goddamn."

"Don't you ever let Momma hear you talk like that." Ned watched Jamie slide toward the dock. "She'll switch you till you can't dance anymore and then she'll let your momma know and you'll get it all over again."

Ned laughed as he floated on his back. "Yeah, well."

At supper that night Jamie's father piled potatoes on his plate. "I talked with Snow today about a better way to use you boys than whitewashing."

Jamie heard his mother behind him at the stove scrape the cast-iron frying pan. "Yessir?"

His father grabbed the bowl of beans, heaped them onto his plate and passed it on. "He told me he wants to go ahead and crank the engine tomorrow. Needs your help to work on it."

The stovetop scraping stopped.

Jamie had heard the engine but never up close. If you were in the garden and stopped hoeing to listen, a body could hear the big bang start and then the deep irregular throb in the wind. "Tomorrow?"

"That's right, first thing. So let's not be dragging our feet getting' up."

"Yessir."

"I thought you said it wasn't going to be for another couple of days." Jamie kept his head down so he wouldn't need to look at his mother, but then Gloria began to kick and fuss and his mother had to take her upstairs.

"Eat up there, clean your plate." His father sawed at the meatloaf with his fork. "Turns out we need it earlier than we thought. It'll be you two, Snow and maybe Marshall. There's a lot to do to get it ready to run."

Jamie heard Ned muffle past the food stuffed in his mouth.

His father leaned his head in Ned's direction. "What's that?"

"Marshall. Lord, he's a big one. Hate to get on the wrong side of him."

Jamie's father chewed and swallowed. "I haven't spoken with him all that much myself. He seems to be a good man and he's got the strength of ten horses but he just doesn't talk a lot."

On the way back to his room from his bath Jamie overheard his parents.

"You told me he wasn't going to be near that thing."

"He isn't gonna be when they crank it. I do need him to help Snow work on it though. They'll just be getting tools and holding things, honey. They're not going to be close when it turns over."

"That's not what you told them."

"Well, they'll be close enough to see it, but nowhere near close enough to get in any trouble."

"Grant ..."

"Honey, it'll be fine."

After that Jamie just heard a slight heave of rustling and then silence. He ghosted back to his room, careful to avoid the creak boards in the floor. Ned was asleep, or seemed to be, but Jamie couldn't, not now. He lay back in his bed, hands crossed underneath the back of his head and thought about that engine. He hoped his father wouldn't keep him too far away. He ached to smell it run.

Chapter 12

Hit and Misses

"Rise and shine, boys. Time's a wastin', up and at-em'."

"Yessir." Jamie yawned at his father.

"Or you could just stay in bed today."

He looked at the shadow of his father lean in the doorway. Never had his father relented once he had awakened Jamie. "Huh?"

"Well, we're just going to crank the engine today, that's all. Not much else goin' on, so if you want to stay home … "

But Jamie had already vaulted out of bed. "Oh no, we're comin'."

"Speak for y'self." Ned's voice was muffled by his pillow.

He shook Ned's shoulder. "Come on, you want to see this thing run just as much as I do."

"Shake a leg, boys." His father's shadow vanished from the doorway.

Ned turned his head sideways on his pillow. "Sleep never hurt anybody."

"Come on, we gotta get up."

Ned rolled over, yawned and shook his head violently, then fell back down to the pillow. "All right, but my git-up-and-go done got up and went."

Breakfast was quiet, except for Jamie's father.

"The CCC wants to work a deal. They've had their budget cut so they're lookin' to tighten their belts a little. They need lumber and they've got plenty of timber. So the idea is that they

94

cut the timber and send it to us, we saw it up and sell it back to them at reduced rate, but I have to send in a bid."

"Doesn't sound like much money, honey." Jamie's mother poured coffee, blue hand towel wrapped around the coffeepot handle against the heat.

"It's not. But if I can keep the sawmill making money while we get logging up and off the ground for the army contracts it'll be worth it."

"Are you taking the work other mills won't? Is there something you don't know?"

"I don't know what I don't know." Jamie's father snorted a laugh. "But I do know if the big mills won't take the work I'm not going to sniff my nose up at it." He looked at nothing, pursed his lips. "I could make it a one-time trial contract though, just to see how it works out." He looked around the table. "Eat up, boys. Let's go."

Jamie felt oatmeal was the worst thing a body could eat fast. He did his best, but jamming the food down his throat made the oatmeal feel like concrete before it even got to his stomach. The bouncing trip down the dirt road to the mill didn't help at all.

When they arrived at the mill the gate was open but there was no one to be seen. Jamie's father pulled the truck up to the office cabin, killed the engine and got out. "Snow and Marshal are supposed to be here somewhere."

Jamie heard Snow call out, turned around toward the sound and saw Snow leaning out of the narrow open door of the engine shed just beyond the saw pole shelter. He waved them over. "Over here."

Jamie looked at his father. His father nodded at him. "Go on. I'll get the coffee this morning."

They trotted over to the engine shed. They ducked sideways to come through the door and blinked the sun spots out of their eyes in the darkness.

They heard an unfamiliar rumble of a voice echo in the small space. "Mr. Snow, I think we prob'ly need to lift up those big side doors and get some light in there 'fore we start workin'."

They could hardly see Snow's shadow turn back and forth. "I think you're right. Hold on a minute." Jamie heard the rattle of keys. "You boys stay right here. Don't touch nothin'. "

Snow pushed by them and out the narrow door. Jamie felt a little spooked waiting in the dark with someone they had only heard speaking, but then they heard rattling chains and a streak of light sliced into the dark interior. The hinges on the top of the wall door creaked but the door stayed put. Streams of light flickered and lashed and showed Marshall the mountain, his face shining like anthracite. He wore overalls with no shirt and a felt fedora set halfway back on his head. He stood still as a stone, hands shoved in his back pockets, while Snow wrestled with the doors against the dirt that had piled up along the bottom over the winter.

"You need some help wid dat, Mr. Snow?" His voice was deep and slow.

The motion of the door stopped and they heard Snow breathe hard for a moment. "You might say. I bl'eve I do."

Marshall blocked all the light coming in through the door for a moment as he ducked through and stepped out to help Snow. With a squeal of rust frozen hinges the bottom of the door moved and there was Marshall, who lifted it as easily as Jamie could a picture frame. He held it up in the air as Snow found and placed the vertical post supports underneath the corners, the lifted door now making a roof overhead.

Jamie looked over at Ned and saw Ned looking back at him with wide eyes. Apparently this man's size was not just bulk. But when Jamie turned back, his attention was caught complete by what rested on the dirt floor.

Jamie had seen engines before. He had seen engines of tractors, cars and his father's truck. He put fuel in the Delco generator at home every night and had even worked on it some. But this was like nothing he'd ever seen. This engine was huge, big as a tractor with two flywheels tall as a man mounted to either side of a great horizontal cylinder. It was love at first sight. "What the hell?"

Jamie did not see Snow jerk in reaction to his profanity nor did he see the hard gaze soften into a slow-grow grin as he saw Jamie's wide eyes riveted to the engine. "It's somethin' ain't it? That's the hit-n-miss. See that?"

Jamie followed Snow's finger to a brass plate mounted to the single massive timber that served as the engine base. It read 'Evans Mfg Co., Butler, PA. 20 HP.' What Snow had said hit him in a half-beat delay. "Hit-n-miss?"

Snow nodded at him. "Yep. It don't run all the time." Snow's grin grew broad into a laugh as Jamie stared. "I'll explain it to you as we go along. You're gonna help me get it runnin'."

"Oh. Okay." Jamie looked back at the metal beast. It was as big as a tractor and looked a little like one with its big rear wheels up off the ground but without wheels on the front. At the end of the cylinder hung a collection of pipes, valves and valve wheels, operating handles, steel springs, brass pipes and rods. The whole conglomeration rested on a cast iron base bolted to a single massive timber that rested on two railroad crossties. He saw that beneath caked sawdust and dirt it was painted a medium green with ghosts of thin yellow pin striping curling around spokes of the wheels.

His hands ached to touch it, but he held his fists tight in the pockets of his overalls, not wanting to break it, not wanting to ruin his chances by messin' something up, though as massive as it was that didn't seem very likely.

"Jamie." Snow awakened him from his reverie.

"Huh?" Jamie looked up. "Oh, yeah."

"Get over to the goo shed there and bring me that can of gas that's sitting by the door, one of them new tin buckets, a spout oil can and a can of grease. And fill one of them metal pitchers on top of the oil drums about half full of oil from the drums. Bring it all back here. And don't forget some grease rags."

Jamie turned back to stare at the engine as Snow talked to Ned.

"Now Ned, if you would, go on up to the cabin and ask Mr. Garrath for the good tool set in the green box." He clapped his hands to get them moving. "Go on now. It'll be here when you get back."

Jamie and Ned turned, grinned at each other and ran.

When Ned reached the office cabin Jamie's dad already had the toolbox set out, along with other tools in a galvanized bucket. "Here ya go. Help him out all you can now, but don't get in his way, understand?"

"Yessir."

Ned grabbed the box and the bucket and ran out toward the shelter. Just before he reached the door he tripped and spilled the tools on the ground. He gathered them all up and wiped off the sand and dirt on them as best he could against the side of his overalls. Fortunately the box hadn't sprung open in the fall, though it was upside down. Tools inside clattered when he turned it over. He picked up the bucket and stepped inside.

Jamie and Snow were laying out flat boards on boxes to make tables.

"Whatcha doin?"

Snow answered. "I'm gonna take apart what needs to be taken apart, then you boys are gonna clean parts for me and lay them out. Then we'll grease what needs greasing, oil what needs oilin' and put it all back together."

"Okay then."

To Ned the rest of the afternoon was a blur of mechanical mystery. Snow pulled the gears and levers of the great engine apart, bit by bit, part by part. He handed the individual pieces to Ned and Jamie.

Ned smelled grease and gas and kerosene. The gas dry-burned his hands as he dipped small shafts and cotter pins and bell cranks and fasteners and rubbed the dirt and grease off with a wire brush and rags.

He dropped parts in the dirt a couple of times and had to reclean them. When they got to greasing and reassembly he handed Snow the wrong ones because he didn't know what the parts were called. Jamie just seemed to know not only what the pieces were but was handing Snow parts before Snow asked for them. It was as if Snow and Jamie had their own language. Eventually Ned just sat on a bucket washing parts and watched Jamie grease and arrange cogs and cams and shafts and spacer washers and bolts and screws on the boards in mystic order.

"You done this before?" Ned asked Jamie. "You look like you done it a hundred times."

Snow laughed. "Yeah, don't he though? You boys makin' this go a lot faster than I 'spected."

To Ned, Jamie and Snow looked like surgeons working on a great mechanical beast. When all the parts were washed he leaned back against the wall of the shed. He felt useless and stupid, seeing Jamie so happy and in his element, smiling with real joy. He hated it. "You guys need anything right now?"

Jamie just shook his head, his gaze never leaving Snow's hands as Snow fitted the parts together and adjusted linkages.

"I'm gonna go get some water then, ok?"

"You come back quick now, we gonna need you for clean up." Snow glanced up at Ned, then right back down to his work. "And find Marshall for me, will you? We need him to get this beast cranked."

"Okay."

Ned left, his hands still burning from the gasoline. He felt like he had nothing specific to complain about, but anger still caught hold in his chest, his heart crusted with black stone. His kinder emotions slid off that glassy surface and fell where he could not find them.

He found Marshall by the water pump, standing by Cyrus. He walked up to them, nodded to Cyrus, who nodded back, then turned to the huge black man. "Mr. Marshall?"

The man nodded at him between sips of water from his mason jar. "Yes? What is it?"

"Snow wants you in the engine shed. I think he's about ready to try to crank the engine."

"That was quick. You helped him?"

"Jamie, mostly." He glanced back at Cyrus, then pumped the handle of the pitcher pump himself and drank from the spout.

Marshall set down the mason jar, set his hat on his head and headed in his constant gait for the engine shed.

"Let me see your hands."

He looked up at Cyrus and wiped his mouth. "What for?

Cyrus just looked at him, so Ned lifted his hands, palms up. This time Cyrus looked at the palms and then turned them over to look at their backs. "Take that soap there and wash the gas off your hands." Cyrus grabbed the pitcher pump handle and pushed and pulled.

Ned grabbed the bar of white soap and soaped up his hands in the stream of clear water. "How'd you know they were burning?"

"Saw the red on your hands and smelled gas. Wasn't too hard to figure."

Ned rinsed his hands under the stream and then wiped them on the legs of his overalls. "Thanks." He turned to leave.

"Hold on a minute."

As Ned turned back, Cyrus reached into the woven bag he always carried over his shoulder. He took out a round tin, opened it and held it out to Ned. "Take a little of this and rub it on your hands."

"What is it?"

"Something that will take the burn off of your skin. Go ahead, you don't need much."

Ned reached out and dipped a small amount out of the tin with his finger. He held it to his nose and smelled. It was fragrant like a plant he couldn't remember.

"Go ahead."

Ned rubbed it into his hands. The burn of the gas stopped. "What is it? I mean, what's in it?"

"Mostly goose grease and whale fat. A few other things."

He blinked up at the man. "Whale fat? Where did you get whale fat?"

"From a whale." Cyrus screwed the lid back on the tin and slid it back into his bag. He nodded toward the engine shed. "You better get back."

"Yeah. Thanks."

Cyrus nodded just once at Ned, then slung his bag back over his shoulder and turned away.

Ned sniffed his hands as he watched Cyrus walk away in his graceful, ground-eating stride.

When Ned neared the engine shed he heard odd puffing and thumping coming from inside. He poked his head in the door and saw Marshall bent over the engine crank on the flywheel. Jamie and Snow bent over the other side peering into what Snow had called the 'magneto.'

Snow spat in the dirt. "One more time."

Ned watched Marshall heave on the starting crank and watched the huge wheels spin over. There was a great hollow throaty metallic puff, then one bang. Marshall backed off. The engine spun, then died.

"Ok, take a break."

Marshall sat down and leaned his back against the wall of the shed.

Snow mumbled as he peered and pushed at the mechanical assembly. "I need for it to move just a skooch forward."

Ned watched Jamie jump around to the starting crank and put his whole weight on the handle. The engine wheels did not move. He bounced and the engine still didn't move.

Marshall pushed up off the ground. "How much you need?"

"'Bout a quarter turn."

Ned watched Jamie back off as Marshall reached out and readjusted the handle position so he could pull up on it and pulled slowly upwards with one hand. "How's that?"

"Perfect." There was a click as Snow adjusted the linkage. "Okay Marshall. Give her one more spin."

101

Ned saw Marshall heave on the crank handle and the spokes of the wheels blurred. The great throaty metallic gulps sounded again, then Ned heard Snow curse, just once.

The train whistle echoed from beyond the woods. Ned watched Snow lean back and wipe his hands on a rag. "All right, fellas, you can take off now. We might not have got her cranked yet but we got a lot done and I think that whistle is God's way of telling us we need a break. We'll give her a try again tomorrow."

Chapter 13

Ned Spooked

Jamie noticed that Ned lagged behind on their way to the lake. "You all right? Not that tired, are you?" He stopped by the worm tree.

"Nah. I'm just still not too sure about that 'Ghost' character. What if he's there?"

Jamie shook his head. "I really don't think he's anything to worry about. He doesn't strike me as a dangerous sort. Not like that Indian. What do you think he's like?"

Ned shrugged. "I don't know. He doesn't say very much. Not unfriendly, just not very talkative. I get the feeling he's a hard person to know."

"I still think he looks dangerous."

"He's strong enough. He's not big, but man is he wiry. I hope I won't have to work around him but it's a different kind of feeling than the Ghost. You know what I mean?"

"Uh-uh." Jamie shook his head. "What do you mean?"

"It's like I just hurt inside when I see him. I don't know what he's been through but it's written all over him upside down and sideways. Whatever it was hurt that man through and through. I don't like to be around him. I just … don't like it."

Jamie looked at Ned a little more closely now. "You can tell what people are feeling? How 'bout what they're thinking?"

He watched Ned look at the ground. "Not so much." Ned drew a circle in the dirt with his toe. "Sometimes. Pop don't like it much."

"So you spook your daddy? That why you're here?"

Ned kept his head pointed toward the ground. "That's about the size of it."

"Well spoon up the grits and call me country. Don't that beat all."

"Ain't no cause to make fun of me."

"Ain't makin' fun. The man's shooting himself in the foot."

Jamie saw Ned lift his head.

"If your daddy had half a lick of sense, he'd be asking you what folks wanted 'fore they walk in the door. Ain't that the whole point of a store? To sell all the stuff you can?"

"Yeah. I guess."

"Well, then I'm sorry to speak ill of your daddy, but he just don't seem too smart."

Jamie watched Ned's face relax. "That ... that's all right."

"Anyway, we got somethin' more important to talk about." Jamie jerked his head toward the lake to get Ned to go ahead of him to he could talk. "We need to figure out how to get that trigger on the rabbit box to work. I know we made it the same was as the old one in the trash pile, but it just don't seem to work that way."

Ned headed on down the path and spoke over his shoulder. "Maybe we could just use the old one and make it work." He laughed. "Or just maybe we could just ask?"

Jamie shook his head. "Nah. It's half rotten and I'm not sure I want everyone knowing we're trying to catch anything. Then everyone might know who did it."

The boys crunched their way along the path in silence, cane poles in hand, the empty bait can dangling from Jamie's hand. "Hope we can find some good worms, it's been awful dry lately ..."

Jamie almost ran into Ned's back as Ned stopped dead in the middle of the path. "Shh."

"Shh? I didn't say nothin' bad."

Ned held up his hand. "Shh. Listen."

"I don't hear anything. What is it?"

"Somebody's in our spot."

"Oh, that's no big deal. We'll just ease off around the side to another one. I was tired of that spot anyway."

Ned shook his head. "It ain't that, it's who it is."

"What? How would you know … ?"

Ned started down the path again. Jamie followed close behind.

They padded as quietly as they could down the path toward the pier.

"Oh hell. I knew it." Ned stopped and Jamie almost ran into his back again.

"Will you stop doing that?"

"It's him again."

"Him who? You mean …?" Jamie tried to peer over Ned's shoulder, but Ned held him off.

"The Ghost, that's him-who."

"So? Let's go talk to him."

"I can't fish with shivers runnin' up and down my back."

"Aw, come on."

"No. I just can't do it." Ned turned, pushed around Jamie and stalked back up the trail.

Jamie trotted up close behind Ned. "What's the matter? Daddy said he ain't never done harm to nobody."

Ned didn't answer, just kept on walking, not looking left nor right.

"You're making ten mountains out of a molehill. Me, I wonder where he got those scars. It was in the war, at least that's what Daddy said."

Ned stopped and turned around, looked at Jamie then glanced in the direction of the lake. "So you said." His eyes looked everywhere but down the path. "Yeah well. Still."

Jamie watched Ned shift from one foot to the other. "Y'know, I bet if we got him to talkin' he'd tell us about it."

Ned shook his head at the ground. "Not likely. Pop says there's two kinds of veterans, those who never shut up about it and those who never let out a peep." He lifted his head toward the lake. "And he don't talk about nothin'. Hell, he don't even talk. What makes you think he'll tell us about the war?"

Jamie shrugged. "I don't know that we can, but what if we could? God, wouldn't that be great?"

Ned just turned away back towards the house and kept walking. Jamie followed, but knew he had planted the seeds. Ned might still have his misgivings, but he had turned Ned's mind to think about it. That was enough for now.

"Daddy, where's the Ghost from?"

Jamie's mother responded as his father waved Jamie off chewing meatloaf. "Silerville, honey. His father was a doctor over there. Why do you ask?"

"I think we saw him down at the Little Lake fishing today."

Hannah Garrath set down her fork and exchanged looks with Grant.

Grant spoke very low and very slow, both indications of how serious he considered this. "We who?"

"Me and Ned."

"Ned and I."

"Yes sir."

"Now don't you go bothering Mr. Wood. He's been through enough in his life without having to put up with a couple of boys nipping at his heels. You hear me?"

"Yes sir, but there's not much chance of that. Ned's scared of him."

"Really?" Jamie's father turned to Ned. "That true, Ned? Why?"

"I don't know. He's just strange, that's all."

106

Jamie' mother spoke. "Ned, he's one of the kindest men I know. But he's been through a lot, that's why he's so quiet. So don't you bother him." Jamie felt his mother's eyes as she turned to him. "And that means you too."

Jamie looked at his mother. "What's he been through?"

Jamie's mother picked up her knife to cut at her beans. "To tell the truth, I don't know a whole lot about it and what I do know is not suitable for young ears. Honey, it's not that you're not capable of understanding, it's that you don't need to be burdened with things like that right now."

Jamie sat silently and looked from his mother to his father and back again, but saw no chinks in the armor, no crack in the unified wall.

Gloria, who had been oddly silent during this, saw the interesting moment was at an end and went about reasserting her self-assumed royal status. "I'm finished, Momma. I want dessert!"

Jamie's mother, more than ready to move on past the conversation, turned to Gloria. "All right, darling. Let's go see what we have in the icebox."

As the two of them got up from the table and went into the kitchen, Jamie turned to his father. "Daddy …"

Grant leaned back in his chair, drew his pack of cigarettes and lighter from his pocket and drew one out of the pack. "Listen to your momma, son." He flipped open the lid of his lighter, thumbed the wheel, held the flame to the tip until it glowed coal red then snapped it shut and exhaled a stream of smoke at the ceiling. "She knows what she's talking about. I know you're probably frustrated at not being told more, but this is one of those times when you'll just have to trust us. You're just not quite ready to know."

"You mean you don't think I'm smart enough yet?"

Grant shook his head and tapped ashes onto his plate. "Oh no, you're plenty smart. I know you boys are not gonna want to hear this; I didn't want to hear it when I was your age, but there are some things … Jamie, I don't know how to say this exactly, but what it comes down to is this. There are things that we just need to be a little older for in order to understand. One of those things is war and what happens in it. It's not a matter of smart. It's a matter of age, of being ready for it."

"Aw, Daddy."

" 'Aw Daddy' nothin', James. You don't throw seeds on the ground 'til spring when the ground is soft enough to plow and damp enough to take fertilizer. It's not a matter of you not being good ground. It's just not time yet. Trust me on this one, son. When I think you're ready we'll talk about it, ok?"

Jamie nodded, but it wasn't ok. He was quiet all through dessert. Rice pudding was one of his favorites, but his mind just wasn't on it. When supper was over Ned asked to be excused and went to take his bath and go to bed. Jamie followed his father into the living room to listen to the radio. When his father lamented again that Will Rogers wasn't around any more with "What did he want to go off on that damn fool flying trip with that damn fool Wiley Post for anyway?", Jamie went to bed.

When he came into the bedroom Jamie saw Ned looking out through the window. He slid out of his clothes and lay down. "It's awful still out tonight. I was hoping for a little breeze to cool it off some, but I don't think that's gonna happen."

"Does this screen come out?"

He lifted his head to look at Ned. "Yeah, you just undo the catches at the bottom then the whole frame swings out. It hinges up at the top. But don't swing it out too far or the whole frame will fall out. I did that once and almost cracked Toby in two when he tried to jump out. That wood frame is heavy."

Ned nodded. "Hmm."

Jamie leaned back in the bed with his hands behind his head on the pillow, closed his eyes and chewed over what it could be that his father said he was not ready for. "Hey Ned, what do you figure that …?" But the rhythm of deep steady breathing told Jamie that Ned was already asleep.

He stared awake up at the ceiling, images of pounding guns and brave men defying death filling his head. He imagined war could be pretty bad, but what could be so bad that they couldn't even talk about it?

Chapter 14
The Ghost

When the pickup stopped at the mill cabin the next morning, Toby jumped right onto the pit of Ned's stomach and knocked the wind out of him, then sprang over the side of the truck, beagle ears flopping. Ned cursed as soon as he could draw breath then jumped down too, but when he hit the ground his feet slammed flat on the hard-packed dirt.

"Ow."

But he could not pause for pain with Jamie pulling on his arm.

"Hurry up, would you? Let's get the coffee done so we can get back on the engine."

Jamie ran ahead. Ned stumbled up the cabin steps after him, but before he could get to the screen door Jamie banged his way back out past him, cleared the steps in a single jump and ran in the direction of the well, coffeepot in hand. Ned plodded to the stove, sat down and tugged the spring handle on the cast iron door. He laid in a fire using fat lighter sticks from the woodbox.

By the time the fire was drawing well Jamie was still not to be seen. Ned stood up to look outside and saw Jamie standing beside his father, Snow and Cyrus. Jamie's father shook his head, climbed in the pickup and drove out. Cyrus tilted his head in a sideways nod then turned and walked away toward the work sheds.

Ned closed the stove door then stepped back outside to find out what was going on. He pushed through the screen door and down the steps. Snow waved at him. Ned shoved his hands in his pockets and walked over.

"You gonna be whitewashing by y'self for a while. Mr. Garrath seems to think I can't pay attention to the engine and but one of you at a time. This mornin' it's just gonna be Jamie with

110

me." Snow turned and laid one hand on Jamie's shoulder. "Why don't you go git the tools, you know where they are."

Ned watched Jamie look down at Toby. "You stay with Ned today, okay boy? I'm not gonna have time to play today." Jamie shoved the coffee pot at Ned, tilted his head in a twisted grin then turned and sprinted into the cabin for the tools.

Ned looked at Snow.

"You know where all the buckets and brushes is. Don't forget to scrape well and slop the whitewash on good and heavy so's we don't gots to do it but once. All right?" Snow slapped the back of Ned's shoulder, then walked away toward the saw shed.

Jamie blasted by, tool box and bucket rattling in hand and caught up with Snow.

As the two walked away beneath the trees Toby gave a low wuff.

Ned reached down and scratched Toby's ears. "I hear you." Toby stood up and rubbed against Ned's leg, then turned away, head and tail drooping down, to plump down hard on the cool dirt underneath the cabin. "Yeah, well."

Ned was just heaving a five gallon bucket of whitewash out of the door of the goo shed with both hands when he felt someone come up beside him. It was Cyrus.

"Here, this might help." Cyrus set another empty bucket down beside the full one. "Sometimes it's easier to carry two half-buckets than one full one." He took the full bucket from Ned, poured half of the whitewash in the empty one and set it down. "Give that a try."

Ned picked up both buckets, one in either hand. They were still heavy, but at least now the load was balanced and didn't pull his shoulders out of whack. He looked up at Cyrus. "Yeah, thanks."

Cyrus nodded just once, then stepped into the tool shed. The tall man picked up a broad file and bent over the bench vise to stroke the edge of an axe.

As Ned turned away, the handles from the buckets biting into the crooks of his fingers, he heard the engine hit just once, then nothing. A sharp curse cracked against the air. Ned smiled just a little, then dragged his feet in the dirt toward the office cabin.

When the morning train whistle blew Ned put down his brush, sat down in the dirt by the cabin and leaned his back up against the clapboard wall. He sipped water from his mason jar and sweated, and looked at the whitewash coating his pants.

Neither Jamie nor Snow nor Cyrus made an appearance at the morning break. The men gathered around the pump, drank their water and sat, too hot for conversation.

Not many minutes after the break ended he heard one large bang, then a series of irregular bangs not as loud in an odd syncopated rhythm. Then the clatter died and he was left with the sloppy squish of his whitewash brush against the rough clapboards.

The noon train whistle wailed. As Ned leaned back to ease the ache in his back, the brush slipped from his hand and dropped into the bucket. The splash soaked his leg. He wiped his hands on a rag, got his lunch flour sack from the cabin and sat down on the oak tree root on the side away from the sun to savor the time off and the food Jamie's mother had packed. As he chewed slowly he saw Toby curled up under the cabin in the cool dirt.

Jamie ran up with the blue toolbox and the tin bucket into the cabin, then burst back outside carrying his own flour sack.

The ground thumped as Jamie almost fell on the ground beside him. "Aw man, you should see it spin."

Ned took a big bite out of his sandwich. He was tired of chicken all of a sudden and spoke through the mouthful of food. "I was there yesterday, remember?"

"Oh yeah. But I was talking about when it runs. It didn't for long, but Snow says now it's just a matter of tweaking a little here and there. That big cold steel thing just comes alive."

"I'm sure it does."

"It's kinda running, so I'm back here whitewashing, but good god almighty that was great. I can't wait to see the saw hooked up to it." Jamie took a huge bite out of his sandwich. "Snow says the saw blade rings when it runs, and there's not much short of throwing a car up on the carriage that'll stop it."

Ned chewed and watched the ground.

"All right then. How 'bout after the afternoon whistle we finish up the box trap, get it set in the woods and then go fishing. What do you think?"

"Mmm."

"I'll take that as a yes." Jamie stuffed another big bite of sandwich into his mouth and slurped on his mason jar. "Sometimes things come together and sometimes they don't, but when they do come together it can be so good you just can't stand it."

Jamie tired quickly of whitewash. Scraping clapboard and slapping on whitewash just didn't compare to seeing big iron wheels spin and feeling the bang of the engine hammer at his chest.

"You gonna hold that scraper till it rusts or you gonna use it?"

Jamie looked up at Ned and realized he'd stopped. "Oh." He scraped at the dirty white flakes on the wood again, but felt Ned waiting at his shoulder with the paintbrush. "What, you wanna switch?"

"Might as well."

They traded tools and Jamie slopped the milky liquid on the heavily scored wood after Ned had scraped, but his head was still full of engine. "It was alive, Ned. It was like we made it wake up."

"Do tell."

The mid-afternoon train whistle wailed. Jamie and Ned gathered up their brushes and buckets and plodded toward the sheds to stash the buckets and tools. As they gathered their lunch sacks from the office cabin, Jamie saw the fishing poles in the corner.

"What say let's just go fish, how 'bout it? I don't feel much like working on the box trap."

"I think I'm just gonna go back to the house."

Jamie stopped. "What's the matter, you sick?"

Ned shook his head. "Nah. Just tired." He turned and went out, letting the screen door slam behind him.

Jamie watched Ned slowly move up the path, hands buried in his pockets. Then he set his hat more firmly on his head, grabbed his fishing pole and went to the lake.

As Jamie approached the dock he saw the tell-tail switch flicking against the sky and as he got closer, the faded fedora of the Ghost. When he stepped out onto the dock the rest of the Ghost came into view, the bones of his back showing sharp through his thin shirt.

"Mr. Wood?"

The Ghost turned his face over his shoulder to Jamie. "Yes?"

"Do you mind if I sit here and fish?"

The Ghost shook his head. "Not at all and I thank you. It's good to meet someone who appreciates the courtesies of fishing."

Now that Jamie was this close to him, he saw a thick fold in the man's face tighten and realized he was looking at a smile, though through the man's smoked glasses it was hard to tell what he was looking at.

It really couldn't be called a smile. One side of the man's face seemed to have thicker skin than the other side with smooth dimples running pocked across the surface. A white scar ran from underneath his eye across his cheek.

"Well, I don't like to be bothered when I'm fishing, so I just figured I don't want to bother nobody else the same way."

"A commendable thought. By all means, try your luck."

Jamie took two steps closer and sat down on the rough dock boards. "There's really not much luck to it, sir. I just put a worm on, set the bobber so that it'll wiggle just a little off the bottom. When a fish pulls the bobber under I pull it out. When I've got a couple or three or four I go on home. No point in catching more than you can eat."

The Ghost twisted his half-smile again as he turned toward Jamie. The other side of his face had a jagged scar that seemed to grow like ivy from his ear and down the side of his neck where the lumpy white rope disappeared under his collar. "Does success usually come so easy to you?"

Jamie shrugged and tried not to stare. "Sometimes not. Sometimes they just don't bite for some reason."

"Did you ever wonder why a fish would bite a worm in the first place?" The Ghost cocked his head to one side. "Your success is proof positive, but why?"

The question rooted around in Jamie's mind, but he came up blank. "I don't know."

"Let's see if we can find out before we meet here again."

"So I'm not bothering you?"

"Oh no. You have the talent for sharing a quiet moment. I thank you."

Jamie's brain stumbled for a moment and then shoveled out, "Sure. Don't mention it."

The Ghost didn't offer anything else and Jamie was too afraid to talk any more. He was about to bust with questions about the war and how the Ghost had gotten those scars, but he felt like he'd blabbed on too long. To ask right then just didn't seem right.

Jamie found Ned with his shoulder leaned under Gramma in the milking shed, steadily filling the milk bucket. "Have I got something to tell you." Gramma turned to him and mooed. "You'll never guess who I ran into at the lake."

"Probably won't." Ned did not look up.

Jamie's mother called them to supper from the back porch. "Jamie, Ned, wash your hands and get in here, supper's ready!"

"Tell you later. You're not gonna believe it."

"Probably not."

Supper was quiet except for Jamie's father talking with his mother about the mill. Ned didn't talk at all.

Jamie's mother leaned toward Ned. "Are you all right, honey? You've hardly touched your dinner."

"I'm just tired is all."

"Why don't you go on, take your bath and get to bed then. Get some sleep."

"Thank you ma'am. I think I will."

By the time Jamie got to bed after listening to the radio with his father Ned was already in bed, turned away and breathing slowly. He wasn't certain if Ned was asleep or not, but if he wasn't, he wasn't in the mood to talk. Jamie blew out the candle and slid into bed as quietly as he could. He listened to the freshening wind through the trees outside his window.

Jamie jerked awake. The sash of his window had always rattled when the wind blew. Now it rattled as a dark shape ducked its way through. Jamie listened like he had a live wire feeding his ears. The window screen banged as the shadow hit his head on the window. The resulting curse revealed the shadow was Ned.

Jamie tried to keep the laugh out of his voice. "You all right?"

The only answer was the creak of Ned's cot.

Jamie slipped out of bed, closed the door as quietly as he could and lit the candle. He pulled the wooden screen frame closed and latched it.

"Daddy'd tan the both of us if he knew you been out like that." He watched Ned slide his boots and pants off and slide his legs under the covers. "Where you been?"

"Nowhere." Ned turned his shoulder to Jamie. "Just out."

"What do you mean, out'?"

Jamie watched Ned's dark eyes slide over on his. "Don't tell me you've never so much as snuck outside at night."

"No, never. What'd you go and do that for?"

"Sometimes I just get to feelin' closed in and just … just to breathe some air."

"You do that at home?"

"Yeah."

"Ever get caught?"

"Not yet." Jamie watched Ned shake his head. "You can blow out that candle now."

"Oh, yeah." Jamie snuffed the candle then opened the door again and slid back under the covers in the dark. "You're gonna get in trouble; you could get hurt."

"I don't wander far."

"What do you do?" Jamie had heard about sneaking out, but in the country where there wasn't a whole lot to see, there didn't seem to be much point.

"Just watch. Watch folks come out of the movie house or the guys in the pool hall a few doors down from the store. I want to see how they move when they're not working or trying to sell you something or … struttin' around in church. I want to see them when they're, you know, out."

"Out of what?"

"Just out. Night breathes easier." Ned lifted his head at Jamie, then turned his shoulder and wrapped his sheet up over his back. "Things just feel different."

Jamie lay back in the dark. It was different all right. The regulator clock ticked in the hall and the wind outside stirred the trees.

Altogether different.

Chapter 15

Eueas

Jamie swung and sweated and hacked at tall Johnson grass around the front mill gate with a sling blade. He heard the scrape and chop of Ned doing the same right alongside, but that was all. Ned hadn't spoken half-dozen words all morning. Clouds gathered gray on the horizon and the hazy air breathed heavy and hard. Every stroke of the blade stirred up dust that stuck to the sweat on his skin and ground underneath his collar.

Hard knocks of a neglected truck engine clattered outside the sawmill gate, so Jamie rested the head of the sling blade on the ground, leaned and looked. A battered dusty pickup truck pulled over and stopped at the end of the approach road with a scraping squeal of brakes. Man-shaped shadows inside the cab sat still until the dust cloud tail blew past, then one of the shadows pushed open the near door and stepped out, rattling a cane against the truck's rusty metal doorframe. When he landed on the ground, he slid a torn black felt hat onto his head, limped one step forward and stood for a moment leaning with the cane against his leg and looked back and forth. The driver shadow inside the truck pointed with his thumb toward the back of the truck. The man with the cane turned slowly and nodded, then heaved two small cardboard suitcases out of the back of the truck. He lifted his hand to the driver in a waveless wave and slammed the door. The driver drove away without another sign, apparently no love lost. The man waited until the dust cleared and then slowly bent over to lift one case up under his arm. He lifted the other case with the hook of his cane in the handle up to his hand underneath the first, and then slowly stilted his way up the road to the mill.

As the man drew closer Jamie saw that he was possibly the dirtiest individual Jamie had ever seen.

He stopped and regarded them with head cocked to one side, then spit a wad of brown yellow tobacco juice on the ground.

The man smiled, which was a mistake. Lonely yellow teeth flecked with green and brown tobacco stains appeared through the horizontal split in his face.

"You boys work here?"

Even at generous talking distance the smell was enough to put off a horsefly, an odd combination of ancient sweat cemented to the armpits of his shirt competing with cheap cologne that irrigated the dirt-filled creases on his neck.

Jamie slid his eyes over to Ned for a second then back to the man, but it was Ned who spoke. "As you see."

"There work here for an honest man?"

Jamie found his voice. "You'll have to talk to my daddy about that."

The grin slipped a little below narrowed eyes. "That so? And where would your daddy be then, boy?" The way he spoke made Jamie want to take a bath.

Jamie pointed at the cabin.

The man shifted his tobacco wad to the other side of his mouth, spit again, nodded just once and leaned on his stockman's cane to grind toward the cabin in his slow stiff-legged walk.

As Jamie watched the man move away he heard Ned's voice behind him. "Who in hell's blue blazes was that?"

Jamie shook his head. "Never seen him before." He turned back toward Ned. "And can't say I want to again."

As soon as Grant saw him he knew what the man was after. It was the same thing all the men who walked up the road wanted. Work. There was little enough here for the men he knew, let alone every Dick and Harry that happened by with a face full of dirt. Grant set himself for turning the man down as he watched him approach the cabin.

"Come on in."

The man climbed the steps, set his suitcases on the porch and stepped inside.

Grant took in the dirt in one glance and sniffed. "State your business."

The man just handed him a sheet of much folded paper. Grant opened it. It was an honorable discharge for one Corporal Eueas Canfield from the Air Service of the American Expeditionary Force, discharged for medical reasons, dated December 1919.

"You were wounded?"

He stretched his mouth into a greasy grin. "They wouldn't call it a wound, exactly. Got my leg broke when I got run over by a hot-shot peach fuzz flyboy when I was pullin' out his wheel chocks. Never healed back right. Since it weren't by the enemy I didn't get no wound chevrons and after the armistice the Army didn't have much use for a broken down man with a wrench."

Grant's conscience grabbed him. "Mr. ..." Grant squinted at the blurred writing on the paper "... Canfield?"

The man nodded. "Call me Eueas."

"You were a mechanic, then?"

He nodded. "That I was."

Eueas Canfield made Grant's stomach crawl, but the man was a veteran. The paper proved it. He folded it back up carefully. "Tell you what, Mr. Canfield. I'll take you on at a dollar and a half a day and see how you work out."

"Hell, that ain't much to live on." Eueas smiled again.

Grant wished he hadn't. "There isn't much here. The only reason I'm considering it is this piece of paper. You still got to prove you're useful. A dollar and a half a day for a six day week."

"Nine a week. That what everbody else is making?"

"No. But it's what you'll make until you prove yourself. There's a dollar a week tent camp back up the road a piece and a worker truck that'll get you here in the morning and take you back at night. It stops by a store for gas on the way back in the evenings so you can get something to eat for supper there."

"Who pays for the truck?"

"Not you, so don't worry about it." Grant held out the paper. "Take it or leave it, Mr. Canfield. That's all there is to it."

Eueas shifted his chew to the other side, looked around for a place to spit, then just held it in his mouth. He took his paper back. "Don't have much choice, do I?"

"Not if you want a job, no. My foreman's name is Snow. Tell him I just hired you on and you're to help him work on the hit-and-miss."

"What's that?"

"You don't know?" Grant tossed his pencil down. "It's an engine. Drives the saw and the planer. Snow'll explain it to you. You can leave your bags where they are 'til you get off work."

"When's that?"

"When it's too dark to work."

"From 'can't see to can't see' huh?"

"That's the job."

The dirty man touched the brim of his hat. "Thank you, sir."

"You'll find him over by the saw."

He watched the man stop at the bottom of the steps, spit then stiff-leg his way over toward the engine shed. Grant rubbed his chin. He hoped the soft-heart Hannah teased him about hadn't just turned into a soft-head. He couldn't afford that if the mill was going to make it.

"I didn't know I was goin' to git another man." Snow was at the door to the office. "And he won't too happy at all when I said my name was Snow, no sir."

Grant regarded Snow. "Didn't care for that, huh?"

"He didn't say nothin', but no sir, not by one little bit."

"Well then he'll just have to lump it, won't he?"

Snow's face broke into a great white grin. "I purely do 'spect so." He laughed, lifted his straw hat, wiped his bald head with a bandana and set it down again. "That man ain't washed in a month of Sundays, though. He work on machinery before?"

Grant nodded. "His papers say he was an aircraft mechanic during the war."

"Thought so. He don't know much 'bout a hit-or-miss, but he knows which way to turn a wrench, I'll give him that."

"Maybe he'll be some use after all." He exhaled through closed lips.

"But you want me to keep an eye on him."

Grant nodded. "That I do."

"All right." Snow pulled out his small notebook and pencil stub from his front overalls pocket. "You got a time we gotta have wood going out of here?"

"Yeah, we need two hundred board feet of pine two bys out of here by Thursday week. Can we get that done?"

"If we can keep the chugger up and running and get some logs in by tomorrow. It don't give Little Foot much leeway in the kiln though."

"He'll do all right getting that first load dried out if we can get him the wood and fuel by Friday, don't you think?"

"We'll give it a shot."

"All right. I don't like to push, but I need money comin' in pretty quick if we're gonna stay open."

"We need some quarter inch chain and some more plow line. The old stuff's so rotten I wouldn't trust it to hold my dog. And I can't seem to find the round whet stones for the axes."

Grant shuffled about on his desk and found his list. He scribbled the items down. "I hope that does it for a while."

"All right now, I'll get back to it." Snow stepped out. The porch screen door slammed behind him as he clumped down the steps.

Grant dropped his pencil and his glasses on his desk, rubbed his eyes and leaned back in his swivel chair. He wondered for the thousandth time if he had done the right thing in opening the mill again. He had the orders, he had the men, he had the mill, and he had timber. He just needed time. And a little luck.

Chapter 16
Boxes

Jamie was sick of lime in his nose. He and Ned were whitewashing the back side of the office cabin in deep shade. Ned still wouldn't meet Jamie's eyes and was still silent.

Jamie couldn't stand not talking any more. "Wonder who came up with the idea of whitewash? I mean it ain't like … "

He saw Ned hold up his hand for quiet.

"Look, just 'cause you decided your mouth don't work don't mean I gotta …"

"No, shhh." Ned shook his head. "Listen." Ned gently laid his scraper aside.

Jamie craned his ears. A pitched voice echoed from the cabin through the open window.

Ned nodded his head toward the window and crept up under the sill. Jamie followed and peeked over the low corner.

Lowell Lowry stood in front of his father's desk with his old felt hat in his hand. "I tell ya it's hurtin', Mr. Garrath. I gotta go get it seen to."

"Well, teeth are nothing to mess with, Lowell. How long has it been hurting?"

"On and off, more than a month now. But it's real bad today."

"Which one is it?"

Lowell pointed to the lower side of his jaw on the back. "Right there, Mr. Garrath. It's hurting so much I can't eat."

"Let's have a look."

Lowell hooked his cheek away from his jaw with one finger. "Et's aht ohn. Eeeh?" He took his finger out. "I hate to spend the money, but you know how it is."

"I'm still a little unclear, Lowell." His father leaned forward. "Which one is it, exactly?"

Lowell reached with his thumb and forefinger and yanked his bottom false teeth plate out of his mouth, leaving his lower lip caved in. He pointed to the last one on the left side. "It'sh 'at one. It'sh been killing me all morning." He clapped the plate back into his mouth and chattered his teeth twice to set it in place. "Hurts something awful."

Jamie watched his father place one elbow on the desk and cover his eyes with that hand. He folded his lips between his teeth, bit down and nodded. "Okay, Lowell. Go ahead."

"You all right, Mr. Garrath? You sound like you swallowed a bug or something."

Jamie's father nodded, held his lips tight shut and waved Lowell out of his office.

Jamie rolled from the window, clamped his hands over his mouth and leaned back against the cabin. He saw Ned slowly fall over in the dirt, both hands on his stomach, eyes shining in silent laughter. His laugh eased into a broad grin. The grin was not for Lowell and his painful false tooth. Jamie had his friend back.

Around midday scraping and slopping on the cabin slowed to a crawl. Jamie could feel the heat of the day drain him flat, sweat dripped from his nose and he wiped it off on his sleeve.

"Hey, Ned."

"Hey, what?"

"You think we'll ever get that rabbit box to work?"

"Hope so." Ned dropped his brush to his side. "I sure am tired of this."

"I talked with him yesterday."

"Him who?"

"The Ghost, 'him who'. His name is Sabastian. He's okay."

Ned narrowed his eyes at Jamie. "What's so okay about him?"

"He's more polite than most grown-ups. And he asks questions like 'Why does a fish bite a worm?' "

Ned shrugged. "I dunno. They just do. So he makes you think about things."

Jamie nodded quickly up and down. "Yeah. He doesn't talk at me like I'm a kid; he talks to me like I'm … me."

"Yeah well. He's still spooky."

"A little. But you forget to look at his face when you listen to him."

"Yeah?"

"And he listens. We're kids, what grown up have you ever known that listens to you?"

"We're supposed to be 'young men' now, according to your dad"

"Daddy just says that when he want us to behave. So he can tell us to act like it."

It was Saturday, so they quit work at noon. On the path to the lake through the woods Jamie heard Ned's voice behind him. "You know, I may be too tired to fish."

As Jamie looked down to avoid a root and saw his feet plodding dusty boot prints in the gray powdery ground he had to agree. "Don't ever tell nobody else that."

"Yeah, 'men' aren't supposed to feel tired or cold or hot or anything, are they?"

"Huh-uh. Nope."

"Can I point out something?"

"What's that?"

"We ain't 'men' yet."

126

They reached Little Lake and Jamie stopped to catch his breath for a moment under the shade of the trees before the dock. "No. I 'spose not." He looked at Ned. "But how is a body supposed to know?"

Ned just clumped out onto the dock. Jamie followed, boots echoing on the broad gray boards.

Sabastian sat in his usual spot with his back up against a piling. He turned his head toward them and smiled. "You're thinking some thoughts today." He didn't have his fishing rod. A couple of books rested beside his flask on the dock beside him. He had a sketch pad atop his propped up knees and held a tiny black stick in his gaunt hand.

Jamie walked up to him. "Can I look?"

Sabastian held up the pad. With only a few lines and sketched-in shapes the tone of the evening sun on the water surrounded by trees was set exactly.

"That's right pretty. How'd you learn to do that?" Jamie sat down at the next piling and leaned against it.

"By doing it."

Ned wordlessly took the next piling further down, laid his pole on the dock and leaned back too. He closed his eyes.

Jamie looked at the drawing again. "What do you mean 'deep thoughts'? We were just wondering stuff."

A heavy crease pulled into one side of Sabastian's face. "That's all the greatest philosophers in the world have done, James. That's what philosophy is when you come right down to it. Just 'wonderin' stuff' and trying to make sense of things."

Jamie shrugged. "We were wondering how to get a rabbit box to work."

"You built one and you can't get it to work, is that right?"

Jamie heard Ned chime in from behind him. "No, we found one and can't get it to work."

"Oh, it's easy once you know the trick." He pulled his shirt sleeves up to reveal bony arms and laid his sketchpad down on the dock. "Imagine the pad here is your box, looking at it from the side." He laid a pencil down flat on the dock with one end about a third of the way down long side of the pad sticking straight out

127

from the edge. "You set one stick like this in a hole in the top of your box about one third of the way down from the sliding door end." He laid down another pencil crossing the first, making a T shape. "Then you make a see-saw on top of the box, see? You attach one end of the see-saw to the top of your sliding door with a piece of string." Sabastian then laid one more pencil down crossing the edge of the pad so it was directly pointing at the other end of the see-saw pencil. "This is your trip stick. You cut another hole in the top of the box big enough for it to slide through and cut notch in the side of the trip stick that will make it catch in that hole in the top of the box. You tie a string from the top of the trip stick to attach it to the end of the see-saw. When the rabbit comes in he'll hit the trip stick and knock it out of its hole. That releases the door and it slides down by its own weight. Simple."

"What about bait?" Again, Jamie heard Ned's voice from over his shoulder.

Sabastian leaned back against his own piling. "For rabbits you don't need bait. They like to hide in dark holes. They feel safe there."

Jamie turned to Ned and saw Ned looking back at him and saw the question in his eyes that they were both afraid to ask.

"What is it?" Sabastian's voice was quiet.

"Well …" Jamie did not want to tell him what they were really up to. Sabastian, for all his isolation from the community, was still a technically a grown-up.

Ned shifted positions, his feet sliding on the boards. "Do you know Mr. Norris, the mailman?"

Jamie swallowed.

Sabastian nodded. "I know him, yes."

"Well … on the way to work in the morning," Ned shifted again. "We've seen him doing something he ought not to be doing."

A moment froze between them that felt longer than a moment to Jamie.

Sabastian rattled a quick cough of a laugh. "Old Nosy is peeking in windows again, is he?"

"What?" Jamie and Ned in unison.

"Oh, yes. Norris has been, ... nosy ... ever since I've known him."

Jamie and Ned's words fell over each other, tumbling to tell Sabastian what they'd seen and their idea of putting a skunk in the widow's mailbox. When they finished, Sabastian let a small half-smile crease the scarred shell of his skin. "There is only one thing I would advise."

Jamie thought, oh no here it comes.

"Don't ever, ever tell anyone what you did."

They looked at each other and then back at Sabastian.

"I know, it will be tempting to talk about it if it works. Sharing joy is a primary pleasure of the human animal. But, in this case, let that joy be just between you two. Keep it secret. When the tongues wag, as they will, feign astonishment. And for God's sake be gentle with the animal. You do not want to get sprayed, believe you me."

Jamie sat stunned. He wasn't sure what 'feign' meant, but Jesus H. Roosevelt Christ, would wonders never cease?

Chapter 17

Trouble in Paradise

Much to Jamie's relief, this time Gloria was the culprit for being late to church. He and Ned sat on the front porch steps in the quiet of the morning and listened to discordant echoes rattle from within the house. "This is just about perfect."

Ned sat leaned back against a pillar of the front porch, cap down over his eyes. If Jamie hadn't known better he would have thought Ned was asleep. "What is?"

"I'm not strong on going to church, but I don't want to get switched for not goin'." Jamie took his own cap off and leaned his head back to feel the breeze. "This kinda fits my ideal."

"Huh." Jamie heard Ned snort from beneath his cap. "We're still goin', we're just late. My ideal would be to spend the day down at the lake, not trapped inside listening to some old broad-in-the-beam fart ass spewing cow flop."

Jamie almost spit. He glanced quickly over his shoulder. "Be careful, would ya? My folks got ears like bats. Talk like that'll get you in trouble quick as a mule kick."

Ned lifted his cap to glance at Jamie, then lowered it again. "Yeah, well."

Gloria sniffed between Jamie and Ned in the back seat all the way to church. By the time they pulled in, the parking lot was full of cars and empty of people.

Jamie's mother pointed one white-gloved finger at them before they got out of the car. "You boys behave yourselves today, you hear me?"

They both nodded. "Yes ma'am."

She reached out and held Gloria's hand. "All right then, you two go on in, we'll be there in just a minute."

Much to Jamie's regret, they were just in time for the sermon.

The Right Reverend Cramphorne spread his arms wide in the pulpit. It reminded Jamie of a buzzard about to dine on a bloody meal. The Right Reverend smiled, waved his nose at the air and dipped his great white head to complete the image.

"My brethren, my brothers, sisters, today I want to talk with you about sin. We are all aware of the seven deadly sins. Certainly all of us here know our commandments, but today I want to talk about a sin that's not discussed much. It seems like such a little sin, a little private sin. Each and every time we're guilty of this it doesn't seem so bad, so the next time it's just that much easier to do it again. It doesn't seem to hurt anyone. Some of you may already have guessed. Yes, my dear friends, my family in the Lord, I'm talking about indolence. I'm talking about being plain old lazy."

The Reverend opened his Bible and spread the pages smooth with his palms. "Now I'm not talking about those who just don't have a job right now, oh no. These are hard times, hard times. The good Lord knows you who are not guilty, who strive and strive and believe me those among us will be rewarded for their steadfast work and dedication. Be comforted my brethren, for you will be soothed and comforted in your pain. I'm not talking about those who try to find work and cannot. I'm talking about those who won't! Won't! These who fill their days with nothing but drink and maybe fishing or reading a trash book or two. You may think yours is a life that doesn't hurt anyone. After all, you're getting by, aren't you? Fishing gives you food for the table and it's not like you've ever hurt anyone, right? Wrong! Again I say, wrong, a thousand times wrong! The Bible tells us in Proverbs chapter sixteen verse nineteen, 'the way of a slothful man is as in a hedge of thorns: but the way of the righteous is made plain.' I can't put it much more 'plain' than that. Brethren, this is right out of our Bible, our holy book. But it's not just the obvious slothful sinners among us that are guilty of this sin. We all are. Every time we put a dish down in the sink rather than wash it and put it in the cabinet

131

then that's a little sin. Every time we don't hang up that coat and just sling it across a chair, that's a little sin. The insidious part is that as all these little sins become habit, they become ingrained in us little bit by little bit and like the wind and sand wearing away the mountains of the world, over time those little sins wear away at our righteousness and make us smaller people, little people. These little sins make us into little people in the eyes of God. And there, my brethren, there lies the great danger because instead of the one great big anchor of sin that weighs the murderer down, sinks him into the very pit of hell, we carry a hundred pound sack of sand that weighs us down, each grain a little sin that each of us drops into the sack worn from the rock of our salvation and we are lost. Lost sheep, lost to God for the sake of a few grains. Don't let that happen, don't let those grains of sand weigh you down so that your soul cannot fly to heaven, cannot float to eternal grace at the right hand of God."

Cramphorne took a deep breath, placed his great pasty pad hands on the podium and leaned forward.

"My friends, my brothers and sisters, we are a hard working community. Let me repeat that, we are a hard … working … community."

He pounded one great meaty fist. "On my way to my errands of my calling I have witnessed, countless times, the burdens of toil you bear, the industriousness with which you discharge you duties to man and to God and I am amazed, amazed and thankful to pursue my calling among such. I see and rejoice, for work, good work, hard work is a blessing unto God. God looks down upon us from his place atop the heavenly host and rejoices to see such hard-working people who will be beside him in the kingdom of heaven, for such virtue is a joy to behold. But as every day has its night, every coin has a flip side, there are those, even among us here, that make their way leaching off the Christian ways of the kind people of God. I have seen it and if I can see it, God can see it. Don't let God see that happen to you."

He took a sip of water. His fat-deep eyes scanned the congregation. There was not a sound, not a cough, not a single wave of a funeral home fan, no smiles or nods to be seen. Cramphorne breathed heavily through his nose, nodded and called for the next hymn.

"Grant! Grant Garrath!"

Jamie watched his father turn around to scan the after church crowd and turned his own head to help. Help wasn't needed. Old Man Mason puffed toward them like a battering ram, his bowed spindly legs pumping like pistons.

"Hello there, Jeremiah. Anne told me you and Sarah are working on the Wednesday night supper. I thought we'd ..."

His father never got the chance to finish, because Old Man Mason's voice steam-rolled, his hand air waving Grant's words away. "Sorry Grant, business first, pleasure later, you know what that sermon was all about, don't you?"

"Well Jeremiah, I can't say that I'm an expert of those particular passages, but seems it was about responsibility and taking care of our fellow man and in so doing honoring God. That about right?"

Old Man Mason shook his head. "As far as it goes, but that ain't the half of it. He's just trying to soften us up before the Thursday night meeting. He wants the Elders to do his shut-in rounds for him."

His father's eyebrows raised just a trifle, but the rest of him was still, his voice very quiet. "Is that so? Where'd you hear that?"

"Sarah overheard old Craphorn talking to Hera at the post office. She happened to be standing in line behind them."

"Did she really? Now that," His father nodded, very slowly, "runs contrary to custom."

Old Man Mason balled his fists and pumped them in the air. "It ain't never been done that way but what the minister was laid up. We're already busy with makin' a livin' and ... sorry Mrs. Hannah," he touched the brim of his hat to Jamie's mother, "but I'll be damned if I'm gonna sit still for him to sit in his own little personal ivory tower just thinkin' thoughts and puttin' on airs. Particularly when it's on our nickel! Dammit," he touched his hat to Jamie's mother again, "it just ain't right, no matter what kind of convoluted cow flop he comes up with."

Jamie watched his father slide his hands into his pockets, press his lips together and nod slowly. "I'll go along with that, Jeremiah. I'll sure go along with that."

Jamie's mother came up behind Jamie, placed her hands on his shoulders and spoke over his head to his father. "Grant honey, we've got to be getting home if I'm going to get that chicken ready for dinner. I'm sorry Mr. Mason."

"That's all right, Mrs. Garrath, you're right. I've got to get to findin' Sarah. She's probably lost in her henhouse of chatterboxes." He extended his hand to Grant. "We'll see you later. Think on it?"

Grant took his hand, shook it and nodded. "I will think on it, Jeremiah. You may be sure. Thanks for letting me know."

"You bet. See you later."

Just then one group of voices in the church crowd rose a bit higher than the rest. Jamie followed his father and Old Man Mason slowly over to where the Right Reverend (the loudest of the loud voices) was in a spirited exchange with Ned's father Gil and Mr. Pete Alderman. They were the other Elders of the church besides Jamie's father and Old Man Mason.

Ned stood a little apart from his father. Jamie sidled over to him and whispered. "What's goin' on?"

Ned whispered back. "I think Old Thunderbuns is trying to pass the buck."

Jamie looked up to watch more of this, but the Right Reverend waved off all protests and attempts to talk and boomed his goodbyes. "Sorry gentlemen, I'd love to talk more but I promised to help Hera this afternoon, can't dawdle."

Mrs. Hera Cramphorne looked a bit surprised at this revelation, more shell-shocked than eager to be away, but no one gainsaid him as Cramphorne pulled on his wife's arm and they were away, leaving both Gil and Pete with wide angry eyes.

Jamie looked at his father and Old Man Mason standing side by side. Both had their hands stuffed in their pockets. Both their mouths were tight.

Jamie heard Ned's voice whisper from over his shoulder. "This should be interesting."

Jamie had been thinking the same thing. He stuck his own hands in his pockets and pursed his lips. He felt his mother's eyes on him and as he turned to her, he saw her watching him with a dimpled smile on her face. "What?"

She reached over and hugged him. "Oh, nothing." Her embrace enveloped Ned as well. "Let's all get back to the house and have some dinner."

As he turned to follow his mother back to the car, Jamie caught just a glimpse of his father and Old Man Mason nod understanding to each other.

He really wanted to know what that meant.

Chapter 18
Boxes Part Deux

After a hefty Sunday dinner, Jamie and Ned waited for Jamie's father to fall asleep on the screen porch, then put their plan into motion.

They eased out the back screen porch and across the pasture to the forest road toward the mill. Jamie led the way. He spoke to Ned as he climbed the fence. "How well can you climb? Maybe one of us can boost the other one over the top of the fence."

"The back gate doesn't have a lock on it."

"How'd you know that?"

"Saw it when Cyrus and I were hacking weeds the other day."

"And you didn't mention it before?"

"No need before."

Jamie just shook his head and turned down the path toward the back gate. True to what Ned had said, it only had a wooden latch holding it shut. "Not much to keep folks out is there?"

"Yeah well. The sheds are locked. Good thing we left the tools out."

Jamie wrestled the box out from under the cabin where they'd stashed it, the tools inside.

Ned stood beside him, hands in his pockets. "You really think this is going to work?"

"Sure. You think Sabastian would lie to us?"

Ned pushed his lips together and lowered his eyebrows. "He still spooks me."

"What he told us makes sense, don't it?"

Jamie watched Ned think for a minute and then slowly nod as if it hurt him. "Yeah, well. Ok. Let's go ahead and get it done."

Jamie and Ned discovered a thing about their relationship this day. They worked well together. As anyone who works with their hands can tell you, there is sometimes a wordless communication between those who work together that goes beyond just asking for help and getting it. It's a communication of observation. One sees the other needs that knife or hammer or piece of string and supplies it before the other asks for it. The other acknowledges with a nod, then later reciprocates in turn. In a perfect working duo this thoughtful courtesy and subsequent awareness and thanks are exchanged back and forth like an improvisational dance. At the end it is never quite clear who did the most work or even who did what, nor does it matter.

So it was with Jamie and Ned. It really did not feel to either of them that they were 'doing' anything. Yet at the end, the box was finished and they awakened from their meditation in movement when they had to reckon with the abrupt knowledge that there was nothing left to do.

Jamie's mind tried to grasp at this nothing. He looked at Ned. Ned was looking back. "That it?"

"I guess it is."

They admired their creation and themselves for a solid minute before Ned spoke. "Time for a test."

They set the trap, door up and trip stick locked in its hole, eased support off the door and then Ned reached a long twig into the box and tickled the trip stick.

"Keep your fingers out of there, you don't want to get them ..."

Slam.

"Smacked." Jamie had to laugh. "By the great gods of gumtrees, it works."

"Yeah." Ned gazed at the box with bright eyes. "Now what?"

"We take it out in the wood and set it, that's what."

"Where?"

"In the kind of place Sabastian told us, but exactly where ..." Jamie lifted his shoulders, let them sag and then noticed that Ned's head was cocked over to one side. "What?"

"I'll bet I know a place."

"All right then, let's get it there. Do you know if there are rabbit runs there?"

"Not specifically. But I'd be willing to bet they're not far from that big patch of briars sitting back from the road leading in here."

"But we're not trying to catch a rabbit, are we?" Jamie laughed. "We're trying to catch a skunk. And that needs bait. And I haven't got any idea what kind of bait to use other than table scraps, which we ain't got."

"We do want to catch something to see if it works as a trap, and we don't want to tell your dad what it's really for, now do we? And besides, wouldn't skunks wander around where rabbits go? It's not like a skunk would have to be afraid of a rabbit."

"We might not need bait for skunk either, not that I'm ready to bet the barn on it. Okay."

They lifted the box.

"Damn. This thing is heavier than it looks."

"Oh yeah."

With Jamie stumbling at the front end and Ned whacking his knees at the rear, they carried it out the back gate and into the woods. After much huffing and puffing along the path they arrived at the briar patch and set the box down.

Jamie breathed hard. "Let's get it in there and get out of here. Daddy'll be wondering where we are."

Ned looked too tired to argue, but nodded.

They shoved the box back in the briars just so it was mostly covered. They lifted the door, set the trip stick and backed away carefully.

They stood there for a moment in a time of infinite possibility, then turned and walked on home.

When they arrived the sky was fading dark, the evening gray casting gradual shadows over the house and barn. Jamie's father greeted them at the door with a question. "Where you boys been? It's almost time for supper and you haven't done your chores."

Jamie looked at Ned. "He's gonna know sooner or later."

"Yeah, well."

They told him.

"We thought we'd surprise you with a rabbit for supper some night."

"You boys act like there's something to be ashamed of."

Ned looked down at his overalls and brushed a bit of dirt and followed his pant creases again. "Sometimes you just want to keep it to yourself."

Grant nodded. "True. But why didn't you ask me for help?"

"We wanted to see if we could do it by ourselves."

Jamie noticed his father dropped into his mill voice. "Well, well. That's good, that's just fine. But you ..." he pointed toward the milking stall. "Have a date with Guinevere."

"Yessir."

They turned off to go to the front porch and Ned leaned in toward Jamie and whispered "I thought you told me everyone called the cow 'Elspeth'."

Jamie grabbed a clean milking bucket off the back porch and the small pot. He gestured with his head at Ned for him to come along. "Gloria calls her that. And because Gloria is such a pain in the butt, whenever she's around that's what we call her. Other than that everybody calls her pretty much what they want to. Daddy calls her Guinevere because she has that red topknot and for some reason he thinks Guinevere must have been a redhead."

"I still like 'Gramma'."

"So do I. Momma calls her 'Bessy'. 'Course Momma calls all cows 'Bessy.' I know. Momma's got a gift."

"So everybody just kinda makes up their own name for her."

"That's about it. it's a lot better than just callin' her 'the cow'."

"That's weird."

"That's a fact."

Jamie swung the milk bucket to and fro, rocking it on the handle. Ned turned to him. "You think we'll have one tomorrow? A rabbit?"

"No telling. It smells a little like rain, so we'll just have to see.

Gramma/Bessy/Guinevere/Elspeth stuck her gray dripping, puffing nose over the fence and gave a low 'mooo-uh'.

"Oh she's full tonight." Jamie watched her shake her head and waddle toward the milking stall. "It's gonna take both buckets."

Ned nodded and held out his hand for the bucket. "Why don't I get her started and you go back and get the other bucket?"

"Okay."

Jamie headed back to the back screen porch where the clean milking buckets were kept after his mother washed them. He paused on the outside of the screen porch, the wire reflecting the low rays of the sun like a golden cloth laid up beside the house. He listened to his Mom and Dad as they bantered about, Gloria complaining as usual and as he stepped back through the screen door he suddenly felt like an intruder in his own home. He stepped quietly, not wanting the others to hear that he was there. He handled the loose bail handle on the bucket carefully so it would not rattle and clank. He pushed the screen door open slowly, stepped down and out and held it back from slamming behind him.

Jamie heard a rumble and looked off to the east. Black thunderclouds rose slowly in the sky. He looked back to the west and saw the sun in its slow fall toward the horizon. He could smell the dusty earth beneath his feet as he had done a thousand times before, but he had never felt so … outside. It did not make sense. These people were his family, people he had known and who had known him all his life and now he felt a stranger. It felt as if he were seeing them for the first time and he did not know if he liked them or not for who they were, for he didn't know who they were; he only knew them inside the house. Ned was right, sometimes there were things you just wanted to keep to yourself. He slowly turned and walked toward the milking stall toward the strange and quiet boy he had not expected to like and who, apparently, was becoming something Jamie had never before experienced and certainly had not expected.

A friend.

Chapter 19
Wet and Slog

"You don't have a raincoat?"

Ned shook his head.

Jamie's father looked out at the steady rain dripping off the screen porch. "I think there's one in the cabin we can let you use. All right, let's go."

Ned felt heavy drops on his shoulders as he ran to the truck and packed in the middle between Jamie and his father. It was a tight fit on the bench seat. Ned scooched over as much as he could toward Jamie to keep out of the way of Jamie's father shifting gears. Water sprayed from the gap between the folding side window and the sliding side door of the pickup and wet his shirt as they bounced along the road.

When they got to the cabin Jamie's father set Ned to laying in the fire in the stove with what dry wood there was in the woodbox and making coffee. He sent Jamie to bring more firewood and stack it on the screen porch to dry.

It was too wet for much real work at the mill. Logging is dangerous in the wet, so Jamie's father set what men showed up to dragging the last logs cut in from the woods by mule. Even that was hazardous. Wrestling heavy logs in slippery wet takes care.

The coffee was just piping hot when the Indian came in, water streaming from his broad hat and long black slicker.

"Sorry I'm late, Mr. Garrath. No one would stop this morning."

Jamie's father looked up from his papers. "That's all right, CC. Just warm up there by the stove and I'll get the belt. You all right to scout trees in this?"

The Indian nodded. "I'll be fine."

Ned bent to load another slab of wood into the stove and slid the door shut by the spring handle. As he stood up and turned he looked straight at the Indian, right in his anthracite eyes. Usually Ned could read a person as quick as he could think but not with this man. He wore a battered oilskin coat longer than his knees and a hat from the Great War with dents in the crown making a peak. With nothing to say, Ned just poured a cup of coffee and held it out to him.

The Indian's long slender fingers slid around the hot cup, cracked blue enamel. When he nodded to Ned the brim of his hat dripped water. "Thanks."

"Don't mention it." Ned backed away from the stove and stepped outside onto the porch where Jamie was stacking wood against the wall under the windows. He watched the Indian through the doorway warming his hands on the stove. He turned toward Jamie. "He kinda …"

But Jamie had already ducked back out into the rain to the work sledge. He spoke as soon as he stepped back up on the porch weighed down with an armload of wood. "Yeah, he spooks me too. That what Sabastian does to you?"

Ned took the armload of wood from Jamie. "No, the Ghost is different." He looked in through the window as he placed short slabs on the stack.

The Indian slid his long oilskins from his shoulders, took the woodman's belt from Jamie's father and slung it about his waist. The belt was a leather bandolier with pockets all around. A flap holster holding a 38 caliber revolver hung from the right hand side. Ned had seen guns in his father's store, in their boxes or in a glass case under lock and key. Those had never bothered him, but seeing this pistol hang from the Indian's waist was different. Ned watched the man warm his hands around the coffee cup and nod in response to Jamie's father as they talked and pointed at woodland plats nailed on the wall.

The rain drummed against the tin roof over his head. He almost didn't hear Jamie call. "Ned!"

Ned turned to him. "What?"

Jamie stood on the steps to the porch holding the screen door open. "There's a pile more wood down by the cross cut saw but I'm going to need help to drag it back up here."

"Okay, hold on a second." Ned stepped inside the cabin. "Mr. Garrath?"

Both men looked up and Jamie's father spoke. "What is it, Ned?"

"Jamie says he needs help to get the wood down by the cross cut saw."

"Yeah, get a rain coat ..." He thumbed over in the direction of the storage room. " ... hold on a minute, CC." He walked toward the back room and gestured for Ned to follow.

"You," Jamie's father looked high on a shelf, "Need a proper hat." He lifted a dark brown felt fedora from the shelf and dropped it onto Ned's head. The hat slid down to Ned's nose. Jamie's father lifted it off again and slid a couple of flat cotton lamp wicks under the sweat band. "Every man ought to have a good hat. Somebody with more money than sense left this behind a few years ago." He dropped it back on Ned's head. The fit was perfect. "Now it's yours. Get one of those slickers from the hook and go help Jamie." He didn't wait for Ned's response and walked back to the office.

Ned shifted the hat on his scalp. It felt good. He lifted the slicker from its hook, slid it on and rolled up the sleeves a few inches so they wouldn't droop over his hands.

Outside, Jamie had loaded one arm with the last couple of pieces of wood from the sledge. He stood still for a moment listening to the spatter of rain on the leaves. Then it came to him that he was just standing in the rain, as in 'not enough sense to get in out of.' He coughed a laugh at himself, shook his head and clumped up the steps onto the porch and dumped the armload onto the pile with a wet thump. As he looked through the window for Ned he felt wet creep onto the back of his collar where water was starting to soak through. The noise on the tin roof was deafening. Footsteps on the porch behind him startled him. He turned toward the sound and saw Snow shaking off the water from his raincoat.

"It ain't quite a frog-strangler, but it'll do." As Snow smiled it occurred to Jamie that as a person grew older their face took on creases based upon how they used it, wore in different patterns like a pair of blue jeans used just for school as opposed to those used for work. Snow had always smiled more often than not.

Jamie followed Snow inside the cabin. He listened to his father talk to the Indian. There was calm in his father's voice he had never heard. It was a warm voice, a caring voice, a voice at home.

Ned came out of the back room wearing a felt fedora and a slicker, rolling up the sleeves. As Ned came toward him, he looked at Jamie closely. "Your face is wet."

Jamie raised his hands to his face and wiped his cheeks, rubbed his eyes and sniffed. "Yeah. Straw hats ain't exactly the best for shedding water. Let's get another load of wood in before it gets washed away."

They clumped across the porch and down the steps into the wind and rain. The drumming ring of rain against the porch roof dimmed as they dragged the wooden sledge across the wet hard packed sandy earth toward the wood pile. The rain had washed off what little soft surface there was and the sledge runners clattered across buried stones left behind. They stopped at the cross cut saw shed where the firewood was piled up in a conical stack taller than their heads.

Jamie heard Ned whistle softly beside him. "They don't want us to be without wood for a while, do they?"

"Gotta have coffee and to have coffee ya gotta have fire. Even if it is in the middle of the summer."

They loaded the sledge piece by slippery piece, then grabbed the rough hemp rope pulling loops of the sledge.

Jamie listened to the rain spatter on the pines. It was not the flat splatter of raindrops against flat leaves but a softer, like the rustle of bedclothes. "Does your daddy talk different at work than he does at home?"

Ned lifted the pulling sling, pulled his hat off, ducked his head through the loop and plopped his hat back on his head. "I guess. When he's talking to folks he wants something from." He settled the loop across one shoulder. "Never really thought about it. But then the only time that Pop is really kind to somebody is when he's trying to get something."

"That's a pretty tough thing to say."

145

Ned shrugged and fingered the rope of the sling in his hand. Rain dripped from the dark edge of his hat brim. "Yeah well." He lifted his head to Jamie with straight pain in his eyes. "But it's true. When he talks with customers he's trying to get money and when he talks with his suppliers he's trying to get a good deal."

The rain dripped around and in between them. Jamie didn't know what to say. Here he was just trying to get a handle on his father and Ned comes out with a thing like that.

"You ready?" He saw Ned lean against the sledge sling, taking up slack.

"Yeah."

By the time they got back to the cabin, both the Indian and Snow were gone and Jamie's father was at his desk staring at papers and scratching his head.

Jamie went ahead to talk with his father. "We got another load, but I don't think any more is going to fit on the porch."

"That's all right. You can get the rest of it tomorrow." His father rubbed his eyes and looked up at them over the top of his glasses. "Why don't you two take the rest of the day off? Go fishing. Snow and Lester are just pulling in the last logs with the mules and CC is out marking timber, so there's really not much more for you to do."

Ned spoke from behind Jamie. "Isn't it too rainy to fish?"

Jamie's father laughed. "Fish aren't afraid of getting wet. I've had some pretty good fishing in the rain. Just don't take the road, I don't want you getting hit by someone who can't see where they're going. Take the path through the woods."

"Okay. See you at home then."

But his father's attention was already buried back down in his work papers. "Right."

Jamie felt a tug on his arm, looked at Ned, then both of them walked off the porch and back out into the rain.

They trudged off through the splatter when Jamie heard Ned's voice behind him. "You want to just go back to the house? Somehow I feel like milking."

Jamie stopped and turned to stare. "Y'know, that's one phrase I never thought I'd hear anybody ever say. 'Somehow I feel like doing some milking'."

"What else we going to do?"

"Go fishing."

"In the rain?"

"You heard what Daddy said. Come on, it might be fun."

"Nah."

"You thinking the Ghost might be there?"

Ned didn't answer.

"Okay, go ahead home. She ain't gonna be ready for a little while, but Gramma likes you better anyway."

"You all right?"

Jamie nodded. "Yeah. I just don't feel like going home. I think I'll grab a pole and maybe catch a couple of grasshoppers and see what they'll do."

They walked in the rain and silence until they got to the shed where the poles were. Jamie grabbed his favorite, a little short whippy cane.

"We might want to check the box first."

Jamie looked up. "Oh yeah, let's see if we got anything!"

As they rounded the curve in the path and saw the box they saw the lid was down, but when they lifted the leather flap over the screen hole to look inside it was empty.

"You think we need to bait it after all?"

Jamie shook his head. "No telling. Let's just set it again and leave it. Give it a week or so. We should have known better than to think it was gonna work first try anyway."

They stood there for a moment, then Ned shoved his hands in his pockets and turned away. "See you later."

"Yeah." Jamie watched Ned disappear up the path. "Give my best to Gramma."

Jamie wiped the water from his face, then slowly, fishing pole in hand, turned toward the path to the lake.

147

Sabastian was there. He sat on the edge of the dock without a coat, his shirt sticking to his back. Jamie thought he saw ripples of scars underneath the wet cloth, but he was afraid to ask.

He sat down beside. "The box trap was empty today."

"You set it up the way I showed you?"

Jamie nodded. "We tested it too. We tickled the end of the trip stick with a long twig and it slammed right down."

"That's all right then." Sabastian nodded. "It's only been one day. When it rains small creatures tend to stay in their holes where it's warm and dry." He smiled with that thick side of his mouth. "It's only man the animal that goes out in the rain to stalk the water for prey. But for fish, this is a fine day for hunting. When they see raindrops ripple the surface, they know that food is coming down off the trees into the water. They also know, probably some genetic instinct of long experience, that their enemies the birds tend not to fly in the wet." He cast his fly out again and began a slow retrieve. "It was the same in the war. I, for one, looked forward to thick rainy days when we would be grounded."

Jamie was felt quiet, looking at the myriad of dimpled rings on the water from the raindrops. He wanted to talk, it seemed the time because Sabastian had mentioned it, but his parents had warned him not to.

Sabastian's quiet voice came to the fore of the drips on the water and on the leaves and branches behind them. "What is it, James? What's on your mind?"

"There's something I want to ask you about, but Momma and Daddy say I shouldn't."

Sabastian nodded. "It's all right, I won't make you ask. It's time for you to know because you're a friend, now. And, I suppose, it's time for me to share a little. That's what the doctors told me anyway, called it 'the talking cure." But I do have to ask something of you."

Jamie nodded.

"What I tell you now is private, only between you and me, all right? Not your parents, not even with your friend."

Jamie felt a chill from the water on the back of his neck again but nodded again and sat very still. "Okay."

"All right." Sabastian turned back to the water and made a little cast along the edge. The fly softly plopped into the water and he began a slow figure eight retrieve with his line hand. His face and neck were wet and the contours of his scars gleamed. "The recruitment posters called us 'Knights of the Air'. Some of us even believed it. I don't know many that held onto that belief as time went on."

"You were a flyer?"

Sabastian nodded. "Joined before America did." He rubbed the water on his face. "Don't let anyone convince you that war is glorious, James. Flying is glorious, but not war. It's only pain ... and blood ... and awful. And sometimes necessary. I know that. That's how I live with it." Water dripped off the brim of Sabastian's felt hat. "There was a sort of freedom in it, knowing we could die any day, at any time and in the silliest of circumstances. That made us live our lives to the fullest when we got the chance. Some chased women, some buried themselves in their bibles and others ... others drank. The heroes died. There are no heroes left, James. There are only survivors."

"Why did you join up?"

"Because I thought it was the right thing to do. Josephine had great misgivings and her concerns turned out to be accurate." Sabastian shrugged. "But that, James, is all in the past. Now I live my life as best I can with what I have left to live it with. What man can do more?"

Chapter 20
Raising Cane

Wet earth steamed in the sun. Every shirt in the mill was sweat soaked by mid-morning. Jamie and Ned had just dragged the sledge to the never-shrinking pile of firewood and leaned for a minute under a shade tree to drink water from their mason jars.

They watched Dancin' Charlie and Caleb Frasier, a tall Canadian with big hands, heft a long slender flexing log. Caleb was strong and a hard worker, but he was molasses next to Charlie's quicksilver. Caleb carried the heavy end and Charlie the slender end, but Charlie fooled around and played like he couldn't hold his end of the log.

"Oop, oop, I got it, I got it ... naw I don't." and Charlie's end of the log banged and bounced on the ground for the nth time.

"Now you stop playing tomfoolery, Charlie. Because you going to be hurt, eh?" Caleb eased his end of the log off his shoulder and held it easily in one hand. He was almost as tall as Marshall and his shoulders were broad as a barn door.

Charlie, for all his slight frame, was wiry and hard underneath his overalls. "Let's try it again, then." As he bent and lifted, Charlie danced about and played at lifting his small end onto his shoulder, letting the pole slide from one hand to the other. "Hey Caleb, I don't know if I can hold this, up up, oop, there it goes, nope, got it, hey watch out ...."

Eueas waited over to the side for Caleb and Charlie to pass by. He leaned on his cane and held a long spout oiler can and a handful of rags. Up to now he had been pretty quiet just thumping around and scanning the place, shifting his eyes from one place to another, from one person to another.

Caleb smiled a little as he hefted his end of the log. "You drop on you foot you going to be 'up up oops' and you work not.

Then where you are with no money, eh? Stop make that damn foolishness."

Jamie felt pressure against his knees and looked down. Toby had moved in front of him and was pushing him back away from the log. He retreated to the other side of the sledge beside Ned to watch.

Charlie rubbed his hands against his hips then raised them in surrender. "Okay Caleb, you win." He lifted the log to his shoulder. "I got it solid, no problem, aww ... there it goes again." The log slipped and flexed in the air.

"Yeah, uh-huh, sure."

"No, I got it, I ... oh damn, look out!"

Charlie's end bounded free as a piece of bark came loose in his hand. The log dropped with such a thump that it bounced and shook the ground. Charlie danced free as Caleb heaved and grunted to control his end, then Charlie darted back in to stop the bouncing roll just as it came to rest against Eueas' ankle and pinned his foot to the ground.

Caleb and Charlie lifted the log away and set it down in a safe spot and straightened up. Caleb gestured toward Charlie. "Mr. Canfield, I'm sorry for this pile of sheep brain here. You hurt, eh?"

There was a solid pause as Eueas turned his greasy eyes on Charlie. "Naw, I ain't hurt, Mr. Frasier. I thank you for your kind concern. But I'm afraid," he turned toward Charlie, "I cain't say the same for this one." Eueas whipped his cane through the air and cracked it down across Charlie's shins. Charlie howled and hopped and cursed and danced away. Eueas stumped after him and whacked him again.

Caleb let out a loud guffaw. "I you tried to tell, you going to hurt, eh Charlie?"

Eueas was the one who answered him as he stumped along in hot pursuit. "You did not lie, Mr. Frasier!" and whipped his cane down again.

Charlie waved his hands and hopped out of range. "Now Eueas, it was just a ... hold on, I didn't mean to ..."

For a time they had their own little one-ring circus. Eueas hobbled around chasing Charlie and whacking him on the shins when he wasn't using his cane for support, Charlie dancing away in alternating ballet.

Caleb laughed and slapped his thighs until the little circus passed by him and Eueas fetched him a crack on his shins too. "What are you laughing at?"

Charlie saw and let out a high cackling guffaw of his own then skittered out of the way of another swing. Eueas started knocking everyone's shins within reach. He raised his cane for one last swing at the last man to arrive, but the cane stopped, quivering in midair in the man's hand and Eueas raised his gaze into the granite face of Cyrus Conner. Cyrus had just come in from the woods and was wearing the wood scout belt with the revolver. He carried a machete in his other hand. He did not smile.

Eueas slowly stretched his green grin at Cyrus. "I guess that's about enough boys, eh?"

Cyrus slowly nodded and released his grip. Eueas put his cane back on the ground.

By now the laughter had shrunk to chuckles. Charlie sidled away from Eueas one last time. "I think I'll go help out the cutting crew, see you later!" and fled the battlefield behind Cyrus and out into the woods.

Snow came up at a trot. "What's all the ruckus?"

Everyone including Caleb looked at Eueas.

Eueas just smiled his big dirty teeth at Snow. "Not a thing, Mr. Snow. Just a little safety lecture. All done now."

Snow scanned the men, who smiled silently and nodded back at him. He tugged on the brim of his hat, glanced around to satisfy himself that no one was hurt and nodded, fists on hips. "All right then, let's everybody stop admiring themselves and git to movin' some wood. You boys, you got enough firewood for now. Mr. Garreth says for you two to knock off and git some fish for supper."

Jamie felt Toby release the pressure on his leg and bound off. "I'll take that." He turned to Ned. "Let's git while the gittin's good, shall we?"

They put the sledge on top of the woodpile by the cabin and grabbed the fishing poles out of the back of the truck.

One pair of shifting greasy eyes followed them as they walked over the rain-packed ground and out the gate. The eyes belonged to Eueas Canfield. "Your daddy way too soft on you, boy. Way too soft." He spat an obscenity past his tight frowned lips and looked back down into the dirt. "Like my old man used to say, you pay for it come time of your come-uppance. Yeah you will."

Chapter 21

Engine Trouble

"You boys stacking wood again today." Snow lifted his hat and scratched his head. "The crosscut team has a big pile all ready for you."

Ned groaned inside. "Where? The side of the cabin's full." He'd hoped they were done with heaving firewood for a while.

"Over by the wood dry kiln. Little Foot gonna need a good supply once he gets that thing fired up. You'd be surprised at how much wood it takes once he gets rolling."

Ned expected a smart-aleck comment from Jamie, but none came. He watched Jamie just nod and turn to plod out the door.

As they leaned into the slings to pull the sledge from the woodpile Toby got right in front of them.

"What are you doing, boy?" Ned reached down to pet Toby but then saw the hairs bristled up on the back of his neck. Then Ned looked up and saw Eueas stump by Rudolph and whack him once on the shins on his way to the engine shed. The man laughed as Rudolph yelped in pain. Then Eueas tried to whack Snow. That was a mistake. Snow turned a stare as mean as Ned had ever seen and pointed his two stiff fingers right at Eueas' face. That froze him. Eueas smiled, gave a little heh-heh laugh, shook his head and stumped off. Toby stood right where he was in front of Ned and Jamie until Eueas was out of range. When Ned and Jamie leaned into the slings again Toby trotted round and round the sled like he was riding guard on a herd. He didn't stop until they arrived at the kiln wood pile, then lay down with a relaxed pant on the cool ground beneath a bush.

Not long after that Ned straightened to ease his back and saw Cyrus talking with Jamie's father. He saw Cyrus nod at what Jamie's father was saying, but the man's eyes were on Toby.

When the morning whistle blew Ned and Jamie sat down on one of the benches by the cabin in the shade, leaned back against the building and watched everyone gather around the well for water. Ned felt the heat of the sun drive all the moisture and all conversation right out of the air.

He saw Eueas fill his jar at the well and turn towards them. When Eueas' eyes landed on them he smiled slowly. Ned felt his skin crawl as Eueas stiff-legged his way over to them and sat down on the bench across from Jamie.

"Hey, boys. I don't think we've been introduced polite. Name's Eueas, Eueas Canfield." He put down his cane and reached out to shake hands.

Ned watched Jamie accept the man's hand for a shake, then wince under the vice-grip of Eueas' hand. The he saw Eueas smile and grip Jamie's hand harder and Ned heard Toby growl just behind him. Quick as thought Ned jumped up, set his hands on his hips and said in a voice loud enough for everyone to hear, "Tell me something Mr. Canfield. Is your name really pronounced 'You-us', 'Ewez' or 'You-ass'? We don't want to get confused, y'know." He backed up a little to the side and stood close to Marshall.

Behind Eueas immediate snorts of laughter rose from the other men coming over to sit. When Eueas released Jamie's hand and turned to growl back he looked right into the eyes of Marshall. Marshall had a half-smirk on his face.

Charlie and Rudolph looked at each other and laughed, then coughed behind their hands to try to hide it. Eueas turned to Rudolph. "What are you smirkin' at, 'Pretty Boy'? You think all that pomade makes you better'n anybody?"

Ned backed off out of range. Jamie followed him up off the bench and away, rubbing the pain out of his hand.

Rudolph swung his hat at Charlie as Charlie laughed loud. "Naw." Rudolph set his hat firmly back on his head.

"That's good, boy. 'Cause' if you know what's good for ya, you'd best ..."

Rudolph laughed again, "Not at all, 'You-ass' " and his chest began to heave. He strolled away and that drew chuckles all around.

Eueas swung back around to the boys and spat at them. "You smart-ass little piles of flop, I'll teach you a thing or three ..." As Eueas' waved his hand behind him to feel for his cane he fell off the stump. His hat fell on the ground too, revealing a big bald spot on the side of his head. He clapped his hat back on is head and scrambled for his cane. It was no longer there.

Ned looked around to see Toby, cane in mouth, loping off toward the engine shed. He followed after, laughter echoing behind him.

Jamie trotted right beside. "Eueas turned mean real quick, didn't he?"

Ned nodded. "We gotta get that cane back, though, or your dad's gonna be mad."

"He's gonna be mad anyway."

By the engine shed Toby dropped the cane in the sand and stood over it laughing like he wanted to play stick, tail waving in the air behind him. Ned picked it up and shook his head at Toby. "You really should'na done that, boy. We're in it now."

Jamie came up beside him. "Wouldn't you just like to get rid of that thing?"

"Sure, but Eueas needs it and then we'd be in bigger trouble, wouldn't we? We'd prob'ly have to buy him a new one."

"Let's hand it back to him at arm's length. We might not be as strong or as mean as Eueas, but I'm pretty sure we can take him in a footrace."

They never got the chance to find out. On their way back to give Eueas his cane they ran right into Jamie's father and Snow. His father had a face like a thundercloud and held out his hand for the cane.

Ned handed it to him.

Jamie's father handed the cane to Snow. Snow left, cane in hand and his face impassive.

"You know better'n this, both of you, but especially you, Jamie. You've been taught to act better'n this. Have you forgotten everything we ever taught you about how to treat people?"

Jamie spread his hands out. "I didn't ask him to fetch Eueas' cane, Daddy. He just did it when he saw that Eueas was going to whack us with it."

"It's 'Mr. Canfield' Jamie. The man's a veteran, wounded in the Great War and I will not have him trifled with. You understand me, boy?"

"But we were bringing it back to him."

"No buts, Jamie."

Ned felt Jamie's father's blood was up and silently willed Jamie to not argue. This was not the time for back-talk.

"Yes sir."

"And another thing, if you can't control Toby any better than that he'll have to stay home. This is a place to work, not to play fetch with other people's property. Toby used to understand that, but you've ruined him. You control that dog, you understand me, boy?"

"Yes sir."

A little of the heat from Jamie's father eased. He spoke a little quieter but Ned could tell the storm was not over by a long shot. "All right. Now you can forget about dinner or taking off at the afternoon whistle. You two go right back to work and stay there. Since you love it so much, I want that engine shed whitewashed, three solid coats by the time you leave today. You understand me, boy?"

"Yes sir."

"Now go on, get back to work."

Ned and Jamie both turned away, heads bowed. Jamie's father's words hit their backs. "And come evening I want that wood box full, you understand?"

"Yes sir." They broke into a run before Jamie's father could say anything else. He did, but they didn't hear it what it was.

Neither wasted a word or a step. They got the whitewash and brushes and headed off to the engine shed.

It was not a big building, but it did house the engine that ran the saw and the planer in the shed behind it, though only hooked up to one at a time.

For a while they painted with a will, silent and focused, but that only lasted as long as the fear of Jamie's father coming up behind them.

Ned and Jamie were fairly covered in white as they finished up the second coat. Ned was the first to break the silence. "It's not like Eueas didn't deserve it." he watched Jamie slap the white liquid on the wall with a will. "How's your hand?"

"All right, I guess. Thanks, by the way." Ned saw Jamie flex his fingers. "The thing that hurts the most is that we didn't do anything wrong. We didn't make Toby get the cane. We didn't do anything."

"He grabbed it to keep Eueas from coming after us."

"You think? I know he's smart and all, but ..."

"I think," Ned slopped a big brush of whitewash on the wall "that Toby's a whole lot smarter than folks give him credit for. I also think," he wiped his arm across his mouth "that I'm getting real tired of the smell of this stuff."

"I don't smell it much by now."

Ned stared at him. "How can you help it, it's all over you?"

"I'm just glad to be away from 'You-ass'. Or would that be 'Ewe-ass', like the sheep?"

Ned couldn't help but snort.

"Anyway, all I want to smell is that engine. Look at it in there, ain't it fine?"

"I can't make heads or tails out of it."

"Neither can I, really."

"You didn't seem to have too much trouble the other day."

A twig crack behind Ned made him jump and the brush went flying from his hand. He spun around and saw Snow and Marshall standing right behind him. Snow looked over the shed wall. He nodded. "Good enough. Time to fill that woodbox now."

Ned retrieved the brush out of the dirt, then both he and Jamie gathered up the brushes and buckets and headed off toward the storage sheds to put everything away.

Marshall and Snow watched them go. Marshall watched Snow sigh and shake his head. "Hey."

Snow turned back around to him. "What?"

"It was funny."

Snow's grin slowly stretched across his face, white in the fading light. He nodded. "Um hmm. That it was." Snow stuck his hands in his pockets. "Close up the shed, would you? I gotta go talk to Mister Grant. I needs a couple of gophers tomorrow to help us work on the engine and I know just the boys for the job." He turned away and walked his hitch of a bowlegged gait towards the office.

Chapter 22

Up And Running

Breakfast was quiet. Jamie and Ned both dreaded the sight of Eueas Canfield.

Jamie's mother noticed their appetites were somewhat less than hollow-leg normal. "You don't like the eggs?"

Jamie's father looked up over his glasses from the papers in his hands. "Don't waste food boys, eat up. You're going to need your strength today."

Jamie stabbed at the lump of eggs. "Why come?"

"Because the hit-n-miss is more miss than hit. I just don't understand it. Usually once we get that thing rolling it doesn't want to quit. And I can't figure out what the problem is."

Jamie grinned at Ned.

"Don't get too happy about it, son. You're gonna work hard today."

Jamie's mother's voice dropped about a quarter octave. "Grant. That saw ... "

His father dipped his head and sighed. He waved his open hand toward the boys. "Honey, it's not the saw. It's just the engine and they're not going to run it, they're going to help Snow work on it. They're won't be anywhere near when it's running." He rubbed his hands over his face. "I don't have anyone else to spare right now." He gathered his papers and tapped the edges even on the table top. "Come on boys, finish up. I'll see you outside." He rolled up his papers, grabbed his hat and walked outside. A few moments later the screen door slammed hard.

Jamie watched his mother stand up from the table to gather up dishes. His father's plate had hardly been touched. She looked out into the early morning darkness and then down into the still half full coffee cup. "You heard your father. Finish up. Your food bags are on top of the ice box." She picked up his plate. "And watch you don't let the screen door slam."

Jamie glanced over at Ned, but Ned was shoveling in food like coal in a firebox going out of business. Jamie quickly bent to his own food and with cheeks still bulging like a scrounging squirrel, stood up and pushed his chair back, grabbed the flour sack that held his lunch and was out the screen door too.

When he got to the truck and hopped in the back, Ned was right behind him.

There was no sign of Nosy Norris or Sabastian as the pickup bounced along. Jamie's father drove a bit faster than usual on the washboard dirt road. Jamie and Ned not only felt more of the bumps but were thrown off balance and had to hang on as they came through the already open gates in a cloud of dust. Snow was writing on his pad, talking to the men and pointing to where he wanted them to go.

Jamie's father didn't even wait to get out of the truck before he began talking to Snow. "The fellas all set?"

"Yessir. Logs'll be comin' in afore noon."

"Can you get it running before then?"

"Do the best we can." Snow waved at Jamie and Ned as they climbed down out of the truck. "Come on boys, let's get to it. Ned, get over to the tool shed and bring me the grease bucket and the big tool chest. Jamie, get me the little blue wrench box out of the back room and then help Ned. And don't forget Thumper. Bring 'em all over to the engine shed."

When Jamie got to the tool shed with the little blue metal box in hand Ned was still peering into the darkness. He stepped inside. He saw the metal tool chest and stepped over to slide it around so he and Ned could lift it by the handles at either end.

He head Ned's voice over his shoulder. "Whaddya think's goin' on?"

"What do you mean?" Jamie only half heard Ned as he heaved on the chest handle.

"I mean your dad just got back into the truck with his fistful of paper and he's wearing a white shirt."

"Yeah. He usually wears a white shirt and he's always carryin' papers around. What's so different? Come on, help me lift this." Jamie grabbed one handle and waited for Ned to grab the other.

"Yeah, but this time his shirt's ironed real neat and he's wearing a belt and his shoes are shined. My dad don't buff up his shoes unless he's meetin' somebody or goin' to church." He grunted as they lifted the chest from the wood floor. "Damn, this thing is heavy."

"Set it down for a minute." He grabbed the grease bucket and handed it to Ned. It was filled with a grease gun, a long spout oil can and wiping rags. "That's as may be. But you know what I'm thinking?"

"No. What?"

Jamie opened the tool chest, made certain the heavy hammer 'Thumper' was inside and closed the lid." He grasped the blue tool box in one hand and bent to grab the handle on the big tool chest. "That if we help Snow all right may be we won't have to put up with 'Ewe-ass' for a while."

Ned laughed. "That would be joy, now wouldn't it?"

Jamie nodded. "Come on, grab on."

He watched Ned glance around the dim tool shed with its oil-stained bench that smelled of steel and grease before he too bent to grasp the chest handle on the other end. "By the way, who's 'Thumper'?"

Jamie lifted, the tool chest handle cutting into his fingers. "Thumper's not a 'who', Thumper's a 'what'. Heavy machinist hammer."

"God, what does he need that for?"

Jamie tried to keep his face impassive. "Hammering things."

"No flop, I missed that."

Jamie could not hold in his laughing snort as they heaved the chest out the shed door and headed toward the engine shed. "For tapping parts in place. It's better than a light hammer because you have more control." Ned stared at him so Jamie kept on explaining. "To get the same whack out of a light hammer you have to put more into it, hit whatever you're hitting a lot faster and harder. When you do that you tend to not hit where you're supposed to, so a heavy hammer used slower has more control."

Jamie watched Ned's eyebrows lift and his mouth open into an 'ahh' then gritted his teeth against the weight of the chest.

Snow already had the front and back doors to the shed open and was crouched down beside one side of the engine, staring at the throttle linkage.

Jamie and Ned came up to him and set their burdens on the ground. Jamie peered over Snow's shoulder. "What do you think the problem is?"

Snow shook his head. "I dunno. It fires but it's got no meat to it. Its git-up-n-go done got up and went. The only thing I can think is that the bang part of it ain't workin' somehow."

"We gonna take it apart again?"

"Got no choice." Snow rubbed his face. "Let's start with the fuel, make sure we're getting flow and then do the carburetor. After that we'll work on the magneto and make sure she's getting enough spark."

And that's what they did. Again they put the parts out on boards in order of disassembly and cleaned them, but this time they looked closely for damage. Jamie turning over the igniter switch contacts in his hand, lost in thought about what part did what where when a dreaded high voice behind him made the skin on the back of his neck crawl.

"What ch'all doin'?"

Jamie almost dropped the piece he was holding, then felt the tip of Eueas' cane on top of his shoulder.

"Careful there, boy. You drop those pieces in the dirt we'll never find 'em all. I told you it ain't nothin' but a bad spark plug. Ya gotta replace those things ever now and again. Happened all the time during the war. It was the heat that done it. We used to get that crap all time."

"Well Eueas, we ain't got no more spark plugs til Mr. Garrath gits back." Snow spit snuff juice on the ground. "Now get over here and hold this carb up so I can bolt it down."

Eueas took a great sniff of air. Jamie felt the cane lift from his shoulder then watched Eueas move over to Snow and sit down next to him. He watched them until the carb was in place, feeling useless now that Eueas was there.

Jamie didn't want to look at Eueas, so he stared at the engine. Directly in front of his eyes was a block with wires attached that looked like a big horseshoe magnet. He looked more closely and saw the wires were old and frayed, especially where they were attached to the block.

"Well, that's it." Snow stood and wiped his hands on a rag.

"Snow, what is this?"

Snow looked down to where Jamie pointed. "That's the magneto. It makes the spark. It's all right. I tested it yesterday."

Eueas let out a loud guffaw. "Little boy think's he's figgered out the problem, huh? You got a long way to go, boy, before you got enough sense to think like an engine. Takes years to know engines."

"Would it make much difference if the wires weren't connected good?"

Snow stopped wiping his hands. "That it would. Why, what do you see?"

"This." Jamie reached out and touched one wire attached to the magneto and pushed it away easy as you please. "It's not attached. It's touching, but it's not attached. Would that make a difference?"

Snow came over and looked hard at the wires. "Will you look at that? And this is for the magneto side, not the battery side." Jamie watched Snow's face widen into a grin. "I don't want to say for sure, but I think you done found our problem. Let's fix it and find out."

Five minutes later Snow had stripped the wires back, scraped them for good contact and reattached them. Five minutes after that they had Marshall in the engine shed to heave on the crank. Two minutes after that, the engine was banging along just as pretty as you please.

Jamie watched Snow slap his hands together and do a right fair imitation of Dancin' Charlie. He shouted over the engine noise. "By the great horned spoon, you done it, Jamie. And that's a fact. Wire was probably almost wore in two from workin' back and forth with the vibration. Somebody what was working near it the other day probably knocked it off the rest of the way by way of clumsy." He clapped Jamie on the back. "Your daddy gonna be proud."

Jamie couldn't keep the smile off his face. He watched the big wheels spin, let the irregular thumping fill his ears and breathed deep with the smell of hot oil and iron. Jamie glanced toward Ned to share a grin and caught sight of Eueas' face over Ned's shoulder. He had never seen a face with that much hate stretched across it. Then it came to him that the only person 'working near' the engine the last time it was running was Eueas. Jamie had seen him with the oil can.

Jamie's stomach was suddenly at war. He was just about to bust with happy at fixing the engine, but now that thought was poisoned by the fact Eueas hated him even more.

Chapter 23
Fear Itself

Their new job was picking up trash. Jamie poked a long stick around in tall grass, a little nervous about copperheads, but at least it did get them away from Eueas. As they dragged the small sledge behind them with a wooden box on top around the lumber stacks they looked for treasure. Alongside an April 1930 'Outdoor Life' magazine (story by Zane Grey and cover with a fly fisher paying a kid with a cane pole for a mess of fish), Jamie found a county resident hunting license button.

Ned was less than impressed when Jamie showed it to him. "What good is it? We don't have a gun."

"It's a lot of money, is what it is. It cost a whole $1.10. Can you imagine somebody paying over a dollar just to go hunt?"

"Seen them a lot at the store. Bunch of yay-hoos got more money than they have sense. But me …" Ned reached into his back pocket and held up the cover of a Spicy Western Stories magazine. "I'd rather have this."

"Wow." Jamie reached out his hand for the picture when he jumped at Eueas' voice yelling from behind the stack of lumber.

"Go on, dog. Git outa here."

They stuck their heads around the corner of the lumber stack just in time to see Toby take a flying nip at Eueas' cane. Eueas dropped his cane, took three solid steps forward and took a double-fisted roundhouse swing at Toby with a sling blade. Toby yelped and darted away. The corrugated blade bit a bright chip out of the stack of wood right above Toby's head with a dull ringing clunk. Eueas hissed curses from between clenched teeth. Brown tobacco juice foam sprayed from his tight lips. Toby dodged the flying viscous juice and fled.

"Hey! What'd he ever do to you?" Jamie jerked at Ned's voice from behind him, challenging Eueas like a full grown man. Jamie turned and stared at him.

Eueas jumped backward and pointed the sling blade at Ned. "Now you keep that damn mutt of yours away from me, you hear me? You don't, he be missin' a few things when I git done with him. You understand me, boy?"

Jamie clenched his fists to his side and took a step in Eueas' direction. "He never done nothing to you but play. And you just tried to kill him."

Eueas stretched a brown greasy smile across his face. "I didn't do nothin', boy. I don't know what you're talking about." The smile froze in a menacing mass as he held up his sling blade and pointed it at Ned again. "I didn't go through the goddamned trenches to be ordered around by a couple of snot-drippers like you. If I'd wanted to kill that goddamn dog, he'd be dead."

A chill grabbed Jamie's spine right between the shoulder blades. He'd read his history books, the opinion of his teacher Miss Huff to the contrary, and he'd looked at pictures of the dead from the Great War in his mother's stereopticon when she wasn't looking. If this man had been through that, there wasn't much he and Ned could do. He turned and spoke low and quiet into Ned's ear. "Let's go see if Daddy can do something."

Jamie watched Ned's mouth tighten. "He's not supposed to do stuff like that, no matter what he's been through. He's not gonna hurt Toby. You go on if you want to."

"Toby's lit out for the woods." He grabbed Ned by the arm. "Ned, we can't fight him, Daddy'd have my hide. We're supposed to be better'n that."

Eueas' smile broadened, showing more gum than tooth in his grin. "You just go running and whining to your papa. You're not growed yet, boy. You best remember that."

Jamie pulled Ned back by the arm, but Ned did not turn his face away from Eueas until he was out of sight behind the lumber pile.

They walked without words toward the office.

Snow and Marshall were unloading lumber from the iron-wheeled trailer and sticking the planks in a stack beside the cabin.

167

"Snow, you know where Daddy is?"

"He ain't here, Jamie. He's gone to pick up some engine parts from the railroad depot."

Close to bursting, they flooded Snow with the story, overlapping each other as they spoke.

"Eueas just tried to kill Toby."

"Toby was just nipping around his cane, wanting to play …."

"… Eueas stood up and tried to hit him with his cane. When he missed with that, he dropped his cane, took off after Toby and swung at him with a sling blade."

"Came near to chopping Toby's head off, you can see the chop mark in the wood where he missed."

Snow slid the board in his hands onto the pile next to the porch, slowly pulled his gloves off and rubbed his eyebrows with his thumb. Marshall pulled a deep blue bandana from his pocket, slid his hat from his head and wiped his face, neck and mostly bald head.

Snow pursed his lips. "Boys, I don't know how to tell you this, but I just can't take what you say as gospel."

Ned and Jamie exchanged disbelief.

"But Snow, we saw …"

"We were there …"

Snow held up his hand. "Boys, let me tell you a couple of things. I don't' exactly warm to the man myself. But that don't make no difference, 'cause you got to learn to work with folks what you don't like. The second thing is I know what you told me ain't true cause he needs that cane to stand up. I seen it in Eueas' paper from the Army. They's no way he coulda stood up solid on two legs and took a swing at Toby."

Ned and Jamie both rushed to speak at once. "But we saw him! He swung that blade like a baseball bat …"

"… nearly took off Toby's head!"

A low rumbling voice replaced Snow's even tone as Marshall spoke. "It ain't right to tell a story, boys. It just ain't right."

Snow nodded to Marshall. "And nobody would want to do that to Toby. He's just too good a dog. Now you can wait till your daddy gits here and tell him if you want to, but he's gonna tell you the same thing and get mad too. Best you just get back to work."

Snow pulled on his gloves, nodded to Marshall and the two men once more bent to their task.

Jamie and Ned slowly turned and with shaking heads and hands in pockets, walked back down toward their sledge.

Jamie was stunned. "It ain't right. It just ain't right."

"You seen Toby?"

"Not since Eueas took a swing at him. He probably just ran home."

He glanced over at Ned.

Ned's mouth was set hard. "We gotta figure something to do about this."

"Like what? They don't believe us."

"Yeah well. I ain't gonna let go of it."

"For now let's just give it a good think while we get the rest of the trash up. And stay clear of Eueas. He's one mean sonofabitch and we're not as quick as Toby."

"We're quicker than he is."

As the boys approached the sledge they saw no sign of Eueas. Not that his work was finished, his sling blade was still there, propped against the wood pile. The grass he was supposed to cut down to make the lumber yard less snakey was still there too.

As he poked in the tall grass and picked up trash, Jamie kept an eye peeled for Eueas. Now snakes didn't seem nearly as dangerous as they had been. Not by a long shot.

Chapter 24

Meeting the Elders

"We're not Elders, Daddy. Why do we have to go?"

Jamie's father peered into the darkness beyond the truck headlights then reached to shift into second gear. "Well, it's about time you got to see a meeting. Your mother and Gloria taking soup to the Widow seemed like a good opportunity to go do something, a chance for you to see how folks can and should do things."

Jamie didn't say anything, Robinson Crusoe in his hand. Ned was quiet too.

"You don't understand, do you?"

"Not really, no."

They bounced from the blacktop road into the church parking lot and Jamie's father steered the truck to a space underneath the pines. "Well, you'll find later in life that there's a right way and a wrong way to do things." He took the truck out of gear, pulled the park brake lever and killed the ignition. "It might not make a lot of sense right now ..." he slid his door open, "but there is a calm and rational approach to solve problems."

Jamie followed his father as he got out of the truck and climbed up the church steps to the heavy front doors.

"And the best way to learn," his father paused with his hand on the door handle, "is to watch and see that calm and rational approach in action."

As Grant pushed the door open and guided the boys through ahead of him, they were assaulted by cacophony of shouting voices.

Old Man Mason's voice was the loudest. "I don't give the hind end of one of my field geese whether the church in Salis is doing it or not, Pete Alderman. Them folks is always doin' stuff like that that don't make sense and stuffin' their noses up in the clouds to keep them from smelling their own stink. It ain't right for us! And when the Reverend gets here," he pounded his fist on the arm of his pew in time with the words, "I'm – gonna – tell – him – just - that."

Old Man Mason turned their way and waved his arm. "Grant, good to see you. Come on over and listen. This load would fill my spreader!"

Jamie's father steered him and Ned into a back pew. "Go ahead and read your book if you want while we get this straightened out. Just stay quiet."

Jamie felt Ned whisper in his ear. "That's different. Now he wants you to read?"

"Yeah."

He and Ned watched Jamie's father rub his face and stroll over.

The Elders of the First Presbyterian Church of Miller's Landing were Jamie's father Grant Garrath, Old Man Jeremiah Mason, Ned's father Gil Custis and Pete Alderman. Pete ran the feed mill, was the town handyman and was the Clerk of the Session, which meant he was in charge of writing down what went on in the meetings. He liked his recordings to read well.

Gil Custis separated himself from the group and came over to Jamie and Ned. He reached down and shook Ned's hand. "How are you doing, son? You aren't giving Mr. Garrath any trouble, are you? And how's the work at the mill?"

"No trouble sir. Everything's going just fine."

Jamie heard behind him the huff and puff of the human locomotive known as the Right Reverend Cramphorne, then felt the floor boards creak with stress and heard the thump of the silver-headed cane as the man steamed past.

Mr. Custis' head swiveled and followed the Reverend. "Work to do."

"Welcome gentlemen, welcome." The Reverend Cramphorne's voice was honeydew soothing. The return greetings were not quite so warm. It seemed kind of odd to Jamie the Reverend should welcome Elders into their own church.

At first, the meeting did not live up to the promise of the animated voices. Pete Alderman began with the first orders of business and read the minutes from the last meeting. When the treasurer began to drone his report, Jamie opened 'Robinson Crusoe'. He was reading it for the third time and had just gotten to the part where Crusoe finds Friday's footprint in the sand when loud voices bit into his concentration. He looked up without moving his head.

The Right Reverend Cramphorne leaned back in one of the large carved chairs to either side of the altar. He spread his meaty hands wide. "Gentlemen, gentlemen, gentlemen. I really don't see what all the fuss and fury is about. After all, this is not so unusual as you seem to think. There are many parishes that do this, where it has been the custom for years, and after all, the Deacons take care of the physical well-being of those of the congregation who require it, why should not the Elders then take care of the spiritual …"

"Not here." Jeremiah Mason rattled his dentures then set his mouth like a mule with the bit in his teeth. "Never here. And I, for one, don't give two twaddles how many other places done it. Those folks down at the county home need a visit … from you. They just can't git to church."

Jamie put his eyes back down in his book, but his ears were tuned to the pews in front. Beside him, Ned slowly turned a page in his own book and whispered under his breath. "Your dad's not sayin' much."

"No, he's not." Jamie tried to talk without moving his mouth.

Pete Alderman tried to pacify both sides. "Now Jeremiah, maybe if we just took a couple of minutes …"

"No, dammit." Old Man Mason crossed his arms and set his mouth harder. "I say no. Period."

Jamie heard Ned's father. "The problem, Reverend, is that we must provide for our families. That's why we have businesses in the first place. We work six days a week, ten to fourteen hours a day. You," he reached in his front shirt pocket for cigarettes, "do not."

"Oh, but I do, sir." Cramphorne leaned forward with ready answer. "I do indeed. In these times I am overrun with parishioners requiring guidance. I must be here when they knock at my door, no less than a doctor must be in his office when his patients come to him with their infirmities. Think of me as a doctor of the soul, a doctor for the spiritual ills of this community."

"If that just don't beat the dog." Old Man Mason cackled. "Might I just git in a little point edgewise to you that doctors around here still make house calls. They might not always around Raleigh or over in Charlotte, but around here good ol' General Practitioners make house calls when somebody's too sick to get to them!" Mason leaned back in his pew. "And as long as they've got good sense they always will!"

"Now Jeremiah ..." Alderman was still trying to play peacemaker, "I'm sure the Reverend ..."

"Don't you 'Now Jeremiah' me, Pete Alderman! I ain't gonna bend just 'cause you don' like to face a little bit of a scrap!"

There was a breath in the proceedings. Strain as he might, Jamie could not hear anything but Old Man Mason breathing hard. He heard the hollow tink of Pete Alderman knocking his pipe into a glass ashtray and then the slide-scrape-click of his father's Zippo lighter. He then heard an odd low rumble that at first he hardly recognized as Cramphorne's voice, the softest tone Jamie had ever heard come out of the man. "Mr. Garrath, you've been most quiet throughout all this?"

Jamie heard his father draw on a cigarette. When he spoke his voice was soft as Cramphorne's, but more even and Jamie heard iron in it. "Reverend, we should continue to do what is customary here. Now don't misunderstand me. I don't believe in continuing to do something the way it's always been done simply because that's the way it's always been done. And I can see where in a very large parish like Raleigh there may well be enough demand for spiritual ministering for the Elders to find it necessary to help out, at least until they can find and hire an assistant minister to carry the load. But in this parish, in this church, particularly to the needs of the county home, I do not believe there are so many demands upon your time as to make that aid necessary."

After that came a silence so sharp the only thing Jamie could hear was a ringing in his ears and the ticking of someone's watch.

Cramphorne's chair scraped so abruptly against the wood floor that Jamie jump-startled. He looked up just in time to see the man pounding his cane on the floor in time with his heavy stomp out of the sanctuary. The man's face was a lumpy red thundercloud creased by deep frown and then he was gone.

Jamie put his head back down.

Pete Alderman's nasal tenor cut through the air. "Well, that went pretty well, don't you think?"

Ned lay back on his bed with hands behind his head, eyes closed. He didn't share this with Jamie, but what he was actually doing was listening to the wind through the open window. In his life there had never been enough time to just lay back, be still and just *listen*. He heard Jamie flip a page of his 'Boy's Life' magazine. Neither of them was a boy scout, but Jamie's father got the magazines because he thought Jamie should have something to read that was his own.

"Hey, you awake?"

"Nope. I'm sound asleep, dead to the world, sawing logs." Ned yawned. "Why?"

"It says here Indians don't own stuff the way we do."

"A body's gotta own stuff. Even Indians can't go around with no clothes on."

"I guess, but not the way we do. It says here they don't own land. Nobody in the tribe does. And if somebody else in the tribe needs something that you have more than you do, you're supposed to give it to them. So if you got a bunch of pencils, say, and somebody else doesn't have any you're supposed to give them what they need."

"Is that all tribes or just that one? Seems like I heard somewhere that the Cheyenne or somebody put a lot of stock in owning horses?"

Jamie lifted the sheet he was reading, looked over the article and shifted the page back. "It doesn't say. It's just a short thing about how not to be selfish."

"What about being selfish?"

"They say it's bad."

174

Ned lifted his head up and looked at Jamie. "Do they?"

Jamie flopped the magazine closed and tossed it on the bed. "Why do you think folks do the things they do?"

"You mean like Eueas takin' that swing at Toby?"

Jamie nodded. "And other stuff. Like why your daddy thought it was such a good idea for you to be here this summer. Don't get me wrong; I'm glad he did, but don' cha' kinda wonder why?"

"You sound like my Uncle Seth."

"I didn't know your daddy had a brother."

Ned shook his head. "Uncle Seth's Mom's brother. Pop don't like him much."

"How come?"

"Says Uncle Seth thinks and talks about stuff that's better off left alone."

"Like what kinda stuff?"

Ned screwed up his face and scratched his nose. "I don't really remember, except for one night last fall. He came over for supper and after Mom took away the plates he and Pop had a grand old time, shouting and hands wavin' in the air and everything. At the end of that Uncle Seth leaned in real close to Pop and says real soft 'Well, where do you think God came from?' "

Jamie leaned back and put both hands behind his head on the pillow. "How did they come to that?"

"I wished I'd listened to half of what they'd been talkin' about."

"Wished you could kinda watch it again, like a movie?"

"I wouldn't want to watch Pop again. Lord All-might-ee. He was so mad he couldn't puff out a single word, face was so red it spread near out to his ears. That was the first time ..."

"What? First time what?"

Ned laid back down. "Nothing.'"

"Come on, what?"

"Snuck outside. I was afraid he'd take it out on me."

Toby lifted up off the floor and pushed his head under Ned's hand where it rested on the sheet.

"He sure seems to like you a lot." Ned heard Jamie speak real soft. A whole lot."

"Yeah well." He scratched Toby's ears. "No accounting for   taste."

Chapter 25

Snakes and Grins

They talked late into the night. The next morning they paid the price. They had hardly dragged themselves upright in bed when Jamie's father poked his head in the door for the second time and told them to get up in a slightly harder key.

Jamie felt Ned poke his shoulder as they bounced in the back of the truck on the way to work.

"Hey, he's at it again."

He knew that was supposed to mean something, but his brain was just too slow to connect. "Who? What?"

"Take a look."

Jamie swiveled his head to focus. Sure enough, Old Nosy stood by the widow's mailbox craning his head this way and that, trying to peer into the upstairs windows.

"Now doesn't that just take and tear the ticket." Jamie turned to Ned as the truck bottomed out in a deep rut. "Ow." He shook his head. "And her sick. That's just …"

Ned leaned back against the truck cab. "It ain't right."

"Ain't supposed to say 'ain't.'"

Ned glared at Jamie. "I'll 'ain't' you."

Jamie grinned.

That little bit of happy only lasted until they saw Eueas. He saw them first, set his hat back on his head and grinned over his shoulder as he stumped toward the woods behind the rest of the logging crew. Jamie had never seen a smile like it, full of pleasure and hate at the same time. His gut churned and he tasted bile at the sight. Toby didn't exactly growl, but the hair in his neck showed proud of his collar and he stood between them and Eueas.

For Eueas, the smile he gave the boys was deeply satisfying. A 'bubble up from ya insides grin' is the way Pappy would have said it and the only time Pap ever showed happy was when he was causin' pain. If his old man could see him now. Damn. 'Hiding out under another name, are you? What the damn hell got into you, boy? I'll teach you be ashamed of ya' name; I'll beat you within an inch …' Eueas spit on the ground. The memories never died, never let him be.

Old Man Cadell Cane, aka 'CC', had been a tough, wiry, cantankerous old bastard even when he was young. His old man was the only person ever made Eueas deep scared. That Indian 'CC', hell, he only thought he was tough. After having withstood Pap, Eueas had figured he could take most anybody. And if he couldn't take them, at the very least he could take anything they could dish out. That notion and his name had changed in the Great War. There his name, his real name, had been Lucas Cane and there he found out there were things no man could stand. Not because he had experienced them personally, but he had seen shattered hulks of men with twitching limbs and hollow eyes. Eyes that had looked into what he didn't even want to think. On the battlefields of France, Lucas Cane had been scared down to his toenails.

Eueas shoved his cane at the ground. Maybe that's why he liked seeing that turd of a kid shake in his brand new boots. It was a right pleasure to watch that little kid work out if he quivered from anger or from fear. Both them little snots needed to have a scare laid into them they'd remember but good. It had been good enough for little Lucas. It was damn sure good enough for the likes of them.

Jamie and Ned were sent out in the lumber yard again to hack out clear space for logs and lumber. They traded off jobs of picking up and stacking trash lumber to go in the firewood box and worrying down tall grass with the slingblade.

About mid-morning Jamie was taking an armload of wood bits to the burn stack when he heard a high yelp from Ned. He dropped the wood with a clatter and came running. "What is it, what's the matter? You okay?"

Ned pointed with the slingblade. "Snake."

And it was. It was a jim-dandy about six feet long. "Will you just look at him?"

"How do we kill it?"

"Oh no, never kill a kingsnake. See the black and white stripes? And the smooth head?"

Ned just looked at him.

"Look, there are good snakes and bad snakes. King snakes are good. They eat rats and mice and better yet, other snakes. They don't bother anybody and I don't even think they're poisonous. The bite might hurt, but ain't gonna kill ya. Same for blacksnakes, we leave them alone too. They don't eat other snakes, but they do eat rats and mice. The ones to watch out for are the copperheads. Them and cottonmouths, but you usually only get them in the swamp." Jamie positively enjoyed himself. "I've heard of running into rattlesnakes too, but I've never seen one."

"Oh, great. So what do they look like? Rattlesnakes, I mean."

"Daddy told me the head is like broad arrowhead and they've got these dark hourglass shaped markings the color of leaves that makes them real hard to spot. That's why they're so dangerous."

Ned pointed his sling blade again. "So this guy isn't poisonous?"

"Nahh."

"So what do we do with him?"

"Leave him alone. Work somewhere else til he crawls off."

"And if he doesn't?"

"Then we get a hoe, lift him up and take him to the woods."

"Okay." Jamie watched Ned push his hat back and take a deep breath. "Had me goin' there."

"I thought you'd run into Eueas."

179

Ned's mouth set hard. "Now there's a snake I'd gladly chop to pieces."

"Oh yeah." Jamie didn't really like the feeling of wishing anybody harm. But sin or not, he had to admit he sure did like that thought.

Chapter 26

Cramphorne's Complaint

To: The Honorable Silas Webster, Executive Secretary of District Presbytery

My dear sir:

I hardly know where to begin to inform you of the happenings of this parish in this week past. As you are well aware, it is and has always been my fervent intent to bring the spiritual ways of the wider world to this positively provincial parish. As one of many efforts to that end, I suggested to the Elders of the church at the meeting last that they, as the leaders of spiritual excellence of the community, should take that example one step further and minister to the spiritual needs of those who by physical impairment and infirmity are not able to attend services on the Sabbath. It was my intent to further deepen their spiritual experience by the ancient maxim of 'I see and learn, I study and know, I teach and understand.' One cannot, of course, reveal to such provincial folk as these the true nature of the exercise; for their primitive sensitivity would most certainly take offense at the mere suggestion that there is more to understanding the deep spirituality of faith than merely studying their bibles and going to church. As you well know, such arrangements as what I proposed are common practice in the larger and, dare I say, more spiritually advanced unions of god-fearing folk. I confess I find it vexing, most vexing indeed, when I attempt to apply the spiritual principals of the refined thoroughbred (if I may be allowed the use of metaphor) to draft horses and mules such as these! A fine thoroughbred belongs amongst thoroughbreds, don't you agree? But no, these folk had the actual temerity to assert that I was in some vague sense shirking my spiritual duties to the flock with which I have been entrusted! At that point in the proceedings I simply could not withstand any more impugning of my character and so rose and left them to consider the error of their ways. In truth, I feel my refined expressions of spirituality are lost on such as these, the subtleties of the figure in the glaze of a Grecian urn compared to the clod of earth turned by the plow, a professorial academician reduced to chanting and droning the alphabet to the stone-vacant minds of the first grade.

I do humbly apologize for any unease or inconvenience this may beget, but I feel it is no less than my duty as your tool of grace and, dare I say, friend, to inform you of the wretched state of affairs in this particular outpost of God. I intend to write a sermon to deliver this Sunday next on the terrible sin of pride of which they are all collectively, well, guilty as sin. I pray that it may have some positive consequence, but frankly do not hold much hope of its effectiveness. Perhaps this long-neglected flock requires a more primitive forcefulness to bring them to heel than my kind and gentle soul has the strength or inclination to exert. I'm sure you will not mind, as it is no reflection on you, if I share my trials and tribulations with my familial relations, who are, I say with all modesty, the very model of tact and wisdom in these types of matters, for advice and counseling.

As always, my kindest regards to you and yours and my sincere wishes for continued health and happiness.

I remain sir, as ever

Your humble servant,

The Right Reverend Costigan Abalicious Cramphorne

Miller's Landing First Presbyterian Church

Chapter 27

The Indian

"Ned!"

Ned was dragging to the paint shed to get yet another bucket of whitewash when he heard Jamie's father call. He turned to the sound and saw him standing beside the cabin with the tall Indian.

Jamie's father beckoned to him. "Come here."

Ned walked over. Jamie's father held a map. The Indian wore his peaked campaign hat and a revolver hung from his hip. The Indian also held a bush axe.

"Today you're going to be cruising timber with CC." He handed the map to the Indian. "Now what I want you to do is follow him around and keep track of the trees he marks. Here's the tree book." Jamie's father extended a small gray notebook to Ned. "Just write down what he tells you. And take Toby with you."

Ned looked up at the Indian then down at the bush axe. "Yes sir."

"Oh, and Ned …"

"Sir?"

"Try to keep up."

Ned felt his spine tingle as he watched Jamie's father turn and climb the steps into the cabin. He had heard about Indians, how they walked vast distances, covering more miles in a day than a man on horseback.

"Ned, is it?"

Ned looked up at the black eyes, his face growing hot at being caught wool-gathering. "Yes sir?"

"We'll be gone most of the morning, maybe longer, so fill up your water jar and throw it in your food bag. Find your dog and meet me over by the tool shed."

By the time Ned found Toby and got to the shed, the Indian had the bush axe clamped in the vice and was applying a whetstone to the heavy curved blade. He leaned his shoulder in with every stroke. Hearing the heavy scrape of stone on metal reminded Ned the axe was whetstone sharp. His chest sank.

He watched the Indian try the edge with his thumb, put the stone away then pull on the vice handle to spin the blade free. "You ready?"

Ned only trusted himself to nod; his mouth was too dry.

The Indian picked up a black woven bag, slung it over his shoulder and strode away.

From the beginning he had a hard time keeping up. He trotted behind the Indian's long strides out the back gate and along the hard dusty road leading into the woods. It got worse when they cut off the road onto a forest track into the shade where tree roots lumped the path. Not only did the Indian just walk faster, but with his long legs he could step over logs and rocks and stumps that Ned had to climb. Toby trotted easily, weaving through the underbrush beside them.

The Indian stopped.

Ned almost ran into him.

The Indian pulled the bush axe from his shoulder. "Sit." He pointed his finger at a nearby stump.

"Sir?" Ned gulped breath.

Ned watched the bush axe as it lowered to the ground. "You're tired. If I was working as hard as you were I would be."

"Yeah, well."

"Then sit. Sit still and listen."

"To what?"

"To what is to be heard."

184

The Indian didn't elaborate and didn't look like he was going to. Ned watched as he sat cross-legged on the ground, crossed his arms over the bush axe laid across his knees and became still.

Ned sat. He tried to not move the same as when he didn't want to be seen when he crept out at night. He tried to listen, but his mind jumbled as rustles and birdsong and whispering leaves all tumbled together in his ears.

"Don't call me 'Sir'. We're going to be out here a while. Call me Cyrus. Ready?"

"What?" Ned blinked to realize that Cyrus had stood up. "Uh, yeah. Okay." Ned pushed up off the ground. Cyrus wasted no voice on preamble before he moved off deeper into the woods.

They had gone no more than fifty feet when Cyrus stopped and signaled for Ned to stand clear with a wave of his hand.

Ned backed off.

Cyrus raised his axe and drove the heavy curved blade all the way through the trunk of a scrub bush about the size of Ned's arm, then methodically hacked a clearing around a large pine. He laid his hand on the rough fragrant bark and left it there for a moment. Then Cyrus backed up and drove his bush axe into the wood about eye level and peeled off enough bark for the yellow tree-wound to be easy to see. "I believe you."

"Believe me? About what?"

"Your friend and your dog, what's his name? Toby?" Ned watched Cyrus consider the tree and lean over to watch Toby quietly sniff the ground and follow a scent. "What you say about Eueas."

Now Ned looked right at his face. "What we say ... did you see it? Why didn't you say anything?"

Cyrus shook his head. "I did not see, so I can't speak."

"Then why do you believe us?"

Cyrus took another controlled chop in the pine bark. "Pine, three feet, quarter."

"What?"

Cyrus pointed at the tree book. "Mark down one pine tree, three feet in diameter, for quarter sawing. It's tall and clear enough to be worth it."

Ned bent his head to scribble in the book.

"Because his eyes are never still."

Ned stopped scribbling and looked right past the book in his hand. Now that Cyrus' words brought the image to mind he could nod at it as true. "Oh yeah. I didn't see that."

"Yes, you did."

"I did?"

"Sure. You remember it now. You just hadn't noticed it." Cyrus moved off, leaving Ned to scramble after him.

Not ten paces further, Cyrus shifted off the path again and peered upward. "Pine, two and a half feet, straight cut. The man is warped in spirit."

"Who?" Ned was scrambling inside and out to keep up with the stop and go and scribbling and conversation all at the same time. When Ned looked down, he saw that Toby, on the other hand, was having a grand old time sniffing over every rock and nettle on the ground.

"Eueas Canfield. Pine, two feet, straight cut. It's harder to work with warped people than it is to work with warped wood."

Ned looked up from the book and saw Cyrus reach up to hack off a couple of limbs. Cyrus' shirt sleeve slid back to show a black tattoo on his arm. "What's that?"

"What's what?"

"Nothing." Ned tore his eyes off the tattoo. "Sorry."

"It's Raven, the symbol of my clan." Cyrus leaned back against the tree and pulled his tobacco pouch and papers from his pocket. He gently rolled the papers around his fingers then tapped tobacco into the trough. "Raven is a messenger from the spirit world where all knowledge lies. That gives us our power. Unfortunately he's also a trickster."

Ned didn't know what to say to that.

"I believe you about Eueas, but there's nothing I can do to help."

"Yeah, well. I don't know what to do either."

"Oh, I know what to do." Cyrus struck a match and cupped his hands around his cigarette.

"Which is?"

He blew out the match. "What can be done. Keep your mouth shut, your eyes open, and remember what you see." Cyrus reached up and tapped his temple with two fingers. "Learn to notice and use this. What to do will come to you."

"I just wish I could help Jamie."

"You can, you have and you will." Cyrus pointed with his eyes. "Watch Toby."

"Why? He's just sniffing around."

"To learn from him." Cyrus smiled. "I've only seen that kind of thing once before and that was my brother's dog. Ugliest dog you ever saw, but oh could he track."

"Yeah well, dog's do it with smell, don't they?"

"Yes, but like Toby he never outran my brother, never strayed, stayed right with him like a friend leading a friend along the path." Cyrus' smile faded. He took a grim drag on his cigarette. "They were like that together until a white hunter killed him."

"Killed your brother? I'm sorry."

"No, killed the dog. But they may as well have."

Ned very carefully kept his mouth shut, the moment precious like a butterfly landing on your shoulder.

"When his dog was killed Hegan lost his way and thunderclouds came into his life. After that he slogged through the mud rather than dancing lightly upon the earth."

"I wish I had a dog like that."

"You do." Cyrus nodded toward Toby.

"Oh no, he's Jamie's dog. I couldn't take him."

"I understand your loyalty to your friend, but an animal makes choices too. The Great Spirit gave them souls and minds to think. They decide if we 'own' them or not."

Ned looked down at Toby, who sat near his feet and glanced from Ned to Cyrus and back. "I don't think he'd be all that happy in town."

"Are you? When two souls find each other there's a spirit bond. They find their place in the world together."

Ned scratched the back of his neck. "I never had a dog." He looked up at Cyrus. "You don't talk much like a lumberjack."

He watched Cyrus take deep drag on his cigarette. "Maybe," he talked through the smoke then took another deep drag, "that's because I'm a teacher."

The revelation set Ned back a step or two. He just could not picture Cyrus in a classroom with a stick of chalk in his hand. "You don't … sound like any teacher I ever had."

"Because I ask you to listen to the wind and to your heart?

Ned nodded.

"That's because schools of my tribe are meant to help you grow." He took one final drag on his cigarette, then dropped it to the loam ground. "I went to the white man school on the reservation. Their idea seemed not so much to teach you, but to bind your soul til it couldn't breathe." He crushed the butt on the ground under his boot heel. "Come on, there a time to learn and a time to work."

"We're done with learning?"

"For now."

Ned stood still. "Did you know there's a place east of here on the Cape Fear called 'Raven Rock'?"

Cyrus shook his head.

"I don't know if there are any ravens there or not, but that's what it's called. There are some cliffs. I've never been there, though."

For a moment Cyrus' dark eyes seemed to warm and he nodded. "I thank you." He glanced up. "Hickory, two feet, straight." He shouldered the bush axe and strode away through the trees.

Ned followed Cyrus down the forest path.

Chapter 28

Wandering in the Wilderness

The Indian called Cyrus Conner opened his eyes. He was immediately sorry for his habit of awakening early and completely once his eyes were open. Sunday was the one day off work and he had intended to sleep in. He lifted up on his elbows and looked around. The migrant worker bunkhouse, a single large room with rough lumber bunks packed together, was filled with snoring lumps. On the whole the lumps were more pleasant when asleep than when awake, so he changed his mind about staying abed.

He eased back the sheet, swung his long legs over the side and stood up. Quick quiet touches made the bed and in very few moments more he was dressed in overalls and boots with his felt campaign hat on his head and his woven carry sack slung over his shoulder. He stepped outside into the soft morning air and breathed deeply. He knelt by the single camp water spigot, filled his Ball canning jar, slid it into his bag then splashed water on his face.

A small store squatted right across the road from the migrant camp. A sign in the window said 'Free Coffee' in huge hand-written letters. He pushed through the double screen doors.

A girl sat on a tall stool behind the counter with one leg crossed over the other. The upper leg bounced in rhythm to a tune only in her head for there was no radio playing, just a fan mounted to the wall rotating back and forth, one blade scraping on a bar of the fan cage, flashing its blades at dead air. One elbow leaned on the counter and with that hand she pulled at her hair. The other hand caressed the slick pages of a fashion magazine.

She didn't hear him until he was at the counter. "Any chance of a cup of coffee?"

The girl jumped, gave a little yelp and held her hand to her throat. Her pale cheeks flushed pink. "Oh! You nearly took my life away, what do you want to come in so quiet for?"

"I didn't mean to bother you."

"I should hope not. It's a good thing I don't make a whole lot of noise or my daddy would be comin' right down those steps there quicker than you could blink." She stopped for a moment, her automatic patter arrested as she looked Cyrus up and down. "Fortunately," she leaned forward with her forearms resting on the counter, letting her sundress blouse out, "I have a strong heart."

Cyrus did not doubt she had a strong heart, nor did he move. It was his habit to freeze in his tracks when faced with a dangerous animal with weapons drawn. "Yes, I can see that."

She tilted her head to one side and smiled slow. "You can see what?"

He returned the smallest smile he could manage. "That you have a strong heart."

She shifted her hips on the stool. "And what can I do for you today?"

"Coffee? The sign outside."

"Ya gotta buy something to get the free coffee. And we're really not supposed to entertain on Sundays. That is, unless you've got an emergency?" She straightened, reached for a cup and the coffeepot, poured him a cup and held it out to him. "See anything you want?"

His grandfather used to call this 'dancing on blades.' In his youth Cyrus could never resist. He reached out and took the cup.

As she let go he felt her fingers trail across his hand. "So what would you like?" Her eyes brushed up and down Cyrus' lean frame.

He took a long sip. It was strong and hot.

She sat back down on the stool. "Well?"

He glanced around the worn wooden counter for something to buy. His eyes landed on the Barlow pocket knives, held in a cardboard card rack behind the register beside the pocket watches. He frowned a smile at her. "I'll just take a Barlow. For now."

Her head turned a little to the side but her eyes never left his. "For now?" A dimple appeared in her cheek. "What about later?"

He drank deeply and then heard a series of leaden thumps from the ceiling above, a heavy smoker's cough and then a deep rough voice echoed from the stairwell behind her. "Charity? You down there? Who you talkin' to, girl? You 'sposed to be up here helpin' ya mamma get ready for church."

Charity smiled at Cyrus and spoke loudly over her shoulder. "Oh, nobody, Daddy. Just one of the single bunk men come in for a cup of coffee." She held out her hand for the cup.

More weight thumped from upstairs and grew louder as they came down the stairs. Cyrus placed the cup gently in her outstretched palm.

A heavy man emerged from the stairwell doorway. "Don't you give him nuthin', 'specially if he's colored, the sheriff'll have our grits for garters for ..." The man stopped talking as he hit the bottom step and saw Cyrus. He filled most of the doorway and jiggled there. A half tied string tie hung between the flaps of his half-open vest. He thumped his cane on the floor as he moved over toward Cyrus, his dark eyes flicking up and down deep in his fat face. Cyrus looked at the man's long ears and thought of the real Cyrus Connor's fat Bassett hound. Evidently the man was trying to decide if Cyrus was 'colored' or not, but just as evidently decided Cyrus looked tough enough to warrant civility. "We can't sell food on a Sunday. The law says we can't, sorry. That's why you have to buy something to get coffee."

"He wants to buy a Barlow, Daddy."

"Oh, that so?"

Cyrus nodded slowly, once. "That is so."

"All right then." Bassett Hound turned, pulled a Barlow out of its slot in the display card and placed it on the counter in front of him. "That'll be fifty cent."

Cyrus picked up the knife, opened it, tested the blade with his thumb and turned his gaze back up to the man's black eyes deep buried in folds of fat. "Your sign says a quarter."

"That's during the week. Sunday prices are higher 'cause there's less business but the overhead of stayin' open stays the same."

Cyrus neither spoke nor moved nor blinked.

Basset Hound coughed. "But today I'll make an exception and give it to you at the regular price."

"I appreciate your consideration." Cyrus lay the quarter on the counter. "I thank you." He closed the knife, slid it in his pocket and touched the brim of his hat to Charity. "Ma'am." He nodded to the man and walked slowly out the door. As he cleared the screen door he heard the man bark at the girl, again much like the Bassett hound of the real Cyrus that was all bark and no bite, but that in no uncertain terms. "Girl, get y'self upstairs and he'p ya momma get ready for church."

Cyrus was glad of escape into open air.

He thumbed a ride from a passing truck. The trucker said he knew where Raven Rock was and dropped him off next to a path leading into the woods. The trucker was wrong. Cyrus didn't find that out until he was deep in and the path dead-ended without track or trace of which way to go. He kept trekking until he came to a small muddy river. He looked to the sky. There was one bird flying very high up, circling like a hawk. So, not Raven. He had looked for ravens and got a slow-moving muddy sorry excuse for a river. Were the gods telling him that's all he deserved?

He wandered back toward the road to hitch a ride back. At the path dead end he spotted a glint of something low down in a crooked hollow tree. He unslung his woven bag and knelt down by the hole. Inside was a canning jar identical to the Ball jar of water resting in the bottom of his bag. He lifted it up, unscrewed the lid and sniffed the contents. His eyes immediately watered so he held the jar away from himself until he could blink his vision back. For all the white man's drawbacks, he sure could make potent moonshine. The question was what was it doing here? He could not say he cared. Raven had, apparently, deserted him here in the middle of a land not his own, a land without an Indian soul. If that be, by damn he'd act like a white man. He took one sip of the clear liquid. It felt like he'd swallowed a lit cigarette as it burned its way down his throat. The first breath he could force-draw into his lungs rushed back out in half whoop, half scream. He screwed the top back on the jar, slid it into his bag and set a pace toward the road. It wasn't too long before he caught a ride, this time in the back of a pickup between bales of straw. That suited him. A bitter fireball burned in his gut and he did not want to lash out at an innocent. He unscrewed the top from the jar and drank again.

Ned tried to sit still, but the hard wooden pew hurt and made him want to shift. Papers and fans rustled about him as the congregation sweated and stuck to the varnished wood in their Sunday best. He prayed, as he was supposed to in church, but it was a pure possibility his prayer would not be appreciated or approved of in any way, shape or fashion by the Right Reverend Cramphorne. He prayed first for wind to blow in through the open windows, then prayed for rain to cool the air and barring those, finally prayed for early release from what he considered a particularly painful form of torture.

This Sunday Ned's folks were gone to visit his mother's family so he sat with the Garraths. On Ned's left, Jamie leaned forward with his chin in his hands. Ned glanced to his right. Mr. Garrath's face was fixed very still and he breathed very slowly. On the other side of Mr. Garrath, Mrs. Garrath sat ramrod straight, her head tilted slightly back. She waved a funeral home fan on its flat stick slowly back and forth in front of her face. He looked beyond Mrs. Garrath and saw Gloria leaned against her mother asleep. Then he looked up to the pulpit. It was time for the Sunday morning's entertainment.

The Right Reverend Cramphorne's massive hands gripped the edge of the big bible in front of him. Sweat streamed down his face.

"Our message today comes from Proverbs. Sermons generally address some aspect of sin. Big sins, little sins, repentance for sin, avoidance of sin, all these things, usually some aspect of fighting the devils within us that make us sin. This sermon is no exception, except the sin I'd like to cover with you today is the granddaddy of all sin, the one that drives the rest, the one we need to defend ourselves against the most, the one from which all the others grow. And that, my dear brethren, is the sin of pride."

Cramphorne paused for effect and waited for that last word to sink in.

"Thomas Aquinas, for those of you who know who he is, said of pride that 'inordinate self-love is the cause of every sin.' It is the paper door between righteousness and self-righteousness and

194

if you do not pay attention to that thin door, the very fires of hell will consume you and you will be broken on the wheel of eternal damnation."

Cramphorne smiled, thumbed a page in the bible and spread his hands. "In Proverbs chapter eleven verse two we find these word, 'When pride comes, then comes disgrace.' And in chapter sixteen verse eighteen 'Pride goes before destruction and a haughty spirit before a fall.'"

He lifted his eyes out of the book and shook his head. "There is nothing new here. My brothers and sisters, from the time of the Garden of Eden, pride always, inevitably, goes before the fall. And it is not just the Old Testament that talks of this. There are more references to the sin of pride than ... " He waved his hand over the bible, "a dog has fleas. The New Testament, our connection with our dear lord and savior and in whose wisdom we place our trust, speaks of pride when Jesus talked to the Pharisees in the book of Mark, chapter seven verse twenty and on, he says 'What comes out of a man is what defiles a man. From within, out of the heart of a man, comes evil thoughts, fornication, theft, murder, adultery, coveting, wickedness, deceit, licentiousness, envy, slander, foolishness and' he paused and cast his eyes across the congregation, "pride."

Cramphorne dug in his pocket and lifted out a white handkerchief. He wiped it across his face, gave it a little wave in the air and then leaned against the podium. "I seem to be guilty of a little bit of pride myself." He took a sip of water from the glass on the pulpit. "I, frankly, was proud enough to think I could stand up here for a great deal longer." He lifted the sheets of paper in front of him and waved them in the air, fanning his own face. "But there seems to be greater use for these pages to make a little breeze than it does for me to keep talking." He took a quick glance at the paper in his hand. "And if my pride in this goeth much further I feel like I'm going to falleth down."

He laughed at his own joke. A couple of follow-alongs flittered in the congregation.

"But you good folks know what I'm talking about. You know what pride is; I'm not telling you anything you don't know already. I'm just reminding you. Reminding you because we must face the world with a clean heart, with a clean soul, with the humility of our heavenly father that gave his life so that we might live forever in the kingdom of heaven. In that place, where there is no blistering heat, but fresh cool air all the time. And speaking of fresh cool heaven, let us pray the Lord's Prayer, 'I believe in God the Father Almighty ….'"

Ned listened to the drone and leaned over to whisper in Jamie's ear. "He shoulda been an actor. He's a big enough ham."

As he straightened back up, Ned heard Jamie snort and laugh into his hands before his father reached out and thumped him on the back of the head.

"Sorry" he whispered.

After the service Ned eased toward the pulpit, hoping to exit the church out the back, away from the press of hot bodies shuffling in file out the front. He glanced at the Reverend's papers on his way by and saw the 'falleth down' joke scribbled in the margin.

It was long past dark when the hay truck dropped Cyrus off at the post office in Miller's Landing. There was still a long walk back to the bunkhouse, but there was no hope and no help for it. As he walked into the darkness beyond the lights of the post office, past striped shadows of black tree limbs under a full moon, he felt anger burn in his lungs, take hold of him. He began to run, run with pumping limbs drawing power from the earth and clenched teeth facing the night and the wind. He pushed off his campaign hat, let it fall down his back and let the night wind flow across his face and head. The real Cyrus Conner had been the only white man he had ever loved and that's why he had taken his name, but now the Indian inside him was bursting to get out, his straining legs not his own. As the wind picked up and worked against him, he saw a trail split off from the road, moonlight marking the path. He plunged straight on it, then followed as it turned right into pine woods, made his way by more stripes of moonlight and shadow and came out on a dock, a pier running out along the edge of a small lake. He stopped at the end of the pier and breathed deeply. The moon shone full and round above. He focused on it, took a deep breath and howled as loudly as he could right at the moon, casting his pain into the night. He collapsed onto the rough deck boards, leaned back against one of the tall posts and began to weep, shaking like he hadn't since a child when he'd had to stay out all night in his cedar canoe at sea because the tide currents had gone against him. But then he'd been with one with the gods, his ancestors had told him to set a sea anchor and wait it out, then had rocked him to sleep with the motion of the waves.

That was then. Now he was alone, grasping to hold together the shattered fragments of his broken soul.

Ned Custis was wild. Though his father didn't understand his own feelings, wildness was the quality that disturbed him about his own only son. Gil Custis thought of his son as wayward, but in truth Ned was simply undomesticated. It was not that he was bad or wished anyone harm, it was just that his heart was not under anyone else's control. To him rules that had no purpose did not exist, no matter what the preacher or anyone else said. If Gil had known of his son's nighttime wanderings he would not have understood that either.

Tonight Ned heard wind brushing the trees call to him. After he heard soft snores from Jamie's bed he crept to the window. The moon lit up the ground like cloudy daylight, so he slid on his shirt and jeans and slipped out the window, boots in hand. When he reached the edge of the yard he pulled them on, swung over the fence into the pasture and trotted down the path across the rolling pasture to the woods.

In town he avoided obvious dangers like billiard halls, alcohol and policemen. But tonight Ned strolled country. Here he was quieter, more careful.

He felt drawn to Little Lake, to see the water in wind and moonlight. When he got there he walked the path around the shore until he found a huge red oak tree. The roots made the tree look like a rough hand of God had reached down from above to push upon the earth. He sat between two roots, leaned back against the trunk and sat very still to feel the breeze against his skin and watch the wind roar through the waving branches in the illumination of the moon.

Then he heard thumping footsteps, first on the path, then pounding out on the dock. He saw a figure stop on the end of the dock with arms spread as if he could not decide if he wanted to

197

jump in the water or fly. Tall and rangy thin, the gaunt shadow stood there breathing heavily with bowed shoulders, then threw his head back and howled loud and long. The man took a deep ragged breath and howled again until his shoulders shook. The man had a bag slung over his shoulder and a round hat hung by its string down his back. Ned realized the shadow was Cyrus.

Unseen against his oak in the dark, Ned watched and felt Cyrus. He'd never been able to read Cyrus before. Now that he could, of all the feelings of all the people he had ever read, this was the strongest. It petrified him. He did not want to know there was that much pain, but it was right in front of him. Ned never wanted to hear a sound like that howl again and he wished he hadn't heard this one. It was a ragged strangled scrape that curled his feet then traveled upward and closed off his throat. He could not breathe, he could not move, even after Cyrus collapsed on the deck and leaned back against one of the pilings breathing in long ragged gasps. Ned had never seen a full grown man cry. He breathed deep and tried to bear the sound. Finally he saw Cyrus tilt over and lay out flat on the deck. The ragged gasps slowly eased into regular breathing. When Ned was fairly sure Cyrus was asleep he lifted up from his tree root seat and stole away, looking back every so often.

After he crossed into the shelter of the woods beyond the road he ran, ran all the way, all the way back to the house.

Chapter 29
Wandering Tom

Jamie flopped down under the oak by the office at morning break. His bones felt like lead. He had been sticking stacks of wood with Marshall. Marshall had picked up six two-by-fours at a time, three in each hand, while Jamie carried two. Jamie could hardly lift even the mason jar of cold water to drink and leaned his head back against the trunk and closed his eyes.

"Hey, Jamie!" Ned slid down beside him.

As Jamie dragged his eyes open he saw Ned was about to bust to spill something between his ears. Ned's eyebrows bounced up and down like caterpillars on springs.

"How can you have so much energy when I'm so tired?"

Ned grabbed Jamie's leaden arm and leaned in close. "Guess what we got in the box."

"I told you, I'm not getting within spraying distance of any skunk. No way, nuh-uh."

"It ain't a skunk."

"Then what do we got?"

"Wandering Tom."

Jamie raised himself up on one elbow then gasped himself back down. "Oh, poor fella. We gotta go let him out …"

"No, we don't. He's almost as good and not near as smelly." Jamie watched Ned grin.

"We can't carry the whole box down to the widow's!"

"We could, but we won't have to if we shake him down into a flour sack. We'll leave him in the sack on the path out by the road, then sneak out tonight and put him in the mailbox. Come on, it's perfect."

Jamie felt his face smile, his dead limbs forgotten. "Not a word though." He held up his finger to Ned. "Not one single solitary word do we breathe to anyone, understand?"

"Wait for it, wait for it." Jamie hissed at Ned when Ned's bed creaked in the night.

"For what?" Ned hissed back.

"For Daddy to snore. When he does that we have about ten to fifteen minutes before Momma wakes up and rolls him over. If we can ease out the window then we're good for the night."

There was a long silence from the darkness. "You stay awake a lot, do you?"

Jamie nodded by habit to the dark. "Most nights."

"So you saw me go out before." A statement, Ned's flat voice.

"Oh yeah."

"Why didn't you say anything?"

"No point. Just cause a lot of pain and trouble and I don't need no more of that. I ain't your mammy."

A rumble from the other side of the house gave the signal. Jamie felt Ned ease past him in the dark. He slid out of bed and into his overalls then at the last minute grabbed his flashlight. The light the copper cylinder gave out was pretty weak, but it would be better than nothing if they needed it. Ned held the window open from the outside as he climbed through and then they were off toward the woods as quickly as they could quietly go. Jamie had never known walking across plain dirt to cause so much noise.

Once they were on the path Jamie relaxed a little, then heard Ned's voice from behind him. "What do you reckon your dad would do to you if he found out?"

Jamie dodged a rock and a root in succession on the trail. "You can bet it'll involve a switch."

"That's his chosen weapon?"

"I guess you could call it that." He slowed as they got close to the cotton flour sack on the trail. He didn't want to miss it.

"My dad's is a belt."

Jamie stopped looking for the sack for a minute to look back at Ned. "Ouch and shit."

He could not see Ned's face in the dark but the tone of the reply carried. "Yeah."

Jamie pulled his flashlight from his back pocket and flashed it around, hoping to spot the white of the flour sack. "You get caught much sneaking out?"

"Not yet."

Jamie spotted the bag and switched off the light. "Let's carry it real gentle, maybe we can get him there without waking him up."

"Fat chance of that, Tonto, but okay."

They lifted the bag gingerly, one boy at either end. The lump inside the bag didn't move. They looked up and down the road. There was no sound except for a breeze through the trees.

"Now." Jamie whispered to Ned.

They tiptoed across the road, knelt by the mailbox and set the bag on the ground ever so gently and a low rolling yowl rose from the bag.

Jamie's heart thumped. "He's awake."

Ned stood up and slowly opened the mailbox door. It squeaked just a bit and Jamie could see Ned's teeth bared against the sound.

They untied the top of the bag and the low yowl rose again.

"He was hard enough to get in the bag, now let's see how tough it is to get him out of it."

They slid the whole bundle into the mailbox mouth first. They grabbing the back end and lifted it just a little and closed the door until just the end of the bag stuck out.

Ned breathed a sigh. "This is the tricky part."

"The other parts leading up to this have been not so tricky, have they?"

"Just be ready to run if we can't hold the door shut."

They pulled on the bag slowly until there was a thump and a small cat cry, then more thumps and another cry larger and more irate than the first one then the flower sack was free and they closed the last crack on the mailbox lid with a little thump.

"Think he'll try to push his way out?" Ned held his hand against the lid.

"He's Wanderin' Tom, ain't he? I'd bet on it." Jamie turned his flashlight on again and scanned the ground for a twig of some kind to hold the mailbox lid closed.

Ned's voice hissed in his ear. "Car."

Jamie switched off the flashlight and they both slid down in the ditch in the tall grass. No sooner had the car lights wailed by than the mailbox scratched and thumped. Ned's hand shot up to hold the lid closed. "Do you think they saw us?"

"Hope not. No help for it now if they did."

Jamie lay on the ground until Ned spoke again. "Maybe a little stick to hold it closed?"

"Oh, yeah." Jamie turned his light on again, close to the ground and spotted a twig. It was old, dry and crumbly but it would have to do. He slid it into the mailbox latch hole and turned to Ned. "Now all we gotta do is get back and not caught."

"Piece of cake."

Ned was right. They padded back up to the house, listened at the screen for noise, then eased the screen open, swinging the wooden frame out from the bottom. Jamie expected a squeak, but the hinge at the top was silent as could be. They climbed in through the window, slid out of their clothes and into bed. They lay there breathing, not believing they'd done it.

Jamie's heart thumped so hard it hurt. He thought for certain that at least Ned could hear it. He strained his ears to hear any sound from his parent's room but there was none. Had they really gotten away with it? Or was it just quiet now because his parents had decided to hit them with it in the morning? The only sounds that came to his ears were quiet staccato hisses as Ned failed to hold in his laughter. Eventually Ned shoved a pillow onto his own face to snuffle the sound.

Jamie did not feel like laughing. It had just been too much of a near thing for it to be that funny yet. But sweet god it had been fun and for the only time Jamie could remember he fell asleep with a grin on his face.

Chapter 30
Silas' Struggle

    Silas Webster plucked the next envelope from the pile in the correspondence basket on his desk, sliced it open and extracted the letter, leaned back in his chair and began to read.

To: The Right Honorable Silas Webster

Executive Secretary of the Presbytery, Presbyterian Church U.S.A.

From: Thomas Cooper Parson

Dear Sir,

    Like a lot of folks right about now I am looking for a job. I know you do not know me therefore you will find my seminary credentials attached to this letter. What my credentials do not say is that I work for a living and have done so since I was a boy. I worked my way through college and the seminary without help from family because they were, like so many others, taken by the flu epidemic. I earn my living as a carpenter. I am recently married and my wife is much the same, also without family. We can go about anywhere, so if you know of a small church in need of a minister who wants to help, is not afraid of hard work and whose sermons tend to be short, to the point and not too heavy-handed, then I am your man and theirs. I believe much can be done with a listening ear and a kind word in the middle of hard times and hard truths. The world is mighty tough right now and I just don't see any need to add to the difficulty. I've probably gone on too long already, but I feel it helps more to encourage folks in our care to do what they should than to beat on them about what they shouldn't. I think it helps more to give a person a goal to work towards rather than a fear to run from. That's how I was reared, anyway. So if you know of a church that is in need of a minister along those lines I would truly appreciate it if you find a good word to put in for me.

Yours, Sir

Very truly,

Tom Parson

Silas held the letter up to the light coming in from the window behind his shoulder. Then he laid the letter to one side and pressed his hand on top of it. As was his habit, he talked aloud to himself. Or more correctly, he began talking with Tom Parson, who was of course not in the room.

"Tom Parson, I wish I did have a church for you. If you are as you say, then there are a hundred churches that could use you and thousands more that should. Mr. Parson, I am going to keep your letter in front of me and if such a place does open up, it's yours. The trouble is with times as they are, a man would have to be mighty dim to give up his position if he didn't have another lined up solid. Most don't complain." He picked up the next letter from his correspondence basket, saw Cramphorne's name on the return address, hung his head and sighed. "With one very painful exception."

His secretary, Mrs. Wenig, sat on the other side of the room at her desk. She glanced up at Silas' words but immediately lowered her eyes to hide her amusement.

Silas Webster had a good heart. Silas was also disorganized and absent-minded. This constantly annoyed his wife, made him a target to the rest of his family who tried to take advantage and disconcerted his friends who thought him on the far edge of eccentric.

Silas also had very little ambition. He did not want to rise in the church hierarchy. In true fact, it had been an oversight he was there at all. His predecessor Mr. Wilkins had passed on suddenly and Silas, as his aide, was pressed into service for the interim. Silas did such a good job that the short term became the long term and his superiors, since they had no problems, left him where he was in a grand spirit of benign neglect. Over the years his superiors died, moved on or were replaced and he slowly cemented in his position, a seed blown by chance to a place of shelter from the wind that had taken root, grown tall and was now shade and shelter to others.

He sliced open the letter, read Cramphorne's scrawl and was not, in any sense of the word, amused. "You right idiot." he mumbled to the paper in his hand. Silas was tired of the Right Reverend Cramphorne, and every letter made him more tired. He grasped the letter in both hands ready to tear it to pieces, when magical Mrs. Wenig coughed and cleared her throat. She blinked at him through her owl glasses without expression, which was her signal he was about to do something he would probably regret. He gave her what might have passed for a smile if she hadn't known it was actually a grimace, then put the letter back on the desktop and attempted to flatten it out with his palms. He saw her raise one eyebrow.

"Cramphorne."

Her eyebrow lowered in understanding and she offered the slightest of nods.

"I was in hopes that liberal application of neglect might wither that weed, but thus far my efforts are without apparent effect." He held the letter out to her. "Might you be so kind as to put this with the other Cramphorne drivel in the Miller's Landing file?"

She nodded and strode across the room to take the paper from his hand.

"Thank you."

As he regarded her retreating back, his eye fell upon the letter from Tom Parson. He picked it up and read through it again. "Now why can't Cramphorne be more like you?" He glanced up in the direction of the ceiling and offered a quick prayer. "Could you please help me find a little parish somewhere that would appreciate this man? I have good feeling about him and I need a place for him."

He glanced up to see Mrs. Wenig gazing at him from the doorway. "It's time for your nap, remember what the doctor said."

"Yes, yes, yes." He pushed himself to his feet and walked over to the faded lumpy leather couch where Mrs. Wenig waited with an afghan outstretched in her hands. He lay down. Mrs. Wenig lowered it onto him and then carefully pulled his glasses from his face and laid them on his desk.

"Thank you Mrs. Wenig. You're very kind."

"Don't you dare tell."

"Whyever not?" He peered at her fuzzy outline as she tucked the cover about his legs.

"Because I've worked long and hard to get this reputation as someone not to be trifled with. I'm not about to have it ruined by you."

"Of course." He smiled. "Thank you, Mrs. Wenig."

"Yes sir."

The door clicked softly behind her. Silas Webster leaned his head back against the arm of the couch and closed his eyes.

Mrs. Wenig didn't mind eccentricity. She witnessed Silas' odd compassion every day and it warmed her. The biggest trouble these days was with that odious Cramphorne man. Oh, he was awful, just awful. From the time when Mrs. Wenig heard Silas talking to Tom Parson's letter, it would be she who was to keep Tom in mind and his letter on the top of the piles on Silas' desk. She would have denied it were it put to her, but Mrs. Wenig was Tom Parson's guardian angel.

Chapter 31

What Goes Around

Nosy Norris was nothing if not dependable. He delivered the mail at precisely the same wee hour every morning. His promptness provided Jamie and Ned with an unexpected ringside seat as they rode in the back of the pickup to the mill.

"Jamie."

"What?" Jamie squinted at Ned. He was half-asleep. He wanted to be full asleep, but banging around in the back of the slow-bouncing pickup truck did not help his cause.

"You're gonna miss it."

"Miss what?" Jamie followed the lifting jerk of Ned's head toward the road ahead. "Oh! What was I thinking?"

"You weren't."

Their timing could not have been more perfect.

Norris' nose once more pointed at the widow's windows as he pulled down the mailbox lid and felt inside for letters. After his night-long captivity Wandering Tom was a pent-up wound-tight fighting spring. The instant the mailbox lid scraped open he launched into the air in an explosion of flour dust and screeching blood thirst, claws out and fighting the first moving thing he saw. That first thing just happened to be Nosy Norris. As the ragged yellow cat flailed claws into his face, Nosy let out a high hollow bawl more screech than yell. He tripped backwards and raised his arms, tried to beat at the scruffy old cat with his mailbag, twisting like an off-center flopping windmill.

The Widow Morrison's timing was perfect too. At that moment she opened her door to lift her daily milk bottle from her doormat. She took in the combat at a glance and was out of her door like a shot, punching a hole in the air with her finger directly at Norris. Wandering Tom saw his chance of escape and bolted to safety, a fuzzy yellow streak right into the widow's house.

"Nathan Ichabod Hindmarsh Norris, you leave that cat alone!" The Widow stomped to a stop directly in front of him, her fists jammed on her hips, her face thrust forward, eyes blazing.

Under her fierce spotlight glare, the wind-milling arms ground to a slow halt. Nosy slowly shook his gaping mouth from side to side in denial. He was winded. He was scratched. His ashen cheeks slowly spotted pink. One white shirttail hung out beneath his disarrayed blue postman's coat. His mailbag dragged on the ground, the leather strap dangling from his scrawny hand.

"But ma'am, he ..."

She stabbed the air with her finger, stiff as her blazing blue eyes. "I don't care what he was doing, that animal couldn't have done anything that bad to you! You just go on now and leave him alone!"

"But ..." Norris waved his open hands through the air to her.

"But nothing! You git!"

That was all Jamie and Ned had time to hear. The pickup moved out of earshot just before the turn down to the mill but Jamie and Ned could still see the widow giving Nosy a solid piece of her mind, fist on one hip, the other hand's finger poking at his chest then pointing down the road.

Norris slowly nursed his scratched cheek with one hand and pleaded his case with palm outstretched with the other, but to no avail. He backed away, having clearly lost both the battle and the aftermath.

Then Norris turned and saw Jamie laughing and Ned rolling holding his stomach in the back of the truck. His glare was visible from beyond earshot and even at that distance if looks could kill, both boys would be sizzling country fried steak on the grill.

Jamie watched until the scene was lost behind trees on the road. He tore his eyes back to where Ned had fallen over in the back of the truck bed, curled up with both arms across his stomach, silent tears of laughter rolling down his face.

"You okay?"

Ned could only nod and gasp for air.

Chapter 32
The Gift

Ned stumble-trudged behind Cyrus Conner. The tall Indian had been silent the whole morning, striding without pause except for once to sip water without even a glance at Ned before they were off again. It was after the midmorning train whistle when they stopped. Even then Cyrus did not sit down. Ned watched him, breathed hard and sweated in the quiet of the woods.

"Mr. Conner?" Ned could not get the dark image of the Indian screaming at the moon in the deep night out of his mind. "Mr. Conner, is this where we start marking trees?"

Cyrus' head swung on Ned so quickly Ned jumped. He felt more than saw Cyrus' eyes burning into him and Ned's eyes stole to the gun at Cyrus' hip.

"What? No, we passed that point some time ago."

"Do you need the map?"

"No, I know where I am." Ned watched Cyrus' shoulders lift then slump before he raised his axe with one hand and drove it deep into the nearest tree. "I know exactly where I am." He motioned Ned toward the log of a fallen tree. "Sit down. Rest a minute."

Ned watched him move to another tree, sit down and lean back against it. The Indian slid the round campaign hat from his head and rubbed his other hand over his face. "Don't call me Mr. Conner. Call me Cyrus. There's only the two of us out here and we're not in a white man church."

Ned sat on the ground and leaned up against the log. "Okay."

"Now close your eyes."

"Sir?"

"Don't 'sir' me, just close your eyes."

Ned swallowed and did so.

"Now listen. Don't talk, listen. A body can learn as much from what you hear in the woods as what you see. And at night even more, so just listen."

Ned bit his tongue. He wasn't too sure about what Cyrus would say if he told him about his night jaunts. He listened all right, expecting to hear at any moment a rustle of leaves that meant he was going to get chopped into small pieces.

"Now tell me, what do you hear? Don't tell me what you think you should hear; tell me what you do hear. Listen quiet."

Ned tried to relax his ears. "Birds, mostly. One has a single sharp whack at the air every now and again, another one has a long quivering trill and then an answer of the same coming from another direction. Then there's another one that sounds, well I can't exactly place it, but," he opened his eyes and looked at Cyrus, who was still leaning safely against the tree, his hat hanging by the brim between his hands, "it sounds like the call is twisting and falling."

"Good. Try it again. This time don't try so hard. Relax, and don't try to go out and get them, let the sounds come to you."

"All right." Ned closed his eyes again. "There's leaves brushing against each other in the wind. Mostly pine, I think. They sound different than other trees. Pines have a kind of quiet roar. Other trees rustle."

"What else?"

"Nothing else. Unless you mean the thunder way off."

"Good. That's enough for now."

Ned opened his eyes. "How'd I do?"

"Better than some. Not as good as others."

Ned's heart deflated. He had hoped he could be good at this, good at something.

"Don't worry about whether you're good at it. That's another way for evil words to steal your faith in yourself. Don't worry about how good you are; just enjoy doing what you can do."

The thought occurred to Ned that Cyrus might have the same gift of reading people that he did. He focused on Cyrus. Cyrus' hat still dangled from his fingers by the brim. "Is that what you do?"

Cyrus looked at his hat. "Not ... as much as I used to. I'm kinda out of practice."

"You have to practice? That sounds like piano lessons. Yuck."

Cyrus smiled at Ned, flipped his hat around with his fingers and onto the top of his head. "If your teachers let you enjoy the music it would be a lot more fun."

Ned had no answer to that. Fun and piano lessons were all oil and water inside his head. When he tried to shake them together all he got was a foamy mess he couldn't see through.

Cyrus wasn't finished. "You ever watch a squirrel jump? Or a blue jay dive-bombing a cat or a hawk floating on the wind way up high? Did you ever watch a thing just for the joy of it, just 'cause it's fun to watch?"

"Sure. Usually that's when Pop comes down on me. 'Quit that daydreaming, boy. Pay attention, boy. Keep your mind on what you're doin'.'"

"Ripped that fun off right in the bud, did he?"

Ned bit his tongue. He felt somehow he'd betrayed his father with the truth.

"Yeah, I hear." Cyrus' mouth tightened a little as he nodded. "Let's mark some trees. Got your pad and pencil?"

"Sure." Ned reached into his bag. The pencil tip was broken off. "Dammit."

"It's all right. Here."

Ned looked up to see Cyrus rise to his feet and dig in his jeans pocket. He tossed something to Ned. Ned caught it and turned it around in his hand. It was a Barlow pocket knife.

As Ned sharpened his pencil he noticed Cyrus stood very still. That seemed more normal for the Indian than the rushing pace they had set this morning. He closed the knife and held it out. "Thanks."

There was a half-heartbeat pause while Ned held the knife out.

"Keep it."

"What?" No one had ever given Ned anything like this, on the spur of the moment. "I can't take this. It's your knife."

The tall Indian shook his head. "I have one my grandfather gave me. Man always oughta have a knife on him of some kind."

"I don't understand. Why would you just up and give me a knife?"

Cyrus scratched his cheek with the back of his thumb. "Because right now your need is greater than mine. And you're not taking it from me; I'm giving it to you. Don't try to understand it like a white man, just think on it and let your brain be."

The best Ned could do with that was nod. He stuffed the knife in his pocket.

Cyrus took a deep breath. "We'll start here and work our way back to the log road, then we won't have so far to walk to get back."

They did just that, slowly moving, talking trees, Ned very aware of the weight where the knife nestled in his pocket. It was a quiet kind of warm thing that he didn't want to share and he allowed himself the private pleasure.

That afternoon Ned looked up from scribbling in the notebook to see Cyrus down on one knee peering at the ground. "Here, take a look at this."

Ned looked. It was a single animal track sunk in the soft forest loam. "What about it?"

Cyrus shook his head, leaned back and sat on his leg beside the trail. "That's not a question that occurs to me when I look at a track. I wonder what the animal was and what it was thinking."

"How can you tell that?"

"Look at it. You tell me."

Ned imitated Cyrus' stance and peered down at the track. He shook his head and looked back up at Cyrus.

Cyrus tapped one finger on the side of his head and pointed down.

Ned looked back again at the track. "From the size of it, it looks like a dog." He frowned. "Not a very big one, not as big as Toby. But what it's thinking I have no idea."

Cyrus shook his head. "Look again."

"It's just a dog track."

Cyrus smoothed a bit of ground. He drew with his finger on the ground a triangular lobe footpad, then dotted four toes and scratched claws at the tips of the toes. "That's a dog track."

Ned looked from Cyrus's drawing to the track and back again.

Cyrus spoke softly. "Look at what's there, not what you expect. What's different?"

Ned looked more closely. There were no claw marks on the trail track and the footpad was not triangular, but had two lobes at the top and three lobes at the bottom. "It's not a dog? Then what …?"

"You know these woods better than I do. What kind of animal could it be?"

Ned looked out into the woods in thought, scanned his memory for … what? What besides a dog would be that size? The hair on the back of his head electrified. "It's a bobcat. Son of a bitch, it's a bobcat."

He looked up at Cyrus, whose usually taciturn mouth was drawn slightly at the corners for what passed for a smile. "Can you tell what he was thinking?"

Ned jumped up and scanned the ground for more tracks.

"Whoa, whoa, hold on young stalker, slow down. Sign don't disappear unless you look too hard for them. Take your time."

"I don't see any more prints. What else can do I look for?"

"Claw marks, scat, and whatever else there is to be seen."

Ned looked and looked, but did not find anything. "I've heard of them being in these woods. I've even seen the skin of one, but I didn't know ... I knew they were around here, but I didn't know they were around *here*."

Ned heard rustling behind him and turned. Toby came bounding out of the trees, ran up and rubbed against his leg. Ned laughed, reached down and rubbed Toby's head. "Hey, boy. They said you couldn't come to the mill anymore but they didn't say you couldn't come out here, did they?"

Cyrus straightened and brushed off the seat of his pants. "Now you know. Animals travel, just like people. You just never know when one is going to come into your life."

A voice inside Ned's head spoke to him. 'Learn, but don't get too attached. He won't be here long. Your time has not yet come.'

His time for what, Ned had no idea. The voice had spoken to him before at the oddest times, but sometimes it left things out. The gift bothered him like that.

Chapter 33
Becoming

The next morning Ned plodded after Cyrus through the woods in misting rain. Their feet beat against the forest floor muted, wet and soft. Water dripped from the branches and leaves with little splashes that filled Ned's ears. His head hurt deep inside.

Cyrus called a halt some time before the part of the woods where work was to begin. "Stop here for a minute."

Ned found a clear spot next to a pine and sat on his heels leaned up against the trunk to rest and stay a little dry. Toby wagged up to sit beside and leaned against him. He felt wet on his shoulder and inhaled Toby's wet dog scent.

Cyrus' voice was quiet. "You feelin' all right today?"

"I guess."

"Your dog don't seem to think so."

"Yeah well." Ned reached out to rub Toby's head. "He's smarter than he looks, I guess. I just feel jangled, like somebody's been rattling my insides."

"You feel jangled out here?"

Ned shook his head. "Not here so much, I like the rain. I just feel, I don't know ... nothin' bad's happened, I didn't get yelled at or nothin' ... but last night my insides didn't want to sleep and this morning banging around in the back of the truck ... it just jarred me."

Cyrus lowered himself until he was sitting on his heels. His elbows crossed over the top of his knees. A smile with teeth spread across his face.

Ned had never seen Cyrus smile with teeth. "What? What is it?"

"You're feeling like an Indian, white boy."

217

"What's that supposed to mean?"

Cyrus laughed quietly. "Nothing bad. It just means that yesterday you relaxed enough to let your heart and spirit feel the woods. Out here that's a good thing." He pointed back towards the saw mill. "Feeling the woods helps you see things more than they can understand."

"Then why do I feel bad?"

"Woods listening is much better than white man listening. The bad side of the coin is when you're in the white man's world it's like somebody turned the radio up way past the point where it's too loud." Cyrus took off his broad brimmed hat. He turned his face up the raindrops and ran his hand over his face and back through his black hair. "And them that's playing the radio don't know what it's like to be quiet."

"But I ain't an Indian."

Ned watched Cyrus slowly turn his hat in his hands. "Not your outside; that's true. But inside is a different thing. If you hear that way, you're hearing Indian. It ain't magic, boy." Cyrus looked at the ground and smiled with one side of his mouth. "Well, maybe it is. But a body has to want to hear it. Not many do and not everybody can." He pointed one long finger at Ned. "You can." He jerked his thumb over his shoulder back towards the mill. "They can't. They don't have the ears for it."

"They don't want to hear it?"

Cyrus shook his head and slid his hat back on. "Nope. They might could if they wanted to, but they just don't. So there ain't no use in talking to them about it, no use trying to make them listen or understand. But that's all right; it's not for them. Just keep it close in your heart and listen to the voice of the wind and the earth."

Ned folded one arm over his knees and wrapped the other one around Toby. "If they don't want to feel deep, what do they want, anyhow?"

Cyrus slowly rose to his feet. He smiled at Ned wider still. "If you ever figure out what it is the white man wants, you'll have the eternal thanks of every Indian ever been born. Come on, the trees are calling."

Chapter 34
History

When the afternoon train whistle wailed through the dripping trees Jamie walked to the office to look for Ned. As he approached he saw Dancin' Charlie and Marshal in deep conversation beside the porch. Charlie was incapable of holding still for any length of time. He danced from foot to foot and clapped his hands together when he laughed particularly hard. Jamie had to wonder at the coordination of a man who could manage to do all that all at the same time. As Jamie drew near he slowed to listen.

Charlie poked the middle of the huge black man's chest with his index finger. "Now just you wait, I set me up a new blind hole with Ol' Fred Black, all I gots to do is pick it up. I tell you, we're all set."

The large man frowned down at the little man's finger. "Why don't we just use the same one? Ain't been no trouble before."

" 'Cause Lester Thomas' got himself made deputy sheriff so's he can sit on his ass. He's never got a thing on me and I don't intend to hand him nothing on a silver platter." His wiry legs danced again, "I hated dat little sumbitch in gramma school and I ain't too terribly fond of him now. He don't go out of his way to hit a lick at a snake, let alone git out of that cool office of his with the ceiling fan." He shoved his hands in his back pockets. "Now Fred'll put the jar in there Sunday mornin' and I pick it up Sunday night after we gets home from church. Ain't nobody goin' pick it up before then nohow, Ain't nobody goin' to be gallivanting out in the woods on a Sunday 'cause everbody's in church, see? It ain't Christian. So don't you sweat none."

"Aw, Charlie, Lester ain't never done you no harm. Don't think he's gonna start now."

219

"I ain't gonna give him a chance. But I want it understood when I put that mason jar in your hand you put the cash in mine. I ain't no charity."

"Yeah, you and every other mother's son of a bitch." Marshall shoved his own finger in the little man's chest, pushed him back a few inches. "And it better be the good stuff too, make sure Black don't give us none of his watered down sh ..." The big man caught a darting glimpse of Jamie's approach, the little man's gaze followed and both fell silent. They nodded to Jamie.

Jamie decided it might be wise to play dumb. "You folks seem deep in it. What cha talkin' about?"

Charlie spread his grin wide and shuffled a little step. "Oh, nuthin', just tellin' Marshall here a little story about Toby."

"What about him?"

"You know, Old Toby. Spooky dog." Charlie slapped his thigh.

"Which time?"

"Uhh ... the time he saved you from fever."

Marshall crossed his arms over his massive chest and look down at Charlie. "You never ... get on with the story."

"Hold ya horses, I was just about to get ready to. Like I said , I was ... uh ... working over at the Garrath's place in the garden, sometimes they let me work for vegetables like they do Snow. God, they got the sweetest corn and carrots, Lord they's just as sweet as ..."

Marshall leaned to loom over Charlie. "What ... about ... the dog?"

"Oh. Well, he come up to us. We was hoeing around the beets, you know you gotta be real careful around them ... and Toby comes up and he's a-squirreling around in circles and whining to all gitout. It was Mrs. Garrath figured out Toby wanted us to faller him. We did, and he led us right to this little fella's room in the house right then and there and boy, was he in a bad way."

"That so?" Marshall turned to Jamie.

Jamie nodded. "So I'm told. I don't remember much about it, 'cept feeling bad when I got home from school and had to go lay down. Next thing I know I'm wakin' up cold and sniffin' alcohol."

"Alcohol?" Marshall looked back to Charlie.

Charlie stumbled over his words to chime in. "Rubbin' alcohol. Mrs. Garrath slathered it all over him to cool him, get that fever down."

Marshall lifted his head a nod. "Huh." He turned back to Jamie. "Did it work?"

Jamie shrugged. "I'm here."

Marshall scratched the back of his head. "Well, how 'bout that. Quite a dog you got there." He looked around. "Or maybe not, come to think of it. Where is he?"

"I don't know." Jamie looked around just as Toby barreled in and ran around him in a circle. "Hey there, where ya been, boy?"

Jamie reached out to pet him, but Toby took off like a streak toward Ned and Cyrus walking up to the cabin.

Cyrus nodded to Jamie on his way up the cabin steps. Jamie's father came out onto the porch, looked at Toby and frowned. Cyrus handed him a notebook. His father took it and motioned Cyrus inside.

Ned stayed with Jamie, Toby bouncing right by his side. "Hey."

Jamie nodded toward Toby. "He been with you all day?"

"Pretty much. He does like the woods, doesn't he?"

Jamie reached down to rub Toby's head. "Missed you, boy."

"Go fishing?"

Jamie shook his head. "Can't today and you can't neither. Momma and Daddy's getting stuff ready for tomorrow. We gotta help."

"With what? What's tomorrow?"

"Fourth of July."

"Oh, yeah. That mean we don't have to work tomorrow?"

"Huh-uh, not tomorrow. Daddy says we're gonna set up a big grill over a wood fire for hot dogs and hamburgers and folks bring out dishes of corn on the cob and potato salad and whatnot. Hope somebody brings some watermelon. Ours withered on the vine this year."

"So what do we do?"

"Set up buckets full of water and sand around the grill in case of fire."

"No, I mean tomorrow. What do you do?"

"Stand-up Indian wrestling and foot races and horseshoes and … you've never been to a Fourth of July party?"

Ned looked at his shoes, kicked dirt and shook his head. "Worked. Pop's always had the store open, sellin' flags and firecrackers. You got firecrackers?"

"Huh-uh. Hadn't been able to lay my hands on any, but I'm sure somebody'll bring some. It's gonna be great."

"If you say so."

Jamie didn't understand Ned's lack of proper enthusiasm. As for him, he was more than ready to stuff his face to the gills, drink all the cold lemonade he could hold and listen to firecrackers blast the birds out of the trees. He just couldn't wait.

Chapter 35
Holiday

Fourth of July meant a day off. Except for Jamie and Ned.

"You call this a holiday?" Jamie heard Ned grumble behind him as he drove the bucksaw through another slab. "You said all we had to do was get water buckets and stuff. We gotta saw wood too?"

"Only if we want to eat. We need wood if we're gonna cook up hot dogs and all those hamburgers Momma was patting out last night."

"You grill hot dogs?" Ned lifted another slab onto the sawbucks. "Mom boils ours. Usually with cabbage."

"Yuck."

As he set the bucksaw on the slab, Jamie watched his father and Snow across the way set up a section of iron grating on top of support bricks near the office cabin next to the well. They laid in a fire underneath and set out a couple of garden hoes to rake the coals around underneath. The two men had no sooner nodded at each other in self-congratulation than Jamie's mother drove in the gate.

She was in manager mode. In soundless faraway pantomime, his mother pointed with full extended arm at his father and Snow, directing them to set up tables against the cabin with sawhorses and broad boards. Between sawing strokes, Jamie's heart grinned to see somebody else at the business end of her finger. She paced right along behind his father and Snow, mouth in motion, as they unloaded the cardboard boxes of hot dogs and hamburgers from the back of the car.

"Get another piece of wood and this time help me hold it." Jamie hissed to Ned under his breath as the bucksaw ripped through another slab.

"What?"

"If we don't look busy she'll have us over there quicker than Beauregard said 'Boo.' "

A little before noon Marshall rolled in in his big pickup, followed closely by the flatbed migrant truck chock full of laughing folks bouncing up against the sideboards. The men helped their wives down out of the back, and then carried to the tables their pot-luck dishes of green beans, baked beans, cornbread, Cole slaw and buckets of mashed potatoes with gravy and butter. Mrs. Lowery, Lowell's wife, got Marshall to help heft down two huge pots of lemonade.

Out of the back of Marshall's truck came four washtubs filled with blocks of ice covered in hay for the hand-crank ice cream freezers. Jamie remembered the smell of the sugar cream, vanilla and the peaches his mother had mixed up last night. He could taste the sweet cold on his tongue already.

Last out of Marshall's truck came Dancin' Charlie. He eased down, glancing back and forth, a huge watermelon in his arms and a huge grin on his face. Jamie felt a heavy hand press on his shoulder and heard his father's voice deep in his ear. "You two stay away from Charlie's watermelon, you hear me?"

"How come?"

"Because he's got a smile on his face. That's all you need to know."

"Yessir."

"There's plenty of firewood for now, so why don't you boys go get a half-dozen buckets from the storage shed. Fill half of them with water and the other half with sand and put them over there next to the grill."

"Yessir."

As Jamie's father walked back to the grill, Ned stepped close and spoke quiet. "I'll bet you ten ways to Tuesday Charlie's got that melon spiked with moonshine. What do you think?"

Jamie nodded. "I think we'd best not get caught having ourselves a taste."

They plodded to the shed, got the stack of buckets and a shovel and loaded them on the sledge. They dragged the sledge to the back of the kiln where the sand was soft.

Jamie stopped and leaned on his shovel handle. "How come you ain't home for the 4th?"

"Pop didn't say anything about it." Ned did not look up. He turned the stack of buckets upside down, wedged the rim of the bottom bucket between his feet and twisted one off the top of the stack. "And since Momma's one of 14 ...."

"You're pulling my leg."

"Not a bit. And Pop keeps the store open all the time. When holidays come around everybody and his brother's cousin descend on us. All their wives and husbands and kids and dogs and cats."

"All of 'em?"

"The whole fam damily of them."

"So fillin' buckets is kind of a holiday for you. Ain't too bad, is it?"

Ned smiled at Jamie. "Not a bit."

"Well, happy 4th to you."

"Likewise."

By the time they dragged the sledge of sand buckets to the grill, festivities were in full swing. Everyone grouped around Dancin' Charlie and Marshall, who were squared off in a smooth patch of dirt to wrestle. Charlie, predictably, did not get very far. He tackled Marshall around the midsection but Marshall did not move at all and just picked Charlie up and laid him on the ground.

Charlie stood and dusted himself off. "I just wanted to see what would happen, don't you know."

Howard 'Rudolph' Mohegan laughed and slapped his hands. "And now you know."

"You think you can do better?"

"Against Marshall? I seriously doubt it, but I can take you."

"Well then, Mr. Get-up-and-go, let's get to it." Charlie shoved his shirt sleeves up over his elbows.

225

Rudolph's girlfriend tried to hold him back. "Let's just relax and have fun, Honey. Come on."

He looked at her, then glanced around with a half-grin. "Can't now, Darlin'. I'd never hear the end of it."

She shifted onto one hip and crossed her arms. "Well then, go ahead. It's your own doin'. Your mind's made up no matter what I say."

Rudolph and Charlie stepped forward, spit on their hands and began to circle each another.

"Hey, this is our chance." Jamie heard Ned's whisper.

"Don't you wanna watch this?"

"Don't you wanna try that melon? When they start to wrestle, just ease off in that direction."

The two men charged, immediately cracked their heads together a little harder than they wanted to, then pushed and locked arms. Each tried to drive the other, but there just wasn't enough traction in the sandy dirt, so they mostly slipped and slid and made a lot of dust.

Jamie looked both ways for his father. He was no where in sight, so Jamie eased back behind the cabin and peeked around the corner to the table where Charlie's watermelon had been cut wide open and slices lay in rows across the table. Charlie's wife Lucille and Mrs. Lowery leaned their bottoms against the table in front of it. They leaned shoulder to shoulder with crossed arms and shook their heads, too busy watching the wrestling match to watch the watermelon.

"Norma, that man, I swear. He's gonna get himself hurt one of these days."

"You mean again, don't you Lucille?"

Jamie felt Ned's hand on his shoulder. "Let me."

"Okay." Jamie nodded.

He watched Ned approach the table gingerly, his feet gliding close to the ground. Ned had just ducked underneath the table boards and reached his hand up and around the edge for a nice slice of ripe dripping red melon when Norma shifted her plaid bottom against the board and almost shook the table down. Ned jerked his hand back down out of sight.

Lucille half turned. "You watch yourself, honey. You knock this table down both our men'll have a conniption. They worked a long time on that melon."

"Well, if he don't keep himself out of trouble this year I'll give him a conniption with a tail on it." She reached behind and took the very piece that Ned's hand had hovered over. She turned back around and took a big bite. She gasped and giggled. "Lord, he soaked this thing good, didn't he?"

"Lemme taste."

When Lucille leaned toward Norma to take a bite, Ned took his chance, lifted another slice from the table and slunk back around the corner. They eased back between the trees.

"Let's get back behind the outhouse." Jamie tugged on Ned's arm. "Nobody'll be there for a little while yet."

They made their way around the outside of the cabin, past men on the edge of the crowd sipping out of bottles in paper bags, past stacks of lumber to the outhouse that sat close to the fence. They scrunched down behind it and looked at the deep red watermelon meat.

Jamie couldn't help but laugh. "You ready?"

"Are you?"

Jamie got out his knife, cut the slice in two and handed half to Ned. "Let's both bite at the same time, all right? One, two, three ..." and bit down on the juicy melon. Before he could blink he could not breathe. Tears gushed to his eyes as his mouth exploded with fire. He swallowed hard, spit, pulled a deep painful lungful of air and coughed. "Oh great gobs of Jesus ...."

In between coughs, Ned wheezed. "How in the hell does anybody ever drink that stuff? Holy mother of ...."

They heard the door to the outhouse slam shut. Then they heard Dancin' Charlie humming a tune of his own design.

Jamie pointed to the watermelon in his hand then pointed over the fence. Ned nodded back and they both heaved the evidence over into the woods. They started back toward the cabin for some lemonade to wash the burn from their throats.

And none too soon. Giggles and snorts echoed through the trees behind them. When they turned they saw Rudolph and

Lowell coming up to the path to the outhouse, closely followed by their gals. They held roman candles. Marshall brought up the rear, a full five gallon water bucket in each hand. Rudolph and Lowell stopped at the outhouse door, struck a match, lit both candles and held them right in the little round hole set high in the outhouse door.

No sooner had they heard the first deep puffs of fireballs than Jamie and Ned heard Charlie bellow.

"Hey, hey, HEY, HEY!" Charlie's scream echoed from inside. "What in hell and damnation do you think you're doin'?" Charlie burst out of the door, hopping with his overalls around his ankles like he was in a bare-assed sack race. He tripped, sprawled and tried to flail at the flames with his hat and to cover himself with his smoking clothes at the same time. He was only moderately effective at either.

Marshall upended a single bucket of water over Charlie.

Charlie sputtered and rolled over. "What the sh ..."

Marshall dumped the other bucket on him. "Watch your language. They's ladys present."

Charlie sat up, spit water and wiped his eyes. "Well, thanks. I needed that like another hole in my ass." He jerked his overalls back up and fastened a shoulder strap. "Now wha'd you go and do that for?"

"You was on fire." Marshall's face contorted as he bit his lip. "Had to do my duty, put it out. A body could get hurt."

Jamie heard the strangest hooting. He turned and saw Rudolph literally rolling in the sand holding his stomach, gasping for air he was laughing so hard. "Who needs 'shine when we got this?"

Jamie's father walked up and pointed out that the outhouse was smoking. "Come on, folks, let's get the buckets from the grill." Jamie watched him rub his face to try to keep from smiling. "Jamie, you and Ned get to carryin' water, go on now."

Jamie splashed the last bucket of water onto the scorched wall of the outhouse then straightened up. He noticed Ned smiling. "What?"

"I was just thinking is different. It's nice seeing how other folks ... hey, you hear that?"

Jamie lifted his head. Over the sound of the wind in the pines, came the slow strain of music. Looking neither right nor left nor at Ned, Jamie dropped his bucket and headed toward the sound. He came out of the pines beside the cabin where Mrs. Carter and Mrs. Lowery now leaned more fully against the table, much the worse for wear from Charlie's moonshine melon.

In the dusty clearing, couples danced to the slow one-two-three waltz of a lone fiddle. No high-stepping here, just single slide-slip-step shuffles and quiet murmured laughter as women taught work-booted men to dance. Dancin' Charlie, his moniker notwithstanding, stared more at his feet than at the young girl in his arms. Tall Caleb Frasier held a tiny woman at full arm extension, like he was holding a porcupine about to shoot quills any second. And Rudolph gazed at his gal like he was looking at a sunrise for the first time.

Mrs. Carter took a long slurping sip of another piece of melon. "Who would have thunk that the old goat would've had it in him."

Mrs. Lowery slurped in reply. "Who, Charlie?"

"No, the fiddler. I've never heard Old Jacob Ashby talk but what he's complainin' about something, a right old curmudgeon, but would you listen at that?"

"Sounds right pretty, don't it?"

"More than that, darlin'." Mrs. Carter sniffed. "That sounds like love."

As Jamie followed the nod of her head, he saw what she meant. Jacob Ashby, shriveled scrub pine tree of a man, held a beat-up fiddle against his chest and swayed to and fro on the balls of his feet to the music. His eyes were closed; his fingers caressed rhythms with his bow. Jamie felt his own feet move of their own accord and, for the first time in his young life, Jamie Garrath wished he held a woman in his arms.

Chapter 36
Faith

Silence made palpable by the swish of hand fans settled on the sanctuary. Jamie watched Cramphorne mount the pulpit and stretch his face into a smile of rippled fat. Words popped unbidden into Jamie's head 'Here come the lies.' At that same instant he felt pressure on his right shoulder as Ned leaned into him and whispered. "You think he actually believes this cow splat?"

His mother's hand reached out, squeezed the back of Ned's neck and pulled him back upright.

Cramphorne gripped the edge of the podium. "It is sometimes difficult in this life to determine the difference between needs and what we just want. There are certainly needs in this life and it is perfectly natural to feel in your heart of hearts that those needs are things you must have. Food, shelter, water to drink, clothes on your back and the honest work that makes those things possible are essentials we must have to maintain life and health. We all know only too well in these troubled times there are all too many who do not have even those, folks we see every day, that cannot afford a meal and so do not eat."

Jamie noted the man's girth and wondered how long Cramphorne had been without a meal. He kept that thought silent in his head, safe from his mother's neck pinch.

"However," Cramphorne's smile bent downward into a frown, "there are those things we just want. The sort of things we feel we need, even though we would not be any better off with them, especially things we see another possess. The first of these that springs to mind is that of a new car. How many times have you seen a person driving by in a shiny new automobile and said to yourself 'I need one of those' and your hungry eyes followed that car until it passed out of sight around the next bend in the road. And what about clothes, a stylish pair of shoes or a new hat that is the height of fashion? When that happens, my dear brothers and sisters, you are guilty of sin, guilty of the sin of envy. Envy is a rancorous sin. It is a sin that splits us apart from our fellows. The Lord has in many places in the good book spoken and warned us not to fall victim. In Proverbs fourteen, verse thirty 'A sound heart is the life of the flesh, but envy, envy is the rottenness of the bones.' Again in Proverbs, this time in chapter twenty three, verse seventeen, 'Let not thine heart envy sinners, but be thou in fear of the Lord all the day long.' And when we envy those who prance around in their finery, that's what we are doing. We are envying those who are filled with pride on account of their worldly goods, as the sin is doubled on both parts. Envy leads folks to do horrible, horrible things to each other. It is the instigator. It was envy moved the patriarchs to sell Joseph into slavery into Egypt. It was envy that drove the Pharisees to deliver our Lord Jesus into the hands of Pontius Pilate. In James chapter three verse sixteen 'For where envying and strife is, there is confusion and every evil work.' You see, our Lord is a wise Lord. These sins must not be indulged in not just because they are deemed so by the Lord in his good book, though that should be reason enough for a good god-fearing Christian on any day of the week, but these thoughts and deeds are not deemed sins in any arbitrary way. These thoughts, these acts are sins because they cause division between brothers and sisters in Christ and that division cannot be if we are to remain a healthy, vital Christian community. Honest Christians worshipping together are like logs on a campfire. When the logs are close together they lend heat to each other, they support each other in the flames of righteousness and are warmed mutually by it. When we sin, especially in the sin of envy, we drive wedges between ourselves and our brethren and that hurts not just ourselves, but everyone. Are we our brother's keeper? The Bible's answer to that question is a resounding yes. Yes, we are. Avoiding the sin of envy is one way to do that. It is one way we care for each other in Christ. Let us not pay a whole lot of attention to what that other fellow has. It's really just not that important. Not nearly so important as our immortal souls. Our immortal souls are enough. We need no more than that. Let us pray."

As Jamie bowed his head he felt uneasy, something wrong. He just could not put his finger on what.

On this same Sunday morning John Wanderwood, who called himself Cyrus Conner, awakened to the cry of a baby. The tarpaper shack in the migrant camp was a step up from the bunkroom, but the infant cries next door still felt like a wood rasp drawing bloody strokes across the middle of his brain. The soothing tones of the baby's mother quieted the cries and drew his mind's ear back to his mother's voice, and that drew the eye in his mind to his home, Neah Bay on the far northwest corner of Washington State. John's mother was spiritual, though she seldom spoke of it, only invited him time after time to the Raven spirit lodge of his family clan. Now alone in his cot, he curled up and wished he had listened.

There was a Raven Rock west of here, the boy had said. Cliffs by the river. He'd tried before but just hit a dead end and moonshine, so he knew that wasn't the path. He wasn't sure what Ned had meant by the 'fall line', but the thought of his mother made him want to visit the place. The thought had balance to it.

The dollar a week rent for his shack was more than worth it to be left alone and be able to fix his own breakfast. He swung out of his cot, rubbed his head awake and splashed clean with the water from the bucket. Usually he cooked all his food at night and ate cold the next morning to save time and fuel, but this was Sunday. A tiny fire on the little cast iron hobo stove heated coffee and sizzled strips of salt bacon and the grease flavored the eggs he scrambled after that.

Another piercing squall from next door drove him away from his food. He gulped his coffee, pulled on his one clean shirt, shoved the leftovers into wax paper and into his woven shoulder bag and clapped his round campaign to his head on his way out the door. The fresh morning air soothed his face as soon as he stepped out the door. He pulled the door to behind him then walked over to the road.

He thumbed a ride from a passing pickup.

A black man with shining skin smiled at him. "Where ya need to go?"

"You going anywhere near a place called 'Raven Rock'?"

"Near as tires can take you. There's an old footpath that leads up to it. Come on, jump in." John did, and slammed the creaking door behind him.

As the man ground through the gears he glanced at John and looked him up and down. "What's your name?"

John almost gave his right name. "Cyrus. Cyrus Conner."

The man extended his hand. "Carl. Carl Avent."

John took the man's hand and shook it. "Glad to meet you."

"I used to know a Rufus Conner. You any relation?"

"I doubt it, sorry. I'm not from anywhere around here. Where's he from?"

"Over near Silerville."

"No, don't' think so." He thought of the real Cyrus Conner. "My Connors are farmers from a little place called Churubusco in Indiana. Ever heard of it?"

Carl shook his head and laughed. "Can't say that I have. Where is that?"

"About 20 miles northwest of Fort Wayne."

Carl laughed again. "Don't help much."

"All right, it's a couple of hundred miles north of Indianapolis."

"Try one more time."

"A couple of hundred miles east of Chicago."

Carl grinned and showed a line of uneven yellow teeth. "Now Chicago I heard of, ain't nobody not heard of Chicago. I got a cousin in Chicago, went up there to find work in the stockyards. And you come down here?"

John nodded. "I thought it was too hard to get work up there."

"What happened to the farm?"

"It got taken." John felt like he was lying to the man, though strictly speaking it was the truth. It was just that the farm had not been taken by foreclosure. It had been taken by the real Cyrus Conner's vulture relatives despite the terms of the will when the kind old man had passed on.

"So you down here now. You workin' then?"

"At Garrath's sawmill."

233

"Now them are good folks, the Garreths. Hard work though. I'll just stick to haulin' and doin' chores on the side. There's pretty steady work for a man with a truck, y'know."

"That so?"

"Oh, yeah. Yeah. You sure you got no folks around here?"

"If I do, I've never heard anyone mention it." John shook his head. "No. Just come for the work."

"But a man like you need roots, y'know. A man needs roots."

"That is a fact."

"You know where you git roots like that, don't you?"

"I know you're going to tell me."

Carl smiled his big yellow smile again. "I know'd right off you wuz smarter'd you look, 'cause you look it." He pointed his finger at John. "A man like you ought to be in church. That's where I'm goin, that's where a man gits roots, yes it is. Deep dug down roots that'll hold you when the storms of Satan come, you know that's true."

John hoped to deflect the man's attempt to witness. "So how long you been saved?"

Huge teeth beamed at him. "More that thirty year, oh you bet I am. And why don' you come with me? You won't regret it."

"I appreciate that and thank you, but no. My mother, rest her soul, had an interest in ravens, so I look for them when I can." John rubbed his face. "It's kinda like talkin' to her."

Carl ground the gears for a lower one on a steep grade. "I respect that. Your one day off and you want to get close to God and yo' mamma. I can't take no issue, no sir. But let me tell you the offer still stands now. Anytime you get to feeling the need to go to church you just be waitin' there where I picked you up. But let me tell you one thing ...."

For the remainder of the trip John let the man tell him one thing and then another and many more things besides. John doubted he could have stopped the man if he'd wanted to, but he did enjoy listening. Not to the details of his wife's illness and the low congregation in church or how good his wife's chicken livers were "You ain't lived till you've let one of them melt in your mouth, no sah!" What John loved listening to was the man's vitality. But by the time he was dropped off the novelty had waned and John regretted giving him free rein.

"Here we is."

Carl pulled the truck off the side of the road and stopped near a path that ran into the woods on the other side of the ditch. He pointed one long finger toward the path. "You take that path a ways, you'll git there."

"Thank you, Carl. Appreciate it."

"That's all right. You just remember my offer."

"I will."

And with a wave, Carl ground his gears and was gone.

A jump across the ditch and John was in the woods. Traffic noise gradually dimmed as he passed more deeply into the pines, the needles crunched softly under his feet. He felt himself slide into the gait and mindset of a tracker making time through the woods, eyes open, watching for movement with the sides of his eyes and stepping over rocks and branches he never looked directly at. The trees cleared out just a little before the path opened up to the Raven Rock landing.

Ned had been right. To either side where the path ran into the river there were cliffs over a hundred feet high hung out over the water. They went for as far as he could see in either direction, too high for him to reach with his eyes. He thought of Carl Avent and how the man was devoted to his church and smiled.

John stepped out to a big flat rock that jutted into the flowing water. The sound bubbled and splashed past his ears the same way the water bubbled and splashed past the rock. He sat down and was still, to let the wind speak and let the flutter of the branches and the rippling waters have their say. He leaned back on the warm rock and closed his eyes.

When he awakened the sun was directly overhead and his mind was calm. He dug into his bag for the bacon and found a jar of leftover black eye peas and rice flavored with bacon grease from the night before. He peered up toward the top of the cliffs. He could not see the top, but he did see, circling high above, a single black wing drifting in the air currents. A shiver ran up his spine as he breathed deep free air like a man just released from bondage.

Sweet painful tears welled up in his eyes and he felt the heart of the circling bird, his raven, high overhead. He heard the call, distant but clear and he knew it was time for him to go home. Not his tarpaper shack in the migrant camp, but home to the Pacific Northwest, to the heavy fog of Neah Bay with air so moist and thick a body could feel it draw into lungs, where the smell of sawn cedar boards surrounded sleep.

John Wanderwood spent that day by a tiny campfire on the rock in the middle of the stream, listening.

Chapter 37

Sirens, or What Gals Will Do To A Man

Work at the mill was now habit. This is not to say Jamie and Ned drew enjoyment from it. They were too busy and too tired. It needed doing but by God was no fun at all.

At the noon train whistle they sat, whitewash spattered, on benches by the side of the cabin and ate their sandwiches in silence. The men trudged in from logging and eased to the ground, scattered amongst the trees in what shade they could find.

Howard 'Rudolf' or 'Pretty Boy' Mohegan walked toward Jamie and Ned. Jamie thought at first he wanted to talk, but he stopped in front of them, laid down his sandwich down on the bench and turned his head from side to side at his reflection in the cabin window. He tucked in his shirt tail, took out his comb and ran it through his slicked hair.

Snow called out. "Hey there, Pretty Boy, you spend more time tuckin' in your shirt than you do workin'! It don't make no difference how you look and you ain't nowhere near the far side of purty no-how, so how come you be slatherin' on all that axle grease?"

Howard's hands hovered in mid-comb. 'Ain't nothin' wrong with keepin' up how you look. You never know when somebody might drive in here lookin' for a hard-workin' man who takes a little care he don't look like no hobo."

Snow threw back his head and laughed as he pushed himself to his feet. "Now I done heard most of everthing. There just be three things wrong with that. One, you ain't hardly no man yet. Two, you got to work more than you pretty up before you're 'hard-workin' and three …."

"It ain't no axle grease, it's hair dressing. Besides, I ain't gonna be here forever. Like you say, I'm young. I got plans." He passed his comb through his slick dark hair one last pass before he

237

slid the comb into his pocket and picked up his sandwich, all in the same motion. He took a big bite out of the corner. "We got plans" he mumbled under his breath, mouth full of sandwich.

"We?" Snow had started to walk off but turned back around. "Who is this 'we'? I don't b'lieve you got yourself a girl."

"Oh yes I do, you just wait."

"What's her name then?"

Howard straightened up, chewed and swallowed in a massive gulp. "Her name's Caroline. And as soon as I can get enough for a grubstake, we're gonna get married and start a little business, maybe a little farm."

Marshall spoke, rumbling low and quiet. "You gotta be awful careful about that marryin' business, friend." He struck the rest of his sandwich into his mouth and dusted crumbs from his hands. "Awful careful."

Howard looked at Marshall. "Don't you worry about me, I can take care of my own heart. She's the real thing, I know right down to my bones. And," he lifted his chin at Snow, "my name's not 'Rudolf' or 'Pretty Boy.' It's Howard, Howard Mohegan. You oughta be callin' me by my right name. It's gonna be a respectful name, you'll see." He took a long draught of water, rinsed his mouth and spat it onto the sand. "Maybe a delivery business. That way I'm out and about, using some of my natural goofy charm." He grinned all around. "That's what Caroline says anyway, and I don't know but what that's a pretty good idea."

"How you know she's gonna stay with you long enough to get married? She might bolt with some guy with a lot of money if she gets the chance just to get out from under her momma's apron." Marshall leaned back against his tree. "It's been known to happen."

"She ain't under her momma's apron now, is she? She with me."

Marshall yawned and set his hat over his eyes. "All that marryin' talk might be just that. Talk. How do you know?"

"'Cause we're livin' together, that's how I know."

A chorus of hoots and laughter erupted from all around.

Howard threw his hands in the air. "Go ahead, laugh all you want, that's all right. We got ourselves a little tobacco barn apartment. It's not fancy or nothin' but it's a start and like I said as soon as I earn me a grubstake I'm gonna start a little business and once that business is runnin' good, we'll build a little house somewheres out of the way and get married. Then," he leaned back and smiled, "I'll pass on some of my goofy charm to a couple of kids."

Snow slapped his hat on his leg. "It sure ain't doin' you no good here."

Howard laughed right along. "Now that's a true fact."

Snow clapped his hands, wiped his eyes and pulled his dollar pocket watch out of his overall chest pocket. He looked at it, stuffed it back in and clapped his hands again, this time to get their attention. "All right, that's enough fun for one day. Let's get them mules hitched up and drag in what we cut this mornin'. Come on."

And in the measured movements of working men in the heat of summertime, they pushed to their feet and walked off to work.

In the afternoon Jamie and Ned were blessed with rare weather, perfect for fishing. There were enough clouds hanging to cover the sky, enough so shadows wouldn't be thrown on the water.

"Careful." Jamie called up to Ned, who was leading on the path to the little lake. "Watch where you put your feet."

"How's that?"

"It's what Daddy calls a 'snakey day'. There's enough heat to make them active, but there's not enough sun to make them easy to see."

Jamie heard laughter like silver bells twinkling over the treetops and froze. Ned raised his hand and stopped. Jamie eased up behind him and listened. For a moment all they could hear was the rustle of pine trees brushing the wind. Then it came again, clearly, laughter. Feminine laughter.

"Is that coming from the lake?"

Jamie's shoulders slumped. "So much for fishing."

"Yeah, well. Let's take a look anyway."

Jamie mumbled assent and plodded on after Ned, eyes on the ground, picking his way through slippery pine straw and surface roots washed clear of rusty red clay by rain. The spaces between the trees opened up and now they could hear splashing.

"Somebody's swimming?" Jamie tried to peer through the trees to the water.

"Appa-rantly."

They slowly stepped forward around the last corner before the steps to the pier, and there, hanging on the railing, were feminine clothes. Blouses and skirts to be exact.

Jamie's feet froze. He felt his heart stop, then pound faster to catch up. "Ned?"

"Uh-huh?"

"We might not ought to be here."

"Yeah, well."

Neither boy moved.

"Ned?"

Ned pushed his hat back and rubbed his forehead. "I'm thinking."

Jamie nodded. "I'm thinking too, and I'm thinking we'd best be gone."

A high trill of feminine laughter ran cool fingers up their spines and pushed them forward. A lilting voice caressed their ears, "Are ye going to stand there hidin' in the trees all day, or are ye goin' to be sayin' hello now?"

Jamie shook his head and backed up a step. "Oh my. Oh my, oh my." He looked at Ned.

Edges of a smile creased the corners of Ned's mouth. He swung one purposeful step then another and another as he swept down the path, past the hanging guardians of clothes and onto the edge of the dock.

Jamie followed.

There, floating and gently treading water with hands lightly clinging to the dark wood of the dock, were two girls, apparently fearless.

"Ned." Jamie spoke into Ned's ear. "Let's go. I got my whole life ahead of me, I'm not ready for this."

Ned spoke over his shoulder. "We're just going to talk."

"I can't talk to girls. I think you oughta know that."

"'Bout time we learned don't you think? What have we got to lose?"

"Our lives?"

"Come on."

Jamie watched Ned stride out onto the pier, one hand stuck in his back pocket.

Jamie began to follow, but after two steps his feet forgot they were supposed to be involved in the exercise. He fell flat on his face on the hard boards. "Ow."

He heard a splash. When Jamie raised his head it was to face the most beautiful eyes he had ever seen. They were clear green, surrounded by eyelashes adorned with water droplets, set into the soft angular face of an angel. This face rested on smooth wet forearms crossed on top of the dock.

"Are ye all right?"

Jamie was utterly unaware his shyness and huge blue eyes attracted girls like moths to a flame. All he knew was that girls made him feel so awful funny inside he could hardly stand it. Now as he lay on the warm boards face to face with this water nymph, he only knew his heart had left his chest, perhaps never to return.

"Hi," he managed to breathe.

She wetly blinked at him and dimples appeared at each end of her smile. "Hi yourself. And what would your name be?"

"Jamie."

Her smile grew broader, her dimples deeper. When she spoke, her voice was low and soft. "Hullo, Jamie. I'm Deidre." He watched, rapt, as she closed her eyes and opened them again slowly. She smelled of sunlight and fresh water. "Did you know Jamie was the name of a king?"

He shook his head. She continued to smile and nodded slowly. Jamie tore his eyes from her and looked back at Ned.

Ned had not moved from where he leaned against the railing. He looked at the other girl.

She was long and lean and sliced through the water. Deep auburn hair plastered smooth to her head. She looked like long-limbed pixie and splashed at Ned. "You look after him, do you?"

"We take care of each other."

"And a good thing it is, too, to have and be such a friend. So my Pa used to say." She held up a dripping hand. "My name's Emmaline, but call me Emma. Here, give us a hand up."

Ned reached down and gently shook the small wet hand. "I'm Ned." Jamie watched Ned set his grip to pull her from the water. "Ready?"

"Wait a second."

Emma set her feet against the piling braces. "Ok, give us a pull."

Ned pulled her up and there she was beside him, tall, wet, dripping and magnificent. Her eyes were clear and direct. She crossed her arms.

Jamie felt water splash against his face and turned back to Deidre. She still smiled. "You come to do some fishing, did you now?"

"That was the plan."

"We sorta scared them away, didn't we?"

Jamie thought of the day they had met Sabastian. "It's not like that's never happened before." He rolled over to sit up, unable to keep his eyes from Deidre. "We'll just have to wait for the fish to come back."

He looked at Emma and was suddenly very aware she was dressed only in her shift. Since she was wet she was shielded only by her crossed arms. He looked quickly back to Deidre, realized she was, under the water, dressed just like Emma and waved generally in the direction of the railing adorned with their garments. "Ah … would you like us … to … get your clothes for you?"

Emma smiled at Ned as she answered. "If you would be so kind." She recrossed her arms, leaned her head to one side and one hip against the rail on the dock and waited for Ned to pull Jamie to his feet. He heard them laugh as they gingerly lifted the clothes from the rail.

Jamie stared, not quite believing, at an actual girl's shirt resting in his hand. It felt soft against his palm the way it must feel to their skin and suddenly his heart was beating fast, like a big frog banging around, thumping to break out of his chest. He whispered out of the side of his mouth. "Ned, we shouldn't be here."

"Yeah well, sometimes the best place to be is where you're not supposed to be. Besides, if anybody is in the wrong place, it's them. It's our fishing hole, ain't it?" He gave a little hiccup of a laugh. "Ain't it grand?"

Jamie turned to stare at Ned.

Ned's face was shining in full catbird bloom. "We'll just sit on the dock and talk and wait for the fish to come back. If we catch any we'll share."

"Back to where, where do you think they're from?"

Ned almost giggled. "No idea. Don't know. Don't care." He grabbed the arm of Jamie's shirt. "Don't let it pass you by. Take care of now and now will take care of you."

Jamie stared. "Where the hell did that come from?"

"What?"

"'Take care of now' and all that stuff?" He couldn't help but grimace a smile. "Mrs. Huff'd be proud."

"Yeah well. I don't know about that." Ned half-smiled, glanced over his shoulder at the girls and shook his head just a little. "Matter of fact, I somehow kinda doubt it." He poked Jamie in the chest. "And don't you never tell nobody either. This and them is between you and me."

A clear feminine voice broke into their whispered conference. "If you two are finished with your blather, could you bring us our things?"

Ned swung Jamie around and pulled him forward by the arm. "Sure."

They walked down to the dock and handed the girls their blouses and skirts.

It was a golden moment they did not let pass by. The girls talked and they talked and leaned back against the dock posts. For once catching fish did not seem important and, of course, that's when the fish chose to bite. As anyone who has ever fished more than a couple of times can tell you, fish extend their grace to you the very moment when you really don't care much whether they bite or not. Strange ephemeral creatures are fish. Like love, you never really know when you're going to get a nibble. Then when you've decided it's not so important after all, they come and spread their magic over you and make the world whole. The boys swam in the ether of the gods until dusk turned the evening to mist and magic.

Then the golden moment stopped. The girls looked at each other and frowned.

Deidre looked at Jamie. "We have to go back."

"Where's back? Will you be all right?"

"For tonight in a fallow field Pa found." Deirdre's dimples appeared again. "It's not far."

"But … can we … will you come here again?"

"That depends. If Pa can find work, sure. I'll try." She smiled her dimples at him.

He held out the stringer of fish to her.

Her hand touched his as she took it. "Mind yourself, King Jamie."

The tendrils of his heart tugged as he watched them walk away, down the lake path the other way from theirs. Deidre held her hand to her mouth and called out her thanks for the fish. With one last wave and a giggle to each other, they disappeared into the woods.

Jamie and Ned rose to their feet. Little Lake felt still and empty. They dragged their feet toward home, silent on the path until they crossed the road. Then Jamie felt a laugh bubble up from his chest. Ned looked at him, laughed back, then with whoops of joy they ran all the way back to the house.

Chapter 38

A Trick and a Tale

Ned normally could keep up with Cyrus' long-legged gait if he put his mind and his feet to it, but this morning Cyrus flew and passed out of sight. He clambered through a stand of briars and was just about to yell for Cyrus to hold up when he looked down where he stepped. The yell to hold up turned into a yelp of shock then fear when he saw the sinuous black shape rustling through the leaves just beyond his toes. In the instant before Ned thought he was going to die he thought this was his chance to see a black Cottonmouth Moccasin and what a pity it was his last chance to see anything. Then his body instincts heaved him out of there and he jumped as high as he ever had in the vain attempt to tiptoe on air. He vaulted over a fallen tree, beyond the next two and a stump before he stopped to look back. Only then did Ned hear laughter.

He had never heard Cyrus laugh. He felt his face turn hot and the anger flushed his fear. "Laugh if you want, but that was a Cottonmouth and you'd better be scared too."

"It's all right."

Ned climbed up on the stump. He saw Cyrus laughing, leaning with one hand against a tree.

"You'd better get out of there, that thing's dangerous."

"Not this time."

Realization dropped over Ned like a blanket. "It wasn't real, was it?"

Cyrus laughed again and shook his head no.

Ned scrambled back over the logs and stalked up to Cyrus. "That's not funny!"

His quiet laughter dimmed to a quiet chuckle without teeth. "Yes it was. You're just too close to it now to be able to see the humor. You gotta learn to laugh at yourself." Cyrus nodded over Ned's shoulder. "He thinks it was funny."

Ned followed Cyrus' glance to Toby, who was not only not upset, but sat back on his haunches positively laughing as only a dog can, his long pink tongue bouncing out of the side of his mouth. "Great, now I've got a dog laughing at me."

"A sense of humor is the best sign of intelligence."

"Oh, that makes me feel so much better." Ned turned to work his way back to the path. "You scared me half to death."

"Hold on, sit down for a minute." Cyrus motioned to an old stump. Ned sat and looked around. "By the way, why are we here? It looks pretty well cut over. The pines look too small to be of any use."

Cyrus smiled and nodded. "Good eye. No, Mr. Garrath wants to know if there's any hardwood worth cutting. He's got some sort of a special contract, but don't worry about that. For right now, right this minute, just sit there and breathe."

"How would I not do that? By the way, what was that?"

Cyrus held up the end of a rope. "Just an old piece of old black rope with a string attached to pull it with." He coiled up the line and stowed it in his bag. "Want to learn how to do it?"

Ned's anger dimmed to a dull simmer at the thought of playing it on someone else. "Yeah. Yeah I do."

"The real trick is to set it up to move naturally, like a snake and not move yourself any more than you have to. When animals hide, they don't move a muscle. Even squirrels hide like that. You must learn to be still. Tell you what, don't think right now. Breathe slowly and think of nothing but that. For this moment do nothing but breathe."

Ned closed his eyes, breathed in slowly and let it out slowly. He heard Cyrus' voice in his ear though Cyrus sat a good ten feet from him on another stump. "Now listen."

"I don't hear anything but the wind."

"You're still trying too hard. Don't force it. Let me tell you a story. It is one of many stories of Raven, but this tale is owned by my clan and my family. Let yourself be and listen."

As the wind gentled Ned's nerves, Cyrus began to speak in the rhythm of a storyteller.

"Raven is a spirit being who can do great magic. It's said he put the sun and the stars in the sky. Raven is a shape-shifter and can take on any form he chooses. He is a great teacher and protector of my people and brought the first salmon to us for food. He is selfish and loves to play tricks, but sometimes even Raven is defeated.

One day Raven found a boy walking alone in the great woods. Raven considered the woods to be his and thought 'I will play a trick on this boy'. He shifted to the form of a man and said, 'Hey you, what are you doing out here in these woods alone? You should be back among the women and the other children.'

The boy answered 'I do not want to be a child any longer' and continued on his way.

Raven was a little upset at this. He had thought the boy was lost and had hoped to make the boy feel bad and drive him back to his camp, for Raven liked to have the woods to himself for his mischief. Raven shape-shifted back to his own form and followed the boy. This time he caused every bush and tree the boy passed to be filled with luscious fruit and berries, for he knew the boy had to be hungry, for he was a boy and a long way from his people. The boy ignored all of the fruit, all of the apples and pears and sweet berries Raven put upon his path. The only thing the boy did was to sip a little water from his gourd from time to time, and then kept walking on his way.

Time after time, Raven tried to make the boy go back or turn him from his path, but the boy kept right on going. He tried heat, he tried cold, he made the illusion of raging waters, he turned the sun black to darken the path, but the boy kept right on walking. Now, it's not a good thing to get too tired in the woods or you may not be able to handle what is in front of you. The boy knew this and every so often stopped to rest and sip from his gourd.

At one of the little rests, Raven tried again. Raven knew if the boy died this deep in the forest he'd have to deal with the boy's ghost for all time. Raven didn't want to do that. To Raven, when it was time for people to die they should die close to their own holy ground where at least they would be held away from the woods Raven considered his domain. So he decided to talk with the boy again. He changed into his old man form and smiled at the boy with his best 'trust me' face. The boy's expression did not change.

Raven asked 'Why do you walk so far and so long?'

The boy answered 'I do not want to be a child any longer.'

Raven said 'But to be a child is to be loved and fed and protected. Seems to me, you'd want to stay like that as long as you could.'

The boy did not answer. Raven was so frustrated he changed back into his real shape right in front of the boy and flew away. From high above Raven watched the boy walking, walking, walking deeper into the woods. Raven threw snow and hailstones the size of your fist, he made trees fall in the boy's path, he tried everything he had the power to do and yet the boy walked on, walked on, walked on. Raven could tell the boy was on his last legs now. He was drenched, shivering and starving. There were holes in his moccasins, there were holes in his buckskins where the hailstones had battered him and Raven saw through those holes dripping blood. Tears ran down the boy's cheeks, but still he walked, walked on as if he were stalking his own death, which he was. Raven saw the boy was prepared to die rather than be a child.

So the next time he stopped for a rest, Raven swooped down to the boy in his own form. He said, 'Look, if you keep this up, you will die.' The boy looked at him while he sat and bled, tears running down his haggard cheeks. 'I do not want to be a ...' 'Yes, yes, I know.' Raven said. 'You do not want to be a child any longer.' Raven ruffled his feathers, which for Raven is the equivalent of a shrug. 'I'll tell you what. I'll give you a pair of magic moccasins if you go back. They'll never wear out and your feet will never be wet and never be cold if you'll just go back.'

The boy shook his head. 'I do not want to be a child any longer.'

Now Raven said, 'I'll tell you what. In addition to the moccasins, I'll give you a robe that will protect you from the cold, from arrows, from rain, from everything.'

Again, the boy shook his head. 'I do not want to be a child any longer.'

Raven offered the boy a magic food bag that would always be full.

Again the boy shook his head. 'I do not want to be a child any longer.'

Raven offered a bow that would never miss no matter what warped and crooked arrow was nocked in the string.

Again, the boy said 'I do not want to be a child any longer.'

Raven jumped up and down with both feet and flapped his wings. 'Will you stop saying that?!' Finally Raven screamed as only a Raven can. 'Then what do you want?'

The boy took a long sigh. 'I want,' he said 'three of your wing feathers. And with each feather your promise you will help my people in times of trouble in whatever way you can. When the life of my people is threatened, they will attach one feather to an arrow and will let it fly from the strongest bow into your forest. When you see that arrow you will come to help. If I come back to my people with such a treasure, then I will be a child no longer.'

Raven saw this cold, starving, crying, bleeding boy was ready to face his own death for the simple purpose of helping his people. Raven slowly nodded, lifted one wing, solemnly plucked three feathers, then hopped down and placed them on the boy's lap.

That is how we became the clan of Raven and why three black feathers is the symbol of our clan."

Chapter 39
A Revelation

Ned and Jamie plodded down the path to Little Lake, rods in hand. As they approached the water Ned felt a painful weight in his chest and then he saw the Ghost sitting on the dock, his back leaning against one of the pilings. The man was very, very still.

They walked onto the dock as quietly as they could. Ned stared at his chest for any sign of breath. There was none. The fly rod hung from his open hand, the line curled away sunk into the water like a thin wavy snake. They could not see his eyes behind smoked glasses. They stared at his motionless shape.

"No, I am not dead."

Ned started and nearly dropped his fishing pole. "Oh, Great Granny Ghost!" Then he froze, not knowing if he'd insulted the man or not.

"Close, but not yet." The Ghost took a long deep scraping breath and coughed it back out. The scarred skin around his mouth folded in what for him passed for a smile. "Haven't seen you boys for a while. Please, sit down and tell me what happened with your Mr. Norris trick." He took a sip from a small leather-covered flask, screwed the top back on firmly and slid it into his fishing bag. "Please," he motioned toward the deck "Sit."

They sat and told him, in fits and starts and half-sentences, each breaking into the other's telling. The telling did not take long, but as soon as the Ghost heard of Norris' windmilling arms under the claws of Wandering Tom, he hacked out laughter. "Oh ho, I do so wish I could have seen that." His second deep breath seemed to flow a little smoother than the first. "That would have been something. But getting it from you is like hearing honeysuckle." His smile deepened and he coughed another laugh.

Ned and Jamie laughed with him, both at remembering again but also because as far as they knew, they were the only folks they knew who had ever seen the Ghost laugh.

But the Ghost's laughter swapped into a coughing fit. He pulled his handkerchief from his pocket and pressed it to his mouth until the racking subsided. "Pardon me."

Jamie sat down on the dock by him. "Are you all right, Mr. Wood? Can we help you?" Jamie's mother had hinted at the man's condition, but watching him suffer was downright painful.

The Ghost nodded and cleared his throat. "Oh yes, quite all right, thank you." Ned saw blood on his handkerchief as he carefully folded it and slid it back into his pocket. "And please, when it's just us call me Sabastian."

Ned's question was out of his mouth before he could stop it. "You really hate Mr. Norris, don't you? More than a little."

Sabastian looked up quickly.

Ned began to say sorry, but Sabastian shook his head. "No, no, don't apologize." He held one hand in the air. "I was just surprised at your perception. Perhaps I'm not as unreadable as I'd like to think."

Jamie turned around to look at Ned. "I'm a little surprised myself."

Sabastian slid his fedora back on his head. "What gave it away?"

Ned shrugged. "I don't know. You just seemed to really appreciate the joke and … I just had a feelin'."

"And an accurate one." Sabastian folded his fishing rod into his arms. "Because you are correct." He looked from boy to the other. "I know you are both aware of Mr. Norris' penchant for gossip."

Ned nodded and saw Jamie nodded too. He wasn't quite sure what 'penchant' meant, but he thought the general gist of it was that Nosy liked to keep his nose is buried in other folk's business.

"Let's just say while I was away at the Big Show Mr. Norris plied his personal trade using rumors concerning flyers, particularly me. It cost me … the regard … of a person that meant

251

more to me than my life." Sabastian was suddenly quiet and the stillness Ned had felt when they had first come out settled on the man like a blanket over his shoulders. "So, I find joy in his trouble and find it difficult to extend Christian charity to one who has caused so much grief." His smile was tight. "I shall, no doubt, in future have to pray night and day, long and hard, for forgiveness at finding so much joy in another's misfortune." Sabastian's smile hardened and a dent appeared in his scarred face. "But not yet. After all, if something feels this good, it's bound to be a sin. Isn't that what 'Old Thunderbuns' tells us darn near every Sunday?"

Ned laughed along with both Sabastian and Jamie at that, but with an edge he did not quite understand, feeling both the joy of the moment and a deep pain he knew was not his own. He could feel the same kind of pain in Cyrus. It felt like both Sabastian and Cyrus had been disconnected from themselves, like a flashlight trying to glow in the deep night, but the batteries were low and the switch only worked part of the time.

Sabastian began to cough hard and Ned could hear his chest rattle as it heaved. When the fit eased Sabastian closed his eyes and breathed slowly. Ned glanced at the handkerchief in Sabastian's hand and saw blood.

"I'm sorry boys, I need to be going. No, you stay and enjoy yourselves, I just need to get home and take care of a few things."

Jamie scratched his nose. "Aw. I was going to ask you more about the war. There's nobody else who will talk about it the way you do."

"Then it's just as well, James. There are things that even I am better off not remembering." Sabastian sighed, stood and with a few touches had his gear packed up. He coughed again, waved goodbye and glided in his long-legged stride off the pier into the wood and was gone. They heard one long coughing fit and that was all.

"So you think he's all right?" Jamie stared after him.

Ned looked out over the water. "Depends on your definition of 'all right.' He's hurting, that's for sure."

Chapter 40

A Fall Into Darkness

That night John Wanderwood, who called himself Cyrus Conner, did not feel like eating at the common table at the migrant camp. He did not feel like eating at all. He felt like an animal was eating his insides, chewing at him, making his mind growl. As soon as the bouncing migrant truck dropped him back at the camp he went straight to his tarpaper shack, slid the clear jar of moonshine deep into his woven bag and walked off for the lake.

It was a clear night. A wide curved band of moon was more than enough to cast shadows from the trees and light his way. The dark water beckoned him as he approached. He felt an edge of peace at the sight of it, his inner man breathed easier. The stars were bright as the moon would allow. As he lay on his back on the dock most of his vision was taken up by the black sky dotted with stars cast like seeds across the heavens by the hands of the gods.

He turned over and lay on his stomach to gaze over the water. Bands of reflected night light rippled across the dark water and his mind's eye filled in the smooth pulsing roar of the ocean. He closed his eyes. He was still Makah. Even in this place almost as far from his home as he could get, he was still Makah, still of the 'People Who Live Near the Rocks and the Seagulls.' Seagulls. He cast his gaze around the lake in the darkness and saw black limbs of trees hanging over the water. The lake to him was suddenly a pool where his heart and mind was the lake and the trees were dark threatening arms encroaching on his soul, reaching for the treasure of his spirit. He laughed aloud and rolled over onto his back. He thought his mind growing soft, feeling such things. Was this what a man of the Makah should be feeling when he had a sky over his head, food to eat and a job working for a man whose back was straight?

Memory streamed into his mind of the first time he had been out of sight of land in his small dugout sailing canoe. He had

253

been fishing and lost track of time. The gods had warned him with a splash of rain on his neck and back but only after he had pulled in one last fish did he look up. The landed horizon was not there, only gray cloud touching the water. He remembered his grandfather's teachings to navigate not only by the sun but by breeze and current, but he had not paid attention to the wind and water, so had no idea which way to go. He had rigged a sea anchor to limit drift and waited with his arms wrapped around his knees until the clouds moved away. It was deep night by the time the sky had cleared. It was only then he found the northern star the white men call Polaris and set his sail for home.

Home. The stars could not help him now. Walking with that damn boy Ned had dredged up the stinking muck from his heart. It was the teaching that had done it. He had instinctively begun to teach the boy as his father and grandfather had taught him and that had triggered memories of his home. Why had he started teaching the boy? What good could come of it? What would such knowledge do for a white boy and a town boy at that? He felt a fool. It had been automatic, but was it fair to teach, to lead such a boy when he was lost himself? He cursed and reached for his bag and the mason jar of clear liquid. As soon as the screw lid was off his nose was assaulted, stinging and clearing his head at the same time. He took a swallow. It felt like live fire burning and twisting its way down, churning until hands of flame gripped his empty stomach and twisted it into a knot. He grimaced and his memory flooded with the pain of the past, being severed from his people. Being joined with his tribe, with his clan, was a thing his bones and muscles remembered like dancing with the wind with his hand on the tiller of his sailing canoe or breathing through another set of lungs. Now he felt like an uprooted tree with its roots drying and dying in the sun.

He forced another swallow into his mouth. This time it slid down much more easily.

He glanced about him at the dark tree limbs and the dark water. Raven had spoken to him what, two days ago? Told him to go home? This was not home. There was no smell of salt in the air, no sticky skin, no sand, nowhere any scent of cedar. He took another swallow. He wanted to sing, sing his own private potlatch, but without his people around him the flow of music stuck in his throat, choking him. He could hardly catch breath, the dark wind

254

inside him squeezed tears from his eyes and he leaned his head back against a piling.

He blinked and looked about. The sky showed the first hint of light. Morning already? He looked for the jar and found it lying on its side on the dock, empty. Where had the night gone? Where had the time gone? He could not remember, could not think. He crawled to the edge of the dock and dipped his hands down into the water and lifted it to his face and mouth. He drank deeply, the water cleaning out his raw mouth and throat and he splashed and rubbed water all over his face and neck and head.

Work. Damn. He had to go to work.

His first attempt to stand was unsuccessful. He leaned against a piling and the thought came to him that he needed food if he was to make it to work. He closed his eyes. "I know I do not deserve it, but gods help me, Raven help me. Do not play your tricks now. Help your lost one."

He pushed against the piling, up onto his feet and staggered down the dock and into the trees. It seemed better surrounded by woods and wind blew in his face, but he was empty and his limbs had no strength to move. By the time he got to camp his gut was chewing at him and the other men were already gathered in the little store getting coffee and egg and sausage sandwiches wrapped in wax paper for breakfast. He silently got in line.

When it was his turn to pay he caught the eye of the girl behind the counter, but this time her look was not friendly and his inner man was poisoned and had no power. He saw her look of disgust. 'Just another drunken Indian' her look said. His eyes fell to the dirty plank floor. There was no touch of the hand this time. She slapped his change on the worn counter and her eyes moved quickly onto the next man in line, passed over him like he was nothing, leaving him to scoop his change off the counter and make his uncertain way back out into the dust.

Outside he slurped the coffee and shoved the sandwich into his mouth to fill the grinding hole in his belly.

God, his head hurt. He climbed into the back of the flat-bed truck for the short trip to the mill. The trip was torture, his head spinning, the white man's poison still in charge. It was just as the truck rolled into the mill yard that he remembered the rule

255

about drinking. He could not miss work, but he knew when he was caught there would be no job, no nothing. He looked at the sign of the mill and slowly walked through the gate to his doom.

Chapter 41

Cramphorne Plays Hera

The Right Reverend Costigan Abalicious Cramphorne sat in his swivel chair, pounded a blank sheet of paper on the desk with one meaty palm and gloomed about the Elders. How could he write his sermon when all he could think about was how they'd refused the simplest of requests? It was they who were keeping him from his work. It was they, supposedly the responsible leaders of the church, who refused to tend to the spiritual needs of the elderly and the sick. The Elders were already arranging for physical needs. That Grant Garrath, for instance, already delivered firewood for those who could not get it for themselves and the ladies of the church cooked for those in need. How easy it would be for them to provide the spiritual help at the same time, while they were already there. But no, these folk were consumed with pride, absolutely consumed with it. And this was despite his sermon, specifically on that subject, intended to stave off just such a selfish attitude. They had not taken his words to heart. Cramphorne simply could not understand. They had not listened, even with his references to the bedrock of the good book that clearly and firmly established what they should do. And the worst of it, the worst of all, he did not seem to be able to get his own superior Silas Webster to listen, not even so much as to consider finding him a position where his talents would be more appreciated. There was nothing Cramphorne so believed as the theory that God in all his wisdom designated certain folk to do certain things and he was just as firm in his belief that the place for him was not here. Ahh, well. They would rue the day they forced his hand.

He glanced at the photograph of his wife on his desk. Beautiful dutiful woman, she was, through her brother Everest, one of the best weapons in his arsenal against the unrighteous. Everest had gotten him this position, had he not? Everest, even in his ignorance of holy matters would surely had to admit upon reflection that this little community could only be a stepping stone to greater things. Cramphorne shook his great white mane slowly. It was ironic to him though love of money was indeed the root of evil, that money could be wielded for the sake of the righteous. If this congregation could not and would not listen, there had to be one that would. He leaned into his desk, both fists now resting on the top. He pounded his fists on the desktop once more. He heard a clank and a rustle from the kitchen and his Hera appeared in his office doorway. Her hair was pulled back in her usual bun (none of the new fancy new curled hairstyles of the day for her, she was a proper woman.), her round gold eyeglasses were perched on her long straight nose. She wore her apron for flower arranging and held her gloved hands aloft with open fingers like a surgeon. "Costigan dear, what is it? Are you distressed?"

"I'm sorry to bother you, my dearest lamb," he rumbled, "I'm sorry …"

She spread her hands and waved off his apology. "No, no dear." She stepped into the room. "You tell me what's wrong. Remember dear," she held up one gloved finger "a trouble shared is trouble halved. Now what is it?"

"It's the Elders again. They refuse to do their duty. It's maddening. I can't help but believe their intransigence is a sign from God we're needed elsewhere, where there is more noble purpose, where nobler characters prevail."

"I'm quite certain our dear Lord would never want us to stay in a place of rocky ground where your fertile seeds cannot grow and flourish, my dear." She smiled and blinked behind her round spectacles. "I'll write Everest at once, my dear. He'll set everything right." Her smile broadened and her eyes warmed at him. "My Jupiter." Then, hands still up in the air, she turned in a pirouette and bounced on her toes out of the room.

Cramphorne folded his hands across his broad paunch and relaxed back in his swivel chair. A small smile played at the corners of his mouth as he thought of how Silas Webster would react. It was such a good thing that his wife was such a righteous woman. His smile grew broader. A very good thing.

Chapter 42

A Dark Day

As Cyrus moved behind him, Jamie caught a strong whiff of moonshine. He lifted another shovelful of sand into a fire bucket. He knew his father's rule about drinking on the job. He knew Cyrus knew it too. But Cyrus was older than his father. And he was Ned's friend.

He watched Cyrus out of the corner of his eye. The tall Indian turned a stack of buckets upside-down and put his feet on the bottom rim. As he pulled on the top bucket to twist it from the stack his hands slipped. Cyrus tried to catch them but was just too slow and the whole stack banged to the ground.

"Cyrus, have you been drinking?" Jamie twisted his hands on the shovel handle.

Cyrus straightened and pulled a smile. He took off his hat and rubbed the top of his head. "I expect I better be callin' you 'Mr. Garrath'. You're grown, aren't you?"

Jamie gripped his shovel a little tighter. "Go on home, Cyrus. I'll finish up here."

Cyrus looked at the ground, nodded and clapped his hat on the back of his head. He grabbed his bag and slung it over his shoulder. As he turned to walk away he staggered one step sideways, then steadied and stepped toward the mill gate, hands in buried in his pockets.

Jamie watched him walk away. He set the stack of buckets upright, wrenched them apart one by one and set them on the ground in a line. The shovel rang as he picked it up but that sound died to a fine-grained scrape as he slid the shovel into the sand pile. The sand felt very heavy as he lifted and dumped it into the next bucket.

"You sent him home?" Jamie's father straightened from sharpening the big circular saw blade and passed a wire brush over his file to clean it.

"He wasn't feeling good, something about what he had for supper last night. Probably be back tomorrow." Jamie looked away at the mill engine. "Fire buckets are all done. What's next?"

"All right." Jamie's father chewed on his cheek. "Go grab a sling blade and help Ned. He's clearing out that tall grass around the lumber stacks. Watch out for copperheads."

"Yessir." Jamie bolted. He grabbed a sling blade from the tool shed and trotted off to find Ned. He followed hacking sounds from behind the last tall lumber stack, but as he turned the corner he saw Eueas, swinging a bush axe like Babe Ruth, pushing off his supposedly bad leg, chopping at a chinaberry tree. His cane was on the ground. When Eueas saw Jamie he started, then quickly bent and picked it up. "What you want, boy?" He glared. "You got no call to come sneaking up on a man."

Ned and Toby emerged from behind the next stack. Jamie started toward them and felt Eueas' eyes burn at him as walked a wide berth around the man.

"That's right, boy." Eueas' voice scraped the air. "You just stay out of my way, you and your no-count dog."

Jamie's feet froze on the hard ground. His throat gripped tight. Eueas was too damn mean for him to say anything back, but he just could not bring himself to run.

Eueas stumped toward Jamie, bush axe gripped in his grimy fist. Toby leapt between Jamie and Eueas. His head lowered, ears laid back and a low deep growl ground from his throat.

Eueas stopped, eyes on Toby. His fist drove his steel shod cane into the ground. His head turned a little to one side. "You hear me, boy. You mind me now or you gonna get whupped but good. I don' give a good goddam who yo' daddy is, you hear me boy?"

Jamie felt like his whole body clench like a fist. He could not speak.

Eueas jutted out his chin as though he had and stalked off.

Jamie could not move, could not breathe. He had never before ached to see a man bleed. Fear and anger fought in his gut and churned his stomach into a froth that threatened to burst from him like bile vomit.

"You all right? Jamie?"

As Jamie's vision cleared, he saw Ned standing above him. He didn't understand until he realized he was sitting on the ground. Toby sat on the ground too, right in front of him, looking in the direction Eueas had gone.

"Jamie?"

"Yeah. I'm all right." Jamie gripped the sling blade handle and pushed to his feet. "Just had a little … run-in with Eueas."

"Yeah, I saw. You wanna tell your dad?"

"I don't know what I want."

Which was a lie. He knew exactly what he wanted. He wanted to beat Eueas' filthy face into the dirt. He just wasn't big enough or strong enough and he didn't know how. A moment froze then his body took over. Jamie watched himself grip the sling blade and start hacking at the long grass. He was vaguely aware of Ned doing the same thing. Sweat soaked his shirt as he worked the acid out of his body, out of his mind. He stopped, took a drink of water from his mason jar. The thought struck him this was what hate felt like, smelled like, tasted like. Hate was strength stirred together with poison. It filled his muscles, but his stomach was so knotted and sick he wanted to heave. It eased only a little when he breathed deeply and swore he'd make it even.

Jamie's nerves jangled even after he had something to eat at midday. He ate mechanically, sandwich bread turning to gum inside his mouth. He was able to swallow only by drenching his throat with water. Ned sat beside him silent, just rubbing Toby's head.

Eueas, on the other hand, was jubilant, very talkative as he sat with the men under the big oak by the cabin.

Jamie became aware that Ned was trying to talk with him. "What? I'm sorry, what?"

Ned pressed his lips together before he spoke again. "I said," Ned folded up his flour sack food bag, "let's go down in the woods when we get outa here and set the rabbit box trap. See if we can catch ourselves a skunk."

Jamie looked at the ground then back up at Ned. "You really think we need to? Nosy's gonna be wearing scratches from Wandering Tom for a week."

"I wasn't thinking about Nosy." Ned glanced over toward where Eueas was laughing and then back at Jamie.

Jaime's face stretched into a grim smile. "Best idea I've heard in a coon's age."

"Don't mention it."

When the afternoon train whistle blew Jamie and Ned tossed their tools in the shed and ran to grab their fishing poles. They hefted the heavy wooden box trap between them and lugged it out the back gate of the mill toward the new spot in the woods. They had to put it down several times to rest.

When they came to the spot they collapsed on the box, sitting back to back. In between breaths Jamie heard Ned ask behind him "You seen Cyrus today? I heard he was sick or something."

Jamie gripped his fishing pole. His eyes riveted on a pine tree root, twisted and gnarled. "He ain't sick."

"I haven't seen him today."

"He ain't here neither."

"Where is he?"

Jamie told him.

He felt Ned stand up. When Jamie turned around Ned was looking down into the dirt and leaves between his feet. "Don't you like Cyrus?"

"It's not a matter of like. If I wanna stay at the mill I gotta follow Daddy's rules. It's not like he cares about what people do on their own time."

"Did you tell your dad?" The gentle breeze through the pines almost drowned out Ned's voice.

"I told him Cyrus won't feeling good so I sent him home."

"I don't feel like fishing." Ned shifted back and forth from foot to foot. "See you." Ned turned toward the path to the house.

"I guess so." Jamie watched Ned walk off with his hands shoved straight-armed deep in his pockets, head hanging still looking at his feet. He called out to Ned's back. "Say hello to Gramma."

Ned did not turn around as he disappeared into the trees.

Jamie worked a couple of kinks out of his back, picked up both fishing poles and walked down the path to the lake. The mid-afternoon sun stabbed his eyes, bright on the water. Jamie lifted his sticky shirt off his back and shoulders. It was far too hot to fish and he had forgotten to dig worms. He stepped out on the dock and saw an empty mason jar lying on its side on the dock. He picked it up, smelled it and immediately wished he hadn't. The acrid moonshine lingered strong to burn his nose even without liquid. He didn't know if it was Cyrus' or not, but the smell was certainly the same. He threw the jar into the water and it sank.

Jamie sat down, leaned back against a piling in the shade and tried to think. He'd been afraid for his life, disobeyed his father, and seemingly lost his best friend all in one day. Jamie didn't know about best friend. Maybe. By default.

The sun beat on the leaves of the woods and Jamie with impartial brutality. In the quiet he felt energy bleed out of his body. He closed his eyes.

The light clump of footsteps on the dock brought him awake.

"You're not fishing today?

Sabastian looked down at him. He had never been so glad to see such a face in his life. Then he noticed Sabastian carried a coffee can.

"What's that?"

"Crickets and worms." Sabastian held the can out. "Doesn't seem right to be at the water with your pole and not be able to fish."

Jamie reached up and took it. "Thanks, Mr. Wood."

"My name is Sabastian, James." Sabastian sat two pilings down, slid his fly rod out of its bag and began to fit the sections together. "Tell me what's bothering you. It's not like you to come all the way down here pole in hand and not have bait."

"It's a lot of nothin'."

"Try me."

Jamie told him about Eueas.

"How do you feel?" Sabastian peered into his tin of flies.

"I don't feel much of nothin'. I don't belong at the mill because it's Daddy's and I'm not grown up enough to face Eueas. I don't belong home because … just because."

"Because Ned's there?"

"Maybe. No, I … I just don't." Jamie popped the lid of the can open and three crickets popped out. "Damn."

"You can't blame a cricket for wanting to jump for freedom." Sabastian tied a fly on and waved his rod to make a very short cast that laid the line on the water with only a hint of splash. "It may surprise you to know you're not the only one who feels they don't belong anywhere. I was not always the pariah you see now."

Jamie was suddenly aware of Sabastian's scars. He heard the word a half beat later. "What's a 'pariah'?"

"Someone who has been cast off from society. Like an old pair of overalls you don't want any more."

"I like my old overalls. They're comfortable."

Sabastian's thick skin creased in a smile as he slowly retrieved line. "Out of the mouths of babes."

"What?"

"Nothing, watch your bobber. But you wouldn't wear those old overalls to church, now would you?"

"Oh God, no. If I ever tried Momma would tan my hide but good."

"Exactly. So as far as society is concerned, those overalls are outcast. They're a social pariah. See?"

"I guess."

Sabastian lifted his fly from the water and inspected it between his fingertips. "I told you before, I think, that Mr. Norris cost me the regard of a person very dear to me. It was during the war. I had a lady friend whom I fully intended to marry if I survived. It's surprising how well a man can court a lady through letters if he tries. We'd written back and forth for some time and she had my heart and I had more than a little reason to believe I had hers as well. The trouble was Mr. Norris was interested in her too. Now being a person of pretty fair judgement, she rejected his scrawny officious hide. To save face and get revenge, he spread it around he had lost interest in her because I had ruined her. That not only destroyed her reputation, it destroyed our relationship as well because Mr. Norris also spread it around that I had told the story."

"But you didn't. I mean spread it around or ... uh ...."

"Oh Lord, no." Sabastian shook his head. "The most we ever did was to embrace in the moonlight in the gazebo at her parent's house."

"So what happened?"

"I came home on leave with a brand-new Captain's rank, a brand-new diamond ring in my pocket bought with promotion bonus money and every intention in the world of asking for her hand. Thought I finally had enough of my own to offer her. I tell you, when I walked up her parent's front walk my heart just about pounded out of my chest."

Jamie turned to Sabastian. "So? What happened?"

"She wasn't there. Her parents had sent her to live with relatives and her father drove me off with the business end of a shotgun. Told me if I had ruined her and kept quiet about it, he'd be using the same gun to drive me to the altar, but as I was the one who had spread it around, there was nothing for it now but to send her away from the place of her shame. I tried to tell him the truth, but he was in no mood to listen."

"What did you do?"

265

"Went back to my squadron, shipped out for Europe and the Big Show and developed a taste for whiskey."

Jamie thought of Cyrus Connor and how he had stumbled trying to fill the buckets. "I didn't know you drank."

"I try not to. Men do strange and destructive things in war."

"I saw a man drunk this morning."

He caught Sabastian's eyes flick at him then look back at his fly floating on the water. "Want to talk about it?"

"Not much to tell. He came to work drunk. It's against the rules, right up there on the biggest sign there is on the side of the office. Daddy says it's dangerous around the machinery and stuff."

"He's right, James. It is."

"But it was me who sent him home."

An echo of silence pulled between them for a moment.

"Did you tell your father about it?"

Jamie shook his head. "I told Daddy he was sick. Do you think I did right?"

"Well, let's look at it for a minute. If you hadn't sent him home, he could have had an accident and gotten hurt, right?"

"I guess."

"If you had told your father, the man wouldn't have a job. The way it is, he'll miss a day's pay, but he's still able to work and make a living. Does he have a family?"

"Not that I know of." Jamie turned to Sabastian. "But when I told him to go home he looked like a kicked dog. And then he called me 'Mr. Garreth.' He said 'I oughta be callin' you Mr. Garrath now you're all grown up.' " Jamie shook his head. "I can't be too damned grown up if I feel this bad about it."

"Something you need to remember, James, is what happens to him now is not your fault. You did that man a favor. He might not realize it, but you did."

"So why do I feel so awful?"

266

"Because the world of grown-ups isn't as clean and clear-cut as we'd like everyone to think." Sabastian scratched on the scar on his neck. "Matter of fact, it's mostly pretty damn confusing."

"Isn't doing the right thing supposed to make you feel better?"

"If you mean is it supposed to make you feel happy, that happens sometimes. But if you mean is doing the right thing supposed to free you from pain," Sabastian shook his head toward the water, "then more often than not, no. Doing the right thing is more a matter of just doing the best you can and living with the result than it is a matter of fixing everything. What he does with his life is up to him, James. You are only responsible for own your actions and you have acted honorably and well. Be content."

"But he's Ned's friend."

"Oh, and you feel like you hurt him. What did Ned say?"

"Ned's not talking."

"Give him time. Trust me on this one, James. If the man stays sober it'll be all right."

"And if he don't?"

Sabastian lifted his line from the water and cast to another spot. "Cross that bridge when you come to it. And watch your bobber."

That night at the supper table was very quiet. Jamie's father sat at the head of the table waiting for food. His mother bent to slide a baking dish out of the oven. Ned said nothing, eyes closed.

Jamie's father lifted his head and sniffed. "Cabbage?"

"Now don't you go turning your nose up 'til you've tried it. I got the recipe from Lily Turner; you know what a good cook she is. It's cabbage with ground beef and potatoes. Little bit of onion for flavor. She calls it 'Poor Man's Casserole.' "

He rubbed his eyes. "You just said we'd probably have chicken tonight and my stomach was set for it."

"Well, I was," she put the dish down on the middle of the table "but I couldn't catch one. And we needed to use up the ground beef before it went bad."

"Dig in, boys." Jamie's father stabbed at the cabbage with his fork.

Gloria made a face, but that disappeared when Jamie's mother pointed one finger down at Gloria's plate. Gloria dutifully forked the mixture into her mouth. He wondered, but not too hard, about why his sister didn't complain more. Maybe Gloria hadn't had such a great day either.

The rest of the meal passed quietly. His father made appreciative noises about the casserole when he got up and passed into the living room to read the paper and listen to the radio.

Ned spoke up. "May I be excused, Mrs. Garrath? I think I just want to go to bed."

"All right, Ned. Feeling all right?"

"I'm just tired."

"Go ahead then."

Ned thanked her, rose and pushed his chair back from the table. Jamie watched him pass from the room, but Ned would not catch his eye before he clumped up the hall to the bedroom.

Jamie helped his mother clear the dishes then went into the living room to read. His father slept, leaned back on the couch with his feet up on the ottoman. The newspaper lay spread in his lap, unread.

The radio droned on with 'Easy Aces.' The voice of the woman who played Jane Ace made Jamie want to either run or smash the radio. He liked 'Lum & Abner' and 'Fibber Magee and Molly' all right but Jane Ace just set his teeth on edge. He gently turned the volume down.

He sat down with his book. Less than a page after Crusoe had gotten settled on the island, he felt his mother's hand on his shoulder. He had nodded off just like his father.

She leaned down and kissed his forehead. "Why don't you go on to bed?"

Jamie could only nod. He got up and went to his bedroom. Ned lay on his cot with his face to the wall.

He gathered his towel and toothbrush and went to take his bath. When he got back Ned was gone and the window screen was ajar. Ned hadn't been sleepy after all.

He spoke to the darkness outside the window. "I am not going to follow you all over hell and half of Georgia." He turned and blew out the candle. "Hell with it. Just hell with it."

Chapter 43
Light Dawns

Jamie arose before the sun. Ned was not in his cot, but the window screen had been pulled to and latched. He slid into his overalls and padded into the kitchen.

His father was already at table, forking food into his mouth with one hand and holding up a technical paper with the other. He nodded at Jamie. "Good, you're up."

"Where's Ned?"

"Milking. He was up before I was." His father looked at his mother. "Honey, how about giving the boys a little coffee this morning?" He went back to reading his paper.

Jamie looked to his mother, but her face was impassive as she wordlessly set a cup of coffee in front of him along with a plate of eggs. He lifted it gingerly, slurped just a little to offset the heat. "It doesn't taste like it smells."

"That's a fact." His father smiled at him as he folded up his papers.

Ned emerged through the back door, milk bucket in hand. He didn't speak to anyone, just set the bucket down and sat down to eat.

Jamie tried to ignore Ned's silence all the way through breakfast, through getting ready for work and climbing in the back of the pickup. When they pulled up to Fred and Adam's store Jamie didn't want to stand it any more, so when the pickup pulled to a stop he jumped out and followed his father inside. He glanced back once. Ned had not moved. The screen door hinges squeaked in discordant harmony with the rusty springs as Jamie and his father pushed their way into the gloom.

Fred and Adam's was a dusty little store. It sat out by itself between Miller's Landing and the mill amidst the farms of the county. It was clapboard built, deeper than wide, just broad enough for two large shop windows split in the middle by two wooden screen doors with round metal signs nailed to them, one reading '7-Up', the other reading 'Pepsi-Cola, It will satisfy you'.

Pepsi wasn't the only thing sold here that satisfied. General consensus of conjecture held Fred Black sold mason jars of 'Homemade Disinfectant.' The deputy sheriff Lester Thomas never had been able to find the moonshine still that supplied it. Not that he had tried very hard. Lester had an enviable record of low crime in his county and he was not about to go all over hell and creation to plow some up and ruin his reputation.

Fred thumped his broad broom over toward them, his perpetual smile plastered in place above his starched white collar. The floor was made of narrow pine boards long since ground to a drab gray by the soles of dirty work boots and the oily sawdust Fred perpetually swept across the floor. "How do, Mr. Garrath, how do? And what can we do for you today?"

"Not a lot today Fred, just a pound of twenty-penny nails and a couple of gallons of gas." Jamie's father stepped toward the circular nail bins and reached for a paper bag. "Oh, and fill up the can in the back with kero if you would."

"Yes sir, I'll get that right away, sure will." Fred set his broom aside, slid his hand over his pomaded hair and hurried through the doors.

The deputy sheriff Lester Thomas sat on one of the benches beside the drink cooler sipping a Pepsi, his skinny legs calmly crossed at the knees.

Jamie's father nodded toward the deputy as he picked up a claw hammer and dug a pound of nails out of the bins into the bag. "How you doin', Les?"

"Not too terrible." Lester tipped his smoky bear hat back on his head with the bottle. "Feels like it's gonna be another hot one today. Have a Pepsi. Fred give's 'em to me, so have one on me."

"Not just now, thanks." Jamie's father set the bag on the scales, looked at it then dumped a few nails back in the bin. He looked at Jamie. "You want anything?"

"Not that I can think of."

Jamie's father looked at him a little askance, then nodded. He dropped the paper sack onto the counter and waited to pay.

Fred came back in from the gas pumps wiping his hands on his apron.

"How's business, Fred? You sellin' lots of mason jars these days?"

Fred's plastered smile slipped just a fraction. "Not too shabby, Mr. Garrath, not too shabby. It does help to have Les here, though. Keeps out the riff-raff, y'know."

"And Les does like his free Pepsi's."

The deputy spoke up from behind them. "What's that you say?"

Fred cleared his throat and rang up the sale. "Mr. Garrath's just having a little joke, Mr. Thomas, havin' a little joke. Awful lot of women in this county can an awful lot of vegetables in those jars, more'd you might think. It's hard times friend, hard times y'know. Hard times. Folks gotta do what they can to make ends meet and I'm downright proud to help out if I can."

"Uh-huh." Jamie's father gathered up his bag. "Later, Les."

As they walked out, Jamie glanced over his shoulder. Fred Black pushed his oily sawdust broom over the floor and jabbered at the deputy sheriff.

Ned leaped down as soon as the pickup stopped moving and met Cyrus coming in through the mill gate. He saw Cyrus' shoulders hunched and pain on his face. He stopped right in front of Ned, hat held in his hands.

"I owe you an apology, Ned. Mr. Garrath's boy caught me drunk yesterday and sent me home. I only come in to pick up my pay." Cyrus turned his hat around in his hands. "You bein' his friend I expect you know all about that."

"Yeah." Ned nodded. "Nobody else does, though."

Cyrus looked up quickly at Ned, his eyes dark and unblinking. "You wouldn't kid this old man, would you? I know boys love to play jokes. This wouldn't be a funny one."

"No joke. He was torn, I think, Mr. Garrath bein' his dad and all." Ned shook his head. "I wouldn't count on him doin' it again, but just for the once, he couldn't bring himself to tell on you."

Cyrus straightened, took a deep breath, and let his hands drop loose to his sides. He looked down at Ned. "That friend of yours?"

"Jamie."

"Yeah, Jamie. He's a good boy." Cyrus nodded. "You mean to tell me I've still got a job?"

Ned was about to answer yes when Jamie's father's voice cut through the air between them.

"Hey, CC! You gonna stand there jaw-jacking all day? You gotta show Caleb where you marked those trees for cutting. Come on, get some coffee, let's get a move on!"

Cyrus lifted his hat and called back. "Comin'!" He laid one hand on Ned's shoulder with a smile then strode away, his shoes no longer dragging in the dust.

Cyrus Conner, aka 'CC', aka John Wanderwood, could not believe his luck. When he had walked in the mill that morning he had known with all his heart his demon had gotten him, just as it had gotten his brother Hegan. But the boy Ned had told Cyrus of his deliverance. The gods apparently still smiled on him despite the best efforts of his demons. Raven once again rode his shoulder and gave him another pair of eyes to see what was to be seen. He never knew what it was that made him look down at the ground just then, most likely habit, for a tracker's eyes and mind are never far from the task of reading the shifting history written upon the ground by creatures of the earth. Whatever the reason, his eyes read the foot-writing of the white man Eueas, the divot of the man's cane beside his right foot. In his mind's eye Cyrus saw the stiff legged gait, the rough right hand gripping the curved wooden handle, pushing it against his thigh, then the divot upon the ground disappeared.

Because the reading had been so easy Cyrus had almost fallen into the trap of seeing what he expected to see, not what was there. Almost. He now stepped to the side of the path, knelt down and felt the earth more closely with his eyes. There was the divot, one step, two steps, then it was gone. The man Eueas had stopped, turned right, then left, then made one, two, three steps *without the cane*, then Eueas had stopped, took two heavy decisive steps to the right again without the cane, then the tracks were lost in other prints of men returning from the woods.

Cyrus searched the tracks further, saw Marshall in his mind's eye, huge heavy steps, far apart, regular, straight ahead and there was Charlie, lighter, closer together, deeply worn soles, rounded heels, the prints sometimes twisted sideways on the ball of his foot as he walked beside Marshall, turning to talk to the taller man. Cyrus could almost see Charlie trotting alongside Marshall, filling Marshall's ears with another of his schemes. He smiled to himself about Charlie. There was no real harm in the man; he just didn't know how to be still.

Then Cyrus looked back at Eueas' tracks. He didn't want to make assumptions, especially because he did not like the man and was more than aware that might color his thinking. But Cyrus could not ignore what was in front of his eyes. When Cyrus stepped in the direction Eueas' steps had been drawn to, he saw the round, five pad tracks of a medium size dog. The only dog at the mill was the Ned's. Then memory of Toby stealing Eueas' cane dropped into his mind. If he was reading these tracks right (for tracks never lie, any inaccuracy is in the mind of the tracker) Toby had seen Eueas walking without it. Cyrus was cautious about assuming how much dogs knew and saw, but a chill went across his shoulders at the thought Toby had wanted to show Eueas could walk without his cane.

Cyrus decided to make no noises about it. Not only would explaining a tracker's logic be difficult, but he did not want to draw attention to himself. Eueas was not the only one with something to hide. But the man bore watching. Yes, indeed, the man bore watching.

Chapter 44
Separation

The next morning Ned was down out of the truck as fast as he could. He found Cyrus, got the tree book and followed the swinging machete slung across Cyrus' back and tried to keep up. It wasn't easy. He kept tripping over roots.

Cyrus stopped and peered at his map. "It's here."

"How can you tell?" Ned reached into his bag for the notebook and pencil.

"We're 100 yards past the third cross roads. Now we go east. We mark for hardwoods for boat builders today."

Ned followed as Cyrus wandered tree by tree. Cyrus called out diameters, height and tree type, and slashed through bark with the machete.

"What's the matter?"

Ned started. "What do you mean?"

Cyrus rested the machete on his shoulder. "I mean, you haven't written down the last two trees."

Ned dropped his eyes to the notebook. He didn't know how to answer.

"He's your friend. There are too damned few of those in a lifetime. Man or boy, it don't do to throw them away."

Ned looked at the ground. "I don't know what you're talking about."

"Yeah, you do. Don't talk about it if you don't want to. But just let me say a couple of things and then we can get on with the work."

"You know what really bothers me?"

"No."

"Why he did it."

"Why he held his peace about me?"

"Not that."

"Then what?"

"Why he sent you home in the first place."

Cyrus lowered the machete. "You must be kidding."

Ned gripped the notebook. "No, I'm not kidding; I'm not kidding at all. All he had to do was look the other way, you weren't hurting anybody."

"What if I'd been working a cant hook on a heavy log with someone at the other end? Or feeding the saw?"

"But you weren't, you were just filling buckets with sand. How sober do you have to be to do that?"

Cyrus slowly shook his head. "I was doing that harmless thing only by the grace of God. What if I had been put to doing something that required judgment?"

Ned didn't want to say it out loud.

"I was wrong, Ned."

A high soaring caw screamed, piercing the suddenly silent forest. Ned looked up and saw a huge black bird circling above. "Kinda odd for a crow to be in these woods, isn't it?"

Cyrus chuckled. "If that were a crow, but it's not." He lifted his shoulders and set them back down in a shrug. "It's a kind of a crow, but more. That, my friend, is a raven."

"That doesn't explain what it's doing here."

Cyrus was silent for a moment. "It's looking after me." He looked skyward and yelled at the bird. "Yes, you look after me, don't you? Only your gods know why." Cyrus glanced back at Ned and smiled with one side of his mouth. "I was supposed to be a shaman, you know. I had the gift and wasted it. Now it only comes to me now and then, when I least expect it. Like the gift is testing me to see if I'm ready to take it up again."

"I don't understand."

Cyrus popped a slap on the back of Ned's head. "Stop thinking like a white man." His eyes bored into Ned's. "You have

276

the gift, boy. Don't waste it now when you need it. Look at what's in front of your eyes and then feel for what's true."

Now Ned really did not know what to say.

Cyrus pointed behind Ned. "Look at Toby."

"What?"

Ned backed up a step but then followed as Cyrus reached out to his shoulders and turned him around. Cyrus' hand and arm pointed over his shoulder at the dog.

"Why? What?"

Toby was sitting as still as a dog can be, the only movement the blinking of his eyes.

"What?" Ned half-turned back toward Cyrus and was rewarded by Cyrus' open hand against the back of his head again. This time it hurt. "Ow, stop that."

"Then start seeing."

"Just what am I supposed to see?"

"What he's *not* doing."

What Toby was not doing was laughing. Toby lifted from the ground, walked over to Ned and ducked his head under Ned's hand.

"So why did Jamie do it?"

"Jamie's turning into a man. He did the only thing he could that was right and responsible to his father's mill and that was right and responsible to you too. I can do a lot of things, Ned, but drink is my weak heel, as you white folks say."

Ned stroked the top of Toby's head. "Your Achilles heel."

"My what?"

"Achilles heel. Achilles was a hero of Greek mythology who had divine protection all over except for his heel."

"What happened to him?"

Ned turned to Cyrus. "He got shot in the heel by an arrow and died."

Ned watched the edges of Cyrus' mouth tighten as he nodded. "Sounds about right. Goddamn. Here I am, supposed to be a shaman and I'm learning lessons from a white boy." He slung his blade into the tree. "Not even a white man, but a white boy."

"I'm confused."

Cyrus turned back to Ned. "About what?"

"Does being a shaman mean you're not supposed to learn anymore?"

Suddenly Ned felt that Cyrus had frozen to the ground, turned to stone. The question had been the first dead certainty out of his mouth since before he could remember.

Then Cyrus nodded to the air. He spoke very quietly in a distant dead voice. "Pick up your book. Two trees, two feet diameter, twenty feet of useful length to the first limbs, red oak."

Ned pulled his notebook out of his pocket and lifted his pencil to write. Then he looked at Toby, whose mouth was now open, drooling and laughing.

Jamie had watched Ned followed Cyrus into the woods. Mixed thoughts churned in his head. He knew he had disobeyed his father, that was one. Another was that Ned had given him the silent treatment as if he had done something on purpose to hurt him, to hurt Cyrus.

"Hey, boy, you gonna day dream all day or you gonna so some work?"

Jamie was jerked out of his reverie by Eueas' rasping drawl that filled the air within earshot. He looked up and saw Eueas and Snow standing together and Eueas grinning so wide his missing teeth gaped. Jamie forced his feet toward them and saw Snow turn to Eueas and tell him something Jamie could not hear. Eueas nodded, tipped his hat to Snow and turned to stump with his cane toward the open engine shed with one last grinning glance over his shoulder at Jamie.

Jamie walked a little more quickly toward Snow. "What is it, Mr. Hackett?"

Snow smiled his wide white smile. "I need you to help me with the engine today."

Jamie remembered his mother and father's talk about his getting anywhere near the machinery, but he wasn't about to say anything that would put him back to whitewashing. "Okay."

Snow talked as they both turned and walked toward the engine shed. "The chugger ain't running right and I can't seem to figure out why come. And we got orders to fill."

"Is Mr. Canfield helping?"

Jamie listened to their boots crunching against the sand as Snow paused for a moment. "He worked on airplane engines during the Great War, Jamie. An airplane engine has got to be more complicated than this old chugger, so watch him and learn if you can. You're gonna be my engine man. He's a migrant, can't count on him to be held in one place, so we're gonna see how you do."

Jamie could not believe his luck, good and bad. Good that he got to work on the engine. But his stomach gripped at the thought of working with Eueas Canfield.

When he and Snow got there Eueas was already rattling wrenches around.

Snow brought him up short. "Hold on there. We're not gonna go tearing into this thing willy-nilly, no sir." He pointed his two fingers at Eueas. "I'm gonna go to the cabin and get the book for this thing. You just hold on there till I get back." Snow looked at Jamie. "You find us a big piece of canvas. One of those old drop cloths out of the paint shed oughta be about right."

Before he started to the paint shed Jamie saw Eueas' jaw clench as he looked at Snow, but Eueas didn't say anything and leaned back on his haunches to wait.

When Jamie got back with the canvas Snow was already there and had the engine book open. Snow handed the book to Jamie. "Hold this for a minute and give me the canvas."

Jamie watched Snow and Eueas spread the canvas underneath the end of the cylinder opposite the giant wheels.

Snow straightened up and rubbed his back. "Now we start with the easy stuff and work right down to the hard stuff. Jamie, take that monkey wrench and pull the spark plug." He handed Jamie the wrench and extended his hand for the book.

279

Jamie handed over the book and took the wrench. It was heavier than he expected and his hand almost slipped on the greasy wooden handle. He spun the adjustment screw and applied the wrench to the spark plug, but Eueas piped in.

"Hadn't nobody ever told you how to use a wrench before, boy? Shit. Turn that wrench the 'tother way 'round. You supposed to put the wrench on the backside of the nut as you're pullin' to you. Here…" Eueas spit on the ground, leaned his cane up against the engine and took the wrench out of Jamie's hands. He applied the wrench to the plug and looked back at Jamie. "Now try it. It'll stay on the nut better that way."

Jamie pulled on the wrench, then pulled harder. The plug didn't budge. He put his foot up against the foundation and pulled as hard as he could and the wrench slipped off the plug and Jamie found himself on his butt in the dirt. He looked up. Eueas was half-smiling, half his teeth showing against his filthy face. He evidently enjoyed Jamie in the dirt.

"Try it again, Jamie." Snow put down the engine book. "We need some parts. Be back." He looked at Jamie. "Try again." Jamie watched Snow walk off and he was suddenly uneasy.

Jamie pushed himself to his feet. He dusted off his bottom and put the wrench back on the plug and pulled as hard as he could, his anger at Eueas feeding his strength. The plug still didn't budge.

Eueas moved forward and took the wrench out of Jamie's hand. "Shit. Let me at it, boy."

Jamie moved out of the way, feeling utterly useless.

Eueas applied the wrench to the plug, held his left hand over the wrench and plug together and pushed down on the handle of the monkey wrench, using his weight against the stubborn plug. It gave with a slight squeal. Eueas continued to turn it, not offering the wrench back to Jamie. He spun the plug out with his fingers. "Here. Scrape the carbon off that." He tossed the plug out to Jamie.

Jamie reached, but the flying plug fell just short of his reach and dropped in the dirt.

"Don't drop it in the dirt, boy. Spark plugs is just like people, they don't like dirt." Eueas turned away from Jamie.

"How the hell would you know about that?" Jamie muttered under his breath."

Eueas whirled back to Jamie with fire in his eyes. "What'd you say to me, boy?"

Jamie didn't answer.

Snow's footsteps approached.

Jamie held Eueas' eyes but nothing more was said and Snow made his appearance through the doorway with a wooden box under his arm. "Got the parts." He put the box down and picked the engine book up again.

Eueas looked at Snow then back at Jamie as he spoke. "We don't need that book none."

Snow opened the book and spoke to Eueas as if Eueas hadn't said anything at all. "We're gonna do everything by this here book. One thing right after the' other. You want to take a look here, Eueas?"

Jamie saw Eueas' face shift, his eyes shifting from Jamie and over toward the book in Snow's hands. "They got any pictures in there?"

Snow flipped a couple of pages back and forth and shook his head. "A few, not many."

Eueas turned directly back to the engine, wrench in hand. "I guess I'll just turn the' screws then. That's what I'm good at."

"Suit yourself. Jamie, come on and help me with this."

Jamie did. He read the instructions one by one. Snow did what the book said with Eueas helping here and there, usually after saying "You sure that's what it says, boy?"

When Jamie read it again just the same, just as it was printed, Eueas cursed under his breath.

They went all the way though the fuel pump, the governor, the mixer where the fuel was mixed with air and finally the cam that drove the exhaust valve connecting rod.

For a wonderful little space of time, Jamie actually forgot Eueas was there. When they had completed all the work Snow wiped his hands on a rag and dug his pocket watch out of his front overalls pocket. "'Bout time for that mornin' break whistle. Let's knock off and crank it after." He looked at Jamie. "Better get

281

cleaned up now. Gather up the tools and bring them up to the cabin."

Jamie noticed Eueas was no longer happy. He glanced at Jamie a couple of times while they were gathering and straightening tools. Jamie got a particular glare when he reminded Eueas he still had an open end wrench in his back pocket. Eueas stopped and slowly reached into his back pocket and handed it to him. "I know, boy. I don't need you to tell me how to put tools away." Eueas spat on the ground right in front of Jamie. "I done it a few times before. Just a few, you understand." Eueas' eyes were slits.

Snow spoke up from the other side of the engine. "Come on, Jamie, let's get them tools put up." Snow walked off, papers in hand.

Eueas finished wiping his hands with a rag and dropped it in the dirt at Jamie's feet. "That's right, boy." He stuck one hand in his overall strap and lifted his cane into the air before he leaned on it. "You get them tools put up now. Don't you miss nothin', cause your daddy'll tan your hide."

With that Eueas turned and stumped with his cane over toward the cabin and did not look back, leaving Jamie to clean everything up.

The train whistle blew just as Jamie walked into the cabin with the box of tools under his arm. His heart flipped a beat. Nosy Norris stood there, a package in hand, standing in front of his father's desk. He stretched a smile underneath his hatchet nose at Jamie.

"Mr. Garrath, I have something to discuss with you."

"What's that?"

Norris drew himself up to his full scrawny height. "They laughed at me, Mr. Garrath. They laughed at me."

"Who?"

"Your boys, is who." Nosy nodded toward Jamie.

Jamie's father shook his head. "I don't have but one son and he works here."

Norris nodded. "They were riding in the back of your truck, Mr. Garrath, the morning this happened. I saw them. I work early morning and you was on your way to work."

"Oh, you mean ..." He waved at the scratches on Norris' face.

Norris dipped his nose in a grave nod, crossed his arms and his mouth pressed into a frown.

Jamie's father tossed his pencil down on his desk and leaned back in his chair. "Nathan, you can hardly blame them for laughing." He smiled, open and easy. "Now I know it wasn't at all funny to you. But even you have to admit that a couple of fourteen year old kids might, just might, find the sight of somebody fighting off a tomcat funny, no matter who it happened to or who set it up. They're just boys."

"You know about it?"

"They told me." Jamie's father interlaced his fingers, placed his hands on the back of his head and leaned back in a stretch. His easy smile did not ease or slip in the least. "They see a lot of things. And usually tell me."

Norris' face froze. "They tell you what they see."

"And did."

Norris stared at Grant for a long still moment, his mouth growing, if anything, even tighter and thinner and paler. He nodded just once. "Here's your package, Mr. Garrath."

Jamie held his face tight to keep his grin down.

His father leaned forward and nodded back. "Thank you kindly. It was nice of you to bring it all this way. I appreciate it."

Norris turned and walked out of the office. Jamie caught a glimpse of his face as Norris climbed into his truck. It was dark red and tight.

Snow came into the office. "What's eatin' him, Mr. Garrath? That man got a come-up-a-cloud on his face for sure."

"Nothing. He's just learning to live in the light is all."

"I sure am glad to hear it, Mr. Garrath. Maybe he'll go to church now. I know he got nothing to wear 'cept that postman's hat and a Carolina tuxedo, but that'd be all right. Sunday-go-to-meeting do everbody good."

"Carolina tuxedo?"

"Come on, Mr. Garrath, even Jamie knows that." Snow's smile beamed white. "That's a new pair of overalls with the hammer loop ironed down flat."

Jamie couldn't help but grin and breathed easy when his father did too. "Well I'm sure God wouldn't mind as long as he shows up."

At the mid-morning break Ned leaned up against the big oak tree by the office and closed his eyes. Cyrus sat down beside him. They both sat in silence, Ned because he had a lot to think about and Cyrus because that was just Cyrus. Ned knew it unnerved a lot of people Cyrus didn't seem to care whether they liked him or not, but to Ned that was a thing he could stand to have more of himself. Ned was glad they had finished working trees a bit early. He liked the quiet spells. They felt like a crack in the millstones of the workday where he could stick his nose up to the sky and breathe. Seemed like the older he got the narrower and fewer between those cracks got. He had just leaned his head back and was feeling the stillness of a good snooze taking hold of his head when he heard Dancin' Charlie's high cackle sear the air.

"I told' him that when I leave the cash in a blind hole that I expect a return now, that I expect a return. I don' mean to get mean or nothin', but a man ought to do what he says he gonna do, that's the way it is, that's the way it's 'sposed to be, now ain't it?"

Ned opened his eyes and looked over at the next tree to see Marshall ease himself down onto the ground in the shade. Marshall's tone was patient as he watched Charlie jump around. "What did he say?"

Charlie punched holes in the air with his finger toward the ground. "He said he done it, that he put it in there just like he said. He says it won't his fault that somebody up and got it 'fore I got there. And I says 'How likely is that?' "

Ned watched Charlie wave his arms all over the air. The man was in a right state. But Ned got the feeling it wasn't the loss of money itself that bothered Charlie so much as it was Charlie had planned on having his moonshine.

"And I told him I was standin' there like a wagon without a mule and places to get to. And he says again that won't his fault and I says again 'how likely is that, with that holler tree bein' so far deep down in the woods almost to the river like it is. Ain't nobody 'round here coulda found it or followed me in, no sir. No sir! That blind hole's as good a blind hole as I ever see and now he's tellin' me it ain't good no more and that's damn sure, now ain't it?"

Charlie plowed on, but Ned was no longer listening. He turned to Cyrus. Cyrus looked right back and then with a movement so slight that only Ned could see it he lifted his eyebrows and his shoulders at the same time.

Ned closed his eyes, leaned his head back against the tree and thought. Charlie was right. No one from this part of the country had found that hole. Cyrus had to have come across it in his wanderings, not knowing who it belonged to. Weren't Indians that way anyway? They didn't understand personal stuff as personal the way white folks did? And hadn't Cyrus given Ned a Barlow knife when he found out he didn't have one? That truck drove both ways. Possessions didn't mean much to them so it wasn't like it was really stealing to him anyway. And Jamie had not told. Jamie had decided Cyrus could keep his job, even though it was against his father's rules, as long as he stayed safe. Ned knew part of all this talking to himself was just to convince himself of what he was going to do anyway. He had already swallowed the lie, felt like a stain was darkening his insides like wild blackberry juice on a clean white shirt. But what choice did he have? To have stood up and shouted his anger would do more harm than good, cause nothing' but hurt. Damned if he was gonna spout off like fat old Craphorn. No, he'd keep the stain. He didn't need to be 'burned clean by the searing fires of righteousness' as old Thunderbuns had put it. He'd be damned if he was gonna do that.

285

Chapter 45

Castaway

Jamie felt Ned's silence as they rattled and shook in the back of the pickup as it bounced over the washboard road to the mill. Not only did Ned not say anything, but whenever Jamie glanced over Ned was looking the other way. When they pulled up to office cabin in the mill yard Jamie leapt out to get away. He was trotting toward the chugger shed before the dust had settled.

Snow's call brought him up short. "Hold on there, young fella!"

Jamie turned to see Snow walking toward him. "Hey."

Snow spat snuff on the ground. "Not today, sorry."

"But it ain't run yet."

Snow grimaced, cleared the snuff out of his mouth then spat again. "If it runs, we gonna be sawin' today. And your mama would have my hide and your daddy's nailed side by side on the smokehouse by sundown if we let you within' spittin' distance of that sawblade."

Jamie's gumption gushed out like someone had pulled a drain plug. He swallowed and stuffed his hands in his pockets. "So what today then?

Snow smiled with one side of his mouth. "Both you boys gonna be whitewashing."

"Whitewashing what? We've done everything in here twice over."

"Kiln."

Jamie's mouth dropped, words dead in his mouth before they were born. The wood-drying kiln had never been whitewashed. It was made of brick.

Snow pulled his dollar watch from his front overall pocket. "Time for me to get going. You know what's to do. Once I get everybody to workin' the saw I'll come t'check on you."

'Come to check on you.' Jamie muttered as he watched Snow hitch his way to the saw shed lean-to. Snow was the sawyer. He would not be 'checking on them' any time soon.

Jamie turned and trudged back to the truck.

Ned leaned against the truck door, hands deep in his pockets, pulling on the shoulder straps on his overalls.

Jamie walked over and kicked the back tire of his father's truck.

Ned pushed himself up from his lean. "What?"

"Snow says we're whitewashing today."

"Again? I was waiting for Cyrus, gonna be in the woods today."

"And I was gonna be on the chugger. But that ain't the worst."

Ned just looked at him.

"They got us whitewashing the dry kiln."

Ned's head swiveled toward the brick building at the back of the mill yard. "He's just keeping us out away from the saw, isn't he?"

Jamie nodded. "That's about the size of it."

Ned lifted his shoulders and let them drop again.

Jamie turned toward the paint shed.

They passed by a bit away from the saw and the engine shed. The engine hadn't been cranked yet.

Jamie looked back over his shoulder and saw Ned lift his head up a little and walk on tip-toe to see better. He had to be looking for Cyrus. Jamie wondered about his father. He slowed to a stop to look and Ned passed him by.

He heard the jingle of harness behind him, then 'Git outa way, comin' through." Jamie stepped to the side just in time for the mule 'Mrs. Ace' to thud past, followed closely by Lester Jones, who pulled on long cotton plow line reins wrapped across his shoulders and dodged the heavy log as it rolled to one side. Lester laughed as he drove Mrs. Ace past him. "Sorry 'bout that, once she starts to pull she don' wanna stop."

Jamie watched the log dig a dirt-brown serpentine score in the path to the base of the ramp that fed the sawmill carriage platform. He ducked his head and around to peer past the trees. Snow pointed and talked, showing the men what to do and what had to happen. A couple of men leaned on their cant hooks as Jamie's father and a tall thin man with sandy hair showed them how to use the hooks to work the logs up the ramp.

"Who's that tall fella?" Ned whispered over his shoulder.

"New to me. He seems to know what he's doin'."

"We better get going."

"Hold on. Whitewashin's just busywork to keep us from underfoot. As long as we stay far enough away we can't get in too much trouble. I want to see what's going on."

Jamie worked his way through the trees until he found a good view of the saw under its pole shelter and the platform of horizontal beams that fed logs onto the carriage.

Jamie glanced over at Ned. Ned had not moved from his spot, so Jamie motioned for him to come over and look. Ned had just put his hands in his pockets to amble over toward Jamie when a loud bang rocked the air. Ned jumped a foot sideways and literally left his hat in the air.

Jamie clapped his hand over his mouth to keep from laughing out loud.

After a short pause several more bangs followed in succession, then the explosions leveled out to the irregular chugging heartbeat of the twenty horse hit and miss engine. Though it was out of his vision, in his mind's eye Jamie could see the huge wheels spinning, the green spokes a blur and the rocker arms at the end of the cylinder, heavy metronomic motions on springs ticking and clicking back and forth in the midst of irregular explosions. What Jamie could see from where he stood was the wide flat belt coming from inside the engine shed out over to the broad drive pulley at the saw gear box drive shaft. He had not seen that belt before. As Snow pressed down on the lever the belt tightened and began to move. It twisted and turned like a great tortured flat snake in the air. The teeth of the blade disappeared in motion and a sandpaper ring filled Jamie's ears as the saw teeth ground the air.

The tall man with sandy hair showed Howard Mohegan how to use a cant hook. They wrestled the first log across the loading platform and onto the sliding carriage works that held the log and ran it into the blade to be sawn off plank by plank. Three mechanical columns that looked like car bumper jacks stuck straight up from the edge of the carriage and Sandy Hair and Howard cant hooked the log up against them, always rolling the log uphill. Snow came over and lowered the downward pointing spike attached to these columns onto the log and cranked a screw to hold it down tight.

Jamie watched Snow step over onto the sawyer's platform next to the blade and grasp the tall black handle coming up out of the box of gears and shafts and pulleys next to the blade. Snow moved the handle, a magician with his giant wand stuck into the ground, and the log began to move toward the blade. As the log rode up and touched the edge of the blade, the blade sang a high one-note wavering ring that sent a shiver up Jamie's spine until the log disappeared on the other side beyond Jamie's view. He saw Snow wave his wand again and the log returned, sliding back along the way it had come. The log had a great tapered yellow stripe across its side where the saw blade had taken the first cut of the season. Jamie knew that was not the first board. The first cut on any log produced what was called a 'slab' or an 'outsider', sawn surface on one side and round bark on the other. The second cut would produce the first real board, but with the first cut Jamie felt this place turn from logging camp to saw mill. The storage areas he and Ned had sling bladed clean of high grass and weeds would be filled with stacks of bright yellow lumber which would, in turn, disappear and be replaced by other stacks. In that moment the mill became real, a sort of living thing. He was truly glad to be where he was.

"If you've finished admiring yourself, we got work to do."

Jamie turned to Ned. "Don't you want to watch this?"

Ned nodded small. "I guess. But it's awful loud, emphasis on the awful. I'd just as soon be away from it."

"You go ahead. I'll be there in a minute."

Ned turned without another word and walked away, hands in pockets and head down.

Jamie turned back just in time to see the tall man and Howard turn the log on the carriage works until the flat side was face down and they spiked it in place again. Then he watched Snow wave his long black wand and the log slid forward into the next cut.

Then he saw Cyrus walk up with logging chain strung across his shoulder. He spoke to the tall sandy-haired man. They turned to Snow, talked, pointed at the logs and gestured with their hands, then Snow nodded in understanding. They were laying out lengths of chain along the inclined loading rails when Snow caught sight of him. Snow cocked his head over to one side at Jamie and threw his thumb over his shoulder.

Jamie tore his eyes away and slumped toward the paint shed.

When he got there Ned was already gone from the shed. Jamie had no idea how Ned had managed to carry a five gallon bucket of whitewash all by himself, but found out when he caught up. Ned had the bucket handle in both his hands and had bucket sitting on his left foot so as he picked up his foot he lifted the bucket at the same time.

"Need any help with that?"

"Oh, all you care to give."

Jamie reached out and grabbed the bail handle and together they carried the bucket, one on either side, over to the kiln.

Little Foot Carson was waiting for them. "Took ya long enough."

Jamie heard Ned respond in gasps. "We was watching them get started on the sawing." They set the bucket down on the ground between them.

"Ah." Little Foot smiled, a tight white grin against his coal black skin. "It don't pay to get too close, I can tell you from experience, get hurt you don't watch out. You young folks better off right here with me." He looked down at the bucket. "What's that for?"

"Snow said we're supposed to whitewash the kiln."

Little Foot shook his head. "Nah. Kiln don't never get no whitewash. Tell you what needs doin' though, and that's sawin' them scraps over there into short pieces so I can use 'em to fire up the kiln." He pointed to a pile of lumber off to the side.

Jamie looked over at the pile. It didn't look too bad. "I guess we can do that."

"Don't smile too soon. You get to saw up the slabs when they get here too."

"Slabs?" Ned's voice in Jamie's ear was flat.

Little Foot nodded. "The stuff what comes off the log when they first start to saw. It's bark on one side so it ain't a board as such. Only thing it's good for is burnin'. Once the kiln's loaded up and cookin' I gotta keep it going for up to a month. Takes a lot of wood."

"Okay, but Snow told us to whitewash."

Little Foot nodded again. "Tell you what, I'll go tell Snow what I got for ya to do. Get started on that pile there and I'll be back in a minute." He set off in his hitch-n-swing stride, but half turned back and made a cutting motion against his arm about the elbow. "Cut 'em 'bout arm's length, fingertip to elbow, what the good book calls a cubit, that's what I need." He turned back around and swung off toward the noise of the saw.

Jamie watched him go. "Well, at least it ain't whitewashing."

Ned didn't answer, so Jamie put down his brush on top of the bucket and walked over to the sawing cross bucks next to the pile. There was a one-man crosscut saw leaning up against it and a short pile of firewood already started. "You want to hold or saw first?"

"I'll saw."

So they went at it. First they lifted the piece of wood, whether a slab, a small log or a board too checked and damaged to use onto the crossbucks. Then one held while the other took the one-man cross cut saw and buzzed away at it till the piece fell on the ground. They wordlessly worked out a system where the holder picked up and stacked while the sawer took a breather, then they'd switch places and start again.

By the time the afternoon whistle blew Jamie felt like his arms were going to drop out of their shoulder sockets.

Little Foot limped out of the kiln house wearing his great white grin and glanced at the pile they had sawed and stacked. "You boys done pretty good."

Neither Jamie nor Ned moved or answered. Jamie could only grasp that he didn't have to work any more that day. He felt the weight of the saw disappear as Little Foot lifted it from his hands. "You boys go on now; I'll take care of this. See you tomorrow."

Jamie and Ned plodded in the dust away toward the office cabin.

Jamie's father was just coming out the door and down the cabin steps when they reached it. "Hey, you fellas want to go to the post office with me?"

Jamie nodded. The thought of just sitting down appealed to him immensely and the thought of sitting in the moving truck with a breeze in his face appealed to him even more. He looked at Ned, but Ned already had his fishing pole in his hand. Jamie shook his head. "I'm sorry. I never thought I'd ever say this, but I'm just too tired to fish."

Ned just nodded, turned without a word and headed toward the gate and the path to Little Lake.

Jamie watched him go, then walked to the pickup, slid open the door and climbed into the cab. He had never been so glad to sit down in his life. He watched his father through the windshield talking with Snow. They both nodded at each other, then Jamie heard them say 'See you Monday' and his father stepped over to the truck and climbed in. His father slid his door shut with a heavy tin can bang and leaned on the starter button. The engine turned over with a sandy grind and coughed to life.

Eueas stumped up to his father's window. "Mr. Garrath, did I hear you say you headed for the post office?"

"That I am."

"Can I hitch a ride? You mind? I'd like to check for mail."

"All right, sure." His father inclined his head at Eueas in the direction of the back of the pickup. "Hop in the back."

They waited for Eueas to clamber in the back of the truck, then Jamie leaned his head back on the seat and held on to the door as his father backed the pickup around then drove out of the yard.

"I hope we get some rain soon. Not too soon 'cause we got to get those logs in that we cut yesterday and get them cut up, but we sure could use some rain."

Jamie lifted his head and turned to his father but his father was looking at the windshield. "How come Eueas is getting off early?"

"He's not." His father glanced over at him and give a slight smile. "It's Saturday, Jamie. I'm kinda surprised you and Ned weren't already gone fishing."

"Oh, yeah. I guess we forgot." Jamie leaned his head back down. He really wanted nothing more than to go to sleep, but his head was bouncing too much and after one particularly nasty pothole jerk that banged his head all the way up off the seat, he kept his head up against the motion.

When they pulled out on the main road the motion and the breeze both got much better. Jamie felt like he had just put his head back down when it seemed they pulled into the parking lot of the post office.

Jamie's father pulled into a parking place and pulled the park brake. He turned to Jamie. "You can stay here if you want. I just want to see if the contract checks are here." His father's smile was a little tight.

"No, I'll come in."

Jamie slid the pickup door open and out of his seat onto the ground. The time was just past midday and the sun beat down on the ground and the truck and Jamie. He placed his hands on the truck door to close it with his hands but it was already too hot to touch so he left it be. By the time he pushed through the door his father and Eueas were already inside. His father was opening the sawmill PO box and Eueas was at the counter. Jamie clumped over to the bench where the best flow of air was coming off the ceiling fan. He sat on the bench, leaned back, stretched out his legs and closed his eyes. His shirt was wet with sweat even after the ride and he could feel the crust of dirt from the dusty ground of the mill. The breeze felt cool on his face and neck. He heard the rustle of papers and opened his eyes expecting to see his father sifting through the mail on the side counter but it was not his father. It was Eueas. He was rifling his way through the clipboard stack of wanted circulars. About a half inch into the stack one seemed to hold his interest but he dropped it with a start and quickly crushed the stack closed flat with his hand when his Jamie's father came up behind him.

"Lookin' for someone in particular, Eueas?" His father smiled at Eueas, then looked down to his own papers and began to sort. "No one you know, I trust?"

Jamie saw Eueas' face freeze for a moment then grip into a sudden forced smile. "Oh no, Mr. Garrath. Nothin' like that. Just like to keep up with things is all."

His father just kept sorting the mail, eyes down on the papers. "Well, that's fine, Eueas. That's just fine." His father looked up over his shoulder as the door rattled open behind him. "'Scuse me, Eueas, but there's a man I gotta talk to." His father scooped up the mail between his two hands, placed it in Jamie's lap and turned to talk with Old Man Mason.

Jamie grasped at the mass of mail in his lap to keep it from falling on the floor. He gripped the pile with his elbow and with the other hand arranged and sorted until it was under control. When he looked up, he saw Eueas looking right at him, Eueas' grimy hands rubbing down the front of his overalls down flat. Jamie felt Eueas' eyes on him as he sat there with his arms full of the newspaper and letters.

"Not at all, Mr. Garrath. Not at all." Eueas' eyes bored into Jamie, flicked over to the stack of wanted circulars. The man hitched up his overalls, set his hat with the brim down over his eyes, then pulled the glass door open and stepped out, letting the door bang behind him to the tune of the door's little signal bell at the top hanging from its little flat spiral spring.

Jamie had a feeling that something different had just happened, but couldn't put it together. He rose, placed the pile of papers on the counter and looked through the mass of wanted circulars.

From the top, most were wanted circulars for individuals for murder, mayhem, assault, robbery, mail fraud and abetting, whatever that was. Some had photographs on them, grainy images of disheveled men with anger in their eyes.

Jamie looked over his shoulder and saw his father across the room deep in talk and hand gestures with Old Man Mason.

He turned back to the stack and sifted deeper until he came across one with a deep fold across the middle where Eueas had slammed the stack shut. Jamie flattened the paper out with his hand and read.

The circular offered a one thousand dollar reward for an Indian named John Wanderwood. The description said he was about six feet four inches in height, approximately one hundred and sixty pounds in weight, of medium dark complexion with black hair and black eyes. The man had a tattoo of a black bird on his right shoulder. Professions included fisherman, fishing and hunting guide, tracker, and lumberjack. He was of the Makah tribe. He and his brother Hegan were wanted for assault and battery against five men who were having a private party near Port Townsend, Washington State. The man was said to be armed and dangerous.

Jamie folded the papers back down and hung the clipboard back up on the wall. The only Indian around here was Cyrus Conner. He shrugged. There was just no figuring Eueas.

Chapter 46
In Spite of Faith

It was dark when Jamie awakened to a slow splatter of rain. He drew off his sheet and padded over to the window to slide it closed against the wet, but with no wind just the odd few tendril drips slid down the screen. He breathed in cool moist air, felt it waft softly against his skin and listened to the drizzle slop on the walkway stones outside.

It was Sunday. The rain and a day off suited him. He was tired, tired to his bones from hard work, not sleeping and watching over his shoulder for Eueas, alone and without the strength to either fight or run. He didn't trust the man as far as he could have heaved a house. At least for today, he would not have to be afraid.

Ned's bedclothes rustled behind him. "It's gonna be hard logging tomorrow."

Jamie glanced to the voice. Ned had pushed himself up to sit and rubbed his eyes.

"That so?"

Ned yawned into the back of his hand. "So Cyrus says. Rain makes hard logging but good tracking."

Jamie turned away from the rain. "Tracking?"

"Yeah. Cyrus is teaching me."

"Is it hard to do?"

"A different kind of hard." Ned scratched his head. "You have to hold yourself still so you can see what's in front of you. Know what I mean?"

Jamie shrugged. "I don't know. Never paid much attention to it. Look," Jamie glanced out the window, "if it stops raining in time, you want to go fishing after church?"

"All right. But right now all I want is to sleep some more." Ned fell back and buried his head under his pillow.

Jamie turned toward the window. The rain gently dripped in the soft gray early morning light. After the rain fishing might be good. Or not. It just depended if the fish gorged themselves on bugs falling in the water the way Sabastian had told him.

The Right Reverend Costigan Abalicious Cramphorne gripped the podium and took a deep breath to fill his barrel chest.

"This morning, my brethren, I wish to speak with you about a subject both near and dear to my heart. I want to speak with you about personal responsibility. If we ask ourselves what that is, the answer could not be any easier, it is in the very words themselves. It is responsibility for oneself, taking the traces of righteousness in our hands," Cramphorne held his meaty fists in front of him like he was holding reins, "and guide the steed of our lives down the straight and narrow path. We must not" he raised one finger into the air above his head "allow our petty desires, our petty little selfishnesses to get in the way, to drive us into the tangled undergrowth of the devil. We must sit tall in the saddle and keep our eyes focused on that straight and narrow path."

Jamie felt pressure on his shoulder and heard Ned whisper in his ear. "What in the ever-lovin' blue blazes is he talking about?"

Jamie leaned a little back towards Ned. "Sounds to me like he's been listening to too much 'Death Valley Days' on the radio."

"You know when we go fishing the girls might be at the lake."

"Oh, yeah." Jamie's memory of sun-burnished auburn hair was splintered by a painful pop on his skull as his father thumped the back of his head. "Ow."

"You boys hush." His father's voice right in his ear. "You are not too old to be taken outside."

His father's pew creaked as he leaned back again. Jamie rubbed his head before he looked at the minister. Cramphorne smiled directly at him with happily narrowed eyes. Jamie set his mouth and looked at the hymnal rack on the pew in front of him.

297

Cramphorne's voice boomed and echoed. "We need to make certain we take care of ourselves and those within our care. Our responsibility does not stop there, oh no. We must take responsibility for our church and all who come within, for that is our sacred duty to assist where and when we can, for the church is not these walls." He spread his hands to encompass the sanctuary. "The church is a fellowship, a fraternity of brothers and sisters in Christ; the Bible tells us so. We must help our brothers and sisters who ask it of us and feel the power of God, of righteousness as we do so and woe be to him that does not, for he ..."

Right about there Jamie's ears stopped listening to the reverend. Soft water sounds drew his attention to the window where the covering patter of rain on the ground just outside drowned out the bombast. He noticed streaks of drops scatter on the surface of the glass like God was waving a giant sprinkler can above them. Cool moist air reached in the window and caressed his skin. He felt warm and still inside and wondered if that was God talking to him.

His serenity did not last. A loud bang echoed through the sanctuary and he jumped. Again his ears were filled with the harsh grind of Cramphorne's bombast.

"I tell you my brothers and sister, I tell you I know as much as I know anything that good Christians are seared, tempered, burned clean of all their nasty greasy sins by the searing white hot fires of righteousness. We should be like a bar of iron fresh from the blacksmith's forge, white-hot with the glow of righteousness, ready to be hammered straight and strong and tall by the forge of God known as this Good Book." He lifted the huge podium bible over his head and shook it. "This good book is the anvil and hammer of God and it is our duty to bend and be forged into the shape and temper of truth and righteousness. It is only our pride that keeps us from doing God's work when we think it is beneath us, when we think that we are too good to get our hands dirty and feel the sweat upon our brows. Be not arrogant, my brethren, be not arrogant and keep yourself from God's holy work."

After the service Jamie and Ned slipped out the side door. Ned went in search of his mom and dad, so Jamie found a dry spot on the ground under one of the pines that sheltered the church. The rain had almost stopped and Jamie felt only an occasional drip onto his scalp. Quiet steam rose from the ground and hung in the air.

He sat and leaned his head back against the tree. As he looked out over the fields beyond the churchyard he saw the lonely figure of Sabastian, shadow black against the gray mist, collar up and hat down against the wet, walking in his oddly graceful loping stride away from the church, hands stuck deep in his pockets.

When Sabastian disappeared behind the trees around the bend in the road Jamie turned back toward the church. From his vantage point he saw the congregation slowly thread piecemeal past the one man gauntlet of the Right Reverend Cramphorne at the door. After being filtered through this bottleneck by the meaty hands of the reverend, they flowed out onto the church grounds and collected in small shifting groups to exchange news. They fanned church bulletins in front of their faces and several pinched shirts and blouses by the shoulders and lifted against the sticky air.

At the church door his father shook hands with the Reverend. His father nodded and moved to step away but the reverend held onto his hand and kept talking. His father turned to move away again. Once more the reverend clung to his hand. His father's back stiffened straight. Then Jamie saw his father slowly reach and take the reverend's wrist hard with his left hand and jerk his right from the reverend's grasp. His father turned and walked away with firm fists swinging at his sides. His father never broke stride all the way to the car.

Jamie's mother trailed behind and pulled Gloria along with her. Gloria tottered on tiptoe, hugged her stuffed monkey and talked up to her. Jamie's mother stopped and responded, then straightened and scanned the crowd. When she saw Jamie she waved him over with one white-gloved hand.

Jamie pushed himself to his feet and trotted over. "What is it, Momma?"

"Do you know where Ned is?"

"Not really. He went to find his folks, but I don't know where they are."

"You go on and sit in the car with your daddy." She extended Gloria's hand to him. "Here, take Gloria and I'll be with you as soon as I can find him. Understand?"

"Yes ma'am."

She walked off at a brisk pace, her church pumps crunching the gravel and one hand holding her white straw bonnet in place while her head swiveled back and forth scanning the crowd.

Jamie bent to his little sister. "All right Kid, what happened up there?"

Gloria's shoulders rose and fell again so quickly they almost thumped. "I don't know. We just came out and I was just talking to momma that one of Monkey's eyes was gone and then I ran into the back of Daddy. He and the preacher were talking about a garden and weeds or something and then Daddy got mad and Momma dragged me over here."

"Come on kid, let's go to the car."

"Where's Momma gone?"

"You heard her, she's going to find Ned. She'll be back in a minute."

"So Ned's coming back? He's going to stay?"

"He's gonna be with us all summer. I thought you knew that." He drew Gloria slowly over toward the car.

Gloria smiled and hugged her stuffed monkey closer. "Okay."

When they got to the car his father already sat in the driver's seat with the door ajar and one foot propped on the running board. He was smoking a cigarette. He had seen his daddy smoke before, but not a lot and never at church.

Jamie opened the back door and helped Gloria into the back seat.

As they settled in his father spoke without turning around. "Where's your momma?"

"She went looking for Ned. He's talking with his folks somewhere."

"Soon as she gets back we're goin' home." His father drew another drag into his lungs. He held the cigarette out of the window but when he exhaled the smoke was still heavy and acrid in the small space of the car.

His mother and Ned soon returned. She had one hand still on top of her straw bonnet and the other on Ned's shoulder, though Ned's pace didn't look as though he needed any urging. When they reached the car she opened the back door for him. "You sit in the back with Jamie and Gloria now, honey."

"Yes ma'am." Ned slid in and closed the door behind him. Gloria looked up at Ned slowly and grinned her gap-tooth smile. Ned looked down at her and smiled back but there were no teeth in it.

As soon as his mother's bottom hit the seat Jamie's father pulled his door to with a bang and had the car cranked and grinding through the gravel out of the church yard.

Gloria leaned up toward the front seat. "Why are we going home so soon, Momma?"

"Hush now honey, we're just going to get an early start on dinner, that's all."

"But why, Momma?"

Jamie's father took another drag on his cigarette and spat his words, expelling smoke like an angry dragon. "Expects me to weed his garden, he says. 'Expects', can you believe the unmitigated gall of that man?"

Jamie's mother was quiet. The back seat riders followed suit. She laid one hand on his father's shoulder as he drove.

Another drag and more smoke speaking, "We already mow all the grass around the manse as it is when we mow the churchyard and now he thinks we're going to weed his little personal garden? The man wouldn't lift a finger to hit a lick at a snake." Another drag. "The man's got more money than Croesus and he 'expects' us to weed his damn little … Well, if he thinks that he'd damn well better have another think comin' 'cause that ain't gonna happen, not in this lifetime it ain't. God-damned pile a'…"

"Grant, honey?" Jamie's mother rubbed his father's shoulder again.

Another tight-lipped drag on his cigarette. "All right. All right, you're right. Enough." He took one more deep breath drag and spoke under his breath and he tossed the cigarette butt out the window. "Damn right enough."

His mother drew another cigarette, lit it and handed it to his father.

Jamie leaned back against the seat. He thought about Sabastian's shabby clothes, thought about Cramphorne's money and thought about the garden that needed weeding. And smiled.

Chapter 47

Slogging Part Deux

"Do we really have to leave him behind?" Jamie held on to Toby, who stood in the bed of the pickup. Rain dripped from the brim of his hat. "He'll just come through the woods anyway."

His father dropped the tailgate. "Not today. You won't have time for him and neither will I." He beckoned at the dog standing in the back of the truck. "Come on down, boy."

Toby looked at Jamie's father then licked Jamie's face. He jumped to the ground, loped over to the front porch and plumped down on the grass doormat out of the rain.

Ned spoke from over his shoulder. "He's all right with it."

"Yeah." Jamie waved at Toby. "Sorry, boy. See you this afternoon."

Toby gave a soft woof in response and laughed an open mouthed pant.

"All right, troops." His father slammed the tailgate back up and attached the chains. "Jump in, let's get at it."

Jamie climbed into the cab of the truck. Ned squeezed in beside him. Jamie had to put his elbows in front of him and hold his legs to the side out of the way of the stick shift and brake lever. His father's shoulder shoved him to one side as he leaned forward to press the starter button. The engine ground and coughed to life then his father jammed the truck into gear and released the brake lever.

They rolled out of the yard and turned left onto the main road, splashing through a big mud puddle at the end of the lane. The windshield wipers plopped back and forth giving intermittent images of the world. Water sprayed in from underneath the sliding door windows.

They passed by a field of corn, small splintered stalks reaching for the rain.

"Rain's too late for that corn." Jamie's father had his window cracked in the vain attempt to keep fog from the windshield and peered through the slit as he steered. "Bad Luck Byron."

Byron Thomas was the farmer whose land adjoined theirs. The family had little to spare. Only the eldest boy and girl ever had anything like new clothes and those not often. The rest lived in hand-me-downs. Quiet and well-favored, they were always too busy making ends meet to be very social.

The smell of the rain was cool in Jamie's nose. All his body wanted to do was go back to sleep.

When they entered the road through the woods he gave in to it, leaned his head back on the seat and closed his eyes. Beneath his eyelids he saw Deidre, all long legs, brilliant smile and auburn hair. A blink later he was jarred back to the present. He looked around and saw they had just banged through the big mud hole in front of the mill gate with a splash of thick brown water.

Snow was waiting for them in his old yellow slicker with what men had shown up for work. Those that had them wore slickers. Those that didn't stood wet in the rain with their hands in their pockets, soaked shirts sticking to their skin.

"We're short this mornin'. We got enough to do logging, but we don't have a man to handle the mules on the drag carts too." Snow turned and spat snuff in the wet dirt.

"Use Eueas as the hook up man."

Snow shook his head. "He says he can't. Says he ain't nimble enough."

"Dammit. And I need Cyrus and Ned to scout today." Jamie's father frowned and shook his head. "Do we have enough timber close enough to work off the logging road today?"

Snow nodded.

"All right." Grant rubbed his eyes under his glasses. "Instead of two mules on the drag carts, hook up one for the woods trail. We'll hook up the Fordson for the logging road. I'll have Jamie drive it. We'll just transfer the logs from one to the other where the woods path meets the log road."

Jamie's heart jumped. His mother had hated his dad's Fordson tractor every since she'd read an article about one that reared up on its hind wheels and flipped over backwards, killing the driver. The magazine had recommended Ford paint a message on every tractor 'Prepare To Meet Thy God.'

"More work for the mule and mule driver." Snow spat again.

His father nodded. "They'll have to slow down in this wet anyway. We won't get much done today is all. But watch'em close, no accidents now. If we work steady we should still have enough to start sawing tomorrow."

"If it don't rain tomorrow."

"Is Lester here to drive the mules?"

Snow spat in the mud. "Oh yeah."

His father nodded. "Good. Let's get done what we can."

Snow touched his cap and headed off towards where the men were gathered on the office porch around the morning coffee station.

"Jamie, come on, let's go."

Jamie trotted in the mud behind his father's long strides. "Yessir?"

His father didn't speak again until they were at the tractor shed.

"You're going to be pulling logs today."

Jamie nodded, afraid to say anything that would make his father change his mind.

"Climb up and sit on the fender now." His father stood by the engine, turned a switch and adjusted something under the gas tank. He reached across Jamie and shifted a long lever with a ring for a handle.

"What's that?"

"Gear lever. Hold on." His father stepped to the front of the tractor, bent down, and heaved on the crank handle. The tractor coughed and wheezed to a stop. His father reached underneath the gas tank on top, made another adjustment and stepped to the front again. This time when he heaved on the crank handle there was a hit, two hits and it died again. Twice more and the engine came to life with a series of heavy breath thuds and the smell of exhaust.

"All right." Jamie's father climbed up into the seat. He leaned over and shouted over the engine noise as he pointed at the various controls. "That's the gear lever, that's the clutch, that's the throttle. Don't touch the throttle." He pushed in the clutch, heaved on the gear lever and let the clutch back out. They jerked forward and his father steered for the back entrance to the mill that opened onto the logging road behind it. There was only the puffing grind of the engine as they drove up to the end of the logging road where there was a widening to turn around and several dragging paths leading into the woods. Lester was waiting with the mule and dragged the first log over to the back of the tractor and started hooking up the chains.

His father stopped the tractor and shouted over the engine noise again. "You, young man, are going to be careful. No daydreaming, I don't want you getting hurt."

"Yessir." Jamie sat on the fender, itching to get into the seat.

"I want you to pull logs from here to just inside the back gate. Somebody will be there to unhitch them from the tractor, then come back here to meet the mule driver and pick up another one. If he's not here when you get here, just take the tractor out of gear and wait for him. More than likely he'll be waiting for you, because you're gonna drive slow, no faster than we just did and you keep it in first gear. If you have trouble just stop and get somebody to help. Do not, I repeat, do not try to shift or hook a log by yourself, that's a good way to get a broken leg. You got it?"

"Yessir."

"You're really helping me out here and I appreciate it, son." We'll see you later." His father got down from the tractor and walked back to talk with Lester.

It was done. Jamie was working logs.

At first it was exciting and new, and Jamie drove carefully up and down the road and every pine cone crunch beneath the steel rim tires was special. But as the day wore on, he began to watch the woods more and more and he smelled the musty swampy earth right along with the tractor exhaust. The clink of chain in the drag cart became an old experience to one so young, so he played the movie of Deidre over and over in his mind.

By the end of the day he was helping with the chains in hookup and Lester the mule driver was smiling at him, glad for the help.

When the afternoon train whistle blew Jamie and Lester had just hooked up a log for Jamie to drag back to the mill though the whistle was hard to hear because of the tractor engine.

Jamie looked at Lester and yelled over the throb of the tractor. "You want a ride back to the mill?"

"Naw, thanks." Lester shook his head then leaned it in the direction of his mule. "Gotta take care of Mrs. Ace."

"How'd she get her name anyway, 'Mrs. Ace'?"

Lester grinned. "When she bitches at me she sounds a lot like that gal on the radio box."

Jamie could not help but laugh. "And I thought I was the only one that thought that."

Lester smiled, very white teeth with gaps on the side. "You go on, I'll be there directly."

Jamie climbed back up into the metal seat of the tractor and sat down. His legs burned with the heat coming up from steel casing beneath him and he held his legs away. Glad this was his last trip, he turned around in the seat to make sure Lester was out of the way, then stood on the steel clutch pedal and rammed the shift lever into low gear. The tractor jerked into motion and chugged down the rough forest road. As he looked back behind the heavy log slewed to one side before it straightened out and dragged a dark line in the wet packed sand. He saw Lester give him one last wave before turning to Mrs. Ace.

By the time he got back the afternoon break was over and everyone was on their feet and moving around under the saw shelter. He stopped the tractor across from the shelter. His father came up and hit the kill switch and after a couple of extra puffs out the exhaust pipe the engine died. Jamie's ears rang in sudden silence.

"You all right?"

Jamie nodded at his father. "Oh yeah. Just a little wet is all. And I can't hear too well."

"Rain never hurt anybody." His father nodded off toward the cabin. "Ned's waiting for you and I got things to do, so I'll see you at the house."

Jamie nodded and watched his father turn toward the men under the saw shelter.

The rain had almost stopped. The wet sandy earth was beaten hard and smooth, with dim pockmarks where slower raindrops had fallen.

Ned was standing by the cabin waiting for Jamie, a fishing pole in either hand.

Jamie nodded at the poles. "I guess we're going fishing."

Ned nodded and grinned. "Yep. Any objections?"

"Nope, not a one."

The wet dripping branches made soft interlapping rings on the water. Jamie's ears still rang. He felt a vacuum in his heart when he saw that Deidre wasn't there. None of the girls at school or church had ever made him feel this way. Georgiana Applegate sniffed at the world, Betty Bridges was certainly healthy in body, but she just could not stop talking and Jenny Cray was, well, a greasy bucktooth rat came to mind. But Deidre … she was different. Jamie had never thought of himself as particularly wild, but something inside him churned and made him want to break away like a hound pulling on his chain.

Jamie walked out to the end of the dock, sat down on the edge and dangled his feet over the water. He heard Ned's footsteps behind him and then felt the vibration through the planks as Ned clumped down beside him. Jamie laid his fishing pole down on the dock and laid back on the rough boards.

"You ain't gonna fish?"

Jamie shook his head. "I'm gonna sit a minute." As he stared out over the water he heard Ned's boots shuffle on the deck boards then a great plunk as a worm-laden hook hit the water.

Jamie's arms ached after man-handling the tractor. But more, he was tired of. That girl had shown him a glimpse of something different, something really different and he felt his insides trying to get outside. He wanted more of that.

At supper that night, Grant spoke to Jamie as he lifted beans onto Jamie's plate.

"Lester had good things to say about you today, Jamie. Thank you, you helped us out of a spot."

"You're welcome, sir."

"I still don't want you doing that as a regular thing, but good job."

Jamie's mother asked, "What did he do?"

Grant stabbed at a slab of country style steak and forked it onto his plate. "Our son dragged logs today."

"You told me he wouldn't do anything dangerous, Grant."

"He just drove the tractor up and down the log road, Hannah. Nothing dangerous, he's fine."

Jamie's mother looked down to her plate and began to crush her fried okra with her fork.

His father gave Jamie one quick look and raised his eyebrow. His father had to know from Lester how Jamie had helped with hookup and handling chains. A log that rolled or dropped or shifted the wrong way could hurt you. He felt the first tendril of a new relationship with his father, the first seed of strong sharing. It gave him deep pleasure, not like the grins from the Nosy Norris thing, but deeper, quieter, the acknowledgement that though still young he was not a little boy any more.

His attention drew back to the supper conversation with the mention of Nosy Norris.

"... apparently our postman had a run-in with the Widow Morrison the other morning." His father smiled and swallowed.

"Something about a cat in her mailbox. You see anything like that on our way by? Jamie? You all right?"

Jamie couldn't speak. He was choking on a mouthful of mashed potatoes. Finally he nodded and took a sip of iced tea.

His mother leaned forward. "I heard about that. Lily Turner told me the Widow heard a racket and when she looked outside Nosy and Wandering Tom were having a fine disagreement. You know how the Widow loves animals, especially stray dogs and cats, well when she came out of the house and saw old Nod wrestling with Tom she just about had a hoppin' duck fit. Apparently she gave him a talking to like he was still in her fifth grade class. Lily said the best they could figure out was that somebody put Wandering Tom in her mailbox and by the time Nosy opened it up old Tom was in no mood for play."

Jamie looked at Ned. Ned's face was completely calm, devoid of guile. Jamie didn't know how Ned did it, holding his face that still, but thought it was something it might be handy to learn.

Chapter 48

Cramphorne's Complaint Part Deux

The Right Reverend Cramphorne drummed his fingers on his desktop. The letter he had to write was delicate. Now that he had Hera's assurances of speaking with her wealthy brother, he felt he had the wherewithal, the required pry bar to wrench a wealthier church from the parsimonious grip of the Secretary of the Presbytery, Silas Webster. The man might be simple and unsophisticated, but smooth hints to a simple soul to achieve higher ends had often been effective for him.

He stretched out his hand, dipped his pen in his antique inkwell and began to write.

To: The Right Honorable Silas Webster

Executive Secretary of the Presbytery, Presbyterian Church U.S.A.

Dear Sir:

I was with some fervent anticipation that I have been expecting an answer from you to my missive of some two weeks past. The situation I described has not experienced improvement. Nay, if anything, the situation has deteriorated and grows more grave with each passing day. I shall not trouble you with the details; suffice to say it involves the simple maintenance of the church grounds and its ancillary properties and involves a member of the congregation that heretofore has been a model of decorum and restraint

311

compared to and for his fellows. But I'll say no more of that, I do not wish to burden you further. I only wish to say I wish to remain the humble servant of both you and God, though obviously not in that order (my little joke, my apologies) and it would pain me more than I can express to be forced to take advantage of alternate opportunities that have recently availed themselves within my humble sphere through the efforts of my inestimable relation for which I thank God for every day that passes. As always, my kindest regards to you and yours,

Yours very truly and humbly

I remain sir, as ever your humble servant,

The Right Reverend Costigan Abalicious Cramphorne

First Presbyterian Church of Miller's Landing

Chapter 49

Works In Progress

The midday train whistle blew, far off and forlorn. Jamie and Ned gratefully dropped their brooms. His mother had been silently furious when she learned Jamie had driven the tractor, so Jamie's father had assigned them to clean the cabin from top to bottom, far from any kind of machinery. They headed for the cool shade of the tall oak standing beside the cabin and flopped down to eat and sip from their water jars.

Jamie had just taken a huge bite of his sandwich to fill his rumbling belly when he heard the high grating voice of Eueas. It was like listening to stones rubbed together with nerves crushed between.

Jamie had almost forgotten about Eueas. He hadn't run into him since he'd seen him flipping through wanted posters at the post office, but now dark remembered fear turned the food in his mouth to paste. He washed his mouth with water, but that didn't stop the voice.

"Hey Jacob, don't you know a lunch pail is supposed to have a handle on it? A handle, Jacob, not some raggedy-assed piece of string. Spring a little of that money you squirreling away! I know you got it 'cause you work like a dog and I don't see you never spend none of it. Be a man and get yourself a real lunch pail."

Jacob Ashby sat on a big root of the break tree quietly eating a thin sandwich. Jamie knew Jacob from church. He and his family sat at the back, very quiet, very polite when they were spoken to. His wife was much younger, pretty, but tired circles under her eyes. Their three stair-stepped sons stared at their shoes most of the time and the three girls always hid behind their mother's skirts. They always wore the same clothes to church, though clean and in good repair. With seven mouths to feed in addition to his own, Jamie thought Jacob's single white bread sandwich was probably all he could afford.

Eueas stumped over to Jacob. "Did ya hear me?" Eueas whacked Jacob on the leg with his cane. "Did ya hear me, ya half-deaf old coot?"

Jacob stopped chewing. "I heard you."

"Well?" Eueas stood over Jacob, nodding and waving his hands. "Well?"

Jacob did not stir. "Well, what?"

Eueas waved his cane at Jacob's lunch pail with its string.

Jacob slowly chewed his sandwich.

Eueas hammered his cane in the dust a couple of times before he laughed and turned away. Jamie caught Eueas' eye, though he had not meant to. Eueas laughed again, this time at Jamie, then hobbled back to his spot, sat back down and took a deep drink from his water jar. His twisted mouth crinkled into a nasty grin.

When the afternoon break whistle blew, Jamie and Ned bolted. They grabbed their cane poles and were out and gone before Eueas or anybody else could say a word.

As Jamie trotted along the path, he felt the bands wrapped around his chest release and he smiled with the maybe thought of Deidre at the lake. Then Ned's voice behind him brought him up short.

"Did we check the rabbit box today?"

Jamie stopped. "No. God, I didn't even think about it."

"We didn't get there yesterday either. It was raining, and …"

There was no help for it.

They turned around and trudged back up the trail and branched off to the place where they'd left the box.

As they walked up near the leaning tree, Jamie smelled it. "Uh-oh."

Ned stopped. "What?"

Jamie sniffed the air. "Can't you smell it?"

"Oh yeah. What is that?"

"Polecat."

"There skunks around here?"

Jamie looked at him. "You bet. Around here, anyway."

"That doesn't smell too bad. I mean it's not great, but what's all the fuss about?"

Jamie laughed. "That's because we're not close. If you get hit by the spray, we'll have to burn your clothes and you'll have to take a bath in tomato juice."

"Aw come on, you're not doing that to me again. I didn't fall off the turnip truck yesterday."

Jamie placed one hand on Ned's chest, holding him back from the trail to the box. "I'm not kidding. It's either that or a bath in vinegar."

"Yuck."

"Oh yeah. And the thing is that neither really works. The smell has to kinda wear off. I heard Doc Voyce talk about using hydrogen Per-something-or-other, but we don't have none of that." Jamie looked up and down at the trail and all around for the little black and white creature. "From here on we gotta be careful."

"What do they look like, anyway? Really. I mean other than black with a white stripe down the middle of their back?"

"The only one I saw had two stripes down its back. They look kinda like a cat with a great huge bushy tail except the front legs are short and they kinda waddle when they walk. I didn't care to get no closer. Come on, let's get to that box, but keep your eyelids peeled back. We don't want to get within spitting distance."

As they continued down the trail the smell got stronger and stronger. A bad thought occurred to Jamie. "Ned. I'm wonderin' right about now."

"Aw, don't say it."

"All right, I won't say it." Jamie kept walking, his eyes trying to peel back the leaves and underbrush and then they were there.

The box had been sprung and there was an odd sort of cat-like mew coming from inside. The smell here was much stronger and when they stood closer to the box it was stronger still. Jamie turned to find that Ned was already looking at him with wide eyes.

"I think what you didn't say just happened. What do we do now?"

Jamie shook his head. "We can't just leave him in there. He'll die."

"Better him than us."

"We gotta get him out of there." His lips tightened. "What we'll do is just slide the door up, throw it clear and then run as fast as we can. By the time he's out of the box we should be out of range."

Ned laughed, a slight quiver in his voice. "What's range?"

"Not sure. Never been close enough to have to worry about it."

"All right. Let's get it over with."

Jamie grabbed the cord attached to the top of the sliding door and set his feet to pull the cord straight up and then run. "Ready to run?"

"Like the wind."

"All right then. On three. One, two, … three!"

Jamie jerked the cord. The door slid up smoothly and cleared the top of the box. He tossed it to one side and scampered back down the trail until he judged he was out of range and then turned around to look back.

Nothing came out of the box. Jamie noticed Ned's fishing pole where Ned had leaned it up against the tree.

"Ned! Your pole!"

Ned cursed then clomped back up the path. Just as Ned's hand closed around his pole the little beast stuck his black head out of the hole, swiveled his nose around and sniffed directly up at Ned. A moment froze while Ned and little black eyes stared at each other. Ned was a statue, fishing pole in hand then the little beast waddled out and stamped his short little front feet. It pointed its little nose up at Ned again and stamped its little feet faster.

"Ned, git outa there!"

Ned flew toward him. There was a heart-stopping moment when his pole caught on a branch. Jamie dashed forward to pull it free, then they were both off and running, flying over root and rocks, laughing. They didn't stop until they were at the road. It was all they could do to breathe deep to catch their breath and laugh at the same time.

They were deep in conversation, laughing about the skunk and the close escape but as soon as their boots clunked against the boards of the dock they heard a musical feminine voice sing out.

"Do ya always make such noise? There be no Indians about, I take it?"

Jamie looked at Ned and Ned looked back. "They're here!"

An edge of Ned thought of Cyrus as they walked out into the sun. There was one Indian about, but the explanation was too involved for the simple question.

The girls were dressed this time, in overalls and simple blouses. They were leaning over the edge of the dock to fill water buckets.

"Well, if it's not our noble knights." Deidre straightened and smiled, her slender arms cradling a wooden bucket.

"We do aim to please." Jamie promptly put down his pole to help Deidre and just as promptly dropped her bucket into the water. He knew just as sure as he knew his name she was going to think he was a complete fumble fingered idiot. The bucket bobbed happily in the water, mocking him. He dropped his eyes, his face burning as much as he thought it could, but he was wrong. When he turned to grasp his fishing pole to get the bucket his fingers touched hers. He looked up and was wrapped in her clear green eyes.

317

"Hi." Impossible as it seemed to Jamie, her face and eyes were relaxed and smiling, a vision of smooth clear dreams. He felt he should, had to, say something, anything to release the pressure in his chest.

"Nice buckets."

The words were gone, flung like a mud pie splattered in all directions from his fumbling mouth. His breath choked in the frozen block of his chest and he was certain his heart had stopped for good. He was going to die right now. He knew it. The air rang in a vacuum between them.

But she only bit on her mouth, her dimples deepened, and her voice was quiet and smooth. "Pa made them. He can make most anything out of wood."

"Really?" Jamie's chest breathed without him. "Your dad's a cooper?" This time he was careful as he grasped his fishing pole and extended the butt end out over the water to pull the bucket back towards the dock.

"That and a lot more. You know how some men are jack-of-all trades and master of none?"

Jamie nodded, his eyes carefully on what he was doing, his entire side next to her tingling.

"Well Pa is master of just about anything a body can do with wood. He made most our furniture back home in Galway and he built all the cabinets inside our caravan."

Jamie looked over at her. "Caravan?"

"I think you call them trailers?"

"Like the ones at the migrant camp?"

Time slipped a pause in the sudden gap between them before she answered. "Only on the outside."

Jamie felt a chasm opening between them. "We're glad you're back."

She smiled and the gap slid closed again. She dipped in a quick vertical curtsy, her fingers pinching the legs of her overalls. "We are glad to be back, Sir Jamie."

This time Jamie just felt a trace of blood flush to his face, but that trace became a torrent when Deidre's laughter trilled like musical birdsong in his ears. Even so, he could not peel his eyes from her. "So you're not at the camp any more?"

"Oh no. Pa found a field not far off that seems to be fallow."

"Where is it?"

"Just there." She pointed toward the other side of the lake. "It's a tiny bit of a triangle of land at the other edge of these woods with yellow wildflowers. We'll leave naught but tracks when we leave, so it's not like anyone should mind. Do you know who belongs to it?"

Jamie knew the field. The land was indeed fallow, a small bit parcel planted in corn for so many years the ground was exhausted. It belonged to his father. "I don't think they'll mind."

"So what are you two doing here?" Emma's voice had a husky edge and she coughed. She stretched out on the deck with her hands laced behind her head holding it up and her feet propped up on the lower wooden railing.

Jamie drew breath to answer but Ned answered first. "We just got off work."

"Oh you work, do you now? Whereabouts?"

"At the sawmill."

Jamie jumped in. "We come here to fish to put a little something on the table."

Ned sat on the dock beside Emma and wrapped his arms around his knees.

She lowered her head back down to the boards. "We could use some good fish. The only thing we've had to eat for weeks now has been potatoes and beans." She coughed again.

Ned's eyes flashed up. He nodded at Jamie but spoke to Emma. "We might be able to help out."

They did just that.

Jamie let Ned do most of the talking. This was not the same Ned he had known at school. At school Ned had been smart but quiet, but with these girls from a land across the ocean he came out and told them all he knew about fishing. It helped that Ned caught fish.

He was watching his own cork bob in the water when he felt Deidre lean against his shoulder. "Are you the quiet one then?"

Jamie's nerves turned to fire. The sun behind her lit her hair in a halo of flaring red gold. He heard her voice emerge from the vision of light. "He seems to be a good fisherman."

Jamie smiled at the thought that a little more than a month ago Ned had first held a fishing pole in his hand. "He's a natural."

Ned glanced 'thank you'.

"You're the quiet one today, Sir Jamie. What would be wrong then?" Deidre's face was calm and open.

"It's … work. A fella tried to hack my dog with a sling blade. He's too strong and mean to fight and nobody'll take the time to believe me." He felt the bands tighten around his heart at the thought again. "It makes so mad I could spit."

"A bit of a temper, have you now?" Deidre's dimples appeared.

Jaime was glad she smiled. "I don't know. I guess."

"Pa's a bit quick as well. We came here because he had a job lined up building furniture, but when he spoke to the man the position had been filled, said Pa had taken too long. Gobsmacked he was and he was in a right state when he got back."

"I can imagine."

"The thing that sent him over the edge was hearing after the man hadn't known Da was Irish when he'd arranged it. When he found out Pa didn't get the job."

"Wouldn't your name have tipped him off? What is your last name, by the way?"

"Dunne. It's not so obvious as O'Connell or something like that, but there's no way of tellin' and nothing to be done but look for other work. It's been hard." She looked out across the water and her voice slipped a notch. "Though that's not exactly news, now is it? And when he caught a couple of moppets at nothing about the caravan he gave out he would wear the shirts off them sure if they didn't do a legger."

"Oh?" Jamie felt his stomach tighten at the thought of her 'Pa' seeing her leaning against his shoulder. "He didn't like any of them?"

Deidre's dimples came back. "Well, none he'd be wanting consorting with the apple of his eye."

Jamie wasn't certain what Deidre meant by the word 'consorting', but the way she said it told him it wasn't a good thing.

"Pa dropped us off for getting water. We're close enough to walk back, but with the buckets full he said he'd drive us. He should be here in a little while. You could meet him, like?"

Suddenly Jamie was scared. Not specifically of her 'Pa', but what he would think and what he would say and how. "Love to, but we'd probably be best getting on."

"And we got chores." Ned got to his feet and looked at Emma. "You going to be all right?"

"I'll be fine, sure." Emma coughed again.

Deidre took Jamie's hand. "Mind yourself, now and come back when you can."

"We're here a lot."

Jamie had never been so torn. Letting go her hand made his chest was rip apart, but he just didn't have it in him right then to face another hostile grown-up. The girls exchanged dimpled grins.

They bolted. They paused for one last look from under the cover of trees when they heard the backfire of a truck. They saw a big man wearing a flat cap and suspenders, with forearms big as bread loaves walk out onto the dock. They watched him listen to the girls and placed his fists on his hips but leaned back and laughed when Deidre lifted the stringer of fish from the water.

"At least if we do meet him he might think better of us that we fed them." Ned's voice over his shoulder.

"Sure. Absolutely." But Jamie wasn't convinced. The man had a face like the beaten granite stones on the railroad track and he thought he was probably right to be afraid.

321

Chapter 50
Possibilities

The next day was designated sawing day and everyone was pressed into service to get ready. Ned had never seen so many people work so hard in such a small space. Snow crawled and poked into every shaft and bearing with grease and oil, Jamie carted sawdust and refuse away in a wheelbarrow and Eueas was set to shoveling. The grumbling Eueas threw in for free.

Ned landed the plum task of digging old sour sawdust out from the deep hole beneath the saw blade with a garden hoe. As he dragged on a particularly heavy lump, the lump slithered, fell and coiled back down in the hole. Ned dropped the hoe and leapt back. He heard a clang behind him and turned just in time to see Eueas fall backwards over his shovel, land right on his butt and scramble to hide behind one of the thick support poles. It was hard to tell because of the dirt, but the man's face looked positively gray around his wide-white eyes.

"What's wrong? Why is Eueas on the ground?" Jamie's voice came from behind Ned along with the rattle and clang of the wheelbarrow.

"Snake in the hole."

"Aw." Jamie picked up the hoe, lifted it by the very end of the handle and chopped the twisting brown rope into bits of scales and blood.

Jamie handed the hoe handle back to Ned. "There you go. One dead copperhead."

"Thanks."

"Nothin' to it. Scoop him up out of there and I'll take him off in the wheelbarrow. Don't get close to the head, it's still dangerous."

Eueas did not resist as Ned pulled the shovel out of his grimy hands. Ned slid the blade up under the snake remains and dumped them in the wheelbarrow, then filled the wheelbarrow from the sawdust pile.

Jamie cursed under his breath as he hefted the wheelbarrow handles and pushed away.

Ned caught sight of Eueas' cane lying in the dirt. He picked it up and handed it to the man.

Eueas took it and climbed to his feet without meeting Ned's eyes. "I'll … uhh … I'm gonna go get some water." He thumped off toward the well outside the office cabin, eyes down.

Ned watched him pass Jamie in the path, but it didn't look like Eueas looked at Jamie either.

As Jamie came up Ned nodded in Eueas' direction. "Did you see that? See how scared he was of the snake?"

"No." Jamie turned to look. "I was too busy being glad he didn't talk to me."

"He was way past terrified, couldn't move for being so scared. He froze as soon as we saw the thing, planted behind that post stiff as last year's cotton."

Jamie's father sang out that everything was clean enough to work. "Any more and better is the enemy of good enough, so let's get to it."

Much to Ned and Jamie's dismay, they were sent off away from the saw. Jamie's father sent Ned out with Cyrus to scout more trees for the next day's logging. He told Jamie to saw slabs for firewood. "You do understand why, don't you?"

"Yessir. We're not supposed to be around the saw."

Jamie's father nodded. "That's right. Now get going, both of you. Go on."

As he turned to find Cyrus, Ned caught a glimpse of Jamie's face. It was completely without joy.

Jamie could hear the high ring of the blade as it devoured the logs and though they were indistinct, he could also hear

323

shouted instructions and laughter. The worst was the laughter. He felt separated and lonely and drove the rough blade of the bucksaw into the wood with the anger that seethed through his arms. Jamie was gut-sickening tired. He had been cutting and stacking slabs for firewood for most of the day and was looking forward going down to the Little Lake to doing a little fishing, but mostly to a little rest.

When the afternoon train whistle blew, he finished the piece he was sawing, put up the saw and walked to the office cabin to meet Ned. Ned wasn't there. His father was, reading glasses perched on his nose, one finger on a line in his account book and holding a paper in the other hand.

"Where's Ned?"

His father looked up from over the top of his reading glasses. "Still out with Cyrus, I imagine. I told them to stay out till they had marked enough hardwood for us to cut tomorrow. They might not be back before dark."

"Could you tell Ned I've gone fishing?"

"All right. It shouldn't be too long. Be sure you get home before dark. In time to have your chores done."

"Yessir."

It was just like his father to remind him of chores just when he was about to go enjoy himself. He thought he knew what it was. For some strange reason, and it was a solid mystery, his father actually enjoyed working. There was just no accounting for taste, wants or needs, but his father did love to work. For Jamie, the smell of sawdust had lost whatever romance it had had. The days were too long, the air was too hot and the hot hard packed ground was just too tough on his feet. Matter of fact as he tromped down the sandy pine-needle trail to Little Lake his feet positively ached inside his boots and every step pressed into the pain. He might even dangle his feet in the water today, even if it did scare the fish. As he came down to the water he saw the flash for a fly rod above the underbrush and below the lower branches of the trees. Sabastian! The pain in his feet forgotten, he thumped down the boards and saw Sabastian sitting quietly on the dock, playing his line in quiet arcs through the air. The dark line floated through the air and the small feathered lure kissed the still mirrored surface and sank, then Sabastian slowly drew the line in, in a continuous back and forth twisting of his line hand.

Jamie was so rapt in watching he was slightly startled to hear Sabastian's voice.

"I was hoping to see you here one of these days."

"Oh yeah?" Jamie walked slowly down the dock, slipped off his hat and sat down. "How come?"

"I wanted to ask you about an altercation between a certain small meddlesome mailman and a certain rather more than malevolent feline and any possible untoward aftereffects."

"Huh?"

"Did you get caught?"

Jamie's heart brightened immediately. "Oh, no." But he forgot to talk as Sabastian lifted his line from the water, floated it back and forth a couple of times in the air in lazy curves and laid it gently back on the water.

"Well, what about it?"

"What about what?"

"Has anything happened? Has anyone found out?"

"Uh ... no ... nobody knows nothin' about ... Can I try that?"

"Try what? My fly rod?"

Jamie nodded and swallowed, suddenly aware he had probably asked too much. "Yeah, I'm sorry. It looks like it's hard to do, but it's real pretty to watch."

Sabastian laughed quietly. "Correct on both counts, James. But not today, I'm afraid. Today I'm running out of time to catch supper. And generally when fly-fishing lessons are on the water the fish, sad to say, are not." He shook his head. "It seems to be some sort of rule of God, I haven't figured out the right prayer for it. But I'll let you try sometime."

"Promise?"

Sabastian turned his head toward Jamie and looked at him over the top of his smoked glass lenses. "Yes, James. I promise." He pushed his smoked glasses back up on his nose and turned back to the water. "So how are you and your friend Ned getting along? You on speaking terms again?"

"Yeah." Jamie could not tear his eyes from Sabastian's hands. They were white and heavily scarred like parchment but there was a grace and ease to their movements.

"Do you have any more nasty surprises for Mr. Norris planned?"

"We thought about putting a skunk in the mailbox if he didn't stop what he was doin'.'"

Sabastian laughed, coughed and laughed again. "I find myself wishing Mr. Norris could have profited by your acquaintance earlier in his life. It would have saved a lot of folks, me in particular, a lot of trouble. If you do that, be sure not to tell anyone what you've done, much as I'm sure you'll want to."

"Earlier in life? When was he ever my age?"

"Even then he was nosy." Sabastian nodded, eyes on his line and the water. "I told you he ruined a perfectly good relationship of mine. By the time she found out the rumor wasn't true it was too late. His evil gossip had already done its work. So, you see, I don't mind Mr. Norris getting a bit of comeuppance. He's ... due."

"We caught one the other day. A skunk, I mean. In the rabbit box."

"What did you do with it?"

"We let it go. And ran."

"Smart boy. You have to be careful with those things." Jamie caught Sabastian looking at him out of the corner of his eye. "Is there something wrong?"

Jamie thought about Eueas, but wasn't sure he wanted to talk about it. "Nah."

"All right." Sabastian flicked his line through the air again. Silence fell as smooth as lake water on a calm day.

Jamie unwound the line on his fishing pole and dug in the dirt in his can of worms, but stopped before he baited his hook. "Mr. Wood?"

"I told you to call me Sabastian."

"Have you ever been afraid? I mean really scared?"

For a moment Jamie thought Sabastian hadn't heard him. He thought Sabastian had turned to stone he was so still. Then Sabastian's hand moved again in that slow twisting motion to gather in line.

"Yes, James. Yes, I have." Sabastian's voice was so different for a moment Jamie did not recognize it. It was both deeper and farther away the air silently echoed. "I have most certainly been afraid." Sabastian drew his line up out of the water and inspected the small wet tendril of feathers at the end of the line. "Who are you afraid of, James?"

Jamie tried to look at his eyes, but Sabastian was looking at his line.

"Has he hurt you James?"

"No. He did take a swing at my dog Toby with a sling blade." Jamie shook his head and dug in his worms again. "He and Toby don't get along too well."

"Who?"

"A man at work. His name's Eueas. Eueas Canfield. He's got to be the meanest son-of-a-bitch I've ever known." He glanced up and down again. "And he said that he'd whup me if Toby ever got in his way again."

"Where's Toby now?"

"At home. Some days he's been goin' in the woods with Ned. Ned's workin' with the tree scout. That's where he is today."

"Tree scout?"

"That's the guy that marks the trees ahead of the logging crew before they go out to cut timber."

"Ah. And this man Eueas took a swing at Toby? Do you have any idea why?"

"Toby stole his cane one time and his hat fell off while he was grabbin' for it. It showed a big bald spot."

"A lot of folks are bald, James. I'm not exactly full-haired myself."

"Maybe. But this bald spot's on the side of his head. He snatched that hat back and clapped it on his head so fast he fell over on the ground." Jamie wound his hook through a worm. "Everybody laughed at him. Oh, he was mad. He's ready and willin' to pick on and laugh at anybody else, but he don't like the tables turned, no sir." Jamie saw Sabastian's head tilt a little to one side and the line twisting motion slowed just a fraction.

"How old is this man, James?"

That seemed like an odd question to Jamie. "I don't know. Old. But it's hard to tell 'cause all his wrinkles are so full of dirt. I don't think he ever takes a bath."

Sabastian pushed his smoked glasses up on his face with his forefinger and lifted his rod to cast again, but this time when the line floated up behind him it tangled in a tree branch. "Damn. Could you get that for me, James?"

"Sure." Jamie got to his feet and reached for the line. It was the first time he had ever touched it up close. The line was dark brown braid, but it had a clear coating on it that made the surface fairly smooth. As he followed the line up into the tree he saw that tied to the end of the braided line was a length of line that was different. It was brown and clear. "What is this stuff?"

"What stuff, James?"

He turned to Sabastian, holding the clear brown line in his hands. "This."

"That is called the 'leader.' Theoretically the fish are not supposed to see it. Practically, I think it's just less visible than the braided fly line."

Jamie looked at the line more closely. "But what is it?"

Sabastian lifted his chin. "You mean 'what is it made of?' It's made of gut."

"Gut?"

"Yes. Animal intestines."

"You're kidding."

Sabastian laughed. "I'm not inventive enough to make up something like that. I don't know quite how they do it, but it's true. But that's not peculiar to fishing, y'know. Violin strings are made of cat gut. That should give you some idea of how tough it is."

"Wow." Jamie pulled on the line to draw the tree limb within reach, grabbed the limb and started unwinding the line from around the leaves and twigs. "Y'know, it's the oddest thing about Eueas."

"What's that, James?"

"He's pretty tough with that cane of his, but he's scared to death of snakes."

A pause hung in the air. "Is he really?"

"Oh yeah. We found a big copperhead in a sawdust pile when we were cleaning out today. I killed it with a hoe, but he just huddled behind a post the whole time."

Jamie heard Sabastian speak very quietly. "You know James, men can be afraid of the strangest things sometimes. Sometimes things that make no sense at all."

"Are you? I can't imagine you afraid."

A slight smile played about Sabastian's lips, as much smile as he could manage given how stiff his facial skin was. "Oh yes." Jamie could hardly hear him and watched him lift his pocket watch and snap it open and closed again. "And at a later date we'll discuss that at great length and in alphabetical order if you wish. But now I must go. Clara's waiting for me."

"But I didn't tell you."

"Tell me what?" Sabastian began to reel in his line.

"I think I maybe found a way for you to make a little money."

"Oh?"

"Yeah. The preacher's garden."

"Cramphorne?" Sabastian's eyebrows lowered to touch the top of his smoked glasses as he cranked in his line on the small brass reel. "He has a garden?"

"Yeah. I heard about it at church last Sunday after you left. He wanted the elders to weed it for him and Daddy and him had a big fight about it. So the Elders aren't going to be doin' it and I figure Cramphorne's not going to and he wants it done, so maybe …"

"He would be willing to pay a small stipend to keep his hands clean?"

"Something like that. Just an idea."

"Interesting." Sabastian gathered his bag and stood up, rod in hand. He laid one hand on Jamie's shoulder. "I don't know if he'd be willing to part with cash for such a thing, but I'll think about it. But whether it works or not, thank you James. Thank you for thinking of me."

"Sure."

"See you later."

Jamie watched Sabastian make his long graceful strides back up the path to the road until he was out of sight, then turned back to the water. He pulled off his boots and splashed his feet and smiled.

Chapter 51

A Friend In Need

After the afternoon whistle the next day Jamie and Ned strode into the woods to check on the rabbit box. They approached it gingerly, eyes scanning for the skunk.

Jamie stopped right over the box and sniffed. "Just a whiff, but we still can't use it again. There's no way any self-respecting rabbit's gonna come within a country mile of this one."

"So what's to do?"

Jaime shrugged. "Build another one."

With many grunts and much complaining the two hefted the box to their shoulders and carried it like a little coffin to their little hidden work area in the back of the office cabin.

There ensued a period of sawing, fitting, nailing, pulling nails and renailing.

And cussing.

When Jamie saw Ned hit his finger with the hammer for the eleventy-seventh time his ears were opened in wonder. He had never heard anyone cuss that well. It wasn't so much that Ned used foul language, his didn't. But the colorful comparisons and images just made Jamie laugh out loud.

"How do you do that?"

"Do what?"

"Cuss like that. How do you come up with all that stuff?"

Ned shrugged. "I don't know. Some of it I heard in the store. Pop doesn't notice when I'm standing right there a lot of times. Either that or he doesn't notice I'm listening. The rest just kinda comes to me."

"I wish I could do that." Jamie shook his head. "'Course there's a lot of things I'd like to do."

331

"Like what?"

"Make Eueas go away." He scratched his nose.

Ned laughed a single cough. "Speaking of ol' Ewe-ass, I wish I could help Mr. Ashby."

"Jacob? Help with what?"

"Puttin' food on the table is what."

"Don't he get paid enough? Daddy's payin' pretty good wages this year, considerin'. Everybody says so."

"Mr. Ashby's problem ain't the wages. His problem is he's got eight mouths to feed including his own." Ned picked up nails and put them between his lips. He spoke out of the side of his mouth that wasn't holding nails as he tacked on the strips to hold the door in place. "That's a powerful lot of food when you don't have a garden."

"Mr. Ashby don't have a garden?" This was news to Jamie. No one he knew didn't have a garden.

"They live in a boarding house in town."

"How does he get out here if he lives in town?"

"He don't. During the week he stays around here with somebody that's within walkin' distance. I don't know who."

"How come you know all this, anyway?"

"You'd be surprised what a body can pick up on if you keep your mouth shut." Ned pulled the remaining nails out of his mouth as he spoke. "I heard something else just this morning."

"What's that?"

"Jacob don't have any meat to feed his family, ain't had any in a month. Just potatoes and beans and macaroni."

The thought of Jacob's family sitting down at the dinner table to nothing but vegetables made Jamie was silent at the thought of that.

They kept working on the box until they drove the last nail, had mounted the trip sticks on top and tested the door. They made a couple of improvements over the old one. One was a screen wire window covered with a hinged lid over it to shut out the light. The other improvement was handles on the sides to get a grip when they were carrying it.

"All right, now where?" Ned kicked scrap wood out of the way.

"Not where we had it, that's' for sure." Jamie scratched his chin. "Maybe somewhere a little closer so it'll be easier to check on."

"I think I know of a good spot."

"Where's that?"

"A little stand of hardwood Cyrus and me looked at, but the trees ain't big enough to cut yet. It's right next to a field of clover."

Jamie could not help but smile. "Perfect. Let's go."

By the time they got the box there and set it, it was too late to get their fishing poles.

"Tell you what, you want to trade chores tonight? Want to gas up the Delco?"

Ned shook his head. "I like milking. Gramma's a pretty nice little cow."

"All right, if that's the way you want it. I just thought I'd give you a little break from the same old stuff. That's what friends do, y'know."

"Oh, is it really?"

"Yes, it is really … and other thing …"

As they walked up the path to the house on the hill, their words relaxed and flowed between them back and forth, to and fro and the music of their laughter echoed against the pines.

The next morning Grant Garrath was not quite clear of the woods, both figuratively and literally. On the figurative side, he was worried about his toss of the dice. The mill was paying for itself, but only just. He shared it out loud only with the woods. He could not talk with Hannah or anyone else about it. She would worry and probably had idea of what was going on anyway. He couldn't share it with any of his friends because it would, in spite of faith, get back to his workers. If they thought their jobs stood as the hymn went 'on sinking sand,' they would look elsewhere for solid rocks to stand on. He needed his workers if this thing was going to fly. He thought about sharing it with Jamie, but he didn't want to worry him. The boy was only fourteen and did deserve some kind of childhood, not the working from 'can't see to can't see' like he had grown up with no matter how tough times were.

He walked along the edge of a stand of hardwood Cyrus had told him had some good trees in it, but not enough to bother with harvesting yet. Cyrus was usually right about such things, but at this stage Grant just could not leave any stone unturned. He skirted the edge of the woods looking for easy hardwood for furniture makers and just under the edge of a bush he saw the rabbit box. He knew it was Jamie and Ned's, had seen the boys building it from the office cabin window. He also saw the trap had been sprung. He strode through the tall grass and over a fallen log and kneeled beside it. His first thought was to reset it, thinking that the boys hadn't taken the time to set the trip stick properly, but when he lifted the lid over the screen just a crack to look inside two dark bright eyes stared up at him. "Well, ain't that just ...."

He thought about telling them, but thought better of it. He didn't want to throw a wet rag over their joy. Grant lowered the lid, stood up and brushed his pants off, then walked away smiling.

Jamie spent the morning in slow torture. He was assigned to clean out the sawdust from under the saw again. It just wasn't fair to smell the sawdust and not be able to watch it run. At midday he had just collapsed between two roots of the oak tree by the mill office cabin with his food bag and Mason jar of water when Ned thumped down right beside him. "Hey."

"Hey yourself."

Ned unknotted the top of his lunch sack. "You look kinda tired."

"You could say that." Jamie bit off a bite of his peanut butter sandwich and mouthed it around. "I never knew sawdust could be so heavy."

He watched Ned reach into his sack and draw out his sandwich and noticed Ned's arm and hand had a dusting of flour on it. Apparently Jamie's mom had used a fresh flour sack to pack their lunches one that morning.

Ned followed Jamie's eyes and looked at his arm. "Oh yeah. Your momma gave me a new one this morning. Apparently she didn't beat the flour out of it first."

Jamie peered at the bag. "What's yours? 'Tidal Wave' flour?"

"So?"

"So nothing, she usually buys White Rose."

"Yeah, well. Feeds the same." Ned took a bite, chewed, frowned, then swallowed hard. "Or not. The extra flour gives it that certain special texture. Like eatin' dust."

Eueas' voice slapped through the dead dusty air from under the trees across from them. "You so great, why don't you getcha self a new strap for that jim-dandy lunch pail y'got there, huh, Mr. Ashby? Oh, that's real executive material there, huh?"

Jacob's response was too quiet to hear. Eueas' cackle rang out again and he stumped away from Jacob and flopped down on the ground.

Jamie had felt pretty good all day, but when he heard Eueas ride Jacob about his lunch pail again, he felt the slim needle of anger slip underneath his skin and burn like a slowly building fire.

"What's wrong?"

Jamie looked up at Ned from cleaning out the ashes from the wood stove in the office cabin. "What?"

Ned leaned on his broom handle. "You've been quiet as a church mouse ever since lunch. That's a bit long for you to go without expressing yourself. What's the matter?"

"Nothing I haven't told myself not to worry about."

"Eueas, huh? I thought that bothered you. You didn't say anything at the time."

Jamie concentrated on the ashes in the little shovel and carefully tapped it into a large empty coffee can. "It don't do no good to complain." He watched the little ash cloud settle. "But I just keep thinkin' there oughta be something we can do."

"Let's just finish this last hour, check the box and go home."

They did just that. At the afternoon break whistle they headed to the woods to check the rabbit box. When they passed by the office cabin the men were settled under the trees.

As they walked by, Eueas' mouth was once again thrashing the air. "Hey there, Ashby, you sure you can carry that heavy lunch pail all by your lonesome? Want me to help you with it?"

Jacob Ashby leaned back against the tree, closed his eyes and slowly chewed his apple.

Eueas thumped over to him and rapped on the tree above Jacob's head with his cane. "You hear me? You need any help?"

Jacob opened his eyes slowly and looked up at Eueas. "Yeah. I hear you. And I'm just fine, thank you."

"Well, I was worried about you. Never can be too careful." Eueas leaned on his stick and laughed, his eyes never leaving Jacob's face.

Marshall slowly got up and walked over and pressed between the two of them. Eueas had to back up to make room. Marshall looked down at Jacob. "Mind if I sit down here?"

Jacob nodded and smiled at him. "Sure, come on. Plenty of room."

As Marshall lowered his mass to the ground he turned his back on Eueas, effectively shutting him out from Jacob.

Eueas watched Marshall for a moment, his smile fixed and not so broad, then he laughed out loud and thumped back over toward the stump he had been sitting on. He yelled over his shoulder as he thumped away, "Yeah, you need plenty of room to carry that fine lunch pail. It's damn near as fine as mine, yeah." He laughed again at his own joke, sat down on a stump and opened his paper sack with sandwiches in it.

Jamie and Ned were glad to leave both the mill and Eueas behind.

As they approached the box they could see the sliding door was down.

Jamie swallowed. "Hope it's not another skunk."

336

But when they lifted the lid on top they saw they had a rabbit.

Jamie laughed. "Well, at least one good thing has come out of today. This is gonna taste good tonight. You ever eaten rabbit?"

Ned looked at Jamie. "I want it."

Jamie looked up at him. "Sure, you're gonna have some tonight."

"That's not what I meant. I want it but I don't want it for me."

"You're confusing me on purpose?"

Ned shook his head.

"What, then?"

"I want it for Jacob."

"Jacob?"

"Remember I told you I heard Jacob say he didn't have any meat for his family? I want to give it to him."

Jamie shook his head. "I wish we could. Your heart's in the right place, but Mr. Ashby's a proud man. He won't want the charity."

Ned nodded back at Jamie. "Yeah. What about ... you know how Eueas has been all mocking Jacob about his lunch pail?"

"Kinda hard to miss."

"Well, what if we fixed it to where Jacob's pail caught the rabbit?"

"Like tangle the rabbit up in the twine handle?"

Ned nodded. "It would put two things right at the same time, give Jacob a little meat and maybe shut Eueas up."

"Do you know where he left his lunch pail?"

"He put it behind the tree where he and Marshall were sitting at lunch. I think he's hiding it 'cause he's ashamed of it."

Jamie pushed his lips together and nodded. "All right. Let's get the little fella in a lunch sack and give it a shot. But we can't let anybody see or the whole things all shot to hell."

They tipped the rabbit into Jamie's flour sack and crept toward the tree where Jacob left his lunch pail. They were almost caught when Snow came by on his way from the office cabin to the logging road. They shrank behind a tree and shushed each other until Snow passed them and walked over to the saw shed.

Snow didn't notice but another pair of eyes did. The eyes were dark, set in a silent scarred face. The tall rangy figure stood in the shadows until they moved from their hiding place and then followed with silent steps. He watched them whisper and struggle with winding the twine strap around both the rabbit's feet and a convenient little root sticking up from the ground to make certain the rabbit would stay and wouldn't make matters worse by dragging Jacob's lunch pail off into the woods. When he saw what the boys were up to he pushed his lower lip into an upside-down smile and nodded. It had been a long time since Cyrus had seen selfless generosity. It was a character trait much prized by the Makah. He noticed Snow was returning and stepped out to buttonhole him about the new stand of trees they could log tomorrow. He put his body between Snow and the boys.

Jamie noticed the two men talking and reached out to grab Ned's arm. "Freeze."

"What?" Ned followed Jamie's gaze and whisper-spat one forbidden curse word and sank to the ground. "Where did they come from?"

They held bated breath until Cyrus gestured Snow away back to the cabin.

"That was too close."

Ned wound the string another turn round the rabbit's back legs. "I think that does it."

"Hope so. Now let's get out of here. Remember Momma's got chores for us; she says the weeds need choppin' out of the corn."

"You don't want to hang around? See what happens?"

"Sure I do, but I can't keep a straight face for beans."

Ned chuckled. "Yeah, well. It's about time you learned. Let's go fishing and come back at the evening whistle. That should leave us enough time for chores. 'Specially if we split them up."

When they got to the lake it was too hot to fish. Which was just as well, for their minds were not on it. Sabastian was not there, neither were the girls, so they gave up and tried to outdo each other skipping rocks till the sun touched the tree tops.

"You reckon it's about time?"

"Close enough. Let's go."

Jamie and Ned walked up to the office cabin just as Jamie's father was locking up for the day. "How's that rabbit box, son? I sure could taste some of that tonight."

Jamie and Ned only had time for a quick glance at one another before great laughter and loud talk echoed from the men slow-striding out from beneath the trees, Snow in the lead.

Jamie's father turned to his foreman. "What's all the commotion?"

Snow walked up clapping his hands in laughter. "You never believe it, not in a hundred years!"

"What?"

"Jacob got hisself a rabbit!"

Grant stepped down off the porch. "What? Let me see."

Snow turned back. "Jacob, come on over here, show Mr. Garrath your rabbit."

Jacob Ashby strode up, his face stretched in a wide smile, one hand swung the rabbit by its hind legs. "Yes sir, here it is!"

Grant reached down and examined the rabbit with interest. He brushed a bit of white flour dust from the mottled brown of its fur. "How'd you get it?"

A huge grin spread all over his face. "It got itself all tangled up in the handle of my lunch pail."

"You're kidding."

"Yeah! I mean no, no kiddin'! Now don't that just beat the straw off the broomstick?" Jacob laughed a high cackle of released joy, for once being on the receiving end of the luck of the gods. "All I had to do was grab the hind legs and whack its head against a tree. Now me and the little ones got meat for supper!"

Grant shook his head. "Well, that sure does beat all. The Lord does indeed work in mysterious ways."

Jacob nodded. "Yes sir, he purely does. I was just sayin' this mornin', you heard me Snow, we was needin' meat for the supper table tonight, been a coon's age since we had any." Jacob slapped his thigh. "Damn if this little fella didn't just come right to me!" He laughed a little lower this time and wiped his eyes with the back of his hand. "I'd love to stand and talk with you, Mr. Garrath, but I got to get home and set Momma gal to get this little fella in the pot!"

Grant smiled back at him. "That's all right Jacob, you go enjoy. You earned it."

Jacob and Snow turned away, still laughing. "We surely will. Goodnight, Mr. Garrath."

"Good night fellas."

Grant turned back around to the boys shaking his head. "If that don't beat all."

Both Jamie and Ned wore Cheshire cat grins. Then he noticed the dusty flour sack in Ned's hand. "Jamie, speaking of rabbits, how is your rabbit trap coming along?"

Jamie's grin vanished. "Oh, uh, it's … uhh …"

Ned spoke up. "It's empty, sir. Sorry."

Grant lifted his chin at Ned. "Do tell, is it now?"

Ned nodded. "Yes sir. We've set it again. If we don't have any luck there, maybe tomorrow we'll put it somewhere else."

Grant nodded, smiled and shifted his eyes from one boy to the other. He spoke softly. "Well, all right." He chuckled. "Let's go celebrate Jacob's good fortune with some supper. In the absence of rabbit, I myself have a hankering for meatloaf and cabbage."

The boys' smiles vanished. "Aww …"

"It's a lovely thing, boys. Balance. You know what symmetry is?"

Ned shook his head. "No sir, can't say I do."

"Well, think of it like this. If someone does a good deed, they feel really good inside, right?"

"Yeah, well. They're supposed to." Ned scratched the side of his face.

"Well, balance and symmetry means that good feeling needs to be balanced by something not so good, or we start feeling too proud. That's the reason no good deed goes unpunished. It's just God's way of making sure we keep things in proper perspective."

Ned bit one side of his lip. "Whatever you say, Mr. Garrath."

"Of course, I personally would like even more some fried fish tonight, if you fellas could manage to catch us a mess before nightfall. Better run quick now. You don't have much daylight left and we don't want to keep our 'momma gal' waiting, now do we? Go on, catch us a mess of fish."

Jamie and Ned both yelled over their shoulders as they ran off to get their poles. "We'll do our best!"

Grant Garrath smiled to himself. Now wasn't that something, the boys wanting to help out a man like that and not take credit for it. Maybe some of church was taking root. More than likely it was just both boys' natural-born hearts only God could take credit for. He took a deep breath, climbed into his pickup and drove away.

Cyrus Conner stood very still in the shadows of the trees. He had watched the boys attach the rabbit to Jacob's lunch pail string with much curiosity. Not since his brother had lost a foot race on purpose against a boy who lacked self-confidence had he seen anyone do such a thing and not sought or expect praise for it. These boys bore watching.

Then Cyrus' eyes were drawn to another who bore watching who was now conspicuous by his silence. Behind the men on their way out the gate, Eueas Canfield thumped along stiff-legged, leaning on his cane, with a face like stone thunder.

Chapter 52

Travelers

"Y'know, if we do ever catch a skunk again …" Ned shouted over his shoulder at Jamie, who trailed along behind him on the path to Little Lake.

He heard Jamie laugh. "Just because I'm in a good mood don't mean I'm gonna go along with catching a skunk on purpose. 'Sides, Nosy'd have to be dumb as a bag of hammers to not look where he's putting his hands now."

"You think he's not? Just think about Nosy with that great beak packed full of skunk after he got blasted. It'd be worth it even if we did get caught."

"Brother, are you rowing with one oar."

As he thumped down the hill through the trees to the water Ned saw a couple of wooden buckets out on the end of the dock. He stopped, still under the trees, and let Jamie pass him, then followed slowly. He looked for Emma and was relieved to see that only Deidre was there. But then as Jamie approached Deidre, Ned felt pretty much like a steering wheel on a mule.

"Oh, it's yourself, is it? Are y'alright? You're just in time to help."

Ned eased out onto the dock and saw Deidre hand one of the buckets to Jamie.

Jamie's hand fumbled with his fishing pole. "Help with what? Oh. Sure."

'We're after needing water." She turned to Ned. "And how's yourself?"

He waved a hand. "Fine. Where's Emma?"

"She's laid up sick with a bit of a cold from the migrant camp. But don't worry your head about it. She'll be right, sure."

Ned was stumped for anything else to say, so he busied his hands threading a worm on his hook. He swung it out over the water and laid it right beside a stump in the water where Jamie had told him fish were.

Deidre turned back to Jamie. "Are there really fish here worth catching?"

Jamie set the bucket down on the dock. "What's say let's find out before we start splashing around."

Deidre smiled at Jamie the way Ned dreamed that someone, sometime, somewhere might smile at him, all sunshine and twinkling eyes. "Can you teach me?"

"Oh sure."

"So what's to be done?"

Ned watched the two of them with their heads together as Deidre watched Jamie lift a worm from the can and showed her how to thread it on the hook then placed his pole in her hand. Jamie guided her hand to swing the line out over the water and laid the worm out in a likely spot.

"Next time, let me thread it on the hook."

Ned watched a smile grow Jamie's face. He had never seen a girl do anything but wrinkle her nose at the sight or even thought of worms. He wondered if Emma would do the same. Ned felt, for the first time in his life, his heart tug with jealousy as he watched a smile grow on her face too. Then he felt a pull on his line as the village idiot hooked himself while he wasn't looking at his bobber. He yanked the fish in and landed it, flopping, on the dock.

He looked up to see Deidre looking at his fish with delight and Jamie's face fallen, but then a fish hit her hook and she squealed as she felt the quivering electricity of a fish on the line.

Sometimes the gods shine upon you. The fish seemed hungry and stupid enough to bite anywhere they tossed a line. It slowed after a while, but by that time there was more than enough laughter for everyone.

Then Ned noticed Jamie's hand resting lightly on Deidre's back as he taught her how to slide the bobber on the line to adjust the depth and a voice inside told him it was time for him to leave.

He lifted his line from the water, stripped the worm from his hook and wound his line around his pole. "I'm gonna run these up to the house and dress them out. See you later."

Ned grabbed the stringer of fish and stood to leave. Jamie followed him to the edge of the dock. "You gonna leave me here? Alone?"

"I'm not leaving you alone." Ned could hardly hold down a smirk as he saw something very like terror in Jamie's face. "She's only a girl, Jamie."

"Yeah but …"

"Have fun." Ned smiled, slung the fish off his shoulder. "Give these to her for supper tonight." He turned away smiling and left, leaving Jamie to his fate.

"I guess we're alone now." Deidre's voice in Jamie's ear was smooth, like warm night wind across his skin. "Have the fish stopped biting?"

He turned around, walked to her and sat down. "Pretty much. It wouldn't be like Ned to leave if they were still biting. He's got a pretty good sense of that."

"That's not the only thing he's got a pretty good sense of."

Jamie's heart thumped and told him to say something but he was damned if he could remember a single thing.

"Jamie."

"Hmm?"

"Ya want to see our camp? I'd like you to meet Pa."

Jamie had never seen a traveler's camp. He had ridden by the migrant camp near Fayetteville, but that seemed like a dry and dusty place to live. "All right. Where is it?"

"I told you before, Pa found a field looked like it was laying fallow, so he thought no one would mind if we used it. We won't be there long and if we don't damage anything it'll be all right."

In for a penny, in for a pound. "Let's go."

The edge of bright had rubbed off the day as they headed through the woods toward the camp. Jamie carried the buckets full of water and Deidre carried the fish. They came out of the woods on a small triangular field. The caravan wagons were gathered in the center. "I know this field."

"Yes? Who owns it?"

"My daddy."

Deidre stopped walking and talking for a moment, but when Jamie didn't stop she started again and caught up to him. "Do you think he'll mind?"

The weight of the buckets pulling down on his shoulders kept Jamie from shrugging. "I don't know, but I don't think so. It is fallow this year, but don't tell nobody else, ok?"

She bounced on her toes beside him. "All right." She leaned in closer to him. "There's a couple of things you have to know before you meet my Pa."

Jamie felt the bottom drop out of his stomach. "Yeah?"

"Don't wander too far from me. As long as you're with me you're not a stranger."

"What happens to strangers?"

"He's very protective of me, especially since Mamma died."

"I'm sorry."

"Thanks, but it's been donkey's years. I was small so I don't remember much. I do remember she was quiet and kind and Pa always listened to her. More than anyone else, anyway."

"I'll be respectful. I know how to do that."

"And for goodness sake, don't be laying your hands on me while he's around, we want him to think I'm safe with you."

"Layin' my hands on you?" Jamie thought of the magic feel of her hand in his and her shoulder under his hand as they had fished. Dread slid under his skin. "What makes you think I'd do that in front of him? I've only … I mean I haven't … you should know you're pretty safe with me."

She smiled just a little and flashed her emerald eyes at him. "I don't want to be too safe, Jamie. But best himself doesn't know that."

"Himself?"

"My Pa."

"Oh." His mouth tried to move in response without success.

"And never, never call him by his first name."

"I don't know his first name."

"It's Seamus."

"But don't use it?"

"No."

"Why not?"

"Because he lets none he does not know use it to his face. There were even those in the migrant camp he wouldn't allow, and them being twice his age."

"Your father's pretty strict, huh?"

"You don't know the half of it."

She reached out and slid her hand up and down his arm and pulled him closer toward the travel trailer camp. Jamie kicked at the old solid dirt rows as they crossed the field. He had a tough time looking both up where they were going and down to avoid tripping with the buckets weighting his hands. They entered between two travel trailer wagons toward the campfire in the middle.

Deidre slowed and peered at the faces around the campfire. "Hmm."

"Hmm, what?"

"My father. He's smiling."

"Where? He's smiling, that's good, isn't it?"

Deidre nodded. "It can be, unless he starts to smile too wide, then his grin grows into a grimace. But I wouldn't worry about it; he promised me he wouldn't do that again, so it's not likely."

Jamie swallowed and his feet felt suddenly leaden. "Do what again? What's not likely?" His eyes scanned back and forth for her father. When he turned back he discovered his quiet question had faded into the empty space where she had been beside him. Jamie glanced about and could not find her. Her warning echoed within his head about him wandering away from her, but there had been no allowance for her wandering away from him.

A grumbling deep voice challenged him. "You're not one of us."

Jamie froze in his tracks and shook his head. "No sir, I'm not."

"What brings you here?"

Jamie ears located the voice. When he turned toward it he saw a man a little above average height with much above average width shoulders that projected the strength of stone. He could not see the face because it was back-shrouded in the setting sun, but the voice was nonetheless deep and serious.

Jamie stumbled out Deirdre's name. The dark imposing countenance eased as the great head nodded and turned toward the fire. Her father was a broad man, deep voiced with a slow smile that told you he knew more of the earth and it's creatures than you did. Jamie reflected there was no reliable means to determine if that were true or not, but the possibility still set him back on his heels. Jamie saw the smile set into a grimace and the voice spoke a half-octave lower. "Another stray. Another damn orphan."

"I'm sorry sir, but I'm not an orphan. I don't understand."

"Then understand this, boy." The head turned back toward Jamie. "We have little enough here for ourselves to be feeding all the strays she brings in."

"I didn't come for supper, sir. She wanted me to meet her father. If you'd be so kind as to point him out, then we can meet and I'll be on my way."

"Then be on your way. I am he. Be off with you now."

Jamie nodded.

"You can put the buckets down."

Jamie did, but then found his hands empty with nothing to do. "Goodnight, sir."

348

One giant spidery hand backhanded a wave to him. Jamie took that as a final signal so he turned and left, picking his way through the growing dark.

"Pa, there you are. I brought someone for you to meet, but when I took the fish to Brigid I lost him."

"Another stray, I know. I saw him, met him and sent him on his way. How many times must I tell you girl, not to bring home every hungry mouth you meet? We're not a soup kitchen, y'know. I can hardly scrape together enough to feed us, let alone more than half the planet you bring home."

"I just thought you'd be wanting to thank him is all. Not that it's at all important."

"And I'd be thanking him for what? For the marvelous opportunity to empty our slim larder for someone I don't even know at the cost of starving my kith and kin? Is that what I'm to be thanking the lad for?"

"Oh nothing so grand as that, just the earth beneath your feet and our supper of fish tonight."

"What? The good earth below belongs to God above and as long as we're here this is home and hearth. Girl, what are you blathering about?"

Deidre stood with her hands on her hip and set her mouth at her father. "Those fine words might work for the heavenly Father, but as well you know it won't work in the land of men. Jamie's father owns this land."

"'Jamie', is it? Well, 'Jamie' never said the first word of it."

She nodded. "<u>He's</u> not the sort to Gabriel his way around."

Her father snorted. "Still. You're young yet to be setting your heart on any boy there is. Especially when we don't know where we'll be from one week to the next. It's worried I am for you."

"Ma was a year younger than me when she married, and you not two years more."

"And both from families each known the other for more than a generation as you well know. You just met this little fella. It's a different thing entire and well you know that too."

She shook her head and stomped off with as much fury as a person can in field dirt. She yelled at him over her shoulder. "He's just a nice gentle boy, that's all. Could it kill you to let me talk to a nice boy?"

Seamus turned to her but she was already gone from the light. He turned back to his drink by the fire. " 'A nice boy' she says, 'a nice boy'." He shouted after her into the darkness. "I don't know there is such a thing." He poked the fire. "And even true, how was I to be knowing that?"

Jamie heard Deidre's voice call behind him just as he reached the lake. "Jamie!"

He turned back to her. "Hi." He peered into the darkness behind her. "Won't your father be mad you came after me?"

She took one of his hands in both of hers. "Can you come back later?"

"Later?" Jamie's heart twisted in too many directions. "He doesn't like me. I might not have all the experience in the world, but I can see that. Besides, I got chores and I'm late as it is."

She pulled on his hand. "Mayhaps you could find your way out after supper some night? He does tell wonderful stories."

"You're sure he wouldn't kill me?"

She nodded and he felt her pull on his hand again. He had never gone out after dark, not like Ned, but his mouth answered before he knew it. "Sure. Okay." He didn't know why he had said that or how he was going to do it but there was no going back now and god his heart was thumping like a jackhammer and he felt shivery cold in the heat of the midsummer twilight. He swallowed. "Here?"

"Yes. Right here." She nodded and her smile glowed. "When?"

This was already Friday night, tomorrow and Sunday would be too hard to get away unnoticed. "Monday? After supper and after everyone's asleep? It's the soonest I can get away without somebody seeing me, I think."

She smiled with her entire face and she squeezed his hand one more time. "Monday, right here, after supper, after the world is abed. And remember Jamie, a king's word is his bond."

Jamie nodded. When she pulled away her fingertips traced across his palm. She looked over her shoulder and waved as she danced off across the field, her slender legs like a new-born filly, long and gliding with an odd slightly awkward grace.

Jamie's heart pounded tight. He felt like his brain was on holiday and his heart was driving while he just bounced in the rumble seat along for the ride. Oh Christ Jesus Almighty in heaven what had he just done?

Chapter 53

A Guardian Angel

Silas Webster leaned back in his wooden swivel chair and rubbed his forehead, another dreaded Cramphorne letter in hand.

"You have to open it." Mrs. Wenig looked at him over the top of her reading glasses.

"You know, I'm not sure that I do."

She pressed her lips together, shook her head and turned back to her own desk across the room.

He sighed and grasped his letter knife to slice through the envelope. He wished he could skewer the Reverend Cramphorne's bluster as easily. He unfolded the single sheet of paper and read. Then he sat very still, buried by thought.

Silas Webster, Executive Secretary of the Presbytery, took pride (though he knew pride a sin) in being a patient man, a man of his word, a man dedicated to peace and rational communication between intelligent individuals. He actively held in his heart that all individuals possessed sufficient intelligence to communicate rationally if only the right words were used and enough effort expended to cross the gap of misunderstanding. But today the letter in his hand challenged those beliefs beyond the breaking point. Cramphorne's reference to his wealthy brother-in-law, the veiled threat, laced Silas with a poison teaspoon of anger. The gut-busting audacity of the man. Here he was threatening to resign and go to a position in another parish, just because he didn't wish to minister to shut-ins. Dear sweet merciful God in Heaven. For two cents on a barrel head, he'd cut old Cramphorne free, if only he ... had another ... *wait*. Hold on just a little minute here. Wasn't there just the other day ... a letter ... oh yes, here. Thomas Cooper Parson, newly graduated from the seminary, older man, newly married, trade of carpenter. Yes. That would do nicely for a rural community, a man who knew what it was like to work with his hands. Not really a great deal about him in the letter, the seminary not familiar, but that could be handled later. Parson could not possibly be worse than Cramphorne, even if he did come from a modest seminary, and just might be a great deal better.

Silas leaned back in his chair, held Cramphorne's letter in his left hand and Thomas Parson's letter in his right. He nodded. If Parson were amenable to a rural parish, and by all indications he was, then he'd just write a letter to Cramphorne 'regretfully' accepting his resignation and expressing his sorrow that things hadn't worked out. Oh my. Sometimes things just fell into place. The Lord in his infinite mercies did, after all, work in mysterious ways.

Anne Parson dried dishes at the tiny sink and watched her husband at the table in their one-room apartment work over papers, mostly bills, mostly unpaid, along with a small stack of work orders.

"If I can get that door repair Nathan English mentioned to me, that should help. It'll pay the rent for next week and the week after. Maybe a few groceries."

Anne picked up another dish and glanced at the pile of bills in front of her husband. She didn't say anything.

"I know, Hon, we'll make out. We will. It'll be all right." He stood up, took the dish out of her hand, laid it gently on the counter and folded her into his arms. She hardly came up to his shoulder.

She laid her hands flat against his chest. "Soon I'll be so big I won't be able to reach around you any more."

"That's all right. I can reach around you. And that means I'm hugging both you and our daughter." He laid one hand on the side of her tummy, just beginning to fill her spare frame.

She giggled. "I told you the baby is going to be a boy. Mrs. Hopper told me ...."

He laid a single finger across her lips. "I don't care what she told you, I want a girl. Mrs. Hopper is our landlady, not a nurse."

353

"She's a lot more than that. She's been very kind to us."

Tom nodded. "Yes, she has. And we deeply appreciate it, but that doesn't make her a nurse. And I want a girl, so that's that."

"Oh you think so, do you?"

"Yes, I do."

"Mr. Parson! Telephone!" Mrs. Hopper's voice rose and fell with her words, echoing from the hall outside.

Tom kissed Anne and headed out the door. "I hope that's Nathan. Maybe he needs that new door sooner than he thought."

Anne listened to his great feet clump down the hall, smiled to herself, rubbed her stomach and picked up the dish again.

Ten minutes later Tom returned, closed the door behind him and leaned up against it. A small smile pulled one side of his face.

"Well? What did Nathan say? Did you get the work?"

"No. Well, I don't know. That wasn't Nathan."

"Who was it then?"

"It was a certain Mr. Silas Webster."

Anne's eyebrows furrowed. "Who?"

Tom's smile grew broader. "The Right Reverend Silas Webster, Executive Secretary of the Presbytery."

Anne's hand flew to the center of her chest. "What?"

The smile on Tom stretched until his face was all teeth. "Honey, we got a church. We've got ourselves a church!"

He held out his arms and danced to her.

She dropped the dish and it shattered, covering the floor with a thousand shards of porcelain. "Oh honey, look at what I've done, I'm so sorry ...."

He gathered her into his arms and waltzed her about the room, humming the only snatch he knew of 'The Blue Danube.' "I'm not. We'll buy another one."

She quick-stepped to catch up with his large feet.

They heard a knock at the door and Mrs. Hopper drove her body, face first, into the room. "Is everything all right in here? I

354

told you I would not tolerate ….” Her shaking finger stopped in mid-air when she saw them smiling and dancing, and the remains of the broken dish covering the floor.

The two of them saw her mouth gape and both burst into laughter.

Mrs. Hopper straightened, put her hands on her hips and shook her head. “I just don’t know what I’m going to do with you two.”

Tom glided with waltz-step, arms open, from his wife to the stocky little woman in the black dress and waltzed her about. “My dear Mrs. Hopper, we are just happy.” He hummed as he swung her around, her long dress sweeping gently against the floor. “And we want you to be happy too.” He looked over at Anne. “Don’t we honey?”

Anne laughed, leaned up against the sink and clapped her hands. “Yes, we do.”

Mrs. Hopper slapped at Tom’s chest and pushed clear, waved her hands in the air as she recovered her wits and humphed her way to the door. “I was just on my way to tell you supper’s going to be a little late when I heard the crash, thought something was wrong up here.”

“Supper?” The two Parsons asked in unison.

Mrs. Hopper stopped and looked back. “Henry didn’t ask you?”

They glanced at each other and shook their heads. “No, no he didn’t.”

“Have you already made plans?”

They shook their heads again. “No. No, we haven’t.”

“Good. You two just come on down this evening about six-thirty, don’t be late now. I’m going to go have a little word of prayer with Henry.” She turned, opened the door and was speaking even before she had completely thumped her way down the stairs. “Henry, you deaf old coot! You told me, you said you’d asked our young folks to supper ….”

Tom bit down to hold in his laughter. Anne held up both palms to her mouth, bent over against the tiny sink.

When they recovered enough to wipe the tears from their eyes, Tom took her in his arms once more. "I cannot tell you how good it feels to see you happy. I hate to see you worry so."

She slid her arms around his waist and nodded into his chest. "I was worried about the baby. How we were going to manage, but now …"

He stroked her hair. "Now it's going to be all right, honey. It's all going to be just fine."

Silas Webster hung the telephone earpiece back on the hook, set the candlestick phone in its place and leaned back in his wooden swivel chair. He drew a deep breath and let out a long sigh. He reached forward once more and drew paper and pen from the drawer.

'My dear Reverend Cramphorne,

It is with great regret I received your letter of this Tuesday past. Knowing as I do of your difficult time and your tribulations, I sympathize with your plight and thus reluctantly accept your resignation.'

Silas lifted his nib from the page. With every word he wrote, a little slice of tension left his mind and heart. He knew it wasn't particularly Christian to find joy in another's difficulties, but decided he would pray later. For now, he accepted the little sin and enjoyed.

Chapter 54
Tracks

"Y'know, every time I get to thinking grown ups are smarter than us, somebody proves me wrong."

Ned's words, shouted over the roar of the wind in the back of the pickup as they rode to work, jolted Jamie from his daydream. He had been daydreaming Deidre's long legs, her coltish grace as she had trotted away after his promise to visit her. "What makes you say that?"

He followed the direction of Ned's nod. Nosy Norris stood on tiptoe at the widow's mailbox, peeking in the widow's windows again. As they rolled by, Norris looked over his shoulder at them and smiled.

Jamie could only stare. "Is he really that stupid?"

Ned coughed. "You did say something about a bag of hammers. We didn't tell what he was doing and it's a lead pipe cinch he didn't. Maybe he figures he got away with it. Maybe he figures your dad gave us a talkin' to in spite of what he said at the mill."

Jamie chewed on his lower lip. "He knows Daddy ain't the kind to go talking.' And the widow ain't neither."

"Meaning?"

"Meaning I'd be willing to bet two nickels to a dead snake in the grass nobody has said word one to him about it. He thinks he's dodged the bullet and that we're too scared to fire another one."

"Well ... we might have another shell in the chamber a wee bit worse than old Wanderin' Tom. We just gotta be willing to pull the trigger."

"I told you I don't hold with that. If it backfired on us we'd be in hot water again."

Ned's smile shifted into what might have been a smirk, but Jamie couldn't tell because the truck turned down the rutted road to the mill and conversation became an athletic event.

Ned did indeed hold back a full-fledged know-it-all grin. He just had a feelin' that one of these days Jamie Garrath was going to bust right open and do something historical. Ned just wanted to be there when it happened.

They made the final bounce into the mill yard and both boys climbed down from the back of the truck. Ned watched Jamie's eyes roll back just a little when Jamie got his work assignment shoveling sawdust again then slumped off to get the wheelbarrow and shovel.

Cyrus was ready to scout wood, the 38 revolver strapped to his hip as he talked with Mr. Garrath over the map and a list of needed timber. Then Mr. Garrath nodded to Cyrus, glanced up at Ned and smiled, then walked away.

Cyrus rolled up the papers and stowed them in his bag. "You all set?"

"Just let me put up my food sack."

"Bring it with you. We're going to be out most of the day."

Ned slung it over his shoulder. "All right."

"You're going to need your hands free to write." Cyrus gazed at Ned for a moment. "Come on."

Ned followed Cyrus to the supply shed, where Cyrus cut off a length of cotton plow line, then followed him out the dirt logging road into the woods. Only after they got clear of the mill yard and off the main path a ways did Cyrus stop. Cyrus breathed deep, looked up into the sky and closed his eyes. "This is better." He turned back to Ned and held out his hand. "Let me see that sack of yours. Not your food, take that out and just give me the sack."

Ned pulled the sandwiches, both apples and the Ball jar of water out of his sack and handed the sack to Cyrus. He bit into one of the apples. "What are you going to do with it?"

"I'm going to put a sling on it so you can carry yours the way I carry mine. That all right with you?"

"Sure."

Cyrus opened his own sack and drew out a small beaded canvas bag. Cyrus' hands were long and slim like the rest of him but immensely strong, nimble in the way they held things. He pulled open the top of the small bag and drew out a tapered wooden rod.

"What's that?"

"What? This?" Cyrus held up the rod and Ned nodded. "Splicing fid. Just a small one, but it comes in handy every now and again." Cyrus slid his knife out of its sheath, unraveled about 6 inches worth of the end of the line then began working them back into the fibers of the plow line with the fid. "While I'm doing this you watch and listen to the woods like I told you before. And I'd be careful around those bushes behind you, there may be a snake in there."

"Snake?" Ned was on his feet in a moment. "Want me to kill it for you?"

Cyrus looked up at Ned from his work. "I don't want you to kill it at all."

"Why not?"

Cyrus shook his head. "No need. He's doing no harm." A small eye splice appeared in one end of the rope in Cyrus' hands.

"How do you know he's there?"

"Sound."

"Aww. You can't hear a snake." Ned went over closer to Cyrus to watch what he was doing.

The eye splice finished, Cyrus turned Ned's bag inside out and folded the top back on itself to make a broad overlap. He pulled out a carved wooden cylinder out of the small canvas bag. He pulled the cylinder open and slid a few large needles out of it, selected one, slid the rest of the needles back in the cylinder and capped it. He threaded the needle with smooth white twine and began to sew the overlap down to the body of the bag. "I heard sound around him. It's hard to explain, but out here in the wood where boots aren't thumping around so much, animals will talk to

359

one another and be affected by one another. Think of ripples that go across the surface of a pond when you toss a rock in to it. Not only do the rings across the surface disturb what bugs might be floating on the surface, but the fish underneath will dive for the bottom of the deepest pool they can find." Cyrus shifted the bag and continued sewing. "Every animal affects other animals and that does include the human animal."

Ned had never seen a man sew before, and now as Cyrus finished the seam around the top of the bag he watched him pick up the rope and measure lengths of it in the air. "So you heard the other animals calling out 'Hey, watch out there's a snake in those bushes over there?'"

Cyrus laughed silently as he threaded the rope through the broad overlap hem he had just created and made it work like a drawstring to close the top of the bag. "More sounds of movement than calls." He spliced the rope to itself in the middle. "In this case I listened to the silent spots, because that's where the animals were not."

Ned was not listening to the forest, he was watching Cyrus' hands now as Cyrus sewed the small eye splice to the bottom corner of the bag. "Listening to silence?"

"Yep." Cyrus held up the bag for Ned. "Here you go."

The bag now had a shoulder strap that was also the drawstring for the top of the bag. The plow line was spliced rather than knotted where it attached. Ned had never seen work like it. "Where'd you learn to do that?"

Cyrus lifted his shoulders and let them fall as he put away his tools in the small bag and slid it into his own shoulder bag. "I grew up on the coast working boats with my tribe and family. We fished and did a little whaling. Most sailors can to this sort of thing in their sleep. Goes with the territory."

"Can you teach me?"

"Not today. Today we have work to do and you have other things to learn. Now stow your lunch, sling that bag over your shoulder and let's get going."

At mid-morning Cyrus stopped and sat down and Ned was glad of it. He plumped himself down on the ground and leaned back against a tree. Cyrus sorted through his maps then looked at Ned. He pointed at the ground beside Ned. "What are those?"

Ned followed Cyrus' finger to a human footprint.

"What can you tell about it?"

Ned stared at it. "Well, it's a man. It looks too large for a woman or somebody my age. He's coming from there," he pointed up the trail "and he's going toward there."

"Look closer."

Ned kneeled on one knee down next to the print the way he had seen Cyrus do, peering across the track, low down and from the side. "Old shoes, maybe work boots. They're smooth on the edges, worn on the heels."

"Good. And?"

"And nothing, that's all I see."

"Look at the left track and compare it to the right track."

Now Ned got down on his hands and knees.

"Don't look at just the prints. Look at what's around them. Look at everything and imagine what would fit."

"Why do I get the feeling you see something I'm not?"

"Because I am. But I'm trying to get you to see it by telling you how to see, not what to look at. I'm trying to teach you how to track, not what these particular tracks tell."

"So I'll know how to track when you're not here any more." Ned's knees began to hurt. The ground had lots of sticks on it. "What am I supposed to be looking for?"

"How deep do the tracks sink in the ground? That tells you things, what kind of pressure the foot pressed into the ground, how heavy the person or animal is. You think Crazy Charlie would go as deep in the ground as Marshall?"

"But Marshall's foot is bigger."

"True. But what if a man of Charlie's height were twice his weight? Look again."

Ned did. Again he saw a man's footprints, smooth edges on the soles, slightly pigeon toed and that was all. He told Cyrus as much.

Cyrus crouched down beside him. "A lot of learning to do this is to look at what you see, not what you want to see. Look first, then try to make sense of it, not the other way around."

"I just see ..."

"And don't just look at the prints. Look at what's around the prints."

"But ..."

"Just be quiet and look."

Ned did. He thought he was missing it, but ... there. "Left prints are deeper. Son of a bitch. How in the hell ... ?" In the excitement of discovery Ned forgot not to curse.

Cyrus smiled. "Drop back to where you were before and look again."

Ned did. Beside each right foot print there was a round hole about a half inch in diameter. "What the hell?"

"You see it now?"

"The hole?"

"That's right. Now close your eyes and imagine what could do that."

In his mind's eye he imagined ... a pole or ... "It's Eueas. Son of a bitch, it's Eueas." A shiver ran up his spine like a witches curse.

Cyrus nodded. "It's Eueas. But what's more important is what you've just learned about how to see. See what you see first, then try to make sense of it."

He thought he understood what Cyrus was trying to tell him, but his brain was flooding. Now that he had an image in his mind he wanted to follow the prints and find out more, but Cyrus brought him up short.

"Sorry, we got a lot of ground to cover before dark, but remember how your mind felt when you were looking." Cyrus stood up. "Let's go."

Ned stood and hitched his bag over his shoulder by the brand new strap. He looked backward once at the tracks then followed Cyrus deeper into the woods.

Chapter 55
Sea Change

"Jamie, you're not eating. You feel all right?" His mother laid the back of one hand across his forehead.

"Yes ma'am. Just tired I guess."

But in truth, Jamie was not all right, not all right at all. It was Monday night and supper dragged like molasses in wintertime and his stomach knotted with the thought of Deidre in the moonlight.

"You're not the only one." His father nodded toward Ned, who was leaned back in his chair with eyes closed. "Cyrus walked him to death today. Tell you what, why don't you clear your dishes and go crank the Delco."

Jamie bolted from the table and outside into open air. He walked around the side of the house toward the Delco, hands in his pockets. Was he really going to climb out the window tonight? He had to, he'd promised and she was just … he had to, that's all there was to it. He opened the door of the small shed and ducked inside to be greeted by the smell of dusty earth floor and kerosene. He pushed the switch. The electric starter whined and the little one-cylinder engine turned over with a little cough before settling down to a dim steady clatter. That clatter dimmed to a muffled purr as Jamie ducked back out and closed the door behind him. As he walked back toward the house he looked over in the direction of the lake. He couldn't see it from here, but imagined it just beyond the line of trees at the edge of the field. He sat on the stoop, stared at the trees with his chin in his hands. It occurred to him that he didn't know how to kiss. But would Deidre want him to? His mind's eye gazed on her at the place where she said she would meet him.

He stood up and climbed the steps back into the house and carefully fastened the latch on the screen door behind him. He stepped into the house, following the noise from the living room. His father was already listening to 'Easy Aces.' Jamie just didn't understand the appeal. The voice of that woman coming out the radio cabinet would peel paint. He stuck his head inside the living room. "Mom, is it all right if I just take a bath and go to bed?"

"Sure, honey. Ned's just finished and there's water on the stove."

After his bath, Jamie slipped into his bedroom. Ned already snored in his cot. He slid under his own covers and waited for the tell-tale thump of his parent's feet upon the floor to tell him they were going to bed, but he never heard it. The next thing he knew moonlight washed his face. He had fallen asleep. Gosh, what time was it? He eased up out of bed and slid into his clothes and boots. His brain told him he was breaking rules, but his hands and legs and feet felt no questions. They moved to the window of their own volition, propped open the screen, twisted out onto the ground, turned and eased the screen closed and took him toward Deidre.

The bright moonlight cast shadows on the ground from the house and trees in the yard. He trotted past the shed to the path across the pasture to the woods, his footsteps muffled in the grass. He paused at the woods, letting his eyes adjust to the dark. Fear and freedom grappled in his stomach. He breathed deep to quell his shaking and felt his chest fully inflate for the first time. The moon lit his way through the woods, leading him to her and god knew what else, but did nothing to diminish the thumping in his chest.

He paused just under cover of the trees where the path came out of the woods and crossed the road at the Widow Morrison's house. He looked both ways then trotted across, but just before he reached the cover of the bushes on the other side a truck came around the bend and illuminated the trees. He dove into the bushes and looked back, but the single red tail light did not slow at all. The truck looked a little like Norris', but there was no telling in the dark. He waited to let the headlight spots clear from his eyes. When he could see the trail again he stepped carefully along the path, the moonlight casting shadows of the trees across the trail. He slowed as he got to the lake, looking for her, and walked down the dock as quietly as he could.

One of the slender shadows moved and there she was, her smooth willow form illuminated from behind through her thin sundress. He had never seen anything so lovely in his life.

"You certainly took your time, King James. I've been waiting here forever." Her voice reached to him in the darkness, lithe, caressing his ears, the tone belying the words. She flowed over to him and took his hand. "I'm glad you came." She pulled and led him back toward their camp. "What have you been doing since I saw you last?"

As he stumbled over the ground, Jamie told her about the rabbit and how they gave it to Jacob. He swore her to secrecy. "If anybody finds out it was us it would ruin it."

She pulled to a stop just outside the firelight of the camp and he felt her eyes upon his face. "It's a good one you are, Jamie Garrath. You and your Ned, the both of you to do such a thing."

Jamie's voice stuck in his throat. He wanted to speak but his brain just wasn't delivering words the way it should. The only thing he could manage was to throw his head a little toward one shoulder.

She giggled, a silver stream of sound in the moonlight. "Come on, meet Pa for real this time." She tugged on his hand to pull him toward the fire.

There were four lumps on the ground by the fire as they emerged from the dark. One of them was Deidre's father. When he turned his granite gaze from the fire Jamie promptly forgot to walk and tripped on a root in the ground. If not for Deidre's hand he would have fallen. He hoped the dark and the dim light had hidden his gaff and his suddenly burning cheeks, but he had no such luck. When he looked up her father's mouth was pulled to one side as he shook his head, then he lifted his arm and waved them over to the fire.

Three heads other than Deidre's Pa swiveled toward them. One head was Emma's. She was wrapped up in a blanket and leaned against a box. She coughed and her husky contralto sang out. "You're just in time for a story."

The other two people were cuddled under a blanket with their heads together like newlyweds. A pot hung on a hook over the fire. The golden glow played across their faces in waves. There was so much new to his eyes Jamie could not see everything.

366

Firelight scenes from the books he read were no longer in the realm of imagination. This was real.

"Would you like a cup of tea, young Deidre's friend?"

The man of the newlyweds held an enameled cup out to Jamie. Jamie reached out and took it and offered his thanks.

The man nodded. "You're welcome. I'm Paddy and this here's Brigid. We'll be learning more of you later. As Emma said, Seamus was just about to start a tale, weren't you Seamus?"

Deidre pulled Jamie down to a spot by the fire where he could lean up against a log, grabbed a blanket and settled herself in front of him and leaned back into his legs. This gave Jamie a good look at Seamus' face. Perhaps 'good' was not the right word, for his face looked like a stone mountain about to avalanche.

"Give us a tale." Deidre settled into him. "Please Pa."

Her father sipped his cup. "What do you know of Ireland, lad?"

"Only that it's west across the Irish Sea from England, it's green and it's people are gifted in music and stories."

The granite head nodded slowly. "That'll do for a start. Do you know any of the tales?"

"No sir."

Jamie thought he could feel Deidre smile even though her face was away from him.

"Well then open your ears. This is an old one, no one knows how old. Ireland is a lady that has been set upon and fought for since the Irish have had memory."

The man raised his cup again, coughed, took a deep breath and began.

Chapter 56
Seamus' Tale

There was a once great harpist and harp maker in old Ireland, or Eire, as those who know her well call her. He was a fair man with a fair heart and the pure magic of the gods in his hands. The maker's wife was a queen. He made her a special harp like no other in the known world and played this harp and sang for her. She was bewitched by his music and his voice and so she gave up her throne for him and to bear his children. And well she might, for the man had magic in him and knew it. Knew it and used it, though never unkindly.

All was well until there came a rival for her hand, even though her hand was already taken along with the rest of her and by her own choice. This evil article scum of a man cared not a stone underfoot for all that but turned his black mind on taking and having her for himself and so set about his works.

This self-appointed rival put on his best clothing, rigged out his best horse and paid the harp maker a visit, knocked on the maker's door ostensibly for commissioning a harp. The harp maker let him in and asked him questions about what kind of music the man would be playing. From the answers given the maker soon grasped the man was not only dumb as a stump but knew nothing of harps or music. As the harp maker leaned back and rubbed his chin on this, the man pressed on, professed a deep and abiding desire to be at one with the harp, to be so imbued with the music and the instrument that one could not tell where one left off and the other began. Now even to the muddled mind of a midge, this was totally untrue. So of course, the maker's mind twigged that the man was there for some other purpose and set to find out what it was.

The harp maker plied the man with whiskey to loosen his tongue. Soon all manner of compliments flowed from the man about the maker's wife, in the beginning innocent, but by the time the middle of the bottle label were reached, the man's comments had gone beyond the bounds of propriety and the purpose of his visit made all too clear. The maker's wife became uncomfortable and left the two men to drink and talk alone.

The harp maker bargained hard with the man and took the commission, but not because he needed the money. He intended to dig a few feet deeper than this evil man's intent to set things straight.

The maker saw the staggering rival outside and back on his horse and watched until he was certain the man would survive the trip home then and pushed back into his own door.

His wife was in wait for him. "How could you sit here and let him say all those things to me? He's a horrible, horrible man."

And the maker responded, "Are you saying I have something to worry about?"

She softened then, her eyes clear and brimming with unmistakable love. "You know that isn't true."

He nodded to her. "Yes, I know. But if you wish me to do something about him I will. For you."

She told him the man bothered her, so the maker set about his works in his own way, as he had always done. Remembering the old saying 'Be careful what you wish for' he set to making a harp to would give the man what he had said he wanted. He did not make it to satisfy the man's desires.

When the harp was finished he sent word to the man with the stipulation the man must meet him on a certain day at midnight at the remote crossroads called the Godstones, a place of rocks of the aged gods, a place well known to those who pay attention to such things as places of power and death for those who dare to defy the will of the gods or lie to them.

The man came, with some trepidation it must be said, for he was well aware he had said far too much with his loosened tongue at the harp maker's house, but he was undeterred and determined in his course to steal the harp maker's wife. The rogue thought if the harp maker was so stupid as to want to fight him and was so unlucky as to die, well so much the better for him and he would soon talk the grieving widow into believing her dead husband's folly. So he armed himself and went.

They met at midnight on the accorded day in the accorded place. The man was ready for fisticuffs or worse and was surprised the harp maker offered him no violence but only wanted him to sit and try the harp while sitting on the stones of the gods for that was a ritual of his, a kindness to the gods offering the first true notes of all his harps to the gods. The harp maker even offered him a drink before he began. The man complained the only truth he had ever told the maker and that was that he did not yet know how to play. The harp maker laughed and said not to worry, for the harp would do all the work for him. The man laughed, thinking the harp maker simple, indulged him, took a great draught of the drink and then sat down to play.

And play he did. At first he did not know how it happened and marveled at the magic of it but his fingers took to the strings like they were made for it and he played and played and played. He became what the harp maker said he would, for once he began the magic would not let him stop. The music loosened the man's soul and as he played his soul bled into the wood and varnish and the strings of the instrument. Once he had started he could not stop.

The harp maker left him like that, playing and playing, consumed with the harp and the music, weeping with the sadness of the tunes, his tears soaking the wood.

A few weeks later the harp maker's wife asked him if he had taken care of that awful odious man for she did not want to deal with the man again and did not want to be surprised by him at her market trips or any other time. The harp maker responded he thought he had but would look into it to make certain.

He did. He went back to the Godstones and there was the man, or what was left of him, lying upon the ground, nothing left but a skeleton with rotting clothes hanging in tatters from the bones. The harp maker buried what remained of the man and retrieved the harp. The harp, other than being a little weathered, was fine and the harp maker took it to the village and sold it to the first passing minstrel, who was glad to have such a fine instrument at a reasonable price.

And so the harp maker kept his wife, kept his shop and kept his promise to the lying man, whose soul to this day lies within the harp known as the Harp That Gently Weeps.

Chapter 57

Return Passage

The moon had led him there. Now the moon led him back again. Jamie had never been so aware the moon moved in the sky, but that was insignificant beside Deidre, the seed growing in his heart. She hadn't kissed him, but her father had shaken his hand. His body still felt how she leaned into him and grasped his hands as they had listened to the tale. His hand could still feel hers, the memory of physical touch a thing he'd not experienced or even thought possible.

He had no idea of the time. The moon was still high. He knew full well from having seen Ned the morning after one of his jaunts that he was going to pay for his, but it was a debt he would have paid a hundred times over.

The closer he got, the more the house seemed to loom. Was Ned awake? Were his parents? He approached the window and set his ear next to the screen. Nothing but a soft snore. Ned must have been really tired. He eased the screen open, propped it open with a stick and belly-flopped inside over the sill. He had one bad moment when his boot caught on the stick and knocked it with a clatter to the ground outside. Ned stopped snoring, then shifted and settled again while Jamie's heart jumped into his throat. After Ned settled he breathed again, pulled in his feet in and latched the screen closed. He slid off his boots, slid off his clothes and slid under the single thin white sheet. He could not believe he had made it all the way back in without getting caught. Ned's words 'breathing free air' echoed in his mind. Now he knew what it meant, how sweet 'free air' smelled.

Jamie laid his head back upon the pillow, blinked and it was morning.

Chapter 58

Discoveries

Sunlight through the window stabbed the pain already living behind Jamie's eyes. "Oh God." He forced himself to sit up but kept his eyes closed.

"Uff aheet?"

Jamie squinted at Ned. "What?"

Ned slung back the sheet, swing his bare feet to the floor and shook his head like a dog slinging water. He weaved. "Morning safety tip, don't ever shake your head like that first thing." He blinked at Jamie. "Tough night?"

"You could say that." Jamie yawned, rubbed his scalp, and wondered if Ned really had been asleep through the clatter he had made coming back in through the screen. "Couldn't settle down. Mom called yet?"

"Un-huh. Ten minute warning." Ned rubbed his eyes.

"That means five before she calls again. Damn."

Breakfast was slow torture. His father spoke too loudly, every dish clattered through his head and the oatmeal and eggs his mother put in front of him made his stomach flip and turn. He managed to fight down the oatmeal, down a big glass of milk and stagger out the door with his lunch sack over his shoulder. He climbed into the back of the pickup.

Jamie breathed the cool morning air deep to clear his head but the buffeting of the wind just made the pain worse. Light barely showed through the trees on the horizon as they bounced out the lane and turned right onto the main road toward the village. The truck pulled into the dirt drive in front of the post office and pulled to a stop.

Jamie's father got out. "Come on down, boys. If the package I'm expecting is here, I'm going to need your help with it."

They got down and followed him. Their feet sent up little puffs of gray dust into the early morning air with each step.

The post office was a tiny affair, white clapboard except for broad panels of glass on the front. There was a heavy inset door with a glass panel in it as well. The greeting bell tinkled as they pushed through the door after Jamie's father.

"You boys just wait here while I go to the window."

Jamie glanced around and saw the Reverend Cramphorne by his mailbox reading a letter. There was a group gathered around two men talking loudly in the corner.

Jamie pushed forward through the group until he could see the protagonists.

"Well, where'd you get it?" George Pepper was the local skeptic. He was a little wiry fella with salt and pepper hair who wouldn't believe rain was wet if he was soaked to the skin and would argue which side of the nickel the buffalo was on. He also held his cards so close to his chest that often even he didn't know what he was thinking.

"M-my Uncle Charles left it to me." A brilliant white smile spread wide upon the farmer tan face of Bob Cramner. In his meaty palm lay a gleaming silver railroad conductor's watch. Bob didn't have very much, but pushed to tell you what he did have. When he was excited the words driving from his mind tended to overrun his mouth.

George had no better sport in this life than sticking pins in Bob's balloons. His face bobbed like a barn cat with a bead on a mouse. You could almost see his ears work before the pounce.

"Where'd he get it?"

"H-he worked for the r-railroad," Bob slid thumbs under his suspenders, "and a m-man what works the rails g-gotta know the t-time."

Jamie heard Ned's voice quiet and low in his ear. "Neither of 'em can read a watch." Jamie glanced at Ned, got an affirming

373

nod then looked back. He flicked his eyes back and forth between the gladiators.

George drawled. "Your uncle could tell time, could he?"

"Oh yeah. Ya got to to w-work the rails, it's a j-job requirement. Found that out when I applied over at C-Criglersville last y-year." Bob slowly closed the watch, slid it into his watch pocket and patted it down.

"You ain't workin' for 'em?"

"Uhh … naw … t-told me I was t-too old."

"Well, that's too bad." George drew his words out long. "Does it, uhh, keep pretty good time?"

"B-best I've ever seen." Bob waved his finger in the air. "N-never had to reset it once since I g-got it, and that was t-two months ago."

George rubbed his grizzled chin and closed one eye. "Is that so now? Keeps that good a time, does it? And it's how old?" Jamie could feel the trap creak open.

"Uh-ah, w-well, Uncle was s-sixty-three when he died, an-and hired in when he was thirty or so, so that makes it about ..." Bob squeezed his face, "'b-bout thirty year I reckon. M-more or less."

George Pepper could chill a poker player right down to his shoes. His eyes narrowed. His voice came out smooth and natural without a ghost of a hint of an accusation. "That's right nice, it sure is. By the way, what time is it now?"

Bob froze for a half-beat, mouth stuck. Then with the face of the condemned, he pulled the watch from his pocket. He pressed the button to open the cover, and held it out for George to see.

"Th-there she is."

George's Adam's apple bobbed just once and stuck. A frozen moment crept by while one set of pupils bored into the other.

"Well, damned if it ain't."

George's mouth gripped itself. He gathered his mail under his arm. "Well, gotta go, got to get to go doing things. See you later."

"Yep, m-me too, see ya." Bob's face smoothed as he watched George's back out the door.

Jamie and Ned exchanged glances and grins, then pushed back out of the group to look around for Jamie's father. They ducked between the bodies to the service window where Jamie's Aunt Melanie sorted mail.

"Auntie Mel, you seen Dad?"

"What did you say?" Bad grammar scraped against Aunt Melanie like an old corncob. She glared over her wire rim glasses at Jamie then shifted her gaze to Ned. "Hello Ned. I hope you haven't been teaching him to speak that way."

"Oh no, ma'am."

"I'm sure. Jamie?"

"Auntie Mel, have you seen Dad?"

"He's in the back getting a package. He might be needing some help with it." She drew open the bottom of the half-door that served as the counter. "Come on back."

The package was round and wide, like a giant hockey puck covered in cardboard. Jamie's father had just lifted it vertical so it could be rolled along the floor like a tire. It came up almost to his father's shoulder and was about a foot thick. "Come here, Jamie. You get on the front side. Ned, you get on the back side and just roll it slow out next to the outside door. I'll be there in a minute. I got a little more business with Aunt Mel."

The package was heavier than it looked and did not roll easily.

"You boys be careful. If that thing starts to fall you get out of the way now. It's heavy enough to break a leg."

"What is it?"

"New belt for the mill. The old one's about to go, so I thought I'd get a new one before the old one broke and whipped around to kill somebody."

Ned whispered under his breath as they pushed the big roll out of the room. "Yeah, us."

"What was that?" Jamie's Auntie Mel had ears like a bat.

"Nothing, Ma'am."

They worked the roll through the half door service counter and stopped behind the outside door where they'd be out of the way.

The outside door opened. Eueas thumped in, his cane clattering against the doorframe. The man didn't see them as he shifted and slunk up to the counter. "Any letters for me?"

Auntie Mel looked at Eueas like he'd just crawled out of a stagnant pond. "Name, please?"

Eueas shifted his chaw to the other side of his mouth. "Eueas Canfield, just like ever other time I come here."

Auntie Mel sniffed, bent to one side and sifted through a stack of letters. "Nothing today, Mr. Canfield, just like every other time you have come. Next."

Jamie watched Eueas bend as if to spit on the floor, then stop and wither under Auntie Mel's 'Don't you dare' stare. Eueas grimaced a smile at her then sidled over to the side table and sifted through the clipboard of wanted posters.

This was the second time Jamie had seen Eueas page through the wanted posters. He thought about possibilities as to why when he felt Ned tug at his sleeve and whisper in his ear. "Hey, look at Ol' Craphorn. He looks like he swallowed a persimmon."

The reverend stood by his open mail box reading a letter. It was true. For once the man's face was not flopping with bombast. Matter of fact he looked like he'd been gut shot, his jowls oddly hanging still.

Jamie jumped as he felt his father's hand on his shoulder. "Come on, let's see if we can get this thing out to the truck."

Jamie grasped his father's arm. "Dad, look at the Reverend."

His father slowly folded his papers and put them in his back pocket as he looked over at Cramphorne.

"What do you think might be wrong? I've never seen him look like that."

Jamie's father shook his head. "Neither have I. But right now," he looked down at the both of them, "it's none of our business. Our business is getting this belt outside and up into the back of the truck. Come on."

They heaved and struggled and rolled the big cardboard covered disk outside. A couple of times it almost tilted over, but his father managed to catch it in time. They got it to the back of the pickup and leaned it against the edge of the tailgate.

Jamie's father tilted his hat to the back of his head. "We need to wait til somebody comes out to help us, boys. Rolling it's one thing, but it'll take three men and a midget to lift it into the back of the truck."

Eueas Canfield, aka Lucas Cane, gently sifted through the stack of wanted posters on the clipboard. He glanced up frequently at the jabbering gee-haws at the service window. Gatherings of folks who talked as if they liked each other made him uncomfortable. He had never liked anyone that much, not enough to want to stand around and just talk. There was always too much to do, too much look out for and way too many folks out there you couldn't trust as far as you could spit. Papa had taught him that.

Right now the only thing Eueas had in mind was to look through these posters. He had never quite trusted his luck that no one had run him to ground for getting out of the army in independent fashion. He had thought the set of blank discharge papers that had come into his hands courtesy of a wrecked staff supply truck would do him up right if he ever needed to skedaddle and he had been right. New orders came that non —essential airplane mechanics were to go to the front lines to ready the clanking tanks for a new push and to help sappers dig mine tunnels. Neither option thrilled Eueas a whole lot. Since he couldn't read, he got a buddy to fill out the papers and forge signatures. First chance he got after that he just wandered off and never came back. He bald-faced his way onto a troopship back to Norfolk then home in an empty baggage car, but no sooner had he hit the ground than he learned his name was on the list of MIA's and what the hell was he doing home? That tripped him up bigger'n a low sawed off stump. Leave it to the army to be efficient when you didn't want it to. He fled before somebody who hated him turned him. A man just couldn't trust anybody these days. No way, no how, not nobody.

As he thumbed through the newer wrinkled papers for his own name he thought to turn back to that poster he'd seen before when that nosy kid had been staring at him. Eueas couldn't read it, but the grainy picture showed an Indian with scars on his face and there was a drawing of a tattoo of a black bird.

I cain't really tell by this picture, but I wonder. Eueas thought. *Cyrus is Indian. He got scars on his face, but lot of people got scars. I'll just keep a watch for that tattoo, that's what I'll do. It'd sure fix his little red wagon.* He chuckled at his own joke. *Little red wagon, just about right. I'll fix him.* He skulked a glance over his shoulder, tore the poster from the clipboard binder, folded it twice and shoved it deep in his pocket. He'd have to study on it to make sure, but this might just be his ticket to getting that dirty ass redskin off his back for good.

As Eueas eased toward the door he was shoved aside by a huge bulk. He reared up to fend off, but stopped when his cane clattered on another one. The preacher passed before Eueas had a chance to whack him even once. Now what the hell was wrong with that fat old sumbitch?

Jamie saw Cramphorne bull his way past Eueas in the doorway.

"Hey Reverend, could you lend a hand …?" His father's voice trailed off as there was no response whatsoever. Cramphorne kept walking right to his car and drove away.

"What the hell?" His father raised a hand to Eueas, who was thumped out of the Post Office shoving a piece of paper in his back pocket.

Eueas begged off. "I know it's a trial to you Mr. Garrath, but with this leg of mine I'd sure hate to drop it and get somebody hurt. You know how it is."

His father took on what Jamie called 'smooth face.' That was the face when his father didn't want anyone to see what he was thinking. "Yes, thank you for your concern Mr. Canfield. I'll see you at the mill."

"Yes sir, Mr. Garrath. I'm on my way." Eueas walked off, his cane grinding little holes in the ground as he made his way over to the migrant worker truck parked at Fred and Adam's store across the road.

Snow came out of the post office. "That the new belt, Mr. Garrath? You need some help?"

"I sure do and I thank you kindly."

Snow gave his big white smile. "You better hold that thanks til we get it up there without breaking somebody's foot."

With Snow's help they heaved the belt up into the truck. Jamie and Ned squeezed in beside the big package. Snow climbed into the cab beside Jamie's father and they bounced out of the Post Office parking lot.

Jamie leaned back against the side of the truck, his head waving with the motion. The wind didn't hurt so much now his head was clear.

When they slowed down for the turn past Little Lake, Jamie forgot his pain altogether. Deidre walked beside the road, wooden water buckets in each hand on her way to the lake. Jamie leaned up, smiled and waved as they drove by. She saw him and dropped one bucket to wave. When her dazzling smile disappeared behind the turn Jamie leaned back.

"You snuck out last night, didn't you?"

Jamie snapped at Ned's challenge. "What makes you think that?"

Ned stretched a catbird smile. "Yeah well, let me see." He counted on his fingers. "I saw the look in her eyes when she waved at you, you're mighty sleepy this morning and you didn't answer my question. One and one and one generally adds up to three."

Jamie turned his head away. "You're awfully full of yourself this morning."

"Yeah well, tell me I'm wrong and I'll shut up."

"You shut up anyway. What happens between Deidre and me is between me and Deidre, you understand me?"

"I didn't mean nothing by it."

The remainder of the trip to the mill rattled the air between them and when the truck stopped they both climbed down out of the back.

"Just happy for you is all." Ned pushed his hat back on his head. "I thought I'd just rib you about it a little. Remember that thing, fun?"

"I don't know. I've never felt anything like it."

Ned grinned. "Smells pretty sweet, don't it?"

"What?"

"Night air."

Jamie's father came over to the back of the truck with Snow and Marshall to get the belt out of the back. "You boys step back now, so you don't get hurt. Jamie, you go get a wheelbarrow and start cleaning out sawdust under the blade. We're setting up to saw tomorrow. Ned, you go find Cyrus, you're cruising timber today."

"Yes sir." They spoke in unison, turned and walked away in the same direction.

Jamie looked over at Ned. "You're right."

He watched Ned scan for Cyrus and then look back at him. "About what?"

"It smells real damn sweet."

They grinned 'see you laters' and got to work.

Chapter 59

Serendipity

Sawing day was a big day.

Jamie dodged the mule Mrs. Ace as she dragged logs to the saw shelter. Her hooves thudded on the ground in quiet rhythm and Lester danced behind to the side of the log that carved scores in the dry earth. Jamie trotted along behind listening to the faint clink of log chain and the slap of harness. Lester pulled Mrs. Ace to a stop beside the inclined ramp of the log deck that fed the saw carriage. The carriage fed the logs to the singing blade.

Beneath that blade was a lot of old sawdust. Jamie's job, again, was to clean it out.

The good part was he got to watch Caleb Frazier use a cant hook. Caleb was a tall French Canadian with sandy scrub brush of unruly hair and shoulders like an ox that rippled as he drove logs up the incline. Cant hooks are heavy off-balance awkward things, but Caleb could lift and spin one around as easily as Jamie lifted a fishing pole.

The bad part of today was that he was close to Eueas. Eueas handled the safety lines that restrained the logs from rolling back down the incline.

He hoped Eueas would be too busy to notice him.

When packed down, old, damp and mildewed, sawdust is heavy and stinks to high heaven. By the third wheelbarrow load Jamie was staggering. He stopped to rest and watch Caleb.

Jamie had tried to pick up a cant hook a couple of times just to see what it felt like. He could hardly lift the thing off the ground. Now he watched Caleb drive the hook into the log with effortless ease before his muscles clenched into ropes and heaved the creaking log upward.

Chains ran underneath the logs at either end. Ropes were tied to the chains and secured to hold the log in place while Caleb got another purchase with his cant hook. Caleb drove the spike of the hook deep into the log, levered the cant hook and muscled it up the incline. Eueas cleated the rope off to hold it there. Caleb had just bent to take another purchase when the rope cracked like a pistol shot as it broke. The log slid back down, the chain flew up and the shackle on the end whipped through the air and smacked Caleb right in the head with the wet pop-crunch like a chicken bone in the hands of a strong woman.

Jamie watched Caleb collapse to the earth and then saw the log above Caleb's legs, swinging slowly, the second rope creaking strain. Then Jamie watched himself move, as fast as he could but through molasses. He passed Eueas, cleared the log with a single leap and grasped Caleb's collar and overall suspenders and heaved as hard as he could to drag the man out of there. He moved Caleb just a fraction. The rope creaked under load. He yelled for help as loud as he could, pulled, heaved and strained, his heels sliding on the sawdust earth. He glared at Eueas. Eueas looked back, down at his leg, then back to Jamie and Caleb on the ground under the creaking log.

"Help! Please!" Jamie screamed and heaved again. Caleb moved an inch or two, but not enough.

Then over Jamie's shoulder a huge meaty paw gripped Caleb's suspenders. Jamie began to scramble back and then felt himself being dragged back right along with Caleb until they were out from under the log.

The log crashed down, the log deck sagged and the carriage support structure beyond heaved up into the air. Eueas had attached the chains to the rail and now the falling log pried the carriage rail upward and cracked the structural wood underneath.

Then it was quiet, even the birds quit singing. The only thing Jamie could hear was breathing and the thump of his own heart. Then voices made it through the fog in his head.

"Jamie, are you all right? Jamie, talk to me!"

Then another voice, Marshall's, deep and calm. "He's all right, Mr. Garrath. He's all right. He did well, very well indeed. Just let him sit for a little while and be proud of him."

Jamie could not catch his breath. He dimly noticed Ned and Cyrus running up. The disembodied thought came to him they had probably come running at the crash of the log hitting the ground.

The other men gathered around Caleb. He heard his father's voice telling Ned to run get the doctor kit and for Snow to telephone for a doctor and to take the truck to go get him if that's what was needed.

Jamie slowly turned his head to look at Eueas, who still sat on the ground with the rope in his hand.

Eueas' face was white, his eyes wide and his gaze glanced from Caleb stretched out on the ground to Jamie, then to his hands, then back to Jamie, his gaze flicking from spot to spot from underneath the single bushy eyebrow that spanned both eyes. He crushed his fedora flat and twisted it in both hands. Then he took a deep breath, slapped it back onto his head by the brim and wedged it back down into place. He clattered his cane out from underneath him and swiveled himself up off the ground with exaggerated difficulty.

Jamie's father walked to him. "What happened, Eueas?"

"Well sir, Caleb hooked the chains up and started workin' it up the ramp rails with the cant hook. I kept a good tension on it and it looked fine till the rope broke right at the shackle there. The log, she shifted back down and that shackle flew up and cracked Caleb right in the head. Then the log slid down all cattywampused." He coughed. "Jamie here did his damndest best to drag him out of there but Caleb was just too heavy. Just thank God for Marshall's all I got to say. He showed up outa nowhere and dragged 'em both up out the way. I'm sorry, I just couldn't get up quick enough." Eueas trailed off.

Jamie felt his father's gaze shift to him. "Is that what you saw, Jamie?"

Jamie remembered telling Snow when he and Ned had seen Eueas swing the sling blade at Toby, that Eueas' leg worked just fine. They weren't believed. And Eueas would never admit it. He had been willing to let a man die to protect his lie so there was no way Eueas was going to tell the truth now.

"Jamie. Is that what you saw?"

383

He nodded dumbly, never taking his eyes off Eueas, never hating anybody so much in his life.

He felt Marshall's hands on his shoulders. "He's all right, Mr. Garrath. I think he just needs a little break is all."

"That sounds like a good idea to me, that sound good to you, Jamie?"

Again Jamie managed to nod; he'd never felt so tired and sick inside. He knew Eueas was a liar and dangerous. He knew the truth. There was simply nothing he could do about it.

Jamie caught Cyrus' eye. Cyrus had been silent through the whole thing after he and Ned had come up. He watched Cyrus throw a quick glance over at Eueas then smiled a frown back at Jamie. He laid a hand on Ned's shoulder. "Good idea if you go take care of your friend. Go on. Caleb will be all right, I seen worse. He's already coming around."

Ned nodded. "Mr. Garrath, could me and Jamie eat our dinner over at the lake?"

"Mr. Custis, that's a prime idea. You two go on while we get all this straightened out."

Ned reached out a hand to Jamie. "Come on. Let's get the poles."

Jamie took Ned's hand. Ned pulled him up. Then he followed Ned up to the office and got their fishing poles and their food bags.

As they walked the woods path to the lake past the cotton fields Ned turned to look over his shoulder several times. "You all right?"

The dirt crunching under their feet was the only real sound except for the occasional insect buzzing around their heads. The air was dead and still, southern dry hot dead, like the earth was waiting for rain just to wake up. Jamie nodded. "I can't believe it. He just sat there like he was frozen. Didn't even try to get up and help. His lie was more important than Caleb."

"You mean to tell me he just sat there?"

Jamie nodded. "Caleb coulda died."

"You too, sound's like. Caleb going to be all right?"

"Cyrus said so, but I don't know. Snow went to get the doctor."

They got to the end of the dock and sat down.

"I've never seen anyone hurt like that." Ned laid his pole down. "I guess it coulda been worse. He's still alive. And he got hit on the side of the head. If he'd been hit in the face …."

"I don't want to think about that."

"All right."

"I don't want to think about anything." Jamie turned his pole in his hand, unwinding the dark line, then stopped and laid the pole down on the dock. "Goddamn, he's a piece of shit."

The accident kept repeating over and over in his head. He could not get rid of the image of Eueas just sitting there, not moving while Caleb bled. He could understand fear. He could not understand not even trying to help.

"Tell you what." Ned's voice was quiet. He stood and nodded toward the path. "I'm gonna go back to the house and take care of the chores. You catch a mess of fish and we'll clean them together when you get back. That all right with you?"

Jamie nodded. Tears were pressing up against the backside of his eyeballs, but he didn't want Ned or anybody else to see.

"All right, I'll see you later at the house."

The sound of Ned's boots clumping on the deckboards faded behind him.

Jamie closed his eyes and let the tears run down his face.

Then he felt a hand on his shoulder and a soft feminine voice spoke in his ear. "Jamie?"

He jumped a royal foot and yelped. He spun around and saw Deidre standing there, her hand still in space where she had touched his shoulder. "Oh Jesus, don't do that."

"I'm sorry."

Jamie waited for his heart to stop pounding and nodded to her, then remembered there were tears on his cheeks and wiped them away with his sleeve.

"Are you all right?"

He looked up at her. She was, as usual, a vision. Tendrils of auburn hair draped around her face but her eyes were not twinkling now. They were wide open serious deep pools of emerald. She wore her cotton print sundress and light little boots. He had never seen anything so lovely or anything so welcome. "I guess. Just a little rattled from the accident, that's all."

"Accident?" She sat down on the dock across from him.

Jamie told her. He also burst forth with all that was on his mind about Eueas and what happened.

She was silent until he had finished. "Are you all right? Are you hurt?"

Jamie shook his head. "I'm fine. Marshall snatched both of us out of there before the log fell."

"He must be a prodigious strong man."

"Oh, he is. When I first hired on at the mill they needed to shift the main engine to get it lined up. Dad was going to get pry bars to work it in position, but Marshall just put his shoulder to it and heaved it right into place. He's amazing. He grabbed me with one fist and Caleb with the other and before I knew it we were both out of there. Y'know, it happened so fast I don't remember moving from there to where he put us down." He leaned back against a piling. "There's all kinds of work to be done now. The log cracked the rails on the loading platform and cracked the log carriage. We need somebody beyond just a framing carpenter to work on that."

"Pa could probably help you with that. He's a woodworker of the best kind, I told you that. He's off looking after a job now."

Jamie heard a truck drive up. He thought the muffler was shot and needed replacement, but when he saw Seamus Dunne approaching though the trees he thought better of mentioning it. Not only did the man probably already know, his scowl told Jamie the mention would not be welcome. When Jamie glanced at Deidre and saw her slight shake of the head, he knew Dunne had not been successful.

He watched Dunne power his way down the dock, swinging fists. He waved at Deidre. "Come on, girl. We're off for camp." He caught a glance from Deidre toward Jamie and stopped. "You again, is it? I thought I told you to stay away from me daughter."

Deidre stepped in between them. "And that's a fine way to be thanking the man that might lead you to work. And just last night we welcoming him to our fire and you tellin' him your tales."

"What 'man' might that be, all I see on the other side of you is a boy and a scrawny wee one at that."

" 'Better on the thin side and able to be fattened up by the cooking of a good woman than a fat man you have to kick in the pants to get away from his pints', isn't that what I heard mother say more than once?" Deidre had her hands on her hips by now and her feet spread solidly on the planks of the dock. "And as you can plainly see if you want to use the eyes that God gave you, that I'm here getting water for supper and he's just here to fish to put a little food on the table of his family."

Jamie watched Seamus look about the dock and see the evidence of what she said. This long look was followed by a deep frown and a humph like a bull clearing its throat.

"Work, is it?" Jamie felt Seamus' eyes bore into him. "And what kind of work would that be?"

"At the sawmill. There was an accident there today. The log carrier that feeds the saw was damaged."

"And just how would you be knowing that?"

"I work there and saw it happen. Dad said they might need some help with it."

"And how would your Pa be knowing that?"

Jamie didn't know how to answer. He didn't want this man to think he was trying to throw any weight because his father owned the place. "If you have woodworking or construction experience, you could ask."

Seamus's eyes were still dark, but there was a nod with the frown. "That I have, in both. Are you certain they'll be wanting help?"

"Not dead certain, no sir. But the longer the log carrier is broken the longer it will be before the sawing's done and the orders filled. And the mill needs the saw to make money."

Seamus looked at Jamie out of the side of his eyes. "And the worst they can say is no, eh?"

Jamie nodded.

"All right then. First thing tomorrow I'll see." Seamus's frown grew a little less severe. "Come on back, Deidre. There's supper to do." With that, Seamus turned on his heel and stomped away up the path again. They heard his truck start and drive away toward their camp.

"I'll walk you home." He didn't want to be without her just then.

"All right."

Jamie wound his line around his fishing pole, laid it down and dipped Deidre's buckets into the water. She picked up his pole and they walked out to the road.

At the turn off to the camp Deidre spun around. "I'll take them from here. He's not ungrateful, it's just that he's angry at having been so long out of work. He's afraid to hope."

She stepped close to Jamie, grasped the bucket handles next to his hands and slowly and deliberately kissed his cheek. He smelled honeysuckle in her hair. She whispered in his ear. "I'm glad you're all right. I'll see you later." She pulled the buckets from his hands and swung down the dirt road after her father to their camp, glanced a smile over her shoulder and left him bobbing in her wake gasping for air.

As Jamie watched her walk he decided that sometimes it was just better not to think and this was one of those times. It had just been one hell of a day.

Chapter 60

Cramphorne's Panic

It was not a long day just for Jamie. The Right Reverend Cramphorne paced his study and rubbed his forehead. He had not heard a single word of the exchange between George Pepper and Bob Cramner in the post office, not a word, as Silas Webster's letter burned his bridges leaving him alone on the wrong bank of the river. His heart had fluttered to the bottom of his stomach as he rushed out of the post office door, pausing only to sidestep some filthy odious man. He did not remember the drive home to the manse, thinking his intent had never been to actually leave the parish, just to be appreciated, to bring his value into sharper focus, for Webster to support him in his efforts against these intransigent buffoon farmers.

He took a deep breath. A little fence mending, that's all that was needed, yes a little fence mending. He refused to believe the horse had really bolted from the paddock. A slight repair of the crack of misunderstanding. He thumped to his desk, sat down, laid the Webster letter in front of him, took out paper, ink and his best pen and began to write.

'My dear sir,

It was with complete surprise I received your letter of Saturday last. I feel it my sacred duty to advise you, considering the troubled flock here, that a new and inexperienced minister would have virtually no chance of success with the incorrigible individuals here in this parish. I feel it my solemn duty to advise you to delay replacement until a mature individual can be found who will not be completely overwhelmed by these folk so entrenched in their resistance to guidance by the inspired of God. To place an inexperienced man in that position would be as to toss a hen in the middle of a pack of wild dogs. He would be torn apart in a trice. It would clearly be unfair to put any young man into a situation where failure would almost certainly result. New shepherds of the flock must be brought along slowly in order to build their confidence. Only then, when they spread their wings, will they fly straight and strong and true to the course of God. It would be a shame to damage such a good man's career before it truly had begun. If you wish, I can take this young shepherd under my wing and train him to the right way of thinking, to the right way of dealing with these people. My opportunities elsewhere must wait. I strongly feel, at the very least, that my duty lies here in the training of this young man. Fortunately nothing formal has been agreed and I'm certain a minor delay can easily be negotiated. You well know I am nothing if not a man of duty and principle. Duty deems I remain in the field, in the trenches, on the front line of the great battle of our great war against Satan, bearing the banner of the righteous against sin and depravity of all kinds in all ways possible. My place is here, steadfastly toiling, bearing the burdensome mantle of God's work.

I remain, as ever, your humble and obedient servant,

Costigan Abalicious Cramphorne.'

His pickle fingers signed the letter with a great flourish. He folded the paper, applied sealing wax, pressed his signet ring into it, and slid it into the envelope. There. That was done and fixed. Surely Silas would see the reason in what he had written, surely he would. It was a certainty.

Absolutely.

Chapter 61
Fresh Blood

At the post office post office the next morning Grant Garrath was sifting through his mail when he felt a hand on his arm. It was Pete Alderman.

"Hey Grant, take a look at this."

"And good morning to you too, Pete."

Pete adjusted his hat by the brim, gave a short laugh and handed Grant a letter. "It's from Silas Webster at the Presbytery."

Grant unfolded the paper. It was indeed a letter from Silas Webster. Webster expressed his pleasure in informing them of the appointment of a new minister, a promising young man named Thomas Parson, to their church. The Reverend Cramphorne had written him of opportunity that had opened elsewhere and Silas had accepted Cramphorne's withdrawal with his regrets. Mr. Parson had all the required qualifications and would, in fact, be arriving on Tuesday the 28th. Webster concluded with a request to have someone meet Parson at the train station.

Grant smiled. "So that's what he was upset about yesterday."

"What do you mean?"

"George Pepper and Bob Cramner had a little to-do in here yesterday about Bob's watch he got from his grandfather or something."

"Oh, yeah. I heard about that."

"Well, Cramphorne was in here at the time and he didn't even notice it. He was reading a letter and from the look on his face you'd think he'd been gut-shot."

Pete pushed his felt fedora back and scratched his forehead. "Kinda wish they'd given us a choice though. Ain't that usually the way?"

Grant nodded, but cocked his head a little sideways at Pete. "Yeah, but I'm not so sure we want to question this one."

"We'll still want to talk about this at the session meeting."

Grant nodded again, but cocked his head a little more. "What say we call a special session meeting and leave 'Ol Cramps' out of it? After all, it is our decision. What do you think?"

Pete adjusted the crown of his hat, then set the brim with the joy of treason. "I'll set those wheels in motion right now and say thank you." Pete laughed as he stepped toward the door.

"Hey Pete, do me one favor, would you?"

Pete turned back. "What's that?"

"Don't tell Mason what it's about quite yet. I want to see the look on his face."

Pete leaned back his head, pulled his hat brim again and chuckled. "All right."

Grant smiled at Pete's laughter and that faded with the twinkle of the door closing behind him. This was really interesting. He had never known Silas Webster to do anything so decisive. Grant wondered what might be behind it but not enough to look inside the horse's mouth. For now, it was just let it happen.

Much later at the mill, a heavy clumping step and a knock drew Grant's head up from his paperwork. He looked up to an unfamiliar face at the door. He waved the face inside.

"What can I do for you?"

A low rough Irish lilt wafted over him. "And a good morning to you, sir. My name is Seamus Dunne. I'm given to understand from a young lad by the name of Jamie that the mill here might be looking for a man who can swing a hammer and make a wee bit of sawdust."

Grant considered the man. Of little more than medium height, the man more than made up for it in breadth. The hands holding the hat at his waist were broad, steady and callused, and his blue denim jacket was worn but well-mended and clean.

Grant liked what he saw and gestured to the coffee pot on the stove. "Grab a mug, help yourself and sit down. I'll be with you in a minute."

He reached for the phone and called Gil Custis at the hardware store. "Gil? Grant, yes. Listen, did that shipment of nails come in yet? Uh-huh, good. And do you have any post hole diggers on hand? How about half-inch galvanized timber bolts? Uh huh. How soon can you have that packed up and ready? How much is that total?" He scribbled on his pad. "All right. I'll send Snow over to pick it up. We still on for dinner Sunday?" Grant leaned back in his chair. "We'll bring the chicken, maybe some early peas. Nothing much more is up big enough yet in the garden. I'll ask Hannah to bake some bread. Good. All right, see you then. Thanks, bye."

Grant leaned back forward, hung the black ear piece back on the hook and turned to Seamus.

"What kind of woodwork do you do, Mr. ... I'm sorry?"

"Dunne. Seamus Dunne."

"So what kind of ... what's wrong?"

Seamus shifted in his chair and gestured with the coffee cup. "Nothing at all wrong, sir. It's just that, pardon me for blunt, but being Irish, I'm by this time not so very used to being treated like folks on such an immediate basis."

Grant smiled. "Well, don't take it personally. I'm partial to being fairly direct. The unpleasant side comes when someone breaks one of the rules and I'm showing them the gate. I'm just as direct then."

A hard edge of a smile drew one corner of Seamus' mouth. His voice was very soft as he spoke. "And what rules would those be now?"

Grant gestured with his thumb over his shoulder. "They're posted on the wall, plain to see."

Seamus lifted his eyes, scanned the wall until his eyes found the small sign tacked to the bare wooden wall. He read:

<u>Rules</u>

1. No horseplay. This is a dangerous place and we don't   want people hurt.
2. No drinking, see rule #1.
3. Dress to get dirty and to work.
4. Do not cant hook a log by yourself. It's a good way to get a broken leg.
5. The mill is not responsible for marital discord.

As Seamus's eyes passed over the sign, the hard edge of his smile softened and grew broader. He nodded slow and took a deep sip. "Easier rules to live by I've never seen in any place of my employment."

"So no problems there?"

Seamus shook his head. "None whatsoever, sir. Not at all."

Grant nodded. "Good. Now, again, what kind of woodwork can you do?"

"Most any kind. I'm mainly a boatbuilder, but I can do most anything from framing to finish carpentry to furniture. Though my heart and my hands do dear love and claim the first for the best, you understand."

"I'm afraid there's no boat building here, but I think we have something that will occupy your talents for a while. I need repairs done on my saw carriage. It has to be straight, square and strong because it's machinery. The alignment has to be right or it won't work."

Seamus nodded. "Sounds clean enough. I can build that, sure."

"After that I need a small building built, to be a workshop and storage building. Simple clapboard will be fine. Work to be done in it will be everything from light machinery work like engine work to woodwork as a lumber mill may require, tool sharpening, so it needs to have a strong workbench. And it needs storage for both tools and supplies, grease buckets, couple of oil drums, chain buckets, rope and thing like that."

"Office supplies too? That would need two rooms, to keep the dirty from the clean."

Grant shook his head. "No, office supplies are here in the office, but come to mention it, I do need some sort of a writing desk with a lockable drawer for my lead man to keep track of his day to day paper. Could you handle that?"

Seamus laughed. "In my sleep, if need be."

"Let's hope that won't be necessary." Grant leaned to the window. "Snow! Snow, could you come in for a minute?"

Snow looked up from where he was talking to two men and held up one finger, signaling he'd be there in a minute after he was finished.

Grant nodded and turned back to Seamus. "That's my head man Snow. Go with him into town to the hardware store and help him pick up the things you'll need for the job. Understand I cannot guarantee employment after this job is over, but after we'll see. What?"

Seamus was standing again, hat in hand. His eyes passed from Grant to Snow and back again, narrowed.

"You have a blackie for foreman?"

Grant spoke very softly. "He's the best man I have. He knows this mill inside out and he's smart as a body comes. I trust, Mr. Dunne, there's not a problem with that?"

Seamus shook his head. "Oh no, not at all. Just a wee bit surprised is all. What do your community folk say to that, I wonder?"

"What the good community folk do in their businesses is up to them. What I do in my business is up to me. I leave it at that."

The broad man nodded.

"So you have no problem working for a black man?"

A great deep grin spread over Seamus Dunne's face. "Oh no, sir. Not at all, quite to the contrary." He took a deep breath. "I think this be a place where a man can breathe deep and do a day's work under God's blue heaven he can be proud of." He blinked both eyes. "Not at all."

"Good. By the way, I do have one question."

"And what's that, sir?"

"How do you know my son?"

Seamus blinked both eyes again, this time in confusion. "Beg pardon?"

"Jamie. My son. How do you know him?"

Seamus Dunne's mouth dropped for the moment it took him to recover his composure and then he slapped his hat across his leg and laughed aloud. "Little Jamie's yours?"

"Yes."

"Well now, he didn't speak of word of that to me, sir." Seamus smiled and shook his head. "No sir, he did not."

"He didn't?"

Seamus shook his head again. "Never a breath."

"That doesn't answer my question. How do you know him?"

"My daughter, dear one that she is, brought him into our camp. She's always bringing home lost puppies and the like. Takes after her mother, poor child. Wants to nuture."

"So you're Deidre's father?"

"He's spoken of her then?"

"In more than glowing terms, I'm afraid." Grant shook his head. "Sometimes my son is a mystery to me, Mr. Dunne. He has a mind of his own, his own way of doing things, but it's a good mind with a good heart to go with it."

Seamus smiled and a solid twinkle came to his eyes to match. "I understand. I'm afraid I gave him a bit of a rough time, warning him about my daughter, she's the apple y'know." Seamus shook his head too. "Young Jamie may not have told me because he didn't want to look the braggart, like he'd want me to look at him for himself and not what I could get from him, no matter what I saw."

Grant nodded. "That sounds like Jamie. He's quiet about it, but he pretty much likes to look the world in the face. By the way, where's your camp? Are you within walking distance?"

"Oh, no worry, I have my truck, such that it is." And Seamus told him where the camp was. Grant understood it was on his land, but said nothing.

"I do have one request? Can I have my mail sent here? I hope to hear from my family in the old country and I'd like to have an address that's not a migrant camp."

"Sure. Have it sent in care of Grant Garrath, Post Office Box 89, Miller's Landing, N.C."

"Thank you kindly, I'm much obliged to you."

Snow stomped the sand from his boots as he opened the screen door and stepped onto the porch, then stepped across the porch into the office.

"Snow, this is Mr. Dunne. He's going fix the saw carriage and then build us a shop shed. Mr. Dunne, this is Snow, my lead man, you'll be working under him."

Seamus stood and extended his hand to Snow. "Pleased to make your acquaintance, Mr. Snow. And please, I'd appreciate it if you'd call me Seamus, if ya would."

Snow looked at Seamus, smiled sideways at Grant and back again. "All right. Let's go to work."

Chapter 62

After The Rise

Work didn't stop just because there'd been an accident. The next day, after Ned followed Cyrus into the woods to cruise timber, Jamie's father sent him to the engine shed to help Snow with the hit-and-miss while Seamus rebuilt the saw carriage.

As he neared the shed Jamie saw a group of men gathered around Rudolf, clapping him on the back and laughing. Rudolf did not look happy. Matter of fact, he looked pretty miserable. Jamie slipped into the engine shed and found a place where he could listen through the cracks in the shed walls without being seen and looked out. He didn't understand all the talk and only about half the references, but the gist of it seemed to be that Rudolf's girl had thrown him over for another man who owned his own dirt farm. Jeers reminded Rudolf of his laughing brag that no girl would throw him over 'a man as purty as me, no not ever. I look too good, I talk too good and I'm just too good, if ya know what I mean.' Jamie didn't know what Rudolf meant, exactly, but he could see Rudolf was not laughing now, his own words flavoring the crow he was eating. Eueas was at the forefront, throwing his head back as he howled and slapped Rudolph on the leg with his cane.

From his hiding place Jamie laughed as well, though he did not know exactly why. He turned around to leave, to go find Snow, then saw Marshall's bulk in the shadows.

"Hey Marshall, you hear all that?" Jamie laughed as much to be a part of the fun as anything else, not that he understood why. "Pretty funny, huh?"

There was only silence from the shadows.

"Did you hear me? Pretty funny, huh?"

A single ray of light streamed in through a crack in the door. Against deep shadow he saw Marshall's huge hands twisting his soft cap in his hands. Only then he heard the material stretch-crack under the pressure.

The laughter died in his throat. "Marshall?" He peered into the shadows for Marshall's face and barely saw the outline edge of the man's head resting against the wooden wall.

"They ain't so funny as they think."

Jamie froze. The air in the shed felt very still.

"A man work as hard as Rudolf to keep the woman he loves … ought not to be treated like that."

"Like what?" As soon as the words were out of his mouth Jamie wished he had not said them, but it didn't matter because Marshall talked through his question.

"Know how he found out?"

Jamie shook his head. "No. This is the first I've heard of it."

A bark of a laugh cracked from the shadows. "He come home to they little tobacco barn cabin place and she just gone."

"What do you mean, 'gone'? Gone where?"

Marshall barked another laugh. "Just gone. Gone along with all her things and a lot of his. The only thing even like a note was a little slip of paper with her new address on it. Not so much as a 'I'm sorry.' "

"Did they have a fight or something?"

"Nah." The narrow plane of light illuminated one of Marshall's eyes as he looked out at the laughing men around Rudolph. "No fight, no nothin'. He come home from work happy as a bayou clam. The next thing he knows the middle of his heart is just empty echo of what used to be home." The shadow of Marshall's head rolled back toward Jamie. "Can you imagine it, boy? Think how you'd feel if that little girlfriend of yours was just gone. The sweet driving light of your life snuffed out; only thing left the trace of the smell of her hair hanging in the air. Can you imagine that?"

"Girlfriend?"

"Seamus allows as his little girl's your girlfriend. Ain't that so?"

Jamie thought for a moment. Marshall wasn't making fun so he told the truth. "I guess so. Closest thing I ever had anyway. So, yeah."

Marshall chuckled and Jamie saw his white smile for just a wink. "Let me tell you something. Seamus may not act like he likes you too much, but that ain't so. He just worried about his little girl. Every man's the same when he got children. Anyway, you think about how you'd feel if that girl of yours just up and left without a word or a note or nothing about what you might'a done wrong."

Jamie sat down on the heavy wooden beam of the engine support and leaned up against the cold engine. He listened to the talk and laughter outside and the silence inside. "I don't think I want to."

The short bark laugh echoed from the corner again. "That's right, boy." The shadow of his head moved up and down. "Got it right first think, you smarter than you look. You don't even want to try on that suit of clothes. Just hope and pray you never have to wear an ache like that."

Marshall said nothing after that, just twisted his hat in his hands and then even that stopped. He became so still he could have just as well been a huge black mountain. Jamie didn't feel right leaving him and didn't feel much like going back outside and laughing, so he just sat and felt cold steel against his back.

Snow's voice cracked the whip at the group outside, giving orders for working logs from the woods. Very soon after Snow's footfalls ground outside the shed. The door opened, light streamed across the dirt floor and the shadow of Snow stepped into the room. "What you guys doin' here, sittin' in the dark?"

Jamie didn't think he should mention Snow had just asked and answered his own question in the same sentence. He just stood up and heard Marshall do the same.

Snow clapped his hands together. "Come on, let's get to work. Time's a wastin'. Jamie, you go git the engine manual from the office. She ain't running quite right so while Seamus gets that carriage together, we're gonna see what we can do about that."

Jamie started for the office cabin at a run, grateful to change from Marshall's depression. Snow's voice to Marshall to lift the sides of the engine shed faded from his ears as he trotted

400

along. He grinned. They were going to work on the engine. This was gonna be fun.

When Jamie got back with the manual he and Snow got down to work. Jamie read out the maintenance procedures from the book while Snow peered into the internals. Sometimes Snow motioned Jamie over to where he was and handed him the tools and let Jamie turn a few wrenches himself. Jamie lost himself in the work. They cleaned the gas filters, opened and greased the governor weights to make sure they were free and cleaned and greased the linkages from the governor weights to the buzz coil and exhaust valve.

When it came setting the gap on the spark plug, Jamie looked up at Snow. "How much do I make it? How wide?"

"Ya got a dime?"

"What, I gotta pay for advice?"

Snow laughed. "Nah. See if you got a dime. One that's worn down a little bit."

Jamie leaned back from his seat on the work stool and reached in his pocket. Sure enough, he had a dime. The woman's face with the wings on the side of her head was smooth, and he couldn't quite read 'In God We Trust'.

Snow nodded at him. "That'll do fine. Use that to set the gap. You want it just an easy slide, but no gaps, no wiggling back and forth. Understand?"

Jamie nodded and bent once more to work. He slid the dime in the gap and wiggled it around.

"That's too loose." Snow's voice was soft but close behind his ear as Snow watched over Jamie's shoulder. "You need to tap on the little tab there with the hammer and close the gap just a little. Careful now, not too much."

Eueas came into the shed talking louder than he needed to. "So, what's to be done? What we doin'?" He thumped his way over to stand beside Snow.

Jamie kept his head down, working the spark plug while the voices spoke above and behind him.

"We all right here. Jamie's helpin' out all right with the engine. I tell you what I need you to do."

"What's that?"

"While Seamus is fixin' the carriage, we need to clean all the sawdust and them slabs out from around the saw. Make sure it's good and clear down to the dirt. When we git goin' again, we're gonna have to make up for lost time."

"But cleanin' up that shit's his job."

"Not today it ain't. Today he's helpin' me."

Jamie scraped the carbon out of the sparkplug with his penknife but his ears were wired to the silence behind him. Then he felt a thump on his shoulder and he was nearly bumped off the little box he was sitting on. He pushed himself back upright and looked around. He saw Eueas thumping off toward the tool shed, his shoulders high and stiff with anger.

"He ain't too happy."

Snow sniffed behind Jamie. "Don't have to. All he's got to be is workin'." Another sniff. "You finished? You gonna make that plug your life's work?"

"It's done."

"All right, then let's get to the magneto gears, they gotta be greased and set. The way you do it is …."

As they continued to work Jamie wondered what Eueas would do next. Whatever it was, it couldn't be good.

That night after supper Jamie wanted to talk with Ned, but Ned went straight to bed.

"Sweet air tonight?"

Ned shook his head. "Nah, just tired. Cyrus damn near walked me to death."

Jamie was still too awake, so he drifted into the living room where his father sat fiddling with the radio knobs in a vain attempt to get rid of the static. Jamie thought about Marshall.

"Dad, can you tell me something?"

"If I can." Jamie's father still fiddled but with his eyes on Jamie. "What is it?"

"Do you know what happened to Marshall, Mr. Graves?"

"What do you mean 'what happened to him'?"

Jamie told his father what had happened in the engine shed. "And after that he just sat there like a stone, not saying nothing 'til Snow came in to work on the engine."

"I'm not sure I should, Jamie. It's private and painful. I'm not sure he'd want anyone other than who he's told to know."

"Please, Dad. I don't understand him. He just seems to be hurtin'. I won't tell nobody, honest."

"Ok, but you keep this to yourself. Don't even tell Ned, all right?"

"Yes sir."

Jamie's father took a deep breath and turned the radio all the way down. He spoke in a low tone. "Snow knows and I know, but no one else."

"How did you get to know?"

He smiled. "Well, that's another story in itself that doesn't need going into tonight." He looked at the clock. "And isn't it about time you were in bed?"

"Just give me the gist of it?"

"Well, a few years ago Marshall had a little rock quarry business going. He still has the remains of the gravel pit on his place. Anyway, Marshall has a twin brother by the name of Alvin. Alvin kept the books. Marshall came home one day to an empty house and an empty bank account. His wife had left him for Alvin and the both of them ran off with all the money from the business. He'd been betrayed, Jamie. Lied to in the hardest way by the people closest to him." Jamie's father rubbed his forehead. "He had to sell his business. I don't know how he was able to keep his land. Probably because it's got so much stone in it it's not worth much for farming. But I've never seen a man who hates lies as much as he does. Now you know why. Remember now, you promised to keep it to yourself."

"His brother stole all his money and his wife?"

403

His father nodded slowly. "There are people in this world who will hurt you, Jamie. It's a thing to keep in mind."

Chapter 63

Scrap

Eueas Canfield was not having a good day. Not the worst in his life by a long shot, but definitely not the best. He dangled, shoved high in the air up against a pine, the fists of Cyrus Connor dug into his throat, the front of his dirty shirt ripping. And his cane had been thrown all the way 'cross the clearing.

Conner's cigarette breath streamed past his nose. "Remember what I told you, you son of a bitch. You leave those boys alone, you leave their dog alone and you leave Jacob alone."

Eueas smiled a tobacco yellow grin. He'd had worse from his own daddy, he won't about to be told what was what by this red sonofabitch. "Whatcha gonna do if I don't, Indian? You gonna beat up on a cripple? That what you redskins do for fun?"

Eueas expected the fist in the gut. But while his breath left his body for a minute, what he didn't expect was what Cyrus spat next into his ear. "I know you, old man. I know."

He finally got a breath. "What the hell do think you know?"

"I know you ain't cripple. I know you walk just fine without that damn cane. Now you remember what I said."

Eueas found himself flying backward. He thumped on the ground and his head cracked on a half buried rock. He yelled through the blinding pain. "I ain't the only one who ain't what he seems, Indian. You hidin' out at this old sawmill too. I seen that crap bird tattoo on you. You ain't who you say neither."

"This ain't about me, old man. I'm watching you. You let them boys alone. They never done anything to you." The tall man spread a white toothed grimace and spat on the ground. "I've seen your kind before. You're plenty brave when you hurt people from the shadows, attacking who can't fight back. But your heart has no honor and does not know how to look a man in the face.' Cyrus kicked the cane off into the woods and it rattled off a tree.

Eueas watched Cyrus stalk off down the trail, and then looked around to see if anyone was about that could have seen before he pushed himself to his feet and limped, bent over, to retrieve his cane. He fought the pain in his ribs and his hip where he had hit the ground. He wiped spittle from the corner of his mouth. "I'll do more than watch you, Indian." He looked around once more, slapped the dust off his hat against his leg, clapped it on his head and thumped off in the direction of the mill.

Chapter 64
Cramphorne's Knell

To: The Right Honorable Reverend Costigan Abalicious Cramphorne

My dear Sir,

It is with much regret that I convey to you the impossibility of your request to remain. There is always risk in the appointment of any new shepherd to a flock, yet that risk must be faced. Even in the condition of your new position there will be trials which will test your faith and the faith of those around you. But I do not tell you anything you do not already know. I cannot tell you, I simply cannot tell you, how much I appreciate your condition and your concern for the man who follows you. Your footsteps will indeed be difficult to fill for your tracks are large and deep. I am quite certain you will not be forgotten in that small church a generation hence. Your legacy will be remembered for a very, very long time. Again I congratulate you on your good fortune of a more prominent position, where I'm certain your abilities will be truly appreciated for their level of quality. I am also certain your former congregation will be deeply aware of your absence in their quiet ranks. Again, I extend to you my heartfelt good wishes and congratulations,

Sincerely,

Silas Webster

Executive Secretary of the Presbytery

Presbyterian Church U.S.A.

Chapter 65

A Little Adventure

Jamie slumped toward Little Lake, cane pole in hand. His boots had never felt so heavy and he tripped over pine roots as he made his way down the path to the dock. Most of his day had been spent cleaning up and keeping out of Eueas' way. He clumped out onto the dock and stood still, looking at the water, then closed his eyes and barked a single forbidden curse. He had forgotten worms. Again. That was how many times this summer? Second time? Third?

A deep wood creak behind started Jamie out of his skin. He jerked around, hoping the dock hadn't decided to fall into the lake. His luck just couldn't be that bad.

It wasn't. Deidre stood, leaned over on one hip, with crossed arms and a smile. "Not exactly awake to the world, are you?"

"I thought I was."

"Because," she swung toward him and her sun dress swirled about her knees and took away the rest of his conscious thought, "I've been following you all the way down the path. You didn't see or hear any of it. I had an awfully hard time."

"A hard time with what?"

"Getting you to notice me."

"I'm sorry." He held the back of his hand to his mouth to cover a yawn. "My fault. I'm so tired I can't see straight. If you'd been a snake you'd a bit me."

"Where's Ned?"

Jamie sat down slowly on the pier and leaned back against one of the pilings. "He went to check on our rabbit box. I didn't see much point. We haven't caught but a couple of things since we started." He laughed to himself. "And one of those was a cat."

Jamie watched Deidre's legs as she gracefully swung down to sit and lean back against the piling opposite him. Her hair was pulled up with a handkerchief and he could see tiny freckles on her neck and her cheeks from the sun.

"You didn't eat the cat, now?"

"Oh no, we just … the widow that lives in that little stand of trees on the curve took him in."

"You find homes for strays, do you?"

Jamie had to laugh. "That's sorta the way it worked out, yeah."

"Jamie Garrath, there's something you're not telling me. I can see it in your face. Don't ever take up gambling at cards, they'll have your geese for garters. Now give over, what is it?"

He looked at her. Her eyes were bright and her mouth was stretched into a beautiful natural grin. She looked like she was shining and he felt stuck. He wasn't sure he wanted to tell anyone because it would be trouble, but oh, this girl did look like she would love to hear of a 'bit of mischief.'

Thumping footsteps pounded up the path. They both turned to look up the pier. Ned burst out from under the cover of the pines. "Jamie, we gotta go. Deidre, sorry."

Jamie pushed himself to his feet. "What is it?"

"We got one."

"One what?"

Jamie watched Ned raise his eyebrows. It had to be a skunk. Up to now Jamie hadn't wanted any part of a skunk, but now ….

"It's now or never, make up your mind."

Now Jamie thought of Eueas and Norris … and his heart leapt. "We really got one?"

"Oh yeah. And it's prime."

The decision to act clicked into place in Jamie's head and he looked at Deidre. "Honey, I'm real sorry, but I gotta go."

Her small smile caught him off guard.

"What?"

She smiled a little bit larger. "Nothing at all. What is it?"

Jamie was almost jumping out of his boots. "I'm real sorry, but I gotta go. I'll tell you about it later, all right?"

She nodded and Jamie was off and running with Ned through the woods to where their rabbit box lay with its deadly cargo.

Behind them Deidre drew up and hugged her knees, remembered his 'Honey' and smiled at the space in front of her eyes.

That night at supper both Jamie and Ned sat on their hands, trying to act like they were tired.

Jamie's father talked in the midst of dipping vegetables onto his plate. He handed the mashed potatoes over to Jamie.

"We're not going to work tomorrow, by the way. You're coming with me to get some things for the saw. And I thought it might be good to get away from the mill for a day."

Jamie almost choked over the fork of mashed potatoes in his mouth. He looked at Ned. Ned was frozen too.

"Damn, don't get all strange over missing a day of work. What's wrong with you?"

"Grant, it's not seemly to use language like that around young ears at the supper table." Jamie's mother forked watermelon rind pickles onto her plate. "And Jamie, don't stuff your mouth so. It's no wonder you choke sometimes, now just slow down."

"Honey, they probably hear worse than 'damn' every day."

Jamie's mother took on her raised-eyebrow 'Oh?' face.

"Not just at the mill. I'd be willing to bet good money they've heard worse than that at school."

"That may well be true, but nonetheless, they should not get the idea that just because other folks do it it's acceptable for them. They should have an example of how to behave."

"I don't cuss, Mommy." Gloria was not about to let a conversation go on without putting her two cents in. "And I've even heard Jamie use those words, 'specially when he hits his finger or something."

"It's not ladylike to tattle, young lady. Eat your peas." Jamie's mother might have hushed up Gloria for now, but Jamie could tell by the half-an-octave-lower tone he was going to hear about that later. His mother had a memory 'like an elephant', as the saying went. Jamie paused for just a heartbeat about that. Did elephants have good memories? And how did anybody know? "Dad?"

"Just a minute, Jamie. Now honey, I told you that …." His parent's conversation was entrenched.

"Dad, can Ned and I be excused?"

"Uh, sure." His father turned back to his mother. "Now you really can't mean that …."

Jamie and Ned pushed their chairs back from the table and carried their dishes into the kitchen.

"Let's go ahead and get our baths. That way we can go ahead and get in bed and wait for everything to die down."

"God, I can't wait to get out there."

"Got your flashlight?"

"Oh yeah."

They cleaned up and tried to go to bed but discovered a new definition of 'eternity' as they waited for the house to settle down enough to go outside.

Ned leaned back on his cot with his hands behind his head. "Time just seems to be crawlin' right now. I wonder if time moves at the same speed all the time."

"I dunno. Watches do. They'd have to or they would be all over the place to one another, wouldn't they?"

"Yeah well. Let's wait twenty minutes after we haven't heard a sound, then we're out that window."

"Why don't we make it thirty?"

"You're getting cautious in your old age. Or you showing chicken?"

"No good if we get caught, is it?"

Ned didn't answer to that.

The echoes of Jamie's parent's discussion gradually died down, then they heard steps on the stair. "Good night, boys. Sleep tight."

"Good night."

And the house was quiet. Jamie watched his clock by the moonlight from the window. The hands seemed to have stopped they moved so slowly. After only twenty minutes he couldn't stand it any longer and quietly got up and dressed, then loosened the window screen. There was one bad moment when Jamie's father came downstairs, but then he thumped back up the stairs. The house rang quiet and they eased out the window screen and were gone.

The box was right were they had left it. Adrenalin fueled their strength and they picked it up and carried down the path to the road across from the widow's house.

Jamie breathed hard from the effort. "We gotta be careful now. The box is gonna be harder to hide than the bag we had Wanderin' Tom in."

They waited until ten minutes went by without cars then carried the box across the road and down the dirt driveway to the widow's mailbox. They lowered the mailbox door, heaved the rabbit box up on top of it with the gate pointing into the box.

"You ready?" Jamie was underneath the box holding it up. He couldn't see a thing.

"Ok. Here goes."

Jamie heard the wooden rabbit box door slide up. There was not another sound. "Is he moving? Is he in there?"

"I'm afraid to get too close to it." Ned's voice was a few feet away.

"Dammit. Get him in there, I can't hold this for much longer."

Then light footsteps scratched their way from the box on Jamie's shoulder. The box got lighter and then he heard those same little footsteps scratch on metal. "Get ready with the mailbox lid."

"Is he in there?"

"I think so."

"Wait till I slide the door down again."

Jamie heard the wood slide. "You ready?"

"Go. Pull it out of there."

Jamie pulled the box down and heard the tin door slam shut. Then he smelled it. "Oh hell, let's get out of here. Grab the other end."

Ned bent to help him and they were off, out the driveway, across the main road and into the woods. Just as they made the path under cover a truck came up from down the road. The lights flashed above their heads and the truck ground on up the road.

Now it was Ned breathing deep. "That was too close."

Jamie had to agree. "And we ain't even going to get to see it though."

"Come to think of it, I'm not sure we want to. Might be better not to be around."

"Did you get any of it on you?"

"Nahh. We'd both be stinking up a storm if that little fella decided to let go. We lucked out."

"The only thing is we won't know if it worked."

Ned shrugged. "Yeah well. Have to just wait and see."

Chapter 66
Storm Clouds

Hera Cramphorne was a thoroughly gray woman with hair that did not move. She pulled the lace curtains of the front bay window open with the tips of her fingers and peered through the slit into a cold early morning drizzle.

A gaunt man stood outside the manse on the path leading up to the front door. He walked up to the door and raised his hand to knock, but his fist paused in the air a couple of inches from the freshly painted wood. He hugged his arms around himself, trembled, then paced up and down the path looking at the ground, his shoulders shaking. The raindrops dripped from his faded fedora and soaked into the shoulders of his suit, gray flannel turned charcoal in the wet. He finally straightened, took a deep breath, stepped up to the door, knocked twice with a firm hand and stepped back a respectful distance with his hands clasped behind his back. His shoes wetly crunched on the gravel.

Hera opened the door and leaned into the narrow opening. "Yes?"

He touched the brim of his hat. "I'm sorry if I disturb you, ma'am. My name is Sabastian Wood. Is your husband at home?"

"Yes, but he's in his study at his labors and is not to be disturbed."

Hera jumped as the voice of her husband thundered from behind her. "Who is it, dear?"

The door swung wide. Hera stepped back and let Cramphorne's mass fill the narrow space and more. "What can I do for you, sir? And I do not hesitate to remind you that, in polite society at least, it is customary for a man who is addressing a lady to remove his chapeau."

414

The gaunt man glanced up at the drizzling sky, then back to the couple whose four eyes challenged his, then to the ground as he slowly pulled the fedora from his head. He held it in front of him by the brim between his two hands in front of his chest. "Yes sir, of course. I'm sorry."

The great silver head nodded and frowned in satisfaction. "Now, what do you want?"

"Sir, I noticed as I was passing by that your garden might could use a little tending and with all modesty I'd like to help you with it, if you'd consider employing me for a short period."

Cramphorne twisted sideways to slide his belly past the doorframe, stepped out under the cover of the stoop and placed his hands on his wide hips. "Sir, I consider myself a man of the earth and I thrill in feeling God's good earth between my fingers. All this," he lifted and spread his hands to indicate the neglected garden, "is entirely due to my stewardship. Can you for one moment imagine that I could or would turn it over to the hands of the local beggar?"

Hera watched the man glance about at the garden and frown in confusion. "I could, at least, rake the leaves there from around your roses and weed the azaleas. I would, of course, not dream of taking on the pruning. I would leave that delicate matter completely to your discretion."

"Do you further imagine I could or would contribute to your deplorable moral condition, your lack of backbone, your parasitic persistence by stooping to extend to you a handout?" Her husband shook one very thick white finger at the gaunt man. "I know you sir. I will not help to drive you deeper into your chosen depravity of drink by dropping into your outstretched palm one red cent. I do not intend to pour sand into your cavernous rat hole! Do I make myself clear?" The huge man thrust his chin forward. For a brief moment the folds in his neck disappeared, but reappeared as he drew back drew back from the water that dripped from the eaves onto his face. He wiped his hand across his face. "Do I make myself clear?" He stood underneath the shelter of the porch, glaring.

The man blinked the water from his eyes, smiled small and tight, inclined his head to both, placed his hat back on his head and crunched down the gravel walk with his hands shoved deep into his pockets of his coat.

415

Hera peered from behind her massive husband. "The very idea! What a horrid man!"

"Don't worry about him, my dear. People like that always get what's coming to them. You mark my words. And he'll hurt someone before he's through and it'll be a tragedy when it does." He shook his head. "We must pray for him."

"Awful man, awful man!"

"Of course, but now we must return to our labors doing God's work, I to mine and you to yours." With that the massive man turned, slid sideways back through the doorway and stomped to his study. The wooden floor creaked under his weight.

"Yes dear."

Hera peered outside at the receding gaunt man's back, glanced up at the dark clouds, then closed the door to the slowly gathering storm.

Chapter 67
Out Of Town

"I wish we could watch." Jamie whispered to Ned as he shouldered his raincoat on after breakfast. "I like going with Dad, but why did it have to be today?"

"Better if we don't." Ned shoved his feet into his boots then yawned. "Makes us keep quiet like Sabastian said. Besides, I'm tired. Maybe sleep on the way."

"Come on boys!" The hard edge of his father's voice rose over the rumble of the truck engine and cut through the dripping rain. "Time to go!"

"Comin'."

Jamie and Ned scrambled out the door. They squeezed into the front seat of the pickup, Ned alongside Jamie's father. Jamie slid the door shut behind him, folded the tri-pane window closed then leaned back in the corner, squeezed between the door and Ned.

The truck splashed and bounced as Jamie's father swiveled the black steering wheel to dodge the larger mud holes in the driveway. The wet smell of the outside washed in over Jamie through the crack under the window and the rain clear-dotted the glass beside his face.

Jamie leaned forward to relieve the pressure on his shoulders where he and Ned were pressed together and to ask his father a question.

"Dad?"

His father's eyes never left the road. "Yes, what is it?" An edge of irritation ground across to Jamie.

"What are we going for?"

"New sawblade." His father peered through the clear arc on the windshield from the wiper. "That and some heavy log chain. Gil doesn't carry what we need."

"Do we need a new blade?"

His father nodded. "Oh yeah. The old one picked up a vibration. I can't seem to hammer it into balance no matter what I do. Don't like to spend the money, but can't stop work. Gotta work if you want to get paid."

Jamie leaned back again and relaxed into the jolts of the truck as it thumped out onto the main road. It was too great an effort to keep talking in the wind as the truck picked up speed. He had thought about bringing a book, but didn't want to face sidelong glances from his father. He braced himself for boredom.

They drove past fields of cotton and tobacco, and through flickering stands of longleaf pine that shut out the horizon.

Jamie awakened, not knowing when he had dropped off. Ned slumped against him, breathing deep, fast asleep. It had stopped raining but mist still rose from the hard ground. He could tell they were close to the tobacco processing plants because he could smell the smooth sweet textured air of cured tobacco. Whenever Jamie smelled that he thought of wood and aged air.

The truck tires hissed through water on smooth roads as they drew nearer to town. Jamie's father turned into the parking lot of a little restaurant. The sign said 'Butch's Barbacue, We Serve Everbody.'

Jamie's father pulled into a parking space. "I been meaning to eat here one of these days and now's our chance boys. Let's go over to the door on the right hand side, that looks like it's got more tables free."

Jamie folded back the window, slid open the door and got out. He stretched, then followed his father and pushed through the closest screen door into a bright room.

A black man in an white apron came up to them. He wiped his hands on his apron. "I'm sorry sir, but you came in the wrong door. The white section is over there." He pointed the way through an archway into another section that was about half full.

Jamie looked around and saw there was but one table occupied in this room and it was occupied by a black family. They did not speak. The woman fed a fat baby in a high chair.

Jamie's father lifted his hat and scratched his head. "You don't really mind if we sit in here, do you? It's quieter."

"Me? No sir." Jamie saw the man in the apron shake his head and smile sadly. "And I appreciate what you saying, but I gotta live here. You understand, don't you sir?"

Jamie's father slid his hat back on his head. His voice came out sad. "Yeah." He chewed on his lower lip and nodded. "Yeah, I do. All right then, think you could rustle us up three heaping plates of your fine barbecue? Don't go light on the hush puppies now. I don't get the chance to eat out very often and I've been lookin' forward to this all morning."

The man smiled wide gleaming white. "You bet I can, let me show you a table and we'll get right on that." He spread his hand toward the archway. "Right this way."

He led them through the arch to a booth by the front window and brought them stainless flatware wrapped in white paper napkins. "Sweet tea?"

"Oh yeah. Thanks."

"Thank you, sir."

Jamie looked around and watched the waitress move amongst the other customers. She was a big old friendly redhead who seemed to know everyone and what they wanted before they'd even asked. The man in the apron talked with her for just a few moments. She looked over at them, nodded and smiled, then turned back to her table. Jamie watched, riveted to how the woman could chew gum, blow bubbles, talk to customers and never miss a beat, let alone an order.

"Dad, how does she do that?"

His father chuckled. "I'm sure I don't know, Jamie. But a meal and a show, what more could a body ask for?"

Jamie had to grin and looked over at Ned. Ned did not look happy. "What's wrong?"

"I kinda wish we coulda stayed in the other room. It's not as busy."

Jamie's father spoke quietly. "I do too, Ned. But his regular customers wouldn't like it. And, like he said, he has to live here. We don't."

Three dishes of heaped up barbecue with Cole slaw clattered on the table, along with the biggest pile of hush puppies he'd ever seen.

"Wow." He looked up at the waitress. She had the name 'Doris' sewn into her blouse right where Jamie was a little embarrassed to read it when she was looking at him. He tried to look at her strong arms instead. Doris smiled wide and her eyes danced at him. "Well, honey, aren't you just the cutest thing?"

Jamie felt his face grow hot right up into his hair. Then he heard Ned snort, but by the time he turned to throw a dirty look Ned had already twisted his face toward the window.

Doris giggled, then looked at Jamie's father. "You need anything else, honey?"

"No, I think that'll be about all. Just keep the ice tea coming, if you would please."

"Sure will, now you just give me a shout if you want anything else." She touched Jamie's father on his shoulder, then turned and walked away. Jamie could not help but watch her swinging walk back up to the counter. Her high heels clicked against the hard checked linoleum floor.

"Come on, boys, eat up." His father dug into the pile of chopped barbecue on his platter. "We don't get to do this much, so eat it while it's hot."

Jamie grabbed his fork and dug in. From the first forkful the chopped pork flavor exploded with vinegar in his mouth. The hush puppies were sweet golden brown deep fat fried and when he bit into one he tasted onion bits floating around inside. He'd never tasted anything so good in his whole life.

Ned spoke from across the table. "You think this is what they serve in heaven? 'Cause if they don't, who the hell wants to go?"

To Jamie's surprise his father just laughed. "Don't you ever let your mamma hear you say that. Understand?"

Ned grinned back and nodded, his mouth packed full.

Conversation suffered from benign neglect until Jamie's father leaned back and tossed his napkin onto his empty platter. "God, I'm stuffed full as a tick."

Doris clicked up to them. "You all had enough?"

His father looked up at her. "That and more. My sincere compliments to your cook. What's his name?"

"Oh, that's Sammy. It was him brought you in here."

"Well, you thank him for us, will you? And tell him this was the best barbecue I think I ever tasted and the Cole slaw was just perfect."

"He'll be happy to hear it. Here's your bill, now you come back when you get a chance now, hear?" She reached out and ruffled Jamie's hair. "And you just come back anytime, darlin'. You're gonna be a heartbreaker, you are." She smiled deep dimples at him and then swung around back to work with one last glance over her shoulder.

Jamie heard Ned snort again, but this time he slid out of the booth and ducked his hot face until he was outside the door into the moist air, away from the grins and chuckles.

Jamie's father pulled up in front of a large tar paper building that had 'E. Prentice and Son, Ironmongers since 1833' plastered across the side.

Ned spoke up. "Mr. Garrath, are we in the right place? Where's the hardware store?"

Grant pointed to the building in front of them. "Right there."

"Iron-mon-jer?"

"That's Iron-mon-<u>Ger</u>, G-E-R, with a hard G like Gerkin. Ironmonger. That's another name for a hardware store. Here." Jamie's father reached into his pocket, pulled out a couple of dimes and handed one to each of them. "If you see something you like. Come on."

They walked into the store and Jamie had to stop and just look. It was biggest, deepest, darkest hardware store Jamie had ever seen. "Would you look at this?"

Ned spoke beside him. "Yeah. This is the kind of store Dad wants. It is something, ain't it?"

Jamie's father walked to the first man he saw that worked there and introduced himself.

"Ah yes, Mister Grant. A pleasure to meet you sir, it was me what was on the telephone." The man's accent twisted Jamie's ears. "We have it just back there. If you'll please follow me, sir?"

Jamie had never heard anybody talk like that, not even Deidre's father. He was accustomed to people bending words to suit themselves, but this was a whole different kind of warp. He and Ned followed into the depths of the store.

They stopped beside a huge octagonal wooden box flat on a table. The man produced a crow bar and pried the lid up against screaming nails. He unrolled oiled felt beneath to reveal the new blade. It was a shining ragged edge disc. The box smelled of fresh pine and oil.

Jamie's father leaned in and twisted his head to one side to see the numbers on the blade then pulled a paper from his pocket, unfolded it and read it. "Yes, that's it. Can you help me get it out to my truck?"

"It is a huge awkward beast to carry, isn't it? Tell you what sir, we'll do better than that." The man looked up and hallooed to the back of the store. "Samson, could you come here and help for a bit?"

While the other fellow came to the front, wiping his hands on a rag, Jamie's father turned to him. "Find Ned, would you son?"

Jamie looked around. Ned had indeed disappeared into the cavernous expanse of the store.

So Jamie had a good time poking about figuring out what things were for. There was rope and pulleys and chain and paint, just about everything that a boy could want for the things he wanted to do.

He found Ned beside the wood tools, looking closely at a set of wood carving chisels. "Whatcha lookin' at those for?"

"Found myself wondering how all those wooden signs get carved. They must use these."

"Dad says it's time to go."

By the time they threaded their way between the stacks of potential adventure supplies and out to the truck, the saw blade was already loaded, along with the chain and a few other boxes of odds and ends. They packed themselves back into the cab, slid the doors closed and headed back home.

They left the truck windows open on the way home. The rain had passed. Jamie took off his hat, rested his chin on his hand on the windowsill and felt the wind blow through his hair. He ran all kinds of scenarios of Nosy Norris through his mind, trying to think of the one most likely. If Nosy smelled a rat, as it were, it was all up. But since they weren't there driving past him, maybe Nosy thought he was safe, maybe ….

The thought didn't last long. Jamie was still full of food from the diner and he felt his eyes close of their own accord. He leaned back in the corner against the door and slid right off to sleep with the breeze blowing his hair.

Chapter 68
Hidden Joy

Jamie squinted into the mirror and plastered down his cowlick as best he could. In the reflection he watched Ned tie his shoes.

He smiled. He did look forward to playing silent catbird. Normally Jamie couldn't sit still without bursting to tell about a joke, but today Sabastian's words echoed in his head, reminding him to let the world simmer. No one but he and Ned knew, whatever had happened yesterday. Rumors in this community flew on the wings of Nosy Norris. But if the trick had gone well, Nosy was hardly the one to go spreading it around.

On the way to church Jamie felt a grin bubble up on his face. He looked over at Ned, who smiled small back at him and held one finger up to his lips. Jamie nodded, hugged himself with both arms and leaned back in his seat.

He got an elbow straight in the ribs from Gloria, who sat between Jamie and Ned in a sulk. "Ow. What was that for?"

"I want to sit up front."

"You behave yourself, young lady." Jamie's mother spoke without turning her head around.

The little queen crossed her arms and pushed her lower lip out just as far as it would go to give her little huff all the strength and force at her command. Then she leaned back against Ned, who in turn looked like he had swallowed a persimmon. Jamie turned his head away and covered his smirk with his hand.

The little drama inside the car halted when they pulled into the church parking lot. Clusters of folks laughed and talked like they were at the fair. As soon as Jamie's father shut off the engine even Gloria stopped in mid-pout to listen to the buzz. Jamie saw

424

Old Man Mason coming fast towards them as usual, but this time with a smile on his face.

"What is it, Mama, what is it?" Gloria tried to climb over into the front seat.

As soon as Jamie's father stepped out of the car, Old Man Mason jabbered at him. "Grant, Grant boy, did you hear? Hear what happened yesterday?"

"Yesterday? I reckon not, Jeremiah. I was out of town getting a new saw blade for the mill."

"That so? Oh, I want to talk to you about clearing out some timber of mine, but that'll wait."

Jamie saw his father blink a double take, for few were the times Jeremiah Mason did not want to talk 'business first, pleasure later.'

"Why, what is it?"

The old man laid one hand up on his father's shoulder and waved the other hand in the air. "Hold on a sec." He swallowed and looked at Jamie's father with twinkling eyes. "All right, all right. You know old Nosy Norris." It was statement, not question.

"Yeah, uh-huh."

"You know the Widder Morrison."

"Sure do, fine lady. She lives just down the road from us."

"That's right, she does." Old Man Mason rubbed his chin and looked over at Jamie. Jamie felt his throat grip.

His father interceded. "They were with me yesterday, Jeremiah."

"Oh, that so?" Old Man Mason's eyebrows lifted. "Oh well, all right." He breathed deeply. "Well yestiddy, somebody put a skunk in the Widder's mailbox for Nosy to find."

Jamie's mother waved Jamie, Ned and Gloria out of the car. She brushed her hand over Jamie's coat lapels with her head turned toward Old Man Mason the whole time. "No! You don't say! How on earth did they get it in there?"

Mason fairly danced and shook his head. "I don't know Hannah, but I lift my hat to them whoever they are."

"Did it get him bad?"

Mason hooted. "Oh ho, yes ma'am, a di-rect shot. Oh, that man's gonna stink for years!"

His mother giggled and held her white-gloved hand up in front of her face. "He's such a little bantam about that uniform of his, there aren't enough tomatoes in the world to get that much smell out, Land alive."

Jamie's father nodded toward Jamie and Ned. "The boys saw a big tom cat come screaming out at him the other day, didn't you boys?"

Mason turned toward them and Jamie saw his eyes light up like Christmas lights. "That so?"

Jamie nodded and tried not to laugh. "Yes sir, it was a sight. We laughed most all day about that."

Ned piped in. "Any idea who did it?"

"Not a breath." Mason shook his head and scratched his nose. "But I gotta tell you I kinda hope it stays secret."

Jamie's father lit a cigarette and closed one eye against the smoke. "How come?"

"'Cause it's a grand thing just the way it is." Mason turned his head and spit. "I got a feelin' that whoever done it, done it for a pretty good reason. You know how much cow flop and trouble Nosy tosses around." He nodded toward Jamie and Ned. "Happened both times when he was at the widow's mailbox. I mean I ain't no police detective, but like the fella with a rock in his shoe, I 'spect there's somethin' in it." He tossed a glance over his shoulder in the direction of the buzz coming from little groups of people gathered all over the church lawn, then turned back. "Ain't it a show, though?"

He looked at Jamie's father and the grin all but buried his eyes in folds of his cheeks. "The widder's a Methodist, but I've half a mind to suggest we make her an honorary Presbyterian just for her part." He gave an old man hoot. "I just had to come over and see if you'd heard, see if you knew anything about it."

Jamie's mother shook her head. "No, 'fraid not. We're all as much in the dark as anyone else."

Old Man Mason cackled see-you-laters, hitched up his pants and wandered back into the fray.

They started walking up to the church but Jamie's father stopped. His mom stopped as well and looked at him. "Grant? What is it?"

His father held one finger up in the air. "Listen."

"Honey, I don't hear a thing. What is it?"

He smiled, relaxed and broad. "Exactly. What do you not hear?"

Ned's eyes lit up first. "Old Crap… Cramphorne … ah … the Reverend isn't …."

Jamie's father lowered his eyebrows at Ned, but nodded. "Very good, Ned. I wonder why he isn't out here?"

The church bell rang clear then with a thunky tink. Jamie's mother waved her hands about and herded her flock together. "Well, Hera's here anyway, that's her ring. The good reverend is probably inside. Oh, there's your folks, Ned."

Ned's mother came up and hugged him for all she was worth. Ned's father shook his hand. "Doin' all right, are you son? Not giving Mr. Garrath any trouble?"

Jamie's father answered for Ned. "Not in the least bit, Gil. None at all. You've reared quite a fine boy here."

"Hmm." Gil Custis looked slightly non-plussed, as if he expected some reference to Ned's being a bit hard to handle, but he recovered enough to say "Good, good. We'd best be getting' inside then."

The group strolled toward the church just as the Reverend Cramphorne emerged and began to welcome parishioners.

Jamie's father coughed. "Had to know that was too good to last."

"Grant." His mother's tone lowered half an octave. His father did not respond.

Jamie and Ned trailed behind and Jamie heard Ned speak under his breath. "'Reared' is the word for it. He says 'it's for your own good' and that it hurts him as much as it hurts me, but I don't believe it."

Jamie turned to his friend. "What are you talkin' about?"

"His 'rearing'". Ned shoved his hands down into his pockets and looked at the ground. "He's worn out a couple of belts on me. That's why I wear suspenders." He sniffed the back of his hand. "Since you asked the other day. I just don't care for the thought of a belt."

"All right." Jamie felt he should say something, but his words would have been lost because they were now within range of the howitzer boom of the reverend's voice blasting welcome at anyone and everyone within earshot.

Jamie and Ned managed to slip past behind as the reverend clasped the hand of Jamie's father, pulled him close and spoke directly into his face. Jamie turned and watched his father pull out of the reverend's grasp, then pull his white handkerchief out of his back pocket. He wiped first his face, then his hands, then with a great sniff frowned the revulsion from his face.

His father joined them as they filed into the sanctuary, the polished pine beneath their feet creaking in concert with the dimming buzz of conversation. They picked their pew and filed in. His father took the seat right next to the aisle and rested his elbow on the arm of the pew and put his other arm along the pew back around his family.

The Custises sat on the other end of the pew. Ned filled in the middle between the two. His mother patted his knee and whispered in his ear, "We're so proud of you."

Jamie watched the Right Reverend Cramphorne flow down the center aisle through the crowd of waving funeral home fans and mounted the dais. The man spread his arms like a great vulture and announced "This holy day our opening hymn is number 685, 'Temperance'"

As Hera pounded the piano for the opening chords Jamie's father whispered to his mother "Have you ever sung this one?"

His mother thumbed through the hymnal and shook her head. "Never. And from the reaction up there, I don't think the choir has either."

Jamie glanced up. The robed few scrambled and fluttered pages for the right hymn and tried to sight read the notes.

It was painful to hear. Jamie could not understand why 'Gifts of plenty from thy dower' applied. They were in hard times and everyone knew it. It got more painful when Jamie realized they were going to sing all six verses. When they got to 'All that brings us degradation: Quell the forces of temptation' he thought he knew. Jamie sneaked a glance over his shoulder at Sabastian. Sabastian looked calm from where Jamie sat, but then he couldn't tell any more because behind him Mrs. Huff blew like a beached whale in the heat, quit singing and flapped her fan high in front of her face.

When the hymn ended Cramphorne nodded to the congregation "Be seated."

Relief rustled through the church.

The Reverend leaned against the podium. Sweat streamed down his face and soaked his collar.

"My brethren, I stand before you today with a heavy heart. I am sick to death to think of what I must speak of today. It is a classic deadly sin, combined with and fueled by an evil iniquity that curses our world. It is the sin of indolence, the sin of just being fat-lazy. All of us are guilty to one degree or another. Every time we put something off until tomorrow just because we don't feel like it, hammers another nail into the coffin of our souls, splitting our sacred spirits into tiny fragments of damnation and loads us down with sandbags of tiny individual grains of sin. These small sins build up over time. They build up and weigh us down until we cannot move straight upon the path of righteousness. They drag us down into the valleys, where the paths are crooked and winding and never ending until we finally roll to a stop at the crackling hot doors of hell. By then it is too late, too late to recover our wits and climb back up. We will have lost our way."

Cramphorne cleared his throat. "I was reminded of this just a couple of days ago. A member of our community who has been guilty of this sin for years, came to my door begging for money. A man that I am given to understand has not once in years even tried to hold down reputable employment. He offered to help out a little in my garden to justify his compensation, but that was just a transparent ruse. It was a ruse because by this time he is not capable of doing any work at all, broken down as he is by years of consumption of alcohol. And that, my brethren, is a scourge. Alcohol in all its drinkable forms is a scourge to the civilization of mankind and an offense against almighty God. We have come to the point where it can no longer be ignored, no longer be tolerated. It keeps men like that down in the ditches, forever slopping around, wallowing in the muck and mud of sin. I call upon all the righteous here today that if they take even an occasional drink, to cease that depravity. And I know, if you do so you will find it so much easier to fight against indolence, easier to fight against that sin and you will also find that you have more time to do God's work, work you should be doing, work that needs to be done, work that is your holy duty neglected for far, far too long. Let us pray."

Jamie snuck a glance over his shoulder to look for Sabastian, but his face was not there at the back of the church, just the double doors in the back of the sanctuary swinging gently.

After the service Jamie trailed after his father and slipped past again when Cramphorne's meaty grip trapped his father's hand. He ducked past most of the grown ups, no longer listening to the buzz of conversation, and drifted toward the car.

He saw Sabastian at the edge of the churchyard leaning against a slender pine smoking a cigarette. He lifted one hand to Jamie in question. Jamie nodded and smiled in response. Sabastian nodded and smiled as broadly as Jamie had ever seen him against his scars. He gave Jamie one final wave, slid his blue glasses back onto his face and strode away. Jamie thought he saw him whistling.

Jamie then felt a heavy hand on his shoulder and the voice of his father behind him.

"Let's go to the car; we need to have ourselves a little talk."

Jamie felt his stomach take a flying nose dive right into his gut. He turned and saw Ned on the other side of his father propelled with his father's other hand on his neck.

His father stopped at the door to the car. "Look at me, boys"

When Jamie glanced up, his father's face was calm, unreadable. His father was not one to keep anger to himself, yet Jamie still felt he was in a whole tobacco barn full of trouble.

"You boys have something you want to tell me?"

Neither Jamie nor Ned spoke.

His father slowly opened the car door, reached for his pack of cigarettes on top of the dashboard, leaned up against the doorframe, shook one out and lit it.

Jamie's gaze landed inside on the floorboard and saw the round clutch and brake pedals. They were molded with concentric circles of rubber and for the first time it occurred to Jamie they looked very much like two targets standing side by side.

"You see, I've pretty much figured out how it was done, but what I can't figure is why."

"Cause he didn't quit the first time."

Ned's voice jolted Jamie and he looked up. Ned, the quiet one, stood there with fists balled, jaw jutting forward and lips pressed tight.

His father blew two slow smoke rings. "Wandering Tom didn't teach him a lesson, hmm? That about right?"

Ned's jutting jaw nodded quickly and his nostrils flared as well.

"All right." His father laid one hand on each boy's shoulder. "Right now I got just two things to say."

"Yessir." They spoke in chorus. He smelled the smoke rising off his father's cigarette.

"From this day forward don't ever talk about it. Don't … say … a word. You heard Mr. Mason, hmm?"

"Sir?"

"You heard me. And second, don't even think about doing anything like that again. You understand me?"

"Yessir." They both nodded.

"Good. Now let's go home and get some dinner. That is," Jamie's father slowly pushed down on their shoulders and moved off toward the church, "if I can get your mamma out of the henhouse."

They watched him stride slowly, taking another drag on his cigarette, toward the choir loft where the wives usually gathered after services.

"Are we in for it?" Ned's voice whispered in his ear.

Jamie shook his head. "I can't tell. But I do know Nosy got his and he ain't got no way to prove we done it."

Jamie didn't say out loud what absolutely made it worth whatever punishment came his way. It had put a smile on the face of a ghost.

Chapter 69

The Catch of a Lifetime

After Sunday dinner, Jamie felt like a cat when someone left the screen door ajar. His father snored on the screen porch glider with the newspaper across his lap, his mother was teaching a pouting Gloria how to darn socks and Ned slept on his cot with a book fallen on his chest.

Sunshine outside beckoned and he padded out onto the back screen porch. He grabbed his straw hat and his boots and eased out the 'scream' door. A moment later he took his fishing pole from the shed and then he was over the back fence and gone to the lake to see what he could catch.

She was there.

From the shadows of the trees he watched her for a moment. Deidre sat on the end of the dock with the legs of her overalls rolled up, swishing her feet back and forth in the water. Jamie moved forward but at the first clump of his boots on the dock boards she spoke over her shoulder. "You wouldn't make a very good Indian."

"I wasn't trying to hide."

She turned around and looked right at his eyes. "And I am glad of that." She tilted her head back toward the water. "I've scared all the fish, sure."

"Well, there's other stuff we can do." Jamie laid down his fishing pole, walked out to the end of the dock and stood beside her.

Her dimples widened. "Like what, I'm askin'?"

Jamie put his hands in his pockets. "Oh I don't know." He felt coins. "Want to see a train up close?"

"They're pretty much the only way to travel any distance in Ireland."

"Oh, I didn't mean to ride. Ever put pennies on a railroad track? When the train runs over them they flatten right out."

"That's a dear bit of business, sure. Why ever?"

"Because it's fun. Will you come?"

"You've a strange idea of fun, Jamie Garreth, to be doin' such things." Her smile lit him up. "I may as well make a show of meself, sure."

Jamie led her up the path through the trees toward the railroad tracks that ran through the woods behind the back side of the mill. The sun dappled the path as they strode along. He felt her beside him, though they did not touch, like his body crackled with an electrical field and he could feel her in it. His brain seemed to have quit generating words and felt strange and stupid and was scared she thought him so. "It must be great living in a caravan and traveling around all the time. New things to see, it must be an adventure every day."

She gave a short laugh. "It's cramped is what it is. Seems we're always in each other's pockets."

Now Jamie really felt stupid. He needed wonderful words to say but each time he tried to think of something he just felt silent space in his head.

When they arrived at the railroad track he was thankful to be able to do something, even if it was just to reach into his pocket for the coins.

Deidre looked up and down the track. "Now what?"

"We wait for a train." He pulled the coins from his pocket. There were three pennies, a nickel and the dime his father had given him in the hardware store. He looked at her. "I'll put a dime for you, the penny is for me." He leaned down, laid them on the track and backed away.

"What are you doing? It's an awful cost."

"It's for you to remember me by. It's for you."

"You're a foolish man, you are." Her eyes were quiet. "You could be Irish."

"Is that a good thing?"

Her dimples showed. "I'll wait to answer that."

Jamie heard the train whistle in the distance. He took her arm and led her back away from the track. "Cover your ears."

The train thundered its way past, iron wheels squealing against the steel tracks, clicking and clacking, its wind blowing leaves from the trees. She took shelter behind his shoulder.

When it was past, Jamie walked back over to the track and picked up the two flattened coins. He held out the flat dime to her. "Now you'll remember."

"There's no danger of forgetting such a foolish man." She took the flattened silver and ran her thumb over the smooth surface. "A whole dime on remembrance. You could have spent it on a loaf of bread or a steak, for goodness sake."

He couldn't tell if she thought what he had done was a good thing or not. He just knew he would give this girl anything and rubbed the broad flat penny in his hand. "We'd better be getting back. Your father will be worried."

They turned and walked back to the lake. He carried the buckets of water back to the traveler camp for her. About halfway there in the now dimming woods Deidre turned to him and held him back with one hand to his chest. "I was wonderin' could I have your coin too? Just for a while. I wouldn't rob you now; I've just got something in mind and I'll give it back to you, sure." She smiled at him. "I swear by me old Gran's garters?"

Jamie set down the buckets, took her hand, laid the flattened penny in her palm and closed it. The smile in her eyes took his breath away. "I'll hold you to that."

As they neared the camp Jamie saw Seamus settled down by the fire, carving on a walking stick. He had a glass of amber liquid by his left hand.

Deidre pulled his head down so she could whisper in his ear. "You can only believe about half of what he says when he's in his cups."

"In his cups?"

"Oh, aye." She nodded and as she stood on tiptoe and pulled his head down further. He felt her lips against his ear, impossibly soft against his skin. A shiver ran up his spine. "He takes a little sip of the whiskey every now and again."

"He'll want to be careful about that. This is a dry county."

"Dry county?"

Jamie nodded at her. "Yep. It means you can't buy alcohol here." He shrugged. "Not in stores, anyway."

"Jamie, you'll not be changing Pa in his ways at this late date." She smiled at him and he thought that no doubt she was thinking him a great goof.

He shook his head. "I'm not trying to. I just don't want to see him in jail."

Her smile dropped away. "You mean it's against the law, then?"

"Yea. It's not that the sheriff looks all too hard, but if he sees it he'd have to do something. So your dad can do what he wants, he just has to keep it out of sight. Don't get caught?"

Jamie could not believe he had just said those words. Purposeful hiding of a sin was a lie which was a sin in itself, but he really could not see any harm.

"And what are you two whisperin' at over there in the darkness? Come over here in the light and sit down by the fire with your old Pa."

Deidre led Jamie over by the fire and took the buckets from his hands. "Sit down on the mat there and put your feet up."

Jamie lowered himself to the ground and leaned back against a box. He didn't trust it at first, but it felt heavy so he relaxed against it.

"Now what were you two whispering about?"

"Jamie tells me you have to keep your glass hidden from the sheriff."

Seamus frowned and squinted across the fire. "You a teetotaler, boy?"

"Oh no, sir." Jamie shook his head. "We have cooking wine in the house."

"Cooking wine? Personally I'd never put a wine in food that wasn't fit to drink. It would ruin the taste of the food, now wouldn't it?"

"Makes sense, sir."

"Deidre, get a bowl for the boy for some boiled beef and potatoes." He leaned back in his chair and smiled at Jamie. "Put some meat on those scrawny bones of yours."

Deidre sighed. "Pa ...."

"That's all right, sir."

"You wouldn't be turnin' down hospitality now?"

Jamie felt caught. "No sir, of course not. Thank you."

"That's a good lad. No whiskey though?"

Deidre put a bowl in Jamie's hands. "Pa, stop teasing him now."

The stew smelled of cabbage and spices. "Where are the newlyweds?" He shoveled fragrant spoonfuls into his mouth. It was delicious.

"Paddy and Brigid? Oh, they're off. Brigid had a dream of some job and she puts great store in magic does that one."

"You're not denying magic now, are you Pa?"

Seamus leaned back and took a sip of amber liquid. "Never in life, my child."

Jamie scraped the bottom of his bowl. "You believe in magic, sir? I know you tell wonderful stories, but you believe the magic is real? Real human magic?"

"Oh, to be sure there is human magic. It's not like fairy magic, of course, but it's well-laid on powerful for all that." He pointed at Deidre. "I've told you girl, your mother was from fairy stock, though of course it's not a thing I'd ever be able to prove."

"Oh, Pa, stop it." She lifted Jamie's now-empty bowl from his hands, wrapped a shawl around her shoulders and sat in front of him. When she leaned back against him Jamie carefully kept his hands on his own knees and still. Her father's forearms looked like they could rupture a stone.

437

But Seamus only smiled and shook his head. "It's true. I can feel these things. I was just lucky your mother was with us as long as she was."

Jamie did not know how to respond. Death of a loved one was not something that people in his experience joked about. He could not imagine Seamus was not serious.

"Mother was not taken by fairies, Pa." Deidre settled back into Jamie and crossed her arms. "I didn't believe that when you told me when I was a child and I don't believe you now."

Seamus held up his palm to her. "Now daughter, I'm not sayin' she was and I'm not sayin' she wasn't, and that's all I'm sayin' because I don't know. But I do know of one who was taken in the time of long ago when such magic was not questioned and double-answered in a double-pot load of confusion. It's said those times were simpler than ours, but we do them a disservice we do. The folk of old had fairies to contend with and fairies are not a thing to be sneezed at."

Deidre laughed, quiet and low. "Another one of your tales?"

He laughed from the other side of the fire. "You might say. Just relax and I'll tell you what I know of it."

Deirdre pulled her wrap around her shoulders a little more tightly. Then she lifted Jamie's hand from where he had anchored it to his leg, wrapped his arm around her and settled her back into him. She felt warm against him. His breath grew short and at that moment Jamie's heart believed in the power of magic.

Seamus did not seem to notice. He sipped at his glass, leaned against his chair back and began to speak in a low voice.

Chapter 70
Seamus' Tale Deux

It does not do for humans to fall in love with fairies. The magic of human love and the magic of fairies mix oil and water and all usually comes to grief. Long ago in a time we cannot begin to understand a beautiful young man loved to wander in the forest. His relatives tried to get him to work hard at the trade they had chosen for him and tried to get him to work harder at a healthy girl they had chosen for him, but their pleas fell upon deaf ears. At the first chance he always took to the woods to listen to the plants and trees whispering in his ears. Now the sound of trees is very close to the sound of the fairy folk and as everyone knows you can hear fairies if you listen. Most cannot because they do not try, but if you stand close to a tree, put your ear to the bark and listen long and hard enough you can. It's the laughter of ridicule that drives fairies and trees into silence, so if you want to hear what is to be heard you must go far away from the laughter of small minds.

On one of his wanderings to the wood, the young man sat with his back against a tree doing just that, listening, when a fawn stepped into the small clearing. The fawn was of an age when it had not quite lost the dappling in its dark brown coat. Its eyes were dark, darker than any deer's eyes he'd ever seen. He was most afraid to breathe and frighten it, but that did not happen. The fawn left the clearing on its own terms and cast a look over its shoulder at him a final time before it bounded off into the wood.

The very next day the young man returned to the clearing. Again the fawn appeared and looked at him and daintily bounded back into the wood. The young man was so enchanted he returned again and again. Each time the fawn appeared to look at him.

Then came a day when the fawn did not appear. So he searched for it, venturing deeper into the wood in the direction he had seen the fawn go. After a while he smelled fire. He followed the smoke with his nose and came across a young woman stirring a pot of fragrant tea over a cooking fire. She was the most beautiful creature he had ever seen. She was young, with the smoothest skin, the most graceful hands and eyes so large and dark he was caught without speech. That was a thing unusual for he was not a man to put a stopper on his tongue for long, as any that knew him could have told you.

For a moment she startled, but as they exchanged glances but not yet a word, she settled and motioned with her graceful hands for him to sit on a large root of a nearby oak tree and she would share her tea with him. He gratefully accepted, for of a sudden he felt tired, as if he had just finished a long day's trek. She poured him a cup of the brew. He took the wooden cup, drank deep, leaned back against the tree and felt all tension flow from him. The last thing he knew before he fell asleep was her smooth graceful hand sliding into his, her fingers folding with his like they had been made together.

When he awakened they were together in a bed made of bent boughs, she curled up beneath his arm.

From that night he never left her. He found she was a fairy princess and had bewitched him but he never minded in the least and was happy as a man who has talent for it can be.

There was a girl child from their union. The rest of the fairies did not approve. It was one thing for a fairy to take a human into their arms, they had done that often enough, many times, but to make a child with one was not a thing they were comfortable with in the least. So after the child came into the world some of the fairies waited until the two of them were asleep, bewitched the nursemaid, for fairies have nursemaids too, and took the child away. They gave the infant to a young human widow who had been pregnant when her husband died and whose child had just died in the birthing. These fairies bewitched the midwife and switched the dead human infant with the half-fairy child. This woman's breasts were full of milk and no child to suckle and as soon as they handed the infant into her arms, the widow and child were bonded with the suckling. This was a great kindness and a miracle to the widow, for she thought her child blessed by the fairies, but these fairies' hearts were black to have done such a thing to their princess.

The widow told no one of what she saw during the birth, wanting to keep wagging tongues at a standstill, and so became the child's mother.

The girl grew and was the apple of the eyes of the whole town. She was beautiful, with large angular eyes and carried a birthmark upon her shoulder in the shape of oak leaf. There were those who thought her strange, for she knew things before they happened and seemed to know when a person was lying. Those about who tended to bend the truth from time to time for their own comfort were made very uncomfortable.

The girl's father, the young man who had married the fairy princess, had a sister. His sister had a son. This son caught the smooth and gentle edge of the girl's eye. They fell in love.

The night before the two were to be wed the young girl walked out into the main room of their cottage and was amazed to see her whole family asleep where she had left them not a moment before. Two luminous beings stood by the fire with joy and sadness in their eyes. They were her parents, the fairy princess and human husband, both glowing with magic. The joy in their eyes was from seeing her at last, the sadness from what they had to say. They told of her origin, that they were her true parents and the story of her birth. At first the young girl did not believe, but when the princess showed her the royal birthmark of the oak leaf on her shoulder the girl was convinced. They told her the reason they had not come for her sooner to take her back with them was because once a fairy child has suckled at a human breast it cannot come back to the fairies, that is fairy law. Still, they had to tell the young girl she was about to marry her cousin and that was a thing they could not allow to happen.

The next morning the young bridegroom awakened to find that his lovely girl with the angular eyes, his bride, the love of his life, was gone. He searched far and wide, went to every village within traveling distance, but all inquiries failed to find an answer. The young groom mourned her until the day they laid him in his grave, not six months later, struck down dead of a broken heart.

Chapter 71
Irish Lace

After Jamie left, Deidre pulled out her lace making box from her drawer in the caravan trailer and settled by the kerosene lamp. She pulled the flattened coins from her pocket and began knots to weave the string into patterns to cover them with lace. "Pa, do you have any leather thongs? I'm making amulets for us to wear around our necks."

"You seriously like the boy, don't you?"

Deidre turned to her father, who leaned in the doorway of the caravan. His expression was grave.

"Yes, I do. I know he's younger than I, but he's good. There's no hurt in him, do you know like I mean? It's been a long time since. A body doesn't meet many like."

Her father nodded and climbed the steps. He lowered himself onto the cushioned seat, leaned back and laced his fingers together over his stomach. "He's a good boy, my girl. But you well know we'll not be here long. There's boats to be built on the coast, y'know. And furniture here and there that I can make a living wage at. We're not stuck here so fast you need be putting down roots."

"I'm not putting down roots." She fixed her eyes on the lace in her hands. "I just like him, is all."

Seamus shook his head. "I see you stringing the coins and I wonder if you'll be hurting yourself."

"He's not going to hurt me, Pa."

"I don't think he would." Seamus nodded, his voice low and quiet. "All I'm sayin' is you just watch your heart. I well know how fierce it can be."

He got to his feet. She felt the vibration as he clumped down the steps and heard his footsteps as he walked back to the fire. She listened to his chair creak as he sat down then the clink of bottle on glass.

Deidre turned up the wick on the oil lamp for a bit more light. She wanted to finish this quickly. She recalled Jamie's reaction when she had asked him to meet her at the lake tomorrow night at midnight. What was that phrase he'd used about himself? A deer in head lamps? She smiled to herself, bent to her work and shivered in the warm night.

Chapter 72
Last Words

The sun's gold touched the leaves in the deep woods about Ned. It was late in the day and he watched Cyrus hack a blaze on a particularly tall and straight pine. One of his feelings like the ones his father didn't like crawled up his spine, but this time he didn't feel detached. This time it touched him. He didn't like it very much.

"What's wrong?" Cyrus' even voice rang in the emptiness of Ned's reverie.

"You're gonna have to go soon, aren't you?" Ned felt his eyes draw closed as he said it, said the thing that had been on his mind, that thing he hadn't wanted to think but was now staring him in the face.

Cyrus lowered his bush axe to the ground. "I think so. Grandfather has been talking to you too, has he?"

"Grandfather?"

Cyrus nodded. "Everyone has one if they will but listen. It's your inner voice, your connection with … it's hard to describe. But yes, I've been feeling for the right time."

"It's now, I think."

"You want me to leave?"

"God, no. But there's a churning in my gut tells me if you don't something bad is going to happen to you."

Ned sat frozen still. The last time he had felt like this he had told his dad the truck needed work. His father had not been happy because of the money. His dad had been even less happy the next day when the truck stranded him a country mile from the

444

nearest house. His dad had blamed him for everything. That was the day Ned decided never to wear a belt again.

He felt Cyrus' eyes on him. "I'm sorry, I really don't want you to go, but I think you have to."

"I believe you."

He looked up. "You do? I mean … you don't think I'm … you do?"

Cyrus smiled. "I think there is more to life than meets the eye. And yes, I believe you. I've had the same sort of feeling myself. And it's both good and bad. Bad I have to leave, but good that I feel like I'm connected again. Good that Raven has once more touched me and let me feel my people."

"Where will you go?"

"Home. It's time for me to go home."

Ned turned away, tears burning in his eyes. He understood, but also understood his home was no hardware store. He wanted to go home too; he just didn't know where home was.

"I'm very sorry to have to thank you."

It was the oddest phrase Ned had ever heard.

"And you need to thank your friend Jamie for me. You both have been friends to me."

Cyrus shouldered the heavy blade and stepped over to Ned. Ned felt weight as Cyrus laid one hand on his shoulder for just a moment, then lighten as he lifted the hand and walked past.

Ned turned his head to watch Cyrus' back recede down the path back to the mill. He rubbed his eyes, then followed. His feet felt very heavy.

Grant Garrath was roused from his papers by a knock in the doorframe of the cabin and the voice of Cyrus Conner.

"I need to speak with you, Mr. Garrath."

"Oh, I need to speak with you too, Cyrus. Those trees you marked yesterday will do nicely for the mast and spar work for the shipbuilders on the coast and that's top dollar, well done.

445

Tomorrow I need you to find more, 'cause right now they'll take on all I can supply. I'm not certain how long this market will last, to be honest, but I want to strike while the iron is hot."

"I'm afraid not, Mr. Garrath."

Grant looked up. "Pardon?"

"I'm sorry sir, but I need to be leaving."

"Oh? Why? Why the hurry?"

"I'm sorry, but I can't say. But I need to leave."

"I don't need to tell you you're leaving me in a spot, Cyrus. I don't have anybody to replace you."

"Ned'll do you just fine. He knows what to do now. And I'm sorry too. It just can't be helped."

"Do you feel you've been treated badly? Is this something I can sort out?"

Cyrus shook his head. "Oh no. I wish I didn't have to go. I was thinking about settling here but … well, I just got to go."

Grant studied Cyrus' face. It was immutable, immovable, unreadable. He laid his pen down on the work table and rubbed his eyes. "All right. You've got pay coming, but I don't have it in the lock box here right now. I'll go to the bank this afternoon and get it. Tomorrow morning soon enough?"

Cyrus gave a little nod. "Thank you, Mr. Garrath."

"All right then, I'll have it for you tomorrow morning." Grant stood and offered his hand. Cyrus took it, his hand rough calluses. "You need a reference? If you're out this way again and need a job, just drop by. You're a good man."

Grant saw in Cyrus' eyes just a glimpse of a crack in the granite face, but then it was gone. "No sir. But I do thank you."

He watched Cyrus turn and walk down the steps and out the mill gate, then noticed Ned standing by the big oak watching Cyrus as well. The boy's eyes were steady, deep under the brim of the brown felt fedora Grant had given him on that first day of rain. Then Ned hitched his shoulder bag just once and began to walk slowly out toward the path to the house, eyes on the ground.

Chapter 73

Fishing for Answers

Ned wasn't back from tree scouting with Cyrus when the afternoon whistle blew, so Jamie headed down to the lake to fish.

Sabastian was already there. "They're biting today."

Jamie sat down beside him on the rough boards of the pier and unwound the dark braided line from around his cane pole. "I'm sorry. I really thought his garden needed work and that he might let you do it."

"You were right." Sabastian quietly snorted. "I've never seen a garden more in need of basic weeding and pruning. Without being one completely neglected, that is. Your idea was right so you did nothing wrong. It's just that Cramphorne is a fairly odd and very proud man. He would never admit anything about his dwelling is anything less than perfect. A lot of officers in the war were the same way. Don't worry about it, I've heard worse."

Jamie watched Sabastian's lips tighten. He wanted to ask about the war, but Sabastian didn't offer any more. "Didn't it hurt to hear him say all those things?"

Sabastian nodded. "Of course. But a body has to consider the source when you hear that kind of thing. You also have to consider the source on the flip side of that coin which is undeserved praise. It is a hard thing to do, especially when the words are fairly hateful. When your heart hears such the first instinct of the wronged is to hop right to anger and outrage. And that is as it should be were this a perfect world." Sabastian lifted his line from the water and cast it to a new spot, graceful curves flying through the air. "Each of us sees the world through our own painted and muddied window. I have mine, you have yours and the learned minister certainly has his."

"Yeah, but that doesn't explain why. Why he sees you as he does."

"Oh, James. You are beyond your years. Too many of even advanced years do not see the key to understanding is asking the simple question 'why.'"

"So? Why does he hate you?"

Sabastian smiled. "I think perhaps he knows I see not what he wants to be seen, but him as he is. I see his fear. He doesn't want to be reminded of it."

"He doesn't act like he's afraid of anyone."

"'Act' is the operative word, James. He acts his part very well. And he's not afraid of people anyway."

"Then I don't understand."

"Did you ever notice he spends a great deal of time fountaining off about his great abilities, his great experience and knowledge?"

"Hard to miss it."

"I think mayhaps it's not so much an expression of what he thinks he is, as an expression of fear of what he is not." Sabastian drew in the brown silk fly line, then lifted his rod to inspect his fly and the line. "Almost time to re-dress." He clipped off the fly and dug in the pocket of his jacket and drew out a small metal tin. "He doesn't fear people or things so much as he fears his own mediocrity." He opened the tin and plucked out another fly. "Though he would strongly deny it if it were put to him like that."

Jamie's watched his conical cork bobber glide slowly, pushed across the glassy surface by a ghost of a breeze. "How does that make him afraid of you?"

"Because I am not afraid to see his loud pronouncements as anything other than hollow bombast."

A thought struck Jamie. "Then he must hate old man Mason too."

Sabastian glanced at Jamie, smiled and nodded quickly. "Exactly." He laughed, then coughed until the cough faded to a chuckle.

"So why did you want to work for him?"

"Because I'd like a job. I need one that isn't too terribly strenuous to fit my diminished condition, and because I hate to see that garden die in such a slow and painful manner. Better to plow the whole place under than to watch it die like that." He gazed at the water. "James, you're thinking too much."

"Why do you say that?"

Sabastian pointed toward the water, at rings where Jamie's bobber once had been. "Because if I'm not mistaken, you have a fish on."

"Oh!" Jamie jerked up on his cane pole. "Oh!"

Sabastian put his rod down, grasped his net and lowered it into the water. "Not too hard now, he's swimming like a big one, you don't want to break him off. Let him tire; let him come to you, lead him into the net."

"God, he feels heavy."

"He probably is, so don't pull at him too hard, let him fight. Let him get tired."

Just as Sabastian said these words, Jamie's fish broke the surface, twisted silver writhing in the air for a blink of a moment, and then splashed down again in a shower of water droplets rippling the surface of the water. "Oh boy. Ohhh boy."

"Large mouth bass, good fish. Let him wear himself out, there you go, draw him in over the top of the net, that's it, just a little bit more …."

Sabastian lifted his net and the fish was home.

Jamie felt like his lungs no longer worked, unable to draw breath as he looked at the fish sagging and wriggling in Sabastian's net. "Wow."

Sabastian hefted his net. "It has to be at least a three pounds, James. Good man. Good fish."

"I gotta get this home."

After he and Sabastian strung the fish up they walked up the path in the fading light. As they topped the rise at the road they met a woman Jamie had never seen leaning against a Ford Model A. She was slender and dark and when she saw the two of them she stopped, clasped her hands in front of herself and smiled.

Sabastian greeted her, kissed her on the cheek and turned back to Jamie. "James, meet my sister Clara. Clara, this is my friend James."

"Uh, hi ma'am."

She held out her hand to him. "Pleased to meet you, James." She nodded to the fish on his string. "I see you met with success today."

Sabastian laughed. "James has; I'm still learning the lake. I stand a great deal to learn from him."

Jamie was a little embarrassed and shrugged.

Clara smiled at him then looked back to Sabastian. "Are you all finished?"

"Oh yes." He lifted his gear into the back seat of Clara's car. "Quite enough for today." He looked down at Jamie. "Thank you James."

Clara looked at Jamie. "Can I drop you home?"

"No ma'am, thanks. I'll walk. It's not too far."

Jamie said his goodnights, not wanting to tell them he wanted to enjoy the moment for a little longer than the car ride up over the hill. It was a moment and he wanted to savor it, just a little, all by himself.

Clara watched Jamie sling the heavy fish over his shoulder and walk away up the hill.

"Brother mine, I may not know a great deal about fishing like you do, but I do remember enough to know that the lure you have on the end of your line wouldn't catch anything here if you fished a month of Sundays. Why did you do that?"

Sabastian smiled more broadly than she had seen in a long time, the scarred side of his face drawn into hard folds. "You watch me entirely too closely, Clara. I'm really all right."

"I just worry about you, is all."

450

"Tonight I dine on the memory of an uncontaminated boy and his joy at catching what I believe to be his first big fish."

She slid her hand to his arm and grasped his khaki clad elbow. "You will eat with us tonight."

"But your Joe doesn't like me, Clara. He has made that abundantly clear. And he's your husband. I don't want to make trouble."

"Dear heart, tonight he will just have to suffer one of his unreasonable wife's whims, to have her brother to dinner unplanned and unannounced."

"It's not his suffering that disturbs me, quite frankly. It is your suffering after I am gone home."

"Let me worry about that?"

Chapter 74

A Little Night Magic

Jamie could not for the life of him sleep. There had been a lot of excitement about his big fish. It had fed the whole family. He had smiled during dinner but his thoughts had been on Deidre. Had she been serious? Did she really want him to meet her at the lake at midnight?

Ned had been very quiet all evening, had gone to bed early and was asleep when Jamie came to bed. Now Jamie rose up in bed, looked over and saw Ned curled up dead to the world. Jamie slid out from under the covers, slid on his overalls, and with his boots slung around his neck by the laces, slid out the window.

The moon was as bright as he'd ever seen it, so bright it cast lace shadows from the trees on the ground. He slid on his boots and headed toward Little Lake.

As he padded along the path toward the dock, he saw a figure sitting on the end of the dock with feet dangling over the water. It was Deidre. He did not want to startle her so he trod just once upon the dock planks. She did not turn around but spoke over her shoulder. "I wondered how long it would take you to come."

He walked down the dock slowly, mist rising from the water around. He sat down beside her. He thought he saw a shadow of a smile.

"Do you watch the stars, young Jamie?"

He leaned against a piling. "Sometimes. The big dipper is easy enough to find and it shows you the North Star. That's pretty handy to know."

"In Ireland we call it the Starry Plough."

"With the dipper handle being the plow handle?"

452

She nodded. "I'm sure there's a story about it, but I can't bring it to mind right now. I can't seem to remember much of anything lately."

"My Granddaddy told me to tie a string around my finger if I wanted to remember something, but for love or money I can't think of why that would work."

"Did you try it?"

Jamie nodded. "But I couldn't remember what the thing was. I could only remember I was supposed to remember something. That didn't help too much." His hands grabbed each other. "Something tells me your dad's not all that keen on our being together."

"What tells you that?"

"That story from last night, for one thing. He said you were from fairy stock and that humans and fairies didn't mix?"

Her voice echoed very soft. "It's not what my father says that need concern you, young prince Jamie."

He was very aware of her, and how she sat there in the mist swinging her legs over the water. He was almost startled when she spoke again.

"I made something for you."

"What is it?"

"Stand up."

He did, and she stood before him.

Jamie's insides tore against each other. It wasn't that he didn't love her. He knew he did right down to his toenails. It was that he did not know how that love would be received, and he had a sense this thrum in his chest was a precious thing, a thing not to be wasted, a seed not to be strewn on stones to be dried of its life by winter wind. He knew all that but could not, for the life of him, back away.

He was stuck but good.

He thought she knew this, but still watched, frozen, as she reached up to her throat and unknotted her bandana. He saw her naked throat, smooth curved slopes shadowed in the bright gray moonlight, surrounded by mist. He could not read her face, it was in shadow, but her movements were languid as she swung one step toward him and stood close. He smelled her, not perfume, but the light scent of cinnamon, the scent of her. That strummed the strings in his chest and when a serendipitous breeze wafted her hair against his face, it drove his skip-beating heart to the pit of his stomach and held it there.

She lifted one of two cords about her neck and placed it over his head to rest around his. Her hands rested briefly on his chest. He could not tell from the touch if she meant to hold him off or what. But then she lifted her bandana, flipped it around his neck and drew him closer, the bandana now a welcome noose about his neck. He could feel her breath against his face and a tiny voice in his head observed her breath was as ragged as his own, but when she pulled on the ends of the bandana, pulled him close and fastened her lips to his, all thought including the tiny voice ceased and desisted. His hands lifted of their own accord to rest lightly upon her hips and they were frozen, frozen, frozen until he felt her begin to vibrate. The vibration grew until she shook loose, her hands released the ends of the bandana and she backed away. He heard her gasp, had one glimpse of her face, wild-eyed and fantastic and then she was gone, her light boots tapped the dock boards like the fleeting hoof beats of a startled deer, and she disappeared into the shadows of the moon.

Chapter 75

Fear Itself

The Reverend Cramphorne stood at the service window and opened the letter from Silas Webster of the Presbytery while the postmistress searched for the remainder of his mail. As he scanned the page his stomach released from its moorings and plummeted to his shoes. He pushed away from the counter.

"Reverend?"

Cramphorne turned back to the voice. It was the postmistress. He could not for the life of him recall her name, Mel-something? "Yes?"

"Here's the rest of your mail, sorry it took so long to find it."

He forced a smile, but did not trust his ability to hold it in place. He touched the brim of his hat to her and made his way to the door. *Why do these filthy farmers never have the grace to move out of my way?* He bumped physically into one particularly heinous fellow, mud-covered as Cain, who blocked the door. *Will I never be rid of these people?* He fled to his Packard touring car, drove to the church and clambered up the hollow wooden steps into the sanctuary.

Halfway up the aisle he stopped, leaned on his silver-headed cane and gazed up at the crucifix behind the pulpit. He gazed at the suffering image.

The cross no longer shone to him as a beacon. It now seemed just a long lump of cast brass that dangled from the whitewash wall. He breathed deep and set his jaw, chanted the boyhood mantra that had carried him through the pain of ridicule all of his life. "I will not fear. I will not fear, I will not ..." He gripped the silver ball of his cane and pounded it into the wooden floor. "I will not fear, I will not ...." He spat from between tight clenched teeth and he now fully leaned on his cane for support as he barge-poled his way to his study at the back of the church next to the Sunday school class rooms.

Cramphorne slumped heavily in his leather swivel chair. On the desk was an item forgotten, a pack of cigarettes he had confiscated from that infernal boy he had found to work his garden. Forgotten also was his vow to repeat the offence to the boy's parents. Now the pack of cigarettes was only a pack of cigarettes. He reached for it with trembling fingers and shook one out. He found a box of matches in his desk drawer, scrambled one out and struck it. As the flame flared yellow he touched it to the tip of the fragrant cylinder. He breathed deeply, drew the acrid smoke deep into his lungs and willed it to burn and fill the ache in his chest where his heart had been, to burn away the fear he had not felt since childhood, not since the day he had begun to read the good book, since the day of his parent's death.

Scattered on the desktop were his notes for the next sermon. The subject had been 'Roots of Man; how to till the soil of righteousness and send them deep to withstand the tempest of sin.' Now that he had been ripped from the earth; those scribblings seemed pitiful indeed. Cramphorne had always written sermons from what was uppermost in his mind, but now that he had been plowed up by these farmers, the tender roots of his muse dangled uppermost, drying useless in the sun.

No. I will wrestle with this flock one last time. He would show them, had to show these traitorous Cains how a true man of god faced adversity.

"I will not fear."

He drew fresh paper from his drawer.

"I will not fear."

A trace of spittle marred the surface of the paper. He dabbed it clean with his white handkerchief.

"I will not fear."

He took a deep drag on the cigarette, lifted his pen and began to write his last sermon.

Chapter 76

Comings and Goings

"Seamus, there's a letter for you."

"Well, I'll be thanking you kindly, Mr. Garrath." Seamus took the envelope from Grant's outstretched hand.

Grant watched him tear open the letter. A ripple of relief washed across the man's face then his mouth tightened. Finally he looked up at Grant. One side of his mouth drew up in an apologetic smile.

"You have to go."

Seamus nodded slowly. "I hate to do a legger on you, but that I do. And more's the pity for Deidre for we must leave … now. There's not a moment to lose."

"What's the job?"

"Fitting out a yacht for some rich-as-Croesus businessman who needs proper interior joinery, like. But if I don't chance the arm and put a good leg under us it's sure as Cain was guilty he'll think of someone else."

Grant nodded to him. "I understand."

"Could you do me a small favor?"

"Sure."

"Could you tell Jamie for us? I've not time to go find him. Tell him how it is."

"I will. And if it doesn't work out, come back. You're not burning bridges here."

Grant saw a certain tension ease out of the man. "You're a good skin, sure. It isn't a trout till it's on the bank, so that's a great

457

gift I'll hold safe in my pocket." Seamus extended his hand. "I'll be thanking you."

Grant took the outstretched hand. "You're quite welcome."

"What do you mean we have to go now?" Deidre felt a bottomless hole open in her stomach. "This minute?"

"You knew this would happen."

"Yes, but not like this. I don't even have time to find him and tell him goodbye?"

Her father pressed his lips together. "Leave him a note. Tie it to a tree, he'll twig to it."

"None of your neck. It's an ignorant way to say goodbye, as well you know."

"It's got to be done."

"No."

Her father drew himself up and took breath. "Girl, it's a hard thing." His tone was flint. "Now get your things together and into the caravan. Write him a note. We leave. Now."

Her eyes bored holes into his broad back it stalked away from her to hook up the caravan for the drive to the coast.

She gathered clothes in off the line and took them inside the caravan, threw them on the bunk, sat down at the tiny table with paper and pen and wrote.

'Prince Jamie,

I don't know what to write except we must leave. They say the Irish have the gift of gab, magic tongues that bewitch and bedevil and trouble at every turn, but I don't know how to say this. I don't know how to say goodbye to you, so I won't. I will write. I will not say goodbye. Please wear my gift. I wear yours.

Look for my letters,

Deidre.'

She felt the caravan trailer move beneath her as Seamus hooked it up to the truck. She folded the note, scrawled his name on the outside and stepped outside. She pulled the long black ribbon from her hair and tied the note to a branch of a crepe myrtle tree in view where she judged he'd find it. The wind blew her hair into her face.

As they drove away, Seamus grim-faced and she tearful, she watched the white note tied to the tree with black ribbon until it was no longer in sight.

A mere hour later a mother starling needed nest material. She pecked at the ribbon until it fell free, but found that neither the paper nor the ribbon would do once she inspected them on the ground. The paper tumbled away in the wind. The ribbon remained and the black coils fluttered lightly against the ground.

Ned could find nothing to say when Cyrus Conner came in to pick up his pay. He just swept the porch floor of the office cabin quietly and watched Cyrus' back as the man walked away to go say goodbye to Snow. Cyrus was just out of sight when the deputy sheriff's car pulled up.

He stopped sweeping.

Jamie's father stepped outside the cabin. "Hello, Les."

A slow man in khaki and brown uniform pushed himself up out of the squad car and set his felt cowboy hat on his head. "Hello, Grant. How you doin' today?"

"Not too shabby. What can I do for you? Business or pleasure?"

"Business, I'm afraid."

"What about?"

"You got a man here by the name of Cyrus Conner?"

"That I do. Or did. He turned in his notice yesterday so he's off sayin' goodbyes."

"Well, I need to speak with him."

"What about?"

Ned watched the sheriff extend a paper to Jamie's father. "A fella that works for you, a Mr. Eueas Canfield says he matches the description on this wanted poster. Says he's an Indian by the name of John Wanderwood. I just need to check that out."

"All right." Jamie's father called over his shoulder up to the cabin. "Ned! Come here, would you?"

Ned came out the screen door and bounced down the steps. "Yessir?"

"Ned, I need you to do two things for me. First, go find Eueas. Tell him I'd like to see him right now."

Ned nodded. "Anything else?"

"After that, see if you can find Cyrus. Tell him the deputy sheriff is here and would like to speak with him."

Ned heard more words from Jamie's father in his head. *'And warn him.'* Then Jamie's father spoke out loud again. "Understand?"

"Yessir."

Jamie's father turned back to the deputy. "Les, this could take him a little bit, the men are usually pretty scattered by this time of day. Let's have a cup of coffee and you can tell me what this is all about."

Ned ran to find Eueas. The man was in the tool shed oiling chain shackles. "Mr. Canfield, Mr. Garrath would like to see you right away."

Eueas straightened up and wiped his hands on a greasy rag. "Right now?"

"Yessir, now. That's what he said."

"What for?" He spit a spatter wad of tobacco juice in the dirt outside the door."

"The deputy sheriff's here."

Eueas grinned yellow. Then he reached out and slapped the side of Ned's shoulder. "Thanks, boy." Eueas laughed, grabbed his cane and hitch-walked in a hurry off to the office.

Ned tried to shake the feeling he'd been infected with something, then ran as fast as he could to where he knew Cyrus was saying goodbye to Snow.

"Cyrus!"

Cyrus turned toward Ned. "What?"

Ned took a deep breath. "Mr. Garrath told me to tell you the deputy sheriff is here and would like to talk with you."

Cyrus' face turned to stone. "Mr. Garrath said he wanted to speak with me?"

Ned shook his head. "He said to tell you the deputy sheriff wanted to speak with you."

Cyrus blinked once slowly, nodded and took a deep breath.

Snow chuckled and clapped Cyrus on the shoulder. "Sorry, Cyrus. Don't mean to laugh, but you got to have known Mr. Garrath as long as I have. When he says he wants to see you, it means come on up to the office. If he says somebody else wants to talk with you, that means it's up to you. Right now I'd be willin' to bet it means for you to stay as far away from that office as you can and maybe git while the gittins' good."

Cyrus took a deep breath and looked at Ned. Ned nodded quickly. "Yeah."

Snow wasn't finished. "I tol' you Mr. Garrath was a good man to work for, didn' I? Didn' I now?"

A tight smile crossed Cyrus' lips. "And you did not lie."

"You come back when you can. You always welcome here."

Ned nodded in agreement. "What he said."

Cyrus lifted his rucksack onto his back and slung his woven bag over his shoulder. Ned noticed a bundle of three long black feathers hanging from Cyrus' net bag. "You didn't have those before."

"I found them at Raven Rock. It was a good gift you gave me. Thank you."

"My pleasure."

Cyrus reached for Snow's hand and shook it, then turned back to Ned. He laid one hand on Ned's shoulder and with the

461

other pointed a finger at his temple and tapped it a couple of times. "Remember." Cyrus then smiled at him, nodded once and then was gone, his long loping stride taking him out the back side of the woods toward the railroad track.

Ned turned back to Snow. Snow was smiling at him. "He'll be all right as long as you take your own sweet time getting back up to the office to let Mr. Garrath know he gone. Go on now. Go slow."

Ned couldn't help smiling back but his eyes burned too. He took one last look at Cyrus' back, watched him disappear into the woods behind the stacks of lumber then turned to trudge back to the office cabin. He didn't break into a trot until he was almost there.

The deputy sheriff sat on the edge of the porch sipping coffee. Eueas stood alongside Jamie's father and broke into a grin when he saw him coming.

Ned didn't speak until he was standing next to Jamie's father. "I'm sorry Mr. Garrath, but Cyrus is already gone."

Eueas' grin faded. "What? You lyin' sack ...."

"Now you hold on, Mr. Canfield." Jamie's father turned to the deputy. "Cyrus came by yesterday and gave me his notice. I'm not at all surprised he's gone."

Eueas danced with rage. He slammed the point of his cane into the ground. "You're lettin' a dangerous man git away!"

Jamie's father frowned grimly at Eueas. "You don't know that. You have a bad photograph, only a description and not a very good one at that." He turned back to the deputy sheriff. "Like I've been telling you Les, the whole time he's worked here he's been one hard-working man and never offered a minute's trouble to anybody. I personally would be very surprised if he is the nefarious character on that wanted notice."

"But th' scars on his face and arms!" Eueas almost wailed. "I seen 'em clear." He pointed a shaking finger at the paper in the deputy's hand. "And the tattoo! He got the same damn tattoo!"

"Mr. Canfield, you know as well as I do that folks who work around axes and saws tend to have a few scars." Jamie's father rolled up his sleeve. There was a long ragged scar on his arm from wrist to elbow. "I've got a few myself. And as far as tattoos

462

are concerned, they're pretty common. And a lot of them look the same."

Eueas turned to the deputy. "Goddamit Sheriff, you gotta go after him, he's gonna git away!"

Deputy Sheriff Lester Thomas looked sideways at Eueas, then slowly got to his feet, hitched his gun belt once and set his hat back on his head. "No, Mr. Canfield. I don't 'gotta' do nothin'. You told me yesterday this man Cyrus matched the description of … ahh …" he lifted the poster to read, "one 'John Wanderwood' or 'Wanderwoods'. As a duly designated officer of the law I judged it worth comin' out here to have a little sit-down with him." He folded the paper and stuffed it into his shirt pocket. "But I also judge it is not worth chasing a man all over hell and creation who has done no harm around here just cause you want your thirty pieces. You got that, Mr. Canfield?"

Eueas screwed up his face and whimpered in rage.

The deputy sheriff looked back to Jamie's father. "Good day to you, Grant. Sorry to have taken up so much of your time."

"That's all right, Les. Say hello to Mary for me if you would. See you in church."

The deputy got back in his car and drove away.

"Eueas. Time to get back to work."

Eueas pulled his hat down tight on his head and thumped off, kicking up clouds of dust with each anger driven stomp.

"Well?"

Ned looked at Jamie's father. "He headed out toward the railroad tracks. Snow says he's probably on the nooner by now."

"Ned, you do know that if all this is true he won't be coming back. He can't."

Ned nodded. "But I don't like it. It's not right."

Jamie's father smiled at him. "Nor do I. But sometimes that is the way of the world, those that we care for pass from our eyes. At least you know he is alive and well and free. And for a man such as Cyrus, for now that is enough. Now go on back to Snow and tell him that I want you to pick up where Cyrus left off."

"Sir?"

"You heard me. You've been doing it for, what, two months now? No need to fly solo quite yet, we'll let you go out with Snow and let him see what you can do. But from what Cyrus told me, you're doing pretty well. Be a shame to waste all that talent." He pulled his watch from his pocket, pressed the button to open it, looked just once and snapped it shut. "I need to go to pick up the new preacher at the train station, but you go find Snow and tell him what I told you."

"Yes sir!"

As Ned walked back to Snow his eyes welled with tears, torn between gratitude and grief. Cyrus was gone, but at least he could still listen to his friend in the silence of the wood.

Cyrus Conner was no more. The man that stood on the rocking floor of the boxcar was once again John Wanderwood of the Makah, the Kwih-dich-chuh-ahtx, 'People who live near the rocks and seagulls' and of Raven that guarded and guided his life. As brown earth, brown grass and green sweet pines flew past the open door of the freight car he felt an oddly cool wind upon his face. He reached up with his fingers and discovered his cheeks were covered with tears. The stupid white man Eueas might think John Wanderwood was running away, but he would be wrong. Yes, he was running, but not away. John Wanderwood was headed to the land of his fathers.

Then, above the clouds out beyond the pines, he saw Raven soar. The anthracite bird floated toward him with outstretched wings. It kept pace with the train, floated nearer until John thought for a moment it was going to fly inside, close enough to see the long look from its shiny black eye, then with a great cry it lurched upward into the clouds and out of sight.

Raven had brought him an odd little boy and a place called Raven Rock that had lifted his spirit from entangling briars and set him back down on the path to the land of his own soul.

He stood with one hand resting on the wood of the open door and watched the world flow by. As the train passed the lake, his gaze was drawn to water birds cutting vee wakes as they strained their wings and lifted their bodies from the water. He took off his hat and let the wind blow through his hair.

John Wanderwood was going home.

On another train inbound to Miller's Landing there was rebirth of a different kind.

Tom Parsons leaned his head back against the open frame window of the train. He had every reason to be happy and every reason to be anxious. He had been released from the jobs he had been afraid would be his last and sum total of existence on this earth. This was his reason for being happy. But when that fear vanished a new one had slid right into the slot, in ways a fear worse than the old one because this was fear of the unknown. But living side by side with that fear in Tom's chest was a settled heart that sat much heavier on the balance scales, for he knew this was what he was meant to do. This was not something he had to even think about. He simply couldn't not do it.

He felt the breeze in his hair.

His wife Anne held the hand of the arm that was around her shoulders in both of hers as she leaned back against him. It had been a long journey. Tom was tired, but he could not bring himself to miss a single mile of the countryside he and Anne would soon call home.

She shifted against him. "You have such strong hands. I like that you work wood. Now you can do the work you want." She smiled and brought his hand back down and hugged it. "Now you can make furniture."

He lifted his hand not in hers and considered the rough calluses. "You're supposed to be asleep."

"I'm not used to being bounced around. What do you think they'll be like?"

"I don't know." He kissed the crown of her head. "Better to just meet them as they are and get to know them the same way."

"Oh, you're no fun. So practical."

"You make it sound bad."

She lifted his hand in both of hers and ran the tips of her fingers across his palm. "No, I'm just about to burst with waiting like this."

"Do we have any coffee left?"

She sat up, leaned over to their bag and lifted the thermos and shook it, feeling the liquid inside. "Just a little. Want some?"

"Um-hmm, yeah." He pulled his watch out of his pocket and pushed the stem to open it. "There's only about half an hour till we get there and I don't want to meet my first parishioners with a yawn coming out of my face."

Anne stole a glance out the window as she poured cold coffee against the motion of the train. She almost spilled it when they heard a blast from the train whistle. "Drink fast, honey. I think your watch is slow again."

He took the coffee. "Smile when you say that. That's my father's watch you're talking about."

Her eyes twinkled. "No disrespect to your father, honey, but that watch loses about a minute a day and it doesn't help when you keep forgetting to wind it." She slid the long tapered cork back into the thermos bottle.

"You trying to wind me up now?"

"Somebody has to. Especially since we're here."

Tom gulped down the cold coffee, straightened, stood up and promptly bumped his head on the overhead luggage rack. He stayed standing and smoothed over his clothes with one hand as he held the cup out to her with the other. "You're right. How do I look?"

She lifted the cup and screwed it back on the top of the bottle. "As I so often am and you look just fine."

Tom ducked to peer out the window as the train slowed. "I wonder which is them?"

She wrestled a long pin through her straw hat to hold it on her head. "Now who's imagining?"

They gathered their baggage in the crowded aisle of suddenly standing folk and waited to meet their future.

Grant Garrath stopped pacing the train platform. "Damn."

466

Hannah Garrath looked up from where she sat on a wrought iron bench. He did not habitually use profanity. "What is it?"

"Seamus had to leave today. He got a job on the coast fitting out yachts."

"That's no reason to curse."

"I didn't get a chance to tell Jamie."

"Deidre wouldn't leave without saying goodbye. He'll probably see her at the lake this afternoon."

"Not her choice, the job won't wait." Grant shook his head. "By now they're gone."

"Oh my. Where's Jamie?"

"At the mill."

They heard the train whistle just around the bend in the trees, not too far away.

He checked his watch. "No. They're off work. He knows by now."

Hannah stood. "One thing at a time, let's just get the new parson settled and then we'll see to Jamie."

The train steamed into the station, all black paint and squealing steel wheels.

There were only a half dozen folks that got off the train. The only one that came close to fitting the description they had was a tall lean man, with short sandy hair topped with a felt fedora tilted back on the back of his head that tripped as he stepped down from the rail car because he was lookin' up and around rather than where he was going. Grant watched the man recover the small cardboard suitcase he had dropped, then turn and take two more suitcases from the door and then lift a lightly built woman down the steps by the waist.

He felt Hannah's hand tug on his arm and her voice in his ear. "I think that's them. Come on."

"What makes you think that's them?"

"Because they don't know where they're going. Come on."

The woman hardly came up to the man's shoulder. She held his hand in both of hers and looked around.

Grant let Hannah start things. She was better at it.

"Reverend? Reverend Parson?"

The woman lifted her head, saw Hannah, then looked up at her husband. He was still scanning the platform. She gave him a quick elbow in the ribs.

"What?"

She nodded in Hannah's direction.

"Reverend Parson?"

"Oh. That's me." He took Hannah's outstretched hand. "I'm Tom Parson. And this is my wife Anne."

"Glad to meet you, Mrs. Parson." The two women shook hands. "I'm Hannah Garrath and this quiet man behind me," Grant felt Hannah's gaze burn into him as she looked at him over her shoulder "is my husband Grant, one of your elders."

Grant wasn't prepared for the firm handshake of a working man nor was he prepared for the deep crystal blue-green eyes and the low steady voice.

"Hi. Tom Parson. Pleased to meet you."

"Likewise. Welcome to Miller's Landing, Reverend. Can we help you with your things?"

"This is it, for now. The rest is being shipped later, I'm afraid. Is there a place here we can store it until we find out where we're going?"

They stopped by the station master to let him know a shipment of the Reverend's things would be coming in and would he please hold it there until such time as they could pick it up?

The drive to Gil Custis' place was too short for Grant. Hannah and Anne chatted in the back seat while he and Tom Parson sat silently in the front. He wanted to know more about this man, but as they got closer he felt more and more strongly that he had to be honest with this man. "Mr. Parson, there's something I need to tell you."

"What's that?"

"Reverend Cramphorne, the preacher you're replacing, is not exactly happy." Grant grimaced at his own clumsiness. "I hate to open the discussion like this and I'm sorry, but there's a couple of things you need to know."

"What, other than him not being a happy man?"

"There has been some rancor between the Elders and the Reverend Cramphorne. Both sides are pretty tired of it. Now we know the reverend has been writing the presbytery about it. What we did not know until right recently was that he had an iron in the fire elsewhere. Or that's what we've been told by the presbytery. But ever since the word has come down about him goin' elsewhere and you comin' here, he's been actin' kinda funny."

Parson nodded at Grant. "All right, but funny how, exactly?"

"Well," Grant down shifted as they entered the final turn, "a man moving on to greener pastures usually is a happy man. He's not. So it occurs to me he's been acting like a man who just got fired with no place to go." Grant turned into the Custis' driveway and braked to a stop. He turned off the car and toward Parson.

"I'm not saying a man in his position is usually relaxed, because there's always uncertainty when moving on, even if it's a good move. But he's had a tendency to snap like a hurt hound."

"So he's still here?"

"Oh yes. You'll be meeting with him on Friday night. When's the rest of your things getting here?"

Anne spoke up from the back seat. "Should be here on Saturday."

"All right. The Cramphorne's should be out by next week, so that works out. Gil and I will pick up your stuff on Saturday and we'll help you move it into the manse next week. We'll put it in storage in Gil's warehouse behind his store if he's amenable. That might be a little calmer, if you know what I mean."

"I think I do. I feel kind of odd being here on a Sunday and not doing anything though. Are there any folk I can go talk with maybe? Folks too sick to get out to church? I'd feel bad just sitting on my hands on a Sunday."

Grant felt a knot of tension he hadn't even known was there ease and flow from between his eyes and one corner of his mouth drew up in a smile. He drew breath for the answer, but Hannah beat him to it.

"Mr. Parson, there are quite a few folks that would love to have a visit from you, I'm sure. Matter of fact," she laid her hand on Grant's arm, "why don't we talk with Verna French over at the county home? Lily Turner and her group would turn cartwheels for a real sermon if they were able, they haven't had one in a coon's age."

"That henhouse of trouble makers?" Grant grinned at Hannah.

Hannah slapped his arm. "Huh, you. They're just high-spirited, that's all." She turned back to Parson. "I'm more than sure they'd love it. Would that be all right with you Mr. Parson?"

Grant watched the man's face stretch into an easy smile. "Mrs. Garrath, that suits me just fine. And call me 'Tom', would you? That's what I'm used to."

Chapter 77

Holes in the Heart

Cruising timber with Snow was easier than Ned thought it would be. Snow had just handed him the map and told him what kind of wood was needed. Ned found the trees, blazed them and took notes just the way he had with Cyrus. Snow didn't say much but Ned didn't feel talkative anyway. Toby trotted along sniffing the ground, so they pretty much worked quiet.

By the time they returned Jamie's father was gone. It was long past the afternoon whistle, so Snow cut him free. "You did pretty good. Cyrus taught you all right, didn't he?"

"It didn't seem like I was learning at the time."

"That's the best way." Snow smiled. "Take off now before I change my mind and put you to work."

Ned watched Snow's back recede toward the engine shed. Toby sat in the dust and waited as Ned decided what to do.

This was a new experience for Ned, being left to his own devices without orders of what he could and couldn't or shouldn't do. And Jamie was nowhere in sight.

He looked down at Toby. "The lake?" Toby dripped a laugh back at him.

"All right, let's go." Ned retrieved a fishing pole and headed toward the lake, though his heart was just not in it.

Jamie wasn't there.

Toby struck out on the path around the lake so Ned followed. Beside a small stand of cypress Toby stopped and looked back at Ned.

"What have you found, boy?"

It was another trail that branched off from the lake trail. It seemed fairly new but well-worn. He applied Cyrus' teachings and stepped forward along the edge to look for sign. The grass was too matted down for him to pick out a whole track but he spotted Jamie's boot heel by the wear patterns and a couple of what looked like a clean print of a smooth soled work boot. It was smaller than his own, so either a boy smaller than him … or a girl … maybe Deidre.

He continued to track, Toby walking calmly behind. He broke out of the woods in a small fallow field. Jamie sat leaning against a tree on the far side, beating a stick against the ground.

Ned stepped out of the shelter of the trees. Jamie's head turned toward him as he neared, his boots crunching on the dry grass. Toby bounded forward and shoved his nose against Jamie's chest.

"What are you doing here?"

"Tracked you. Or Toby did."

"No getting away from you now, is there?" Jamie's head turned away.

"If you want."

Jamie shook his head and sniffed against the back of his hand. "They're gone."

"Who?"

"All of 'em. Deidre." Jamie broke the stick in his hand and flung away the pieces. "Nothing left but the fire ring and ashes."

Ned went back to tracking. He stepped lightly, as Cyrus had taught him, taking in everything he could without judgment until the vision came clear. "They left in a hurry."

"How can you tell?"

Ned pointed. "Deep heel and toe marks, not running, but walking fast and making a lot of turns and they go back and forth a lot. And the tracks of the truck looks like the tires spun before they caught hold." He straightened. "So them too."

"Too?"

"Yeah. Cyrus took off today. Deputy Sheriff came looking for him."

"Cyrus? He some kind of criminal? Damn. Did Lester get him?"

Ned shook his head quickly. "No. It was just Eueas making trouble. Apparently he wanted the reward on some poster so he said it matched Cyrus."

"I hate that man. I know it's a sin, but there it is."

Ned continued to stare at the ground. "Yeah. Me too." A shiny black ribbon lay on the ground in soft coils. He picked it up and held it out to Jamie.

Jamie reached and pulled it from his fingers. "It's hers. It's her hair ribbon." Pain squeezed his eyes. "You think her dad's some kind of criminal?"

Ned shook his head. "Nah. Sheriff would have been after him too. He just asked after Cyrus and said Eueas had told him Cyrus matched the wanted poster."

"Bastard." Jamie spat. "Cyrus never hurt nobody." He reached out and stroked Toby. "I'm sorry I sent him home."

Ned sat down beside Jamie. "Cyrus wasn't. He said you done the right thing."

"It didn't feel right. It felt awful."

"Yeah, well. That's water, over and done."

He heard Jamie give a two-bark chuckle. "So's Deidre."

Ned watched Jamie sling the ribbon around his neck. He couldn't think of a thing to say, so he just sat quietly and watched the wind blow the campfire ashes into the trees.

Jamie took a deep breath and got to his feet. He walked, hands in pockets, scuffing his feet over to the charcoal gray on the ground where their campfire had been. "She was curled up against me, right here while her dad told stories and we watched the fire."

Now only the beginning wafts of the cool winds of autumn blew powdered ashes across an empty field.

"Let's go home." Ned's voice scraped against his own ears as if human voices no longer belonged in this place, but clear wisdom was there and Jamie nodded.

They crunched along the road together, walking slowly side by side, hands in pockets in the fading golden light. Jamie stopped in the middle of the road and Ned stopped with him.

"Hey."

"Yeah?"

"Let's work on that Snake tomorrow."

Ned looked at Jamie without raising his head and pulled up a half-smile. He felt just a touch of evil healing at the thought of giving Eueas back a little bit of his own. "Yeah, well. Okay."

Jamie's father was already elbow deep in paperwork at his desk in the living room when they got home, so supper was pretty quiet. Jamie caught a couple of looks from his mother, that was all. He skipped dessert and asked to be excused from the table.

He slid into his room, kicked off his shoes and laid on his stomach, rested his face on the backs of his hands and looked out into the dark for stars. A line of light appeared on the wall as his mother came into the room, her knock soft on the wooden panels of the door. "Jamie? Are you all right?"

Jamie rolled over onto his back and laced his fingers together behind his head. "She's gone, Mom."

His mother leaned on the doorframe. "I know. They're off to Woodsville, on the coast."

"Why? What's in Woodsville that has so much more than here?"

She came into the room and sat on the edge of the bed. "A job, Hon. Her daddy is a boat builder, remember? He can make a lot more money there than at the mill and he has to feed his family. They never were going to stay long."

"They were here this morning and now they're gone."

His mom nodded. "Things like this just happen sometimes. Doesn't make it any easier knowing that I know, but what you're feeling is part of being a grown-up. Feeling like this and still going on, having the courage to love again, that's all part of it." She put her hand out and lightly touched his leg. "It did happen awful fast. She may just not have had time to scribble a note."

"I don't know, Mom. I told her I liked her, and all she did was smile at me."

"That's the way some people are. They love but they can't say it. I had to work on your daddy for a couple of years. He acted like he loved me, but it was a long time before he could say it."

"He didn't trust you?"

She shook her head. "Didn't trust himself. It's never wrong to love, son. It's impossible to control how you feel. You can only control what you do. The trick is to live your life as best you can and treat yourself with respect along with everybody else. That's all anyone can do." She patted his leg and stood up. "Get some sleep."

She stepped to the door in the darkness. "Good night."

"Night, Mom."

He watched the line of light at the door narrow and disappear as she closed his door, leaving him in darkness. It was only then, wrapped in the safe blanket of darkness, that tears began to flow.

Chapter 78

Constant Change is Here to Stay

There were times Ned wished he couldn't do what he could do. This morning was one of them. He had seen Jamie tired, but this was different. This morning Jamie sat there like a bump on a log for the entire ride to work.

A man's soul has to rest on something. Whether it's the lessons of the school of hard knocks, the faith of his fathers or the love of a good woman, a man's soul must rest on some sort of foundation, like a piece of machinery bolted to a solid footing. A man can't move without his soul. Without it he is a cart without a horse, a tractor without an engine, a traveler with no place to go. So when Ned reached out to Jamie, he felt like his soul was falling through a gaping black bottomless chasm. Deirdre had been Jamie's first true love, the first deep tap root drawing from the underground spring of his heart. Now his heart was broken, the connection severed. As he drew his mind back again, Ned was torn. He envied Jamie his love, but a part of him was glad, a case of 'there but for the grace of God go I.'

After the truck stopped, Ned and Jamie sat there for a minute while the morning work bustle rattled on around them.

"It just ain't the same, is it?" He looked at Jamie.

"What?"

Ned slid his legs around and stood up. "It just ain't the same without them around."

Jamie sat still as Ned put his hand on the side of the truck and jumped down. His boots made a little cloud of dust as he landed on the ground.

Of all the things Ned might want to hear that morning, Eueas' laugh was not one of them. He saw Eueas standing over to

476

the side, leaning on his cane and watching Jamie. "That boy's lovesick as a weaning pup, look at him."

Jamie's father glanced at Eueas, then clapped his hands. "Sorry, fellas. Hate to split you two up, but I lost two good men yesterday and you two are gonna have to help pick up the slack. Ned, you just hold tight for a minute. Jamie, rail platform and the saw carriage has to be put back together. Seamus did all the woodwork, so today you and Snow are going to mount machinery to it." Jamie's father looked at Snow. "Get it all aligned and drilled out, then take the machinery back off and give it a couple of good coats of red primer. We'll let it sit during lunch, give it another good heavy coat then re-mount the machinery tomorrow and lift it into place."

Eueas piped up behind Jaime's father. "That should be a good job, Mr. Garrath. I'll go git the tools." Eueas turned to go to the tool shed.

Jamie's father spoke over his shoulder. "Not you, Mr. Canfield. Today you work the kiln. Little Foot needs a hand keeping the drying fire fed, so you're gonna be his man today."

"What?" Eueas' face turned to stone. Ned could feel the heat of hate flare up out of the man. "I gotta work with that boy?" He spat a big greasy splatter on the ground. "And all day too, I'll bet."

Jamie's father turned to face the man and nodded. "That's right. The drying don't stop once it starts. Little Foot's been here all night and needs a man to spell him while he catches forty winks. He'll tell you what to do." He turned back toward Jamie and Snow. "Get goin' now. We need that saw running by tomorrow afternoon."

Ned watched Snow reach out and place on hand on Jamie's shoulder. "Come on, let's get the tools. Let's see, we'll need the chest drill, the snap line and the box of wrenches ..." The two turned and walked off toward the tool shed.

Ned felt his skin crawl as he saw Eueas shift his chaw to the other side of his mouth, frown and nod as his eyes followed Jamie and Snow walking away. The man's black eyes flicked over just once toward Jamie's father, then he slowly stumped around, spit and headed toward the kiln.

"Ned."

Ned's head jerked up. "Sir?"

"Come on."

Ned followed Jamie's father up the steps into the office cabin. He waited while he unlocked the desk and drew out the tree scout belt with the pouches and the revolver hanging from it in the closed flap holster. "You're going to be my wood scout and cruise timber."

"I am?"

Jamie's father nodded. "Snow tells me you did pretty well yesterday. Says he didn't help you a bit and the logs came in yesterday evening just fine." He handed Ned a piece of paper. "So today you're going to fly solo. That's what we need for the next order."

Ned glanced down to read the paper. It was a list of wood types, sizes and amounts required.

"I want you to cover this area through here and see if you can find what we need." Jamie's father pointed to an area on the map behind the desk that showed the nearest stand of timber. "Just like always, blaze mark the trees, record what you find and we'll cut those tomorrow. We'll finish cutting today what you and Snow marked yesterday, but that's not going to be enough to fill the contracts I have in hand. You up to it?"

Ned managed to move his head up and down. "I'll do my best."

"Good man." Jamie's father held out the belt. "Go ahead, put it on. You ever handled a pistol?"

"A few times. Pop has them in the store. He made me learn how to clean them and then he took me shooting a couple of times. I gotta tell you though, I never did much like firing them."

"And rightly so, because it's not to be used unless you absolutely need to. If we hear it, everybody and his brother is gonna come running 'cause we'll know you're in trouble. Understand?"

Ned nodded.

"All right, get going. Grab a machete or a hatchet from the tool shed, whatever suits." Jamie's father smiled. "See you when you get back."

Ned slung the belt around his waist. The leather creaked as he cinched the buckle down tight. He folded the papers, stuffed them in his shirt pocket, slung his bag over his shoulder and set his fedora solidly on his head. Then he turned and pushed out the door.

The weight of the belt felt odd as he walked out toward the woods beyond the sawmill yard. He avoided the kiln. It made Ned uncomfortable to feel that kind of hate oozing out of Eueas and he didn't want more coming his way if Eueas saw him wearing the belt. He headed to the woods, where he could breathe, where the air was clean and he could listen to the wind.

Jamie walked along beside Snow. He only heard half of what Snow was saying, especially when they walked up to the saw shed after fetching the tools and he saw the work Seamus had accomplished. There was a lot of it and it was beautiful. Not only was the structure of the saw rails foundation and the carriage rebuilt, but it was not the rough two-by-four and post construction it had been before. It was smooth and clean with tight joints and beaded edges. "Damn. It's better than new. It looks like furniture."

Snow cackled. "You got that right. Old Seamus, he knows what do to with a wood tool, I'll give him that. Almost a pity to paint it."

Jamie ran one hand over the smooth wood. It felt like sacrilege to drill into it. But once the work began he was too busy to think about much of anything except lifting the black cast iron assemblies onto the wood structures, holding, aligning, marking and drilling.

He was helping Snow lift the spike assemblies off the carriage to get ready for painting when Eueas stumped by pushing a wheelbarrow. "You still lovesick, boy?" He cackled high. "That's you problem, ain't it?"

Snow's kind smile faded as he turned his attention to the offending smiling grimace. "Good you come by, Eueas. We need you to take this box of old parts over to the storage shed whilst we get the painting done."

Eueas looked down at the box of cast iron parts. "You know I ain't able to lift that. My leg, you know. How many times I gotta tell you?"

The edges of Snow's mouth tightened. "Dammit, they shoulda named you 'Cain't'"

"What's that?"

"Cause you sure cain't do much, can you? You just ain't 'able', are you?"

"Huh?" Eueas' nasty grin faded.

"Never mind. Just go ask Marshall to come over here and help out. Now git."

"All right, I'm gittin'." Eueas lifted the wheelbarrow handles and stiff-walked toward the kiln, whistling out of tune.

Snow dug his snuff can out of the pocket on the side of his overalls. He pushed his finger deep in the can and filled his lower lip. He chewed a bit, then spit on the ground. "This thing ain't gonna paint itself."

Jamie stood there for a moment, watching Eueas' retreating back. "I hate him. It don't feel good, but I just can't help it. Not today."

"I hear you. Every man's hated at one time or another." Snow gave a single shake to his head. "But it ain't a good thing to do too much of. It'll eat you alive from the inside out, if you go on too long. Leave nothin' but an empty shell ready to fold in on yourself. I reckon that's what happened to Eueas, reckon that's why the good book calls it a sin." Snow reached into his overalls chest pocket and checked his pocket watch. "Let's get the primer. A couple of good coats if it ain't gonna warp. Let's get to work, now. Best thing."

That night Jamie slid out of bed, slid into his clothes in the dark so he wouldn't wake Ned and slid of his window to walk down to the lake. A clear full moon lit the way, all the green and color of the world turned to soft gray and black. He had never felt more alone. Even the crunch of his shoes on the stones of the road seemed a plain rhythm without the syncopation of her dancing steps filling in the space between his plodding notes. He knew it was the same sky above his head, as Sabastian had reminded him not so many days ago, but the sky seemed darker and each star seemed to be shining on its own rather than being as one of a cluster the way they had been when he and Deidre gazed at Cassiopeia.

When Jamie got to the dock Ned was already there. He clumped up the dock. "Hey."

"Hey yourself."

"What are you doin' here? How'd you get here ahead of me?"

"Same as you, I expect. And there's more than one path through the woods."

Jamie sat down across from Ned on the dock. "I guess there is." He looked at the dark still water.

Ned nodded and slapped the reed stick in his hand against the dock boards."

"You ever felt this way before, Ned?"

"Like what?"

"Like … whatever it is that holds up the inside of your chest isn't there anymore?" Ned was silent and Jamie wasn't sure his friend had heard. "I don't want to feel like this."

"I do. I mean I don't but I do." Ned threw the reed into the water. "I mean I want to feel the way I did before, when Cyrus was still here, but I don't want to feel this. I don't want this ever again in this life."

"Dad tried to warn me."

"He did?"

"Yeah. I don't think he had any more warning than we did, but he said Mr. Dunne was looking for work as a woodworker, as a boat builder and probably wouldn't be here very long. It had to be he'd be leaving." Jamie tossed a pebble in the water. After the splash silent dark rippling rings spread across the water and met the reflected ripples of Ned's reed.

"Yeah, well. Stands to reason."

"He also said something I didn't understand at the time."

"Which was what?"

"He said watching folks leave was part of being a grown up. That between folks leaving and folks dying …."

"Yeah well. Amounts to the same thing."

"Well anyway, he finished up by saying 'Loss is part of living, part of life. It's always gonna be there so ya gotta find your own way to deal with it'."

Ned snorted, harsh in the soft night air. "It makes you not want to get close to folks in the first place. I don't think a body can help the folks they're already close to, but it sure makes you not want to get close to any more."

"That don't sound very grown up."

"Yeah, well. Maybe I'm not ready to be a grown up yet."

Jamie listened to the soft fluttering noises of the night. "I don't want to be here no more. Gotta be getting' home."

"Yeah."

They walked back slowly under the dim light of the moon. They didn't say a word while they got to the window, helped each other back inside over the sill and got into bed.

After Jamie slid back under the covers, he gripped the necklace around his neck and her bandana with it. A thought came as his mind drifted in the dark. Though she had kissed him, he had only held her when they had been by the campfire. Now his arms felt empty with the knowing he never would again.

Chapter 79

Back On The Rails

Everything reminded Jamie of Deidre. Riding in the back of the pickup on the way to work, Jamie saw the spot where she had walked and waved to him as they drove by. His mind's eye flashed her smile. Worse was Little Lake where she had kissed him, smooth and calm with steaming mist rising to caress the tree branches in the cool of early morning. Every curve of every limb reminded him of her and his body felt like lead. Ned didn't say a word.

As the pickup bounced to a stop in front of the office cabin, Jamie breathed deep to get a grip on his heart. Ned reached out and grasped his shoulder just once, jumped out of the truck and was gone, up to the cabin for the scouting belt. Jamie made himself follow. Unfortunately as soon as his feet hit the ground, Eueas was right there. He tried to shake the sorrow from his face, but Eueas immediately leaned his head back and grinned.

"Ya over that little girl yet boy? You love-sick, you whipped, that's what you are. Time for you to pull ya head out you hind parts. Hell, she's only a girl." He shook his fist in the air. "Be a man, boy. Git ta doin' what needs to git done."

Jamie couldn't say anything, could not draw any response out of his head. His father was already gone to the cabin.

As Eueas threw back his head and laughed, a couple of faces from the gathered men turned in their direction. Howard 'Rudolph' Mohegan glanced at Jamie then stared at Eueas with his mouth set hard. His shirt collar was open and his fedora wasn't set cocky any more. Marshall's face was lined ebony stone.

Neither man moved. They watched Eueas thump off toward the kiln shaking his head and hooting to himself. Jamie shoved his hands in his pockets and moved off toward the saw shed.

The paint from the day before was dry on the new carriage frame. Jamie looked from the old carriage to the new and felt Snow's hand on his shoulder.

"A little work'll put this thing back on the rails. We'll be up and rolling in no time, you'll see. All you need is a little elbow grease. Then you and me get back to the engine running prime, all right?"

Jamie nodded and Snow set Jamie to reaming dry paint out of the drilled holes on the carriage frame.

Marshall and Rudolph dragged the old carriage out of the way and bolted the cast iron wheel assemblies into place using the holes Jamie had cleaned out. It helped Jamie to work with Rudolph and Marshall. Even though Jamie knew he was not supposed to know, the thought they might understand was calming, though never spoken.

The four of them were enough to put the carriage back on the rails with Marshall being on the heavy side. Then they mounted the log jacks and drive cables.

"Ain't that nice now?" Snow stood back and admired the carriage.

The train whistle signaled the afternoon break. Jamie slumped over to the well and pumped a mason jar of cold water.

"You feelin' a little better today?" Rudolph's quiet voice struck Jamie as unfamiliar this close to his ear.

Jamie turned and looked up at Rudolph. The man had never been unfriendly to him, but also had never so much as offered a word. Now Jamie saw tired eyes and a day's growth of beard, but also calm kind concern. His hat was cocked on the back on his head.

"Some." Jamie's throat gripped. He didn't trust it to release more than one word at a time. "Thanks."

"Don't mention it." Rudolph gave Jamie a gentle slap on the shoulder as he nodded and turned away to go back to where Marshall who held out a mason jar full of water.

As Jamie turned away he heard Eueas' voice once more shouting out to him. He couldn't pick out exactly what Eueas said, but he knew the gist and didn't really need details anyway. The man was hateful.

Ned went out into the woods with Snow that afternoon. That left Jamie on his own to go to the lake to mope. He didn't really know that's what he was doing, but that is what he was doing all the same. Fortunately, Sabastian was there.

Sabastian Wood smiled as he held the wooden teardrop net high to feel the flexing weight of another strong bass. Together with the one he had caught earlier it would make a fine brace for supper. He had caught the bass on a new fly he had dreamed up, a little green streamer with a bit of flash to cut through the murk when swimming deep. He rose and walked to the edge of the pines where his creel lay in the relatively cool shade. He slipped the fish in through the hole and turned back to his rod when he saw Jamie coming down the path and on the walkway to the pier.

The boy was another reason to smile. Before Jamie, Sabastian had almost forgotten the simplest pleasure of friendship. But today Jamie had his head down and his hands buried in the pockets of his overalls.

"Hello, James. Where's your fishing pole?"

"Not really interested in fishing today, Mr. Wood."

"I think that's the first time I've heard you say that. Want to talk about it?"

Sabastian watched Jamie's face shift from one expression to another and back again, as if he couldn't decide what emotion to feel.

"She's gone."

Ahh. "Your Irish girl? Deidre?"

485

"Uh-huh. I know she had to leave because of her dad's job and in a hurry, but it feels like she just got here. I just didn't have enough time to be with her before she was gone."

"I felt the same way about Jo." Sabastian turned and walked back out to his place on the dock.

Jamie's voice followed him. "Huh? Joe?"

Sabastian laughed. "Her name was Josephine. I just called her Jo. J – O. Jo." He saw Jamie's face tightening with a question so he answered it. "She was the woman I was going to marry before I left for France." He picked up his fly rod again.

"What happened? Did she leave too?"

"In a manner of speaking. Apart from the damage that Norris had done, I had changed much more than she from the war. It didn't last once I got back. So she's gone, just like Deidre."

"She's gone and I hate him."

"Hate who, James?"

"Oh, just Eueas. He's been laughing at me because he can see I hurt. 'Be a man, boy' and 'Git to doin' what needs to git done.' As if that had anything to do with the price of tea in China."

A black stone fell into the pit of Sabastian's stomach. "What did you say?"

"About the price of tea in China? That's just something Pop says when …."

"No, about what this man Eueas said to you?"

"Oh that. 'Be a man. Git to doin' what needs to git done.' And the thing is he don't begin to practice what he preaches. All he ever does is hobble around on his cane and beg off work."

Sabastian's attention sank inside. This man Eueas couldn't be who he thought he was. He couldn't be. The bald spot Jamie had mentioned before, the man's fear of snakes and now the 'Git to doin' what needs to git done'? But he was, the man Eueas had to be Lucas Cane. A fire flared in Sabastian's gut, anger he hadn't felt since France, a fire that he thought and hoped he'd never feel again.

"I hate him, Mr. Wood. I can't help it. I hate the son-of-a-bitch."

Oh James, if you only knew. "Call me Sabastian, James. And have you ever noticed that those who tell us not to hate are mostly those who have never felt rage in their veins?"

"Have you ever hated, Mr. Wood? I mean hated somebody so much that you just wanted to pound them into the dirt, pound them til they bled?"

"Oh yes indeed, James." Sabastian took a deep breath. "I have hated."

And we hate the same man. The difference is you want to use your fists whilst my first thought is of my service revolver. What Sabastian wanted to do was shove his Webley 455 barrel hard up under Eueas' chin and yell spit into his face. *You were supposed to fix that petrol leak, Lucas. When it broke for the third time it sprayed me, blinded me and then burned in the crash fire. You bastard. Look at me. Did you think I could ever forget what you did? Did you think you could get away with it forever?* So after all these years, it was him. He had even changed his name. *Lucas Cane, you sorry son of a bitch.*

"Are you all right, Mr. Wood? You don't look at all good."

Sabastian had never been able to confront Lucas Cane, because the man was tribal, never alone; he always gathered about him men as mean and low as he. Military punishment had had no effect. Lucas punished had only been Lucas meaner and hardened with the resolve of resentment at being caught. There was no thought in the man's mind for honesty or a sense of right. But Lucas, as 'Eueas', was now without that kind of friend. Now Lucas was alone.

"Are you all right Mr. Wood? Mr. Wood?"

Sabastian blinked. He looked down and saw he'd dropped his fly line into the water. "I'm fine." *God, I need whiskey.* "I'm sorry, James. I go off somewhere else like that sometimes. Sorry if I troubled you."

"You just had the strangest look on your face. Like you weren't here. You sure you're all right?"

Sabastian nodded. "You just made me think of a man I hated in France who was … very like Eueas. He was my mechanic, matter of fact, and not a very good one. His bad work was the reason my kite crashed." He forced a smile. "I was just lost in thought, James. I just do that sometimes. You can ask Clara; she'll tell you. Don't you ever do that? Just get lost in thought?"

"Sure. And when I do, Dad usually tells me to quit gathering wool. 'Come on, boy. Let's go do something.' "

Go do something. Yes, by all means let's go do something. Let's go kill the son of a bitch whose pure incompetence was to blame for dead pilots in my squadron flight, to blame for killing my friends, to blame for bathing me in liquid fire.. Do I really want to bring all that back? By God, yes. But to do that he needed whiskey, he needed his revolver and he needed his rage.

"James, would you mind too terribly much if we talked later? I have a couple of things I have to do tonight."

The boy shook his head. "No, that's all right. See you here tomorrow?"

"I hope so. I'll certainly do my best to be here. Take care."

Sabastian got to his feet, methodically unrigged his rod and walked home. He did not hear Jamie's voice behind him when Jamie found his stringer of fish. He was long gone, focused on his memories and his whiskey and his hate.

Chapter 80

Cramphorne Meets a Parson

"What's this man Cramphorne like, anyway?"

As he turned the pickup down the long church lane, Grant downshifted and considered Tom Parson's question. He also considered that Anne Parson sat between them on the seat. By habit, by nature and by encouragement from Hannah, he did generally try to give the benefit of the doubt, but in Cramphorne's case he found this a particular challenge. "He is sincere in his beliefs ... and he puts an awful lot of effort into his sermons."

"Hmm." Grant felt Parson shift in his seat. "I don't mean to be rude, but that really doesn't tell me a great deal."

"I'm trying to be fair to the man." Grant steered around a hole in the road.

"It sounds like," Parson ran one big hand through his sandy hair, "you're trying to be nice. Nice and fair are not the same thing."

Out of the corner of his eye Grant saw Anne throw an elbow into Parson's ribs. "Now, Tom."

Parson raised his hand. "I know, honey. I know." He ran his hand through his hair again. "Mr. Garrath, not to put too fine a point on it, I'm here to work and help as best I can using the tools God gave me. But to do that I do need the truth."

"All right." Grant slid a glance sideways. "You want it, here it is. Cramphorne has been a pain in our collective ass since the word go. He preaches generosity, but won't put one thin dime in the plate, sermons on hard work but wants the Elders to tend his vegetable patch. He won't get off his self-righteous can to attend shut-ins, thinks it's beneath his damn dignity and then to beat all, he had the unmitigated gall to sermon us on pride."

Grant gripped the steering wheel. He didn't like the flash of anger in his stomach. This was not good. Hanging out their dirty laundry in front of the new preacher and his wife? Hannah would have his guts for garters. Christ, what was he thinking?

He stole another glance in Parson's direction. Parson leaned back against the door post, a small quiet smile pulled up one corner of his mouth. "That was a long time coming out, wasn't it?"

Grant drew breath and puffed it back out through his lips. "Yeah. It was." He braked as they approached the hard sandy dirt parking area shaded in pines surrounding the church. "That what you want to know?"

"Yes, thanks. Please understand I don't ask to be nosy or be troublesome. I just don't want to go stomping my delicate size 12's into places I don't know where the holes are."

Grant turned his head away and tried not to smile as he pulled the pickup to a stop under the trees.

There were already cars parked around the church. Cramphorne's huge maroon Packard (though he lived in the manse within easy walking distance), Pete Alderman's plain black Model T pickup and Gil Custis' bright green Model B pickup with his store's logo on the side were all there.

They walked up the front steps and through the open doors of the church.

As they entered, Grant saw the Reverend Cramphorne sitting on one of the chairs next to the altar. He wore his black robe. When Grant saw that and the man's great white mane of hair he thought irreverently of a black toad adorned with white bird droppings sitting with squatter's rights on a river stump. Standing beside Cramphorne were Gil Custis and Pete Alderman. Both talked with their mouths and hands.

Gil made introductions all round, but Cramphorne shook Parson's hand without raising his eyes or his bottom from the chair.

Gil turned back toward Cramphorne. "Sir, we need to discuss this."

Grant watched Tom Parson back off a little and guide his wife to a pew to sit down, then wander forward to look at the pulpit.

His attention was drawn back by Cramphorne pounding on the floor with his cane. "No, no, no, a thousand times no, sir. There is no discussion. I have preparations to make for our departure. I have … things – to - do," he pounded in rhythm to his words 'and – I – will – not – be - rushed." Cramphorne frowned and stared straight ahead, the bullfrog image complete.

Parson's quiet voice arced down from the pulpit. "Sir, I'd hate to see you break that fine stick. It's only wood, after all."

Pete snorted, but turned it into a cough when Cramphorne swiveled his white head toward him.

Grant looked up at Parson, but Parson was either a master of control or the comment was made in the innocence of a carpenter respecting his material, for his face was completely calm.

Cramphorne drew himself up to full sitting height. "I think it prudent to cancel services for Sunday. I will be moving my things out of my study. I feel it is my right to cancel services just – this - once." He banged his stick on the floor again and glanced backward toward the pulpit.

Grant looked over at Pete. Pete's mouth waved, soundless going through the motions. Grant knew why. Never in the history of their church had any minister just 'canceled' services on a Saturday for the following day.

Grant reached out and buttonholed Pete, drew him away up the aisle from Cramphorne and motioned to Gil. The three strode to the back of the church.

Pete hissed at Gil. "We can't let him do it. We've never had a church service canceled just 'cause the preacher took a mind to. Even when the preacher's sick one of the Elders takes over."

Gil hissed right back. "I don't know about you, but I don't want that old man around here any longer than necessary. If that's the best way to get him the hell away from here, then so be it."

"What'll old man Mason say? You know how hide-bound he is to do things the way they always been. He'll blow his ever-lovin' stack. And I, for one, ain't in the mood to put up with that kinda shit."

Grant eased the two closer to each other with their backs away from Cramphorne. "Watch your voices, you know how echoes carry in here." He stole a quick glance. Cramphorne still sat like a bullfrog on a stump, face stiff as lockjaw. If the man had heard he certainly gave no sign.

"What do you think, Grant? It's just never been done." Pete's eyes pleaded.

"Pete, y'know … I know. But just this once, it might not be such a bad idea." He held up a hand to Pete's shaking head. "I know, just listen for a minute. A little break might be good just to let folks get used to the change. Give them a little vacation from church. And have a little charity for the new preacher, give him a little time to settle in before we toss him into the fire. That make sense to you? What say?"

Pete frowned, but his eyes were calm.

Gil spoke so quietly Grant could hardly hear him. "Pete, sometimes it's good not to look a gift horse in the mouth. Let Ol' Thunderbuns get the hell out of here and things might settle down. That's what we want, isn't it?"

Pete set into a grim smile, chewed his mouth and tasted the idea. "All right. All right, I'll put out the word tonight."

"Pete, you're a good man."

Pete shook his head. "No, I'm not. I just want all this upset behind us. And if you're right, if this is the way to do that quick as possible, then I'm for it. But I still can't say I like it, and I know Old Man Mason is going to have more than a few words to say."

The very next afternoon Grant drove Parson in his pickup to the train station to get his belongings. Gil had gone on ahead to get the belongings out of storage.

Parson was quiet in the cab beside him. Grant was just before getting nervous when Parson spoke. "Isn't this pickup an old Federal?"

"What?"

"Your truck. It looks like an old Federal."

"Yeah. It is."

492

"Where on earth did you get it? Federal is Canadian, isn't it?"

Grant braked for a bump in the road. "That's kind of a story. A fella by the name of Joe Carter tried to make a go of farming. Had the damn fool idea of spending hard times in the country where it wasn't so hard."

"Oh Lord."

Grant nodded. "As you might expect, it didn't work out. The land was and still is poor, he didn't dig his well deep enough and his whole dream folded up like a Japanese lantern. I had a bit laid by so I paid the back taxes and had the deed signed over to me. The deed included a tractor and this truck."

"So you kind of inherited it. If the land was so poor, why did you want it?"

"It was a good place for a sawmill. Right smack in the middle of a big stand of pine."

"Where'd he get it? Your pickup, I mean."

Grant parked at the railroad station right beside Gil's green Model B at the end of the platform baggage area. "No idea. Parts are hard to come by but it seems to run pretty good."

He pulled the park brake and stepped out into the bright sunshine. He pulled his hat brim down over his eyes, climbed the steps onto the platform and saw Gil Custis and Alvin Hedgepath the train station manager standing next to the baggage storage cage. Alvin lifted his head then walked over to meet them.

Alvin extended his hand to Parson. "I'm sorry, Reverend. We don't seem to be able to locate the rest of your things. I just can't tell you how sorry we are about this."

Parson shook it. "What's missing?"

Alvin scratched his head. "Well, that's just the thing. We don't know. Everything that's on the list I was given is here, but there just has to be more." He pushed his railroad uniform cap back on his head. "I've sent up and down the line to search for the rest of it. I'm sure it'll turn up."

Parson pulled a sheet of paper from his shirt pocket and unfolded it. "This is our list. What does yours look like?"

493

Alvin took the sheet of paper and held it up beside his. "This is it?"

"I'm afraid so. We haven't been married all that long, haven't had time to accumulate."

"Oh."

"So what's missing?"

Alvin looked at the list and back at the pile. "Ahh, I don't know, now."

"Why don't we go over what you have?"

"Right." Alvin nodded, led the three men over to the baggage storage cage with firm step.

The pile didn't look all that big. There was an old wooden desk, four chairs, a plain dining room table, a iron bedstead, two boxes of china, three boxes of books and a couple of trunks of clothes and linens. The only thing Grant saw additional were three tall wooden chests with shallow drawers.

Grant turned to Parson. "What are those?"

"My pride and joy. Those are my tools."

"What kind?"

"Woodworking. It's how I've made my living up to now. Hope you don't mind a working man for a minister?"

A little knot right under Grant's heart unclenched when he heard this. Oddest thing. He hadn't even known it was there. He rubbed the smooth wood of the chest. "No sir. I'd say as we don't mind at all."

Alvin cleared his throat behind them. Grant turned to watch Alvin slide his pencil behind his ear. "All right then, Sir. If there's nothing else, let's get this stuff out of here. I gotta make room for the Reverend Cramphorne's things and there's a passel of that, let me tell you. We're gonna need five men and a midget to get it all out of here."

494

Chapter 81

A Real Parson

Tom Parson did not feel well. Matter of fact he felt pretty poorly. Part of reason was he'd been bouncing over dirt roads for thirty minutes, part of it was he'd only had coffee this morning. Anne had had morning sickness and couldn't stomach the smell of eggs.

But mostly it was panic.

He glanced over at Gil Custis, who drove with an expression as hard as the springs on the Model B pickup they rode in, and put one hand up to the roof of the cab to keep his head from hitting it again.

The sky was blue, pale powder blue, with just enough curling wisps of white cloud to give the eye something to compare against to appreciate the beauty.

They bounced to a stop in front of a rambling old house with a huge wrap-around front porch that sprawled beneath a canopy of oak and pecan trees. As Tom stepped from the cab he saw fields of cotton and wheat beyond. A ghost of a breeze wafted the scent of fresh soil and flowers to his nose.

"See you later, Parson. Things to do."

Tom got a blast rooster tailing from the back of Gil's pickup. He spit dust from his mouth, lifted his hat, wiped his handkerchief across his face and set his hat back down on the back of his head.

"Good morning."

He turned to behold one of the loveliest women he had ever seen. Snow white hair pulled back smooth against her head into a single pony tail, a beautifully shaped head and eyes like deep blue crystal. She was slender and leaned on a plain wooden cane.

"That man is always in a frightful hurry. Seems not to get much of anywhere though." She extended her hand. "You must be Reverend Parson. I'm Lily Turner."

Tom took her slender hand lightly. Her fingertips were smooth and cool. "I'm pleased to meet you Mrs. Turner. I'd introduce myself, but you seem to already know who I am. Do you run the place?"

"Oh my no, dear. I'm just one of the inmates. But I do try to help out where I can to keep busy so I volunteered to be your welcoming committee."

"I thank you." He extended his elbow.

She smiled and he saw true beauty. She took his arm and turned him to walk toward the house. "Shall we stroll to the garden? It's in the back."

"I was a little surprised when Gil drove away so fast."

"Oh I'm not. I was his teacher in grammar school. He doesn't like to be reminded I paddled his little bottom more than once. Even then he was in a hurry and puffed his chest out like a little bantam."

"I know you're used to your old minister. I'll try not to disappoint."

The clear blue eyes twinkled behind soft wrinkles as the white haired woman smiled and cocked her head to one side, like a graceful bird of paradise. She patted his arm with her small cool hand, thin white skin against his deep tan. "Oh don't you worry about that, don't you worry one little bit. You just ply this old lady with a bit of gossip and I'll be just fine."

Tom smiled in spite of himself. "Oh, I haven't been around here long enough to know any gossip, ma'am. And I'm supposed to be tending to your soul, being all spiritual."

She laughed, a silver peal dancing in the air. "Let's get to know each other first, then you'll be able to tell if my soul is even worth saving."

"I already think you have one of the most beautiful laughs I've ever heard."

"Only one of?"

"Well, I'm kinda partial to my wife."

496

Now she grasped his elbow to help her step down stone steps in the walk. "Oh, and I was so hoping you were single."

"Sorry to disappoint."

"Oh, you don't, believe me."

"I'm not sure how my wife will feel about my finding a girlfriend though."

"Oh, you do go on now. Would you like to hear some?"

"If it'll help me get to know the folks around here a bit better, sure."

Lily Turner leaned on her cane and smiled like the proverbial Cheshire. "Oh, it will do that, I guarantee. Where do you hail from?"

Tom told her of his life as a carpenter in Indiana, how he met his wife in the seminary and about their baby on the way. She told him she was the widow of a veteran of the Great War who died of complications of his wounds.

"Gas, you know. He was lucky not to have been blinded. That would have been a shame, Mallie had such beautiful eyes. But his lungs never recovered, just like poor Sabastian Wood. And Mallie did like his cigars and that didn't do any good at all."

"How long ago was that?"

"Oh, a coon's age, dear. That was in 28'. He was such a dear man."

They circled around the path to the back of the house through a stand of magnolia trees and Tom saw the wide porch extended all the way around the house. "You know, it's such a nice day, do you think we could hold the service outside?"

A prim woman in a smooth gray suit with her hair in a tight black bun wearing black high heels clicked her way up to them, her hand extended. "Good morning, Reverend. I'm Verna French. I'm in charge here."

"Pleased to meet you, Mrs. French. Would it be possible to hold the service outside?"

Mrs. French's handshake stopped and a flash of a frown appeared before she promptly pasted a smile in its place. She could not control her eyes nearly as well. "I don't know, we're all set up with the folding chairs in the hall now …."

497

Lily Turner broke in before she could finish. "Oh, Verna. Look at the day outside. We could even go down by the pond, sit in the chairs there around the tables."

"Now Mrs. Turner, we don't want to get sick, do we?"

Tom Parson didn't think he'd ever see such a thing, but lovely Lily's face tightened to a grimace of a smile. Her pleasant tone never changed. "Now Verna, what would be better for health than a turn of fresh air on a day like this? You yourself talked about that just the other day, getting all of us old things outside for fresh air. I heard you myself."

Verna nodded. "That's true." She clapped her hands together and smiled as if the idea had been hers. "Mrs. Turner, would you be so kind as to take the Reverend Parson to the glade? Give him the scenic route so we can get everyone down there. Thank you so much."

And she was gone, organizing orders to everyone in sight. Tom offered Lily his arm again and spoke under his breath. "She does need to be in charge, doesn't she?"

"Oh my yes. She's been giving orders since grammar school." She led him back around to the front of the house under the red oaks.

Tom looked up at the Victorian detail on the porch trim. "You taught her too?"

"Before the school closed down. Few folks know people as well as their grammar school teacher. Maybe their parents, but that can be a close call."

As they approached the glade, it became apparent to Tom Parsons just how effective Verna French's orders were in this place. About twenty well-dressed people sat on wrought iron chairs around round tables beside huge magnolia trees that ringed the pond. Huge creamy flowers blossomed against the deep shiny green of the leaves.

Tom let Lily lead him to a spot by one of the tables. He looked over the lined and life-beaten faces. The sun reflected through white hair on many heads, turning them into halos. He thought it a good omen.

"Good morning. I'm Tom Parson. I feel there is something you should know right up front, right from the start. I do not believe in long sermons. There's already too much pain in the world and I don't like to cause any more."

A gentle wave of chuckles rippled though the group.

He looked about at the magnolias and up at the blue sky. "I know I'm new to you and you are new to me. But I cannot imagine a finer day for a fresh beginning." He held out his hands. "Just look at this. Some folks I know believe ministers are supposed to point out all the sin in the world and what we all can do about it. But I cannot believe a day such as this is meant for a long litany of finger shaking, shalts and shalt nots. I think a day like today is intended to remind us of the need for fresh starts. Fortunately I'm not the only one who thinks so.

In the book of Luke, Christ says 'This cup which is poured out for you is the <u>new</u> covenant.' In the Gospel of John, right up at the front there, 'In the <u>beginning</u> was the word and the word was with God and the word was God.'

And from 1ˢᵗ John 'For this is the message which you have heard from the <u>beginning</u>, that we should love one another.' What a beautiful thought. Such a beginning deserves to be renewed, at the start of every day, as simply as watching a sunrise. Seeing that sunrise should be a symbol for us, a reminder of how simple and beautiful a beginning can and should be.

I need new beginnings in my life. Every day I need new beginnings. We tell ourselves we will begin anew, with fresh purpose, fresh resolve all the time. Our new year's resolutions are one form of that. We are going to lose weight, or exercise more, or eat better, or write more letters or do this thing or that thing that we have been putting off since time knows when. I personally have a whole string of those. Fortunately my wife is kind enough to remind me of them so I don't forget."

More chuckles rippled through the group.

"And rightly so. What finer resolve, what better daily refreshment of purpose could there be than to love one another and perhaps, just perhaps, to tell those we care for how we feel? It doesn't need to be a melodramatic radio soap opera grand gesture. Mostly better if it isn't. A simple flower will do. Or opening a door. Or a warm handshake. Sometimes folks are embarrassed by the expression of love, and though there's logically no reason for them to be self conscious about it, either giving or receiving, that's really all right. Let your loved ones know in a way that won't embarrass them or you. Iron a shirt, oil a squeaky hinge, replace a light bulb in a reading lamp or even just give them an easy smile in passing. It's not necessary to do the world, just what you can. Just do what you can. '… from the beginning that we should love one another.' Every day, begin again. Every day, fresh start. Every day, listen to the voice of God in the sunrise and begin."

He waited just a little bit.

"To that end, I would like to affirm faith with you for the first time with the creed of the Apostles …."

And so Tom Parson began his ministry, in a small garden by water, surrounded by quiet listeners and the rustle and sweet smell of magnolias in the summertime.

Chapter 82

Passing

Captain Sabastian Oliver Wood sat at his single table in his single chair in his single room above Sam Bowden's gas station garage for three days and drank. Or was it four? He could no longer remember. He was not roaring drunk. He was not sloppy drunk. He was thoroughly drunk, the way he used to be before he went into the air, a quiet, mean drunk, balanced on a razor's edge of control. He wore his flight jacket. He stared at his whiskey bottle, his medals and at his service revolver on the table. Cold hate flowed through his veins. The object of his hate was Lucas Cane.

His flight leader had broken up the fight between him and Lucas. His commander told him officers did not behave that way, officers were better than that, officers used their hate against the enemy. He had taken his flight leader's advice. He closed off and harbored his hate for times he could use it. And they had given him medals for his hate.

But now there was no enemy but Lucas or Eueas or whatever the devil the man called himself.

Sabastian raised the bottle and drank deep, one, two, three full swallows the way Shandy Mills had taught him in the withdrawing room of their chateau. Good pilot, old Shandy. Saved Sabastian's hide up there more than twice.

He spoke to the dark. "Shandy, what would you think of your brother in arms taking his honorable weapon and putting an honorable bullet through a dishonorable man's head?" He picked up the Webley Mark IV revolver, deliberately pushed the catch lever and hinged it open. "<u>You</u> know what it feels like. Do I really want to open the door?" He slowly filled the dark holes with dull brass shells. Each clicked into its appointed place and echoed on the walls of his hard and empty room. "But it's Lucas, old man. He calls himself Eueas, but it's still the same son-of-a-bitch that killed you with his stupidity. If I had killed him when I had the chance, might you still be alive?" He clicked the revolver shut. "But we didn't think we would live anyway, did we? We were dead men, waltzing with the bony hands of death every time we climbed in our kites." He stared at the ghost standing in the shadows before him. "Josephine never understood. She feels guilty, I know, but you didn't see her. Sweet Jo doesn't want to think of me in the world."

He grabbed the whiskey bottle by the neck and pushed to his feet. He stuffed the revolver into the deep pocket of his flight jacket, stepped out onto the upstairs landing and stared deep at the midnight mist. Memories flooded into his mind as the humid scent of wet grass came to his nose. He heard the cough and hacking clatter of aircraft engines and felt cold flow into his bones. He began to sing, softly. "Allons enfants de la Patrie, Le jour de gloire est arrivé. Contre nous, de la tyra ... "

He heard a real metallic clatter echo beyond his vision in the mist. No, it couldn't be. "Shandy?" He stared down the wooden steps.

The clatter repeated. He realized someone was at Sam Bowden's gas pumps. He started down the steps and fell, landing beside an old oil drum at the bottom.

The Right Reverend Cramphorne was stealing gasoline. He thought the town owed him at least that much for their mule-headed intransigence.

His wife rolled down her window and sniffed. "Hurry dear, we want to be gone from this place of unholy heathens."

A clatter and a great thump shattered Cramphorne's concentration. "Stay here, dear. I'll be back in a moment." He grasped his great black cane with the silver ball and stalked off into the mist.

Sabastian lay with his back against the wall, half-hidden behind the fifty-five gallon drum. Pain stabbed through his spinning alcoholic fog. He raised the bottle. The amber fluid burned and warmed his stomach. Relaxed relief from the pain had just begun to spread when he saw shining wingtip shoes scrape to a stop on the hard ground directly before his eyes.

He squinted upward and saw a massive white head atop a dark blue linen suit. He also saw the white band of a clerical collar. That drove the warmth from his mind.

"You ought to be ashamed of yourself!"

Sabastian pressed his eyes closed against the noise.

"To be drunk in such a state is one thing, but to do it in public where children and women can see you is so far beyond the limits of human decency I cannot describe it!"

Images of men exploding into abstract patterns of flying flesh and burning blood before his machine guns flashed through Sabastian's mind. He tried to grasp the meaning of 'human decency' this thundering fat man intended. He tried to speak, but was cut off.

"Have you no shame? Have you no honor? Have you not a shred of human decency your precious bottle has not taken away?"

Something inside Sabastian gave way, the see-saw of his soul tipped and his sanity tumbled down the slippery slope. He began to laugh. He could not help it; he laughed longer and louder than he could recall since the war. When it finally subsided he opened his eyes to the reverend again.

"If you don't have the self-respect to put down the devil's draught, by heaven I'll do it for you!"

Sabastian watched the meaty hands reverse the black cane and grip it like a baseball bat. He watched the round silver ball arc around as the reverend swung like Joe Jackson at a low change-up and watched the amber filled bottle in his hand shatter as the silver ball hit.

He set the neck of the bottle delicately on the ground and looked up again. When he saw the red and furious fat man's face, fresh peals of laughter burst from his lips. As he fell over helpless he heard the scrape of wingtips, a car door slam, an engine's cough, the grinding of gears and the correolus engine whine which dropped in tone as it gradually faded away.

As the tone faded, so did Sabastian. He ceased to grip the swirling world, no longer clutched the grinding, slicing shards of the vessel of his soul. He opened his clutched fists and let them fall away. It wasn't a matter of drink. A binding inside just let go. There was no point. Every supreme effort of his life had been ineffectual. Though he knew there were those who loved him, no one he knew needed him, and there was nothing he knew he could do really worth doing. That made it time to leave this mortal coil and greet his old flying companion who had beckoned with skeletal fingers on every flight, had whispered in his ear to leave the chaotic cacophony of his cockpit and invited him to stay in the silent peaceful clouds.

"Yes, old friend. I'll come with you now. I'll take your hand. Lead me out of here. I'm ready." Images swirled before his mind's eye of he and Josephine their last night together before he left for the war, dancing, turning, swirling, he trussed tight in his flyer's uniform, she in her long dress and diamonds, dark tresses caressing her smooth shoulders.

A single blink, and he was gone.

Sam Bowden had been in the war. He struggled through paperwork at his garage desk when he heard Cramphorne's shouts and Sabastian's laughter. He smiled. "Finally. Give that old bastard hell. It's good to hear you laugh, maybe your wicked sense of humor is finally back." Sam looked toward the ceiling. "All right, I know that ain't very godly. Guess I'll have to go to church now. I got to give thanks for getting a new parson to replace that piece of horse dump showing his ass outside. And it's worth a month of Sundays to hear the old Sabastian back. You understand." Sam winked at the ceiling, chuckled and bent back to his paperwork. Organization did not come naturally to Sam Bowden. But with a reason to smile the work came easier.

There is an old adage about what you don't know not hurting you. The adage is only partially true. It is only true until you find out.

Sam's bliss would not last.

Chapter 83

Aftermath

Sam Bowden awakened with a smile stretched across his face. He arose, kissed his wife Nellie and made his way to the kitchen. He brewed a full pot of coffee and poured a cup for himself and Sabastian. Sam didn't like him to drink, but he also thought there were just so many things a man could handle at one time. Hearing Sabastian laugh at Cramphorne deep in the night made his heart light. What had old Cramphorne been doing out there in the middle of the night anyway? He held both cups gingerly in one hand as he stepped outside, turned left around the edge of the building and saw a pair of legs extending out beyond the edge of a fifty-five gallon drum.

"Shit." He set the cups down on the drum and knelt. He felt Sabastian's wrist.

"Goddamn it." The wrist was cold, no pulse. "Goddamn it all."

He straightened Sabastian's collar and combed a couple of cobwebs out of his hair. He saw the revolver in the pocket of the leather flight coat and pulled it out. "We don't want nobody to see this. I sure am sorry." He held Sabastian's cold hands for a full five minutes, then gently folded them across his chest.

Sam pushed himself to his feet, took the cups of coffee and plodded back inside. He set the cups and the revolver on the kitchen table, picked up the candlestick phone and dialed the deputy sheriff.

"Hello, Mary? This is Sam Bowden down here in Miller's Landing. Is Lester there? I gotta talk with him. Sorry to wake you this early, but … yeah, it's important. Thanks."

As he waited for the Lester to come on the line Nellie came out of the bedroom, took one look at Sam's face then saw the

505

still full cups of coffee. When she saw the revolver one hand came up to her face. She turned her head to one side, wrapped her arms around her waist and leaned against the counter. "I'll have to make a casserole for Clara. She won't feel much like cooking." She strode into the bedroom and pulled on her housedress. "I'm going across the road to 'Fred and Adams'. Maybe Adam will have a chicken, so I can make a casserole. I'll be back in a few minutes."

"Honey?"

She looked at him, pain in her eyes.

"You'll want to go out the front."

She nodded, grabbed her purse and left.

"Hello, Les? Sam Bowden, yeah. I'm afraid I've got some bad news. Sabastian Wood is dead. Yes, he's right here at my place. Do you want me to call the funeral home? I'll be making the arrangements. All right. No, no, Clara doesn't know yet, you're the first one I've called. Figured Nellie and me better drive over there, it's not something she'd want to hear over the phone. Uh-huh. Thanks Les, I sure do appreciate it. Sure, I'll wait for you right out front. See you later."

He set the phone earpiece in the hook, then picked up the phone book and found the funeral home number. His mouth set hard. It was going to be a long day.

Gil Custis stopped by Bowden's for gas on his way to deliver paint and Tom Parson's tools to the rectory. He watched Sam closely as he pumped gas up into the glass cylinder on top of the gas tower. "What's wrong, Sam? You don't look right."

Sam turned and put the nozzle in the tank. "A good friend of mine died this morning, fella I knew in the war."

"I'm sorry to hear that. Who was it?"

Sam nodded and coughed. "We got a new parson now, don't we?"

"That we do. I'm on my way to see him now. Seems to be a nice fella, pretty wife, likes to work wood."

"Carpenter?"

Gil nodded. "Some kind of woodworker. He's a lot different from Cramphorne, I'll tell you that. Not a bit afraid to work with his hands. Don't know how far down it goes, how much is hot air and how much not, but he's got good tools, anyway."

"Hey Gil, could you do me a favor?"

"Sure."

"Could you tell the new parson I need to speak with him about the funeral? I'm making the arrangements."

"I'm on my way to pick him up now to go look at the rectory. See what kind of shape Cramphorne left it in. I'll ask him to call you."

"Appreciate it."

"Not a problem. I'll call you later."

"Holy slapping catfish, will you look at this?"

Pete Alderman had only said aloud what Tom Parson was thinking. He hadn't known what to expect on his first visit to the rectory, but it certainly was not this. Everything was gone, stripped. The only thing left in any room was a couple of pipes hooking down from the ceiling where a carbide gas jet had once lived.

Pete lifted his hat by the bill, ran his other hand over his thinning pate and adjusted his hat back down. "Reverend, I … I'm awfully sorry about this. I sh-should have come here first and had the … place a little bit fixed up."

Gil Custis stuck his hands in his back pockets and shook his head. "I'm sorry too, Reverend. We'll get it right."

"That's all right. You didn't do it. And call me Tom, would you?" He thought he caught a blink of a look flash between Pete and Gil but neither man spoke.

He wandered over to the fireplace. "Do I see what I think I see?" He turned to look at Gil. "Did they really rip the finish molding off the fireplace?"

"You're kidding." Gil moved to stare at it himself and nodded. "That was special order, too. Nordic rune stuff, from

507

Norway, expensive as all get out. Thought he was some kind of a Viking."

Tom half smiled. "I wonder if he knew the ancient Danes were heathens. Pagans and pirates."

Pete called from the other room. "I don't know pagan from pogo sticks, but he sure got the pirate part right."

Gil walked to where Pete stood in the kitchen doorway.

Tom looked down at the floor in front of the fireplace. There were little divots in the hardwood floor, little round dents about a half inch in diameter. There were a lot of them.

He wandered to the kitchen.

Pete lifted his hat again. His voice cracked about a half-octave higher. "Not only did they take the woodstove cover plates, but out on the screen porch they took the pitcher pump off the well pipe."

"You're kidding." Tom stepped out onto the porch.

"Nah. Lookit."

Gil reached into his back pocket for his pad and pulled a pencil from his front shirt pocket. "All right. Let's start a list."

When they were finished Gil folded his notebook up. "I'll get the materials." He looked at Pete. "I'll put 'em on the church account. Have 'em here this afternoon."

Tom rubbed the back of his neck. "Could you bring my toolboxes and my sleeping bag as well? I might as well stay here tonight and get some work done on it if I can. Oh, and could you ask Anne to give you a few of my work clothes?"

He saw Gil's eyes blink over to Pete's and back again. "Your tools are in the back of the truck right now. I'll bring your bag and a couple of kerosene lamps, though. And a pitcher pump. We'll go ahead and screw that on so you can have water." Gil took a deep breath. "Oh, by the way, I got something to ask you. Sam Bowden needs to get with you. A friend of his from the war just passed and he needs to talk about the funeral."

"Sam Bowden? I don't think I've met him."

"Not yet you haven't." Gil shook his head. "He runs the garage right across the road from Fred and Adam's."

508

"I saw that place as we drove by. Who is the fella who passed away?"

"A friend from the war, that's all he said and I didn't want to push him."

"He have a phone at the garage?"

"Umm-hm."

Tom looked around. "I'm afraid to ask if the right reverend left the phone. Is it here?"

Pete cackled. "I think the operative words are 'usta-be'."

Tom snorted without pleasure. "I really did not want my first sermon to be a funeral."

"Nobody else to do it."

"Yeah." Tom nodded. "Take me to Sam Bowden's? Come to think of it, I'd like to talk with him face to face. Find out enough about his friend to make a decent eulogy."

Sam Bowden stood at Clara Gracie's door with hat in hand. He glanced back over his shoulder at his wife. "Nellie, I don't know how to do this."

"Nobody knows how, honey. Better you and me, who might be able to ease her a little. Now go ahead and knock." She shifted the casserole dish from one hand to the other. "Go on."

Sam knocked on the door.

Clara's husband Joe Gracie answered the door. "Hello, Sam. What can we do for you? Come on in."

Sam stepped across the threshold. "Thank you, Joe. Is Clara home?"

"She's in the back sorting through old clothes she wants to give to the county home, if they'll have them. She just … what is it?" Joe looked from Sam to Nellie and back. "What's happened?"

"It's Sabastian. He … ah … he died last night."

"Oh Lord." Joe breathed deep. "Come on in the kitchen."

They followed him there and he crossed to the doorway leading to the back of the house. "Honey, could you come out here for a minute?"

"Hold on." They heard her sing-song call. "Be right there."

The clock ticked away long moments until she appeared, wiping her hands with a towel. "You know you never think clothes you've put away in storage can get so dirty just sitting there. I mean I put them away clean but here they are just as dirty as they can be. Why hello you two, you sure are dressed up." She stopped. Her hands stopped wiping. "What is it?"

They told her. Told her about the argument in the night. Sam left out the part about the revolver.

She sat down at the table, pressed the towel to her mouth and closed her eyes. She nodded. "I had hoped this day would be later rather than sooner." She looked up at Sam. "An argument?"

"But he was laughing, you know? Like when we were kids. When you knew he had the devil in him, but you couldn't help but laugh right along 'cause he was just so damn funny, remember?"

Clara nodded, took off her glasses and pressed the towel to her face.

"It was like that. I thought he was back. When I heard the car drive away he was still laughing." He sat down heavily in the chair opposite Clara and slammed his hat on his leg. "I thought he was back. Damn that parson, may he rot and burn in hell."

"Is that who it was talking to him? You're sure?"

"No doubt, no mistaking that voice; he was yellin' at the top of his lungs. But Sabastian laughed right back in his face. Dammit."

"And you found him?"

"This morning. Sitting neat and calm as could be on the bench by the side of the garage."

Clara stared into space.

"His face was peaceful, Clara. With a little smile."

She took a deep breath. "Right. Well, I have a lot to do, then."

Nellie sat by her at the table and laid one hand lightly on her arm. "Most of it's already taken care of, honey. Sam already called the sheriff and the funeral home and they're busy taking care of him. It's just a matter of setting up the church for the funeral."

Clara's eyes burned into Sam's. "You just let me take care of that."

"All right, if you're sure. I'll take care of it now, if you need me to."

"You're a good friend Sam, but no. I'm sure, all right. I'm real sure."

Chapter 84

Building

Tom Parson was working on his life, figuratively and literally. Gil had brought his sleeping bag, his work clothes and a cot, but also two kerosene lanterns, a few books and a little dinner from his wife. Better yet, Gil had brought Tom's desk, a plain wooden pedestal desk that had belonged to Tom's father. Tom sat on an upturned apple box and tried to prepare his first full sermon by lantern light.

It was not going well.

The beginning of the day had been fine. He had begun work repairing the rectory, a symbolic as well as real mending. While daylight streamed in the windows he had replaced the flooring in front of the stone fireplace. As late afternoon passed and evening fell, he replaced the trim around the rough stone hearth and the mantle by the light of flickering kerosene flames. He had been told the trim had been a carved Nordic pattern, but after he fitted the last pieces and stood back to consider his work, he could not imagine anything other than plain smooth wood beside the rough stone would look right. More would be 'gilding the lily' as his grandfather used to say.

Finally he sat at his father's desk, ate a little and tried to apply pen to paper to create the right note on which to begin his ministry.

Unfortunately words would not come.

So he did what he always did when the great white wall of a blank page stopped him cold. He turned to his tools. But there didn't seem to be anything that could be worked without either more materials or light. He stretched and walked over to the church. The church doors were unlocked and he strolled inside and wandered up to the pulpit through streaming moonlight. He tried to imagine a congregation before him. He ran his hand over the bible on the dais. At least Cramphorne had left that. Then he turned and looked up at the cross for inspiration.

It was gone.

It had been an ornate shiny brass thing, gleaming against the plain white plaster wall. His lips gripped together. He nodded, thumped his fist on the dais just once and walked straight back to the rectory, straight to his tools.

He selected a piece of clear oak from the woodpile Gil had left. It was fairly simple to make a cross about the size of the one missing from the back of the sanctuary. Lap joint center using the classic golden ratio of length to width, then he added braces to the center. He took his pencil and drew, laying out the interlaced circles of a Celtic cross. Then he opened his chest and selected tools: a straight chisel, a skew chisel and two rounded gouges, one large and one small. He took up his mallet and began to carve.

As the chips curled, he breathed in the scent of fresh oak and talked as if he were standing in front of the congregation. Occasionally he turned to the desk and noted a turn of phrase, but mainly he let the words flow as his hands moved across the surface of the wood.

Across the road from the rectory, Verna French could not sleep. She did not want to know what time it was because if she found out it was early morning she'd have to get up and go do something. She didn't want to do that. She wanted to go back to sleep. So she lifted herself from her bed, wrapped a shawl around her shoulders and went downstairs for glass of warm milk.

As Verna turned at the bottom of the stairs, out the front door window she noticed a light. She stepped over her cat on the braided rug and pulled the lace curtains to one side. Through the front rectory window on the other side of the road she could see the new reverend working hard, building something. On Sunday at the county home, Verna hadn't told the new reverend her house was right across the road. The subject had never come up. Of course, 'right across the road' in this county meant a good hundred yards from porch to porch, as houses were set back from the road. But that didn't keep neighbors from 'keeping an eye on things.'

Verna approved of work, believed in work, liked hard work. She frowned a steady smile, nodded in satisfaction and went to get her glass of milk. He would do. Yes, the new reverend would definitely do.

Chapter 85

Into the Wood

Jamie's father drove without speaking, jammed the downshift and braked harder than usual as they pulled into the rectory. He had promised to help, but Jamie thought it probable his father was not particularly pleased with taking time away from the mill. The grim silence lasted until they walked in the open door of the rectory and his father looked around. "Well I'll be damned."

A powder of sawdust and wood chips covered the floor and the sound of hammering echoed from the other room. As they passed into the dining room they saw their new reverend in work clothes, sleeves rolled up with chisel and mallet in hand. He looked up as they came in the room.

"I'm sorry; I didn't hear you come in."

Jamie smelled the fresh cut wood as he crunched over the curls covering the floor to the cross lying across the sawhorses.

"Well, it looks like you've been kinda busy." Jamie's father laughed, stuck his hands in his pockets and looked down at the cross too. "Kind of big, isn't it? I mean it's pretty, but I've never seen a cross that big in a house."

"It's not for the house, it's for the sanctuary."

"What for?"

"I went over there last night to take a look around. The brass one I saw the other day when I met Reverend Cramphorne is gone. So I made you another one. It's not real fancy, but I hope that's all right. You think it'll do, at least until you folks decide what you want to do?"

Jamie's father gaped. "Gone? You're kidding."

"I wish I were."

Pounding came at the door of the rectory. His father turned to Jamie. "See who that is, would you?"

At the front door stood Clara Gracie, Sabastian's sister. Her eyes widened as she saw Jamie then her face melted a little. She reached out and hugged him close. Jamie felt her shake a little and could hear her cry. She released him and dabbed at her eyes with her handkerchief. "I'm sorry, Jamie. I don't mean to embarrass you."

"That's all right, Mrs. Gracie. I'm not embarrassed."

"You are such a good boy. Sabastian talked about you a lot, did you know that? You were good for him; he was so very fond of you."

Jamie felt something strange about what he was hearing, but Clara Gracie didn't give him time to think. Her face hardened.

"Is Mr. Parson the new minister here?"

"Yes Ma'am, he's right in there. He's been working trying to get the house in shape to move into."

"Thank you."

She pushed her handkerchief back into her purse, snapped it shut and strode firmly into the room where Parson had his work space set up. Jamie followed at her heels. She strode right up to Parson. Her voice ripped through the air.

"You should be ashamed, sir." She stamped one foot on the floor. Her fists clenched at the end of her ramrod arms held to her sides. "You should be ashamed."

Jamie watched the minister blink once slowly at her, then deliberately place his tools on the sawhorse bench. "I'm sorry, ma'am? I don't know what you mean."

"Don't play the innocent with me, Mr. Parson. Sam Bowden heard you at his garage. He heard you and my brother having an argument on Sunday evening. It was you. How could you do such a thing? How could you be such a beast? You will NOT preach at the funeral service of the man you killed."

Grant stepped forward shaking his head, hands out. "Clara, I don't know what you're talking about, but whatever it is, it wasn't him."

The distraught woman turned her tear-stained face to Grant. "Sabastian's dead, Grant. You think I'm imagining that? What do you mean it wasn't him? Of course it was him."

"It couldn't have been. Reverend Parson was with us on Sunday. He gave a sermon over at the County Home, then Verna French gave him a ride to our house and he was with us for dinner."

She shook her head at Jamie's father, spitting her words through pressed lips. "But Sam said it was him. I remember what he said exactly. He said 'Damn that Parson, may he rot and burn in hell.' I will never forget it." She spoke through trembling lips and pointed a shaking fist up at Tom Parson. "It was him. It was him."

Grant shook his head. "Clara, Sam Bowden is from the mid-west. He says 'parson' instead of 'reverend'. He couldn't mean this man." He shook his head again. "He must have meant the parson. I'm sorry Clara, but Sam had to have been talking about Cramphorne."

Clara clamped her hand up to her mouth. Her eyes closed and squeezed tears down her cheeks. She turned away to hide her face behind her shoulder and sobbed. Her shoulders began to shake and she ran from the room.

Jamie felt a dark hard shiver grab the back of his head and squeeze. "Sabastian?"

His father looked back at Jamie. He did not speak, which was confirmation enough for Jamie's heart to tear its way down through his stomach.

Tom Parson looked at Grant with questions in his eyes. "Who?"

Jamie's father reached over and put one arm around Jamie. "A man by the name of Sabastian Wood. He was a good man." He looked down at his son. "And he was Jamie's friend."

Tom Parson's face cleared. "That's who Gil was talking about then. He told me that Mr. Bowden wanted to talk with me because he's making the arrangements. What happened? Was that his wife?"

Jamie's father shook his head. "I don't know. And no, that was his sister, Clara Gracie. Mr. Wood wasn't married. Other than an invalid maiden aunt, Clara's his only survivor."

Angry lightning tore Jamie apart from the inside out. "There's me!" He twisted away from his father and ran from the house. "There's me!"

Jamie tore across the lawn to the back side of the churchyard and into the woods. Briars and low saplings ripped at his legs and arms. He fought his way through, not feeling scratches nor blood. He ran until he ran right into a low spreading cedar bush, and as he tried to think of how he could get around this, he also thought of how cedar bushes were a wonderful place to hide. He looked low and found a way through the rough and fragrant branches. He crawled in on his hands and knees, made his way past cross limbs and found a place to lie down on the fragrant carpet of fallen nettles. His mom would be angry if he didn't come home, but he didn't care. Right now he didn't care about much of anything. Yeah, he knew Ned was his friend and Toby ... but Toby, for all his magic was a dog. , but Sabastian had been his window to the wider world and now Sabastian was gone.

Several hours later the sun dropped below the treetops and threw golden red fire between the trunks of the trees. Beyond the cedar branches he could see the smooth steel ribbons of the railroad. He ran his hand across his nose, crawled out from underneath the cedar and listened to the wind. When he emerged at the railroad he remembered the train did not run on Sunday. The straight steel path would guide him home, for it ran right through the middle of his father's land.

The hard soles of his shoes rang on the worn surface as he walked the rusty rail. Sabastian's warm laugh rang in his mind, so smooth and musical when he thought of putting a skunk in the Widow Morrison's mailbox for Nosy Norris to find. For the first time since he had heard of Sabastian's death, Jamie smiled. It was a thought that had made Sabastian smile. That was enough then. Now he would stand up for Sabastian, and the target was his nemesis, Eueas. They had taken care of Nosy. He would take care of Eueas. And if Ned wouldn't help him, as unlikely as that might be, he would do it by himself. He would do it for Sabastian. He would make a dead man laugh if it were the last thing he ever did.

Grant leaned back at the kitchen table and held the newspaper spread in the air. "Sabastian's obit is in the paper today."

"Oh my." Hannah finished drying the plate in her hand and slid it onto the stack in the cabinet. "What does it say?"

"Captain Sabastian Oliver Wood, 42, of Miller's Landing, left this world on this Sunday night past. He was a hero of the Great War, an ace flyer with 9 victories in the sky above the Argonne forest and was thrice decorated for valor in action with the Croix de Guerre from France, the Distinguished Flying Cross from Great Britain and the Distinguished Service Cross. He is survived by his sister Clara Wood Gracie and his aunt, Beatrice Robertson, also of Miller's Landing. Services will be held on Sunday with private internment after. Family will be receiving visitors on Saturday afternoon at the home of Miss Beatrice Robertson, 18 Elm Street."

"You know, I don't know if Josephine ever knew any of that. She never mentioned it if she did."

"Wouldn't have made any difference if she had."

"That's hard, Grant." Hannah scanned the darkness outside the kitchen window. "It's awfully dark out there. I'm starting to get worried."

"You weren't worried when they snuck out before. 'They're just being boys.' I think you said."

"He's not just having a little boy adventure now. And Ned isn't with him." She handed Gloria another dish to dry. "I want to comfort him."

"Right now he wants to be left alone."

"Right now he needs to be comforted. He shouldn't be alone at a time like this."

"You mean you need to comfort him."

"It's what mothers do, Grant." She handed Gloria another plate. "It's awfully dark out there."

Grant heard a crunch on the hard earth outside. "That's him. No fussing, now. You hear me?"

They listened as Jamie walked around the side of the house to the back. A few moments later Jamie came in the back screen door stomping off the dirt off his feet and taking the broom to his clothes.

"Hey there, young fella." Grant lowered his paper and watched Jamie come in the door. "What have you been up to?"

"Filled up the Delco."

Grant held his tongue.

Hannah wiped her hands on her apron. "We held some supper for you, hon."

Grant watched his son slowly shake his head. "No, thank you. Is it all right if I just take a bath and go to bed?"

"Sure, honey."

They both watched him pad his way out of the kitchen toward the bathroom.

Grant lifted his paper again and popped it in the air to straighten it out.

"What's wrong with Jamie, Mommy?" Gloria leaned against her mother. "Where's he been?"

"He's just been for a walk, honey." Grant tried to keep his voice even. "Just been for a walk."

Jamie took a bath almost without realizing what he was doing. When he got to the bedroom Ned was leaning back on his cot reading. "You've infected me with this damn reading thing, y'know."

"Oh gee. I'm sorry."

"Yeah well. You should be. Where ya been?"

"Out."

Ned laid his book down in his lap and looked at Jamie.

"Just out in the woods."

"Didn't go to the lake?"

Jamie shook his head. "Nah. Just in the woods between here and the church. You heard, I guess."

"Yeah. The obituary is kinda interesting."

"You read Dad's paper before he got to it?"

Ned smiled with one corner of his mouth. "Yeah well. I was careful. It's not like the words on paper are going to wear out from reading it."

Jamie sat on the side of his bed and stared at the floor. "What'd it say?"

"That he's a hero."

Jamie looked up. "Yeah?"

Ned pressed his lips together and nodded. "Oh yeah. He was a pilot. Flew in the Great War. Nine victories. The man was almost a double ace."

"Damn."

"Oh yeah. And," Ned pushed himself up a little "he was decorated three times for valor. Once by France, once by England and once by us."

Jamie swallowed a hard lump. It made his eyes hurt to think that he had been right about Sabastian. "I'd sure like to know that story."

"Maybe you can ask his sister someday."

Jamie shook his head. "No. She feels worse than I do."

"Not now. Later when she feels like talking."

"You mind if we just blow out the light and go to sleep? I'm tired. I'm just tired."

As Ned put his book down on the floor and blew out the lamp. Jamie turned and laid back on his bed.

The moon shone brightly in through the window. He felt like the moon was now Sabastian, looking out for him, guiding him and shining on him to let him know he was not alone.

Chapter 86

A Little Bit of News

Pete Alderman was not a particularly nervous man, but he did not like surprises. The letter in his hand from the presbytery was certainly a surprise. He closed the little post office box door and lifted his hat off his head three times, once by the crown and twice by the brim and settled it back down. "Now what do you think of that?"

He walked over to the service window. "Mel? You in there?"

"Just a minute." Melanie Coughman came out from behind a stack of cardboard boxes, dusting her hands against her green apron. She was a solid woman with neat iron gray hair. Her pumps thumped against the wooden floor as she walked up to the window. "Mornin', Pete. What can I do for you?"

"You seen Grant this morning?"

She shook her head. "Not yet. But he doesn't come in every day. You know that, you know Grant better than I do. What's gotten into you?"

"Oh, just some church business. If you see him, could you tell him I really need to talk with him."

"Pete, why don't you just use our telephone?"

"Ain't that against the rules?"

"Don't say 'ain't'. And I'm just helping Mary out a little bit so I'm not all up the rules anyway." She winked and opened the lower half of the Dutch door that served as the service window. "You come on in. Phone's on the desk right there and the phone list is right above it on the bulletin board."

"Thanks, Mel."

"And leave a dollar."

He stopped and lifted his hat. "What? For a phone call?"

"Oh, calm down. It was just a joke." Melanie thumped back to sorting packages.

"Oh." He adjusted his hat. "All right." He sat at the desk, reached for the candlestick phone and lifted the earpiece. He peered at the list and dialed the number.

"Hello, Grant? Yeah, it's Pete. Listen, I just got a letter from the presbytery. It's about Tom Parson and there might be a little hiccup. Yeah. Well, listen to this … turns out the man ain't a Presbyterian. Yeah, that's right. He's Lutheran, of all things. I know he don't act like it, but that's what this paper says. Yeah, uh huh. Okay, I'll see you at the session meeting. Bye."

Pete hooked the earpiece back on the phone and took a deep breath. "Damn. Just when I thought we were out of the woods."

Chapter 87
Decision

"Is he all right?"

"What?" Ned turned to Snow's voice behind him as he strapped on the revolver belt in the office cabin.

"Jamie. Is he all right?"

He reached for his shoulder bag from the table. "I don't know, Mr. Snow. He talked about it a little bit last night, but now he's not talking about anything. I've tried, but nothing does any good. It's like he's someplace else."

Snow sat and slipped his hat from his head. Ned didn't very often get the chance to see Snow's bare head and the slender crown of white hair that gave him his nickname.

Snow ran his rough hand over his bare pate. "Well, let me tell you. Sometimes friends don't need words so much as they just need us to be there while they work out what they need for themselves. My granddaddy used to do that. He'd sit there, doin' whatever he was doin', glance up every so often, hardly say a word, just enough to let you know he was listening and didn't think you were bad or some damn fool for feeling the way you did. I remember he did it with Grandma too, saw she was hurting the way Jamie is now and that's just exactly what he done. You're a good boy, Ned, wanting to help your friend. He'll be all right. He's just got to work it out inside for himself. Takes time." He slapped his knees and set his hat back on his head. "And now it's time for you to go cruise some timber for us."

The train whistle that signaled the morning break blew just as Ned came out of the office cabin. He could hear Eueas jaw-jacking about Sabastian to whoever would lend an ear. Ned didn't want to listen so he kept walking.

He found Jamie working on the engine. "You workin' through the break?"

"You're wearing your stuff, getting ready to scout, ain't you? Well, this is me doin' the same thing." Jamie hefted a monkey wrench.

Ned didn't know what to say, so he just nodded and turned to leave.

Eueas' raspy voice grated through the quiet air. "Yeah. I know'd him during the war, used to work on his airplane. Went and got his self crashed right into the middle of no-man's land, right in the middle of a gas cloud the way I heard it. Don't know why they made him up to be such a hero if you ask me. Shit, just makes him a foul-up."

Ned heard a thump. When he looked back the wrench Jamie had been holding was in the dirt and Jamie was running for the woods.

"Dammit."

He followed, trying to copy Cyrus' easy trot while he kept his eyes wide. Jamie passed out of sight pretty quickly, but sign was easy to follow. All Ned had to do was a little bit of tracking then he let himself be guided by sound, heavy thunks against a tree trunk. He followed the echoes. They got progressively louder and Ned came out in a small clearing.

There was Jamie, tears streaking his face, pounding a tree as hard as he could with a broken-off branch, swinging it like an ax, grunting curses. Eueas' name was between every curse.

Ned sat cross-legged to one side and waited silently until Jamie spent himself and collapsed to the ground.

"I hate him, Ned. I hate him for what he did to Toby, I hate him for what he's done to him, I just hate him."

"Done to who?"

"Sabastian."

"He did just say he was Mr. Wood's mechanic, didn't he? Think he was telling the truth?"

Jamie nodded. "Yeah, I do. Something Sabastian said to me one time about a bad mechanic he hated in France because he'd been the cause of his plane crash. That's why Eueas thinks he knows machinery."

"Not very well."

"He can't even read. Can't read a technical manual. How he's supposed to work on an airplane when he can't read the book? He's to blame." Jamie spit on the ground. "Eueas just told the truth for once. Of course he lies about everything, so we don't really know. But we do know he can walk just fine without that cane. Except we ain't got no way to prove it."

Ned thought of the snake trick Cyrus had used on him and looked sideways at Jamie. "Maybe we do."

Jamie looked up. "Huh?"

"Cyrus showed me this trick, well played it on me, matter of fact. I saw a snake wriggle right in front of my feet and it was all I could to not fly off the ground. I nearly jumped out of my skin."

"Cyrus could charm snakes? He was a medicine man, though. We can't do that."

"No, he made a fake snake and danced that in front of me on a string I couldn't see. I'm not all that scared of snakes. But remember how old Ewe-ass hid like a girl behind the post when that copperhead was in the sawdust? If we played that trick on him he'd drop that cane and run like a rabbit, I know he would."

Then Ned saw something he had never seen in Jamie's face. He saw mean. Not just pick-on-your-little-sister mean, but real mean, and when Jamie spoke Ned heard it in his voice.

"If it was in front of other people he'd get beaten to pulp." Jamie had dead serious in his eyes. "I want to see him hurt."

Ned scratched his nose. "Jamie, this ain't like you."

"Will you do it or won't you?"

Ned nodded. "Sure. Happy to."

"We might get in real trouble."

"Yeah well. Been there before. Be there again. Nuthin' new."

"Thanks."

"Why you so strong on doin' it now anyway? I thought you were sour on ideas like this."

"Wasn't mad enough."

Ned waited for more, but Jamie stopped talking. He just didn't feel he could sit still with just that. "That explains why you were sour on it to begin with, but that doesn't explain why you're so strong to do it now."

Jamie tossed his stick away. "Remember when we told Sabastian what we did to Nosy? He laughed, you remember that?"

"Oh yeah. Out loud too and I thought he never laughed."

"And if Sabastian can still see us here, I want to make him laugh again."

"Sound's like what Dad calls 'a cold dish of comeuppance'." Ned felt his face grow grim. "I think it's about time that old Ewe-ass had a taste."

Jamie smiled. It was not a big smile. It was small and mean and without pity.

"Yeah."

Chapter 88

Confrontation

Tom Parson stood high up on a ladder and lifted the wooden Celtic cross in place on the back wall of the sanctuary. It still felt a little tacky to the touch and smelled of varnish, but he wanted it in place before the Elders arrived for their meeting.

"Hey, you up there. You order that cross?"

Tom Parson turned around. An old man in overalls walked up the aisle and pointed at him with one arthritic finger. "Pardon? Order it?"

Grant Garrath followed the man in through the church doors. "Jeremiah, easy there. That's the new preacher you're talkin' to."

The finger kept pointing and started shaking at Tom. "I know damn well who I'm talkin' to and he ain't answered my question yet." The old man stripped his straw hat from his head. "Yes, order it. Did you order that cross? We didn't approve it and the Elders decide any and all expenditures. That's what these meetings are for, to discuss church needs and what to do about it. We had a perfectly good cross up there already."

Behind Grant and the old man, Pete Alderman and Gil Custis filed in.

"Well, that's as may be." Tom Parson turned back around, adjusted the cross to vertical and backed down the ladder. When he got to the bottom he wiped his hands and tucked the hand cloth into his back pocket. He glanced from man to man. "But there wasn't one up there when I got here. That's the only reason I put that one up."

Tom watched Gil and the old man glance over at Grant. He saw Grant nod and Gil's upside down smile and nod in return.

"Oh, Grant, Gil, thanks again for helping us move in. Anne's over there bustling around building her nest."

"Reverend, this is Jeremiah Mason, one of our leading Elders." Grant's mouth twitched like he was trying to suppress a smile. "Jeremiah, this is the Reverend Tom Parson."

"What do you mean it's gone? Where'd it go?" Mason was not a man to let go of a thing until he'd wrung every last bit of understanding out of it.

"I have no idea. Sorry. I just saw you needed a new one."

Mason turned and hit the top of one of the pews. "He just could not leave us in peace, could he? I hope to hell someone fills his drawers with poison ivy." He hit the top of the pew again and looked back at Tom Parson. "But that don't answer my question. What I want to know is, who approved the expenditure?"

"Oh, I see." Tom smiled and leaned against the altar table. "There was no expenditure."

"What?"

"Well, other than for the raw materials. I used a bit of scrap from the new flooring I had to put down in the rectory."

Mason peered up at the cross. "You made that?"

"Yeah." Parson shrugged. "I know, you might not think it's as nice as the one that used to be up there, but I thought there should be one. I'm sorry if you don't like it. Don't worry, no insult to me if you want to get another one, but maybe this will do in the meantime."

For three or four blinks no one moved. Then Old Man Mason mounted the steps to the pulpit. "Let's take a look at this thing." He lifted his head way back so he could see the cross through his bifocals.

The cross was of a slender Celtic design with the circle about the center. The work was clean, neat and finished, and the decorative design carved into the face was also originally traditional. In short, it was a beautiful piece of work.

"Hmm." Old Man Mason clapped his hands behind his back. "We'll have to discuss it, of course."

"Of course."

"But it'll do for now."

"Thank you."

"But fact is, we came here to discuss something altogether different." Old man Mason chewed on the side of his mouth.

Pete chuckled. "I'm glad you took out your chaw plug."

"That's enough out of you, Pete Alderman. Any more of that and I'll show you a spittoon in a hurry."

Tom tried to smile and glanced over the group. "It must be pretty important to take so many of you to say it. Is there some sort of trouble?"

Pete began, "I don't know we'd call it trouble exactly …."

Old Man Mason blasted into the tiny gap of silence Pete left behind in his hesitation. "Some says it is, some say it ain't, but whether it's a trouble or not is what we've come to beat over with you."

Tom held his eyes on theirs. "All right. Let's talk."

Parson sat in one of the chairs by the altar and the Elders sat haphazard in the pews. When they were all seated, Pete began again. "First off, Tom, we want to reassure you we think you are a fine person …."

"Pete, you say the least with the most words of any I've ever come across that didn't have a nervous condition. Get to it." Mason slapped his straw hat on the pew beside him.

Pete solidified and faced Mason. "You think you can do better, Jeremiah, you go right ahead then." He sat back in his pew and crossed his arms.

"All right, I will."

Mason turned to Tom, who leveled his eyes straight into Mason's and waited.

"First off, we wrote the seminary and got some information about you."

Tom nodded and pressed his mouth tight.

Mason nodded with him. "Yes, you see it. You're not Presbyterian, are you?"

"No, I'm not."

"What are you?"

"I was reared Lutheran, so I thought I'd stick with it."

"What changed your mind?"

"Nothing. I couldn't get a position as a Lutheran. Despite my degree, there's not much chance to crowbar your way in unless you know somebody who knows someone else. And I wasn't reared in town where the decisions are made, if you know what I mean. So I started writing letters elsewhere and Mr. Silas Webster accepted me. It's all pretty much the same anyway, isn't it? Same Bible, same Jesus, same God? I'd just be wearing a little different collar in church."

"And?" Mason was not about to let go that easy.

Tom fixed straight on Mason. "And I needed money. My wife is pregnant and I didn't want her and my child to suffer if my carpentry job dried up."

"You a carpenter?" Mason looked up at the cross. "Well, I guess you are, aren't you? What kind of carpenter?"

"Framing and finishing, mostly. But I'm learning carving and furniture building."

"Furniture?"

"Need a crib soon."

Mason rubbed his stubbled chin. "How you feel about taking a little carpentry work on the side?"

"Jeremiah." Pete uncrossed his arms and jumped in. "We're not here to talk about that."

But Tom still looked at Mason. "Be glad to, long as it doesn't keep me from visiting the shut-ins. I have to make sure I do all of this job before I take on more."

The room of men took a deep collective breath and gave a great collective sigh of relief.

"One last thing." Old Man Mason scratched his head.

"What's that?"

"Your sermons."

"What about 'em?"

"From what Verna tells me of your first one at the home … they're too nice."

"Too nice?"

"That's right. Too sweet."

"God's love is too sweet?" Parson laughed and even Mason chuckled.

"Remember, we're Presbyterians. We like a little more flint."

"Flintier than Lutherans?" Parsons' eyebrows lowered and his head cocked a little to one side.

"Think a little bit Puritan. Just not quite to Jonathan Edwards."

Tom could not help but laugh. "All right, Mr. Mason. I'll see what I can do."

"Call me Jeremiah." Mason extended his hand. "I know we shoulda said before, young man, but welcome to our church."

Tom took it and shook it slowly.

Each man followed Mason's example as they filed out, clapped their hats on their heads and walked off, each to tend to their own.

Tom Parsons leaned on the doorframe of the church and watched them walk, filled with relief. Then he clapped his hands, jumped in the air and with the closest thing to a dance his great clumping feet could manage, ran to the rectory next door. He burst into their home.

"Anne? Oh Honey, you'll never guess what just happened …."

Chapter 89
More Revelation

Jamie sat in the pew with his father's arm around his shoulder. Ned sat on his other side, silent but there. He could not believe the casket in front of the altar held Sabastian. Though it was full of people, the sanctuary felt empty, he felt empty, like a hole had been blown through the middle of his chest.

The tall figure of the new minister stood at the dais and shuffled papers. Jaime thought this man knew nothing that could possibly make any difference. He didn't seem anything like Cramphorne had been, but Jamie waited, grim-lipped, expecting platitudes.

The Reverend Parson lifted his head and took a deep breath.

"I cannot fully express what an honor it is to be standing before you today. I certainly did not expect my first words to you from this pulpit would be for a funeral. But it was completely beyond me to think it would be such a man as Captain Sabastian Oliver Wood. I don't know how many or how well you knew this man. I, of course, knew him personally not at all. But in the past few days I have had the rare privilege to spend time with his friends, with his family and with a few of his brothers-in-arms from the Great War. This privilege has taught me once again that there are truly extraordinary people who live among us, and Captain Wood was one. Before the Great War he studied to be in the ministry, had felt the call of God. The war cut those goals short. He felt so strongly about what was going on overseas that, even before the United States became involved, he traveled to Canada to join the Royal Air Corps. There he trained and graduated from flight school. After flight school he went to France and flew above the fields of battle. I am told by those who knew him there that he was a very good flyer. A beautiful and natural flyer is what they called him. As the war went on he collected nine air victories, almost enough to be a double ace and became captain of his air group. For bravery in action and leadership he was awarded the Croix de Guerre from France, the Distinguished Flying Cross from the British, and lastly, from our own government, retroactive to the actions, the Silver Star and the Distinguished Service Cross. These last two are truly exceptional because he was serving in the Royal Flying Corps at the time. When I was told of the medals I knew I was learning of a brave man. When I read the citations I was stunned to learn just how brave. On his last flight he was shot down over the battlefield of the Somme. He had seen from the air how ground troops, stumbling over shell holes and barbed wire, were slaughtered by machine gun fire. He dived down close to the ground to attack machine gun nests, a tactic of ground support from the air little known or used at the time. It is impossible to know how many lives he saved. His machine was hit, caught fire and crashed in the middle of no-man's land. He suffered heavy burns to over half his body and to his face. After fighting his way clear of the wreckage, he crossed no man's land under artillery fire to return to the allied lines. On the way he came across two British soldiers. One was badly wounded. The other was dead. The Germans chose that time to make a gas attack. He placed the dead man's gas mask on his burned face and carried the wounded man on his back under fire, scrambling from shell hole to shell hole to stay clear of German troops until they made it back to friendly lines. When he finally got to hospital, in addition to the burns the doctors found bullet and shrapnel wounds and gas damage to his lungs and eyes. He came very close to being blinded and carried those scars to the end of his life."

Jamie rubbed the water out of his eyes. He watched the minister take another deep breath before he continued.

"The citations speak of his courage, but Captain Wood was also a man of great compassion. He found a small child whose family had been killed and was suffering from shell shock. He made certain the child got proper care and became a father to her. Unfortunately before adoption proceedings could be completed the child wandered into the wrong place and was killed by so-called 'friendly fire'.

Captain Wood endured pain and tragedy, and bore it with quiet dignity without complaint. He was a rare individual, a brave,

534

kind and gentle man. I wish there were more like him in this world. I wish I had had the honor of meeting him. He was admired and loved by his men, his comrades in arms, his friends and by his family. The world is much poorer for his passing and heaven, unless I am sadly mistaken, is very much richer. And now let us pray for the soul of Captain Sabastian Oliver Wood."

Jamie did not hear the minister's prayer. He was too busy with his own. Sabastian had once told him silent prayers were the only ones that counted because they were just between the person and God. So now Jamie prayed silent with everything he had.

'God, I know I don't talk to you much. For that I'm sorry, but that also means I don't ask you for much. That's gotta count for something. I know it probably don't mean a lot comin' from me, but I do want to put in my two cents that you take him up there with you. Seems to me he's seen enough fire and hell. So give him a hand up, if you would please? I know I'm no saint but I'm askin' just the same.' Jamie opened his eyes and looked at the coffin.

The graveside was very quiet. Jamie hung back on the edge of the gathering by himself. He leaned against a large gravestone, not wanting to talk. A single eagle soared in lazy circles against a clear blue sky, high above the trees. No one spoke except for the new minister as he led the last prayer in hushed tones.

When the service ended Jamie watched Sabastian's sister Clara take slow careful steps away from the grave toward her car. She held a handkerchief to her face and her head high.

His eyes were drawn to a small group of men unfamiliar to him who had hard tired eyes and who stood back as well. After most folks had drifted away, these men moved quietly forward to stand in line at the edge of the grave.

Jamie stood very still, hardly daring to breathe.

One of them wrung his hands behind his back, bounced his head and hissed under his breath "Goddamn it. Goddamn it all to hell!" before he turned and stalked away. The second and third stood without a word, hats in hand, granite faces clenched before they too walked away. The next was a short wiry man with bow legs and an odd little flat cap. He slid it off his bald pate, slapped the hat against his leg and spoke in an accent Jamie could hardly understand. "Ah shoor ahm sorry, sur. Sorry, to be sure." He slapped the hat again, set the little cap on his head and turned away.

The last man was tall and as he walked stiff-legged with a cane, the angles of his body poked sharply against the material of his suit. "So sorry, old man." When this man turned, he looked at Jamie straight with clear light blue eyes, sadly smiled and walked away.

Jamie stepped forward and stared down at the coffin in the grave with the handfuls of dirt strewn on top. A half smile came to him and he spoke under his breath. "I've got one more trick up my sleeve, sir. I think you'll like it. I hope I can make you laugh just one more time."

When Jamie turned around his father was waiting. "Ready to go?"

Ned stood behind his father, still silent, still there.

Jamie felt wind in his hair and looked up at the sky for the eagle. It now flew high above the clouds to the west and Jamie waited until it was lost aview. He looked back at his father and nodded, not trusting his voice.

Chapter 90

The Trick is Built

After Saturday midday dinner, Jamie and Ned slipped out of the house and ran for the mill, feet thumping on the thick pine needle trail through the woods. They cut through to the backwoods path to the rear gate because the front was locked.

Unfortunately, the latest batch of lumber was drying in the kiln. James 'Little Foot' Carson, the tall black man with a crippled left foot, sat under the kiln shelter tending the firebox. They knew Little Foot knew they weren't supposed to be there after closing. Not that he would mind if he knew what they were doing, Little Foot didn't care for Eueas at all. But Jamie and Ned had learned from the Nosy Norris trick. Nobody could know they did it.

As Jamie peered around the edge of the gate he heard Ned hiss behind him. "Try to keep your feet quiet, will ya?"

Jamie bit down on his tongue and watched Little Foot move about in the shadows underneath the kiln firebox shelter. They just had to make it though no-mans-land between the gate and the tall stacks of lumber.

Little Foot wore overalls but no shirt. He slowly pulled on his gloves, grabbed a length of wood and banged open the latch of the cast iron firebox door. Then he stuck the wood in the door handle loop and swung the door open on squealing hinges. In the flaring light from the firebox his skin gleamed like high polished ebony. The tip of his cigarette flared as he took one last drag, tossed the butt into the flames and bent to the task of feeding the fire.

With the iron clatter and roar of the fire covering their footsteps, Jamie waved Ned to follow, took one step and a branch snapped-cracked under his foot. Ned ghosted past him to safety behind the lumber stack without a sound. He followed as fast as he could tip-toe, his heart in his throat.

They skirted the smooth brown sawdust piles, slipped past the saw and engine shed. During the day, the engine shattered the air, wide leather belt squealing and creaking. Now the cold dark metal mass bore silent witness as they padded up to the trash bins at the back of the office cabin.

Ned slid his hat back on his head. "All right, now exactly how we gonna do this?"

Jamie turned to stare. "Hell, I don't know. You said Cyrus showed you. How did he do it?"

"He just showed me how. He dragged it in front of me with a heavy piece of thread just as I was coming up to it."

"Well, what did he use for the snake?"

"Dark brown piece of hemp about a half inch round. Smelled like pine tar."

"Dammit." Jamie searched his mind for a way to make a snake. "Let's see what we have to work with." He started digging in the trash cans for materials.

"I did lift some heavy thread from your mother's sewing box to drag it with."

"Good thinking, that's a start."

Trash cans can be treasure chests. Jamie found a holed pair of long black dress socks, a few worn out cleaning rags and, best of all, a big tangled ball of black mail twine. He smiled as the image formed in his head.

There is a knot used in logging called a timber hitch. It is a series of loops tied along a log with a single rope used to drag it along the ground. Jamie filled the socks with slender bits of rag, tied them together and wrapped them with two timber hitches with the black string. He tightened the timber hitch on one side more than the other so the snake would curl just a little. It made a reasonable facsimile of a good-sized black snake if the light was dim.

"I got another question."

Jamie's heart sank. He had just begun to feel good and was not in the mood for another question. "What now?"

Ned sat on the ground crossed-legged. "It's no good if we just scare Eueas. Everybody else has to see it too."

"Yeah, so how are we going to get everybody to see it and not be seen ourselves?"

Ned nodded.

"Damn good question." Jamie chewed his lip. "The only time they're all together at the same time is when they get off work, right?"

"Yeah."

"We'll have to do it in the evening when everybody's coming out together. The dirt road from the mill has mud holes all over it, so we coil the snake up in one of those and lead the string out into the spreading cedars on the side of the road. Those should be good cover for us, don't you think?"

Ned smiled. "Should be. It'll be after dusk, so the light should hide the string, especially if we sprinkle dirt over it. That should work."

Jamie could not help but grin back. "Let's set it up tomorrow."

"We need to practice."

Jamie nodded. "No time like the present. Let's go."

All they had to do was to sneak past Little Foot again.

Years ago, James Carson had made a mistake. He had tried to kick at a log and shoved his foot right into the path of the saw blade. It was only due to the kindness of Mrs. Garrath and the attention of Doc Voyce that he had any foot at all. Extreme pain makes some folks see God, but in Little Foot the screaming had driven the Almighty from his soul and opened the cage of the beast. That's why he liked the kiln. The kiln was also a beast, a beast of fire, a beast that did not rest for day or night nor weekend and Little Foot reveled in the excuse to keep away from church. Here he was his own man and controlled the blaze of the furnace as if he were the fire god himself. He knew he did it well.

The boys did not see the smile on Little-Foot's face as he created more noise to let them pass out the back gate. After he thought they'd gone he sat on his stool and reached into the front pocket of his overalls for cigarette fixin's and a match.

"One day," he whispered to himself, "I gotta teach those boys to move quiet."

He tapped the tobacco into a thin fold of cigarette paper and a rough white cylinder rolled up in his nimble hands. His eyes flicked up from beneath the brim of his sweat-stained fedora toward the dry crack of a twig crunched underfoot. The smile gradually faded as he considered where they were and where he was. His lips formed a slight set around the wrinkled paper of the cigarette and he struck a match.

"No." The match flared through his cupped hands and the cigarette tip glowed in the shadows. The smoke curled briefly around his head. "I don't gotta teach them nothin'."

Chapter 91
Mixed Hearts

Jamie slumped in the back seat of the car with his head leaned back. It rasped against his grain to wear Sunday-go-to-meeting clothes for two days in a row. It added to his already dark heart. Ned stared out the window on the other side. Gloria sat between them and was uncharacteristically quiet, though she turned and twisted like an itchy cat that wouldn't settle. He listened idly to his parents in the front seat.

"I don't know but what we'll keep that cross Mr. Parson made. It's clean and classic, not like that old twisted brass Cramphorne thing."

"And it's made of wood."

"Well, yes." Jamie's father laughed and nodded as he downshifted to turn into the churchyard. "The amazing part is he knocked the thing out in less than a day. And that was in the middle of all the work he did in the rectory. Our Mr. Parson is a working man, Honey."

"Anne seems pretty nice too. She's an orphan, did you know that? Verna, Mrs. Lily and the Widow Morrison have all taken her under their collective wings."

"That speaks well for her." Jamie's father pulled the park brake to a firm ratchet click, then turned off the engine. "Those hens don't take to just anybody. I'm feelin' pretty good about this."

"It is a relief not to dread church, isn't it?"

Jamie's father opened his door with a creak. "All right, folks. Let's go."

Jamie and Ned rolled out of their respective doors. Jamie helped Gloria out and handed her hand to his mother. He and Ned trailed behind on their way across the grass.

Ned gave him a gentle elbow and a chuckled whisper. "I can't wait till tomorrow."

As Jamie glanced at Ned dance-walking with hands in pockets, he felt upside down. When his heart had been light, he had dreaded church because of Cramphorne. Now, with the new minister, the place was light and his heart was weighted with hurt and anger to the point of mean. It was the reverse reason, but he still felt shadows walking in the church door.

He could not meet Reverend Parson's eyes as he shook his hand on the way in. He could not help glancing at the empty pew in the back where Sabastian used to sit. Jamie slid in with his family into their usual pew.

He lost the next little while thinking about Sabastian. When he raised his head to look around, everyone was quiet, waiting for the new minister to speak. Jamie looked up him. He looked taller up there in the pulpit than he had seemed yesterday.

The new minister straightened his tie.

"Good morning, everyone. Thank you for coming. I know some of you will be relieved to hear I do not believe in long drawn-out sermons. I like to say what I came to say and move on. But before I start, I do want to say thank you. Thank you for being so nice to me and my wife and I also thank you on behalf of our child that can't speak for herself, as she hasn't been born yet. From the folks I've met here so far, I believe I'm going to like this place. I can tell you what else I believe." He raised his arms to either side. "Join me, would you? Let's all rise, join hands, and let the Lord know what we believe as we say the Apostle's Creed."

Boots and shoes scraped against the hard wood floor and voices rough and sweet shared and chanted the old words and the bond was affirmed.

The shuffle and shift of boots and clothes repeated as everyone sat, then the air was filled with the sound of funeral home fans. Jamie looked up again at the new minister and felt different air in the church now that Cramphorne was gone.

"My name is Tom Parson. I think it's in the church bulletin this morning, but I still wanted to introduce myself to those I have not met, and to say how happy my wife and I are to be here. We greatly appreciate all your kindness. For us, being here is a kind of miracle. It's very new, and we hope our work and effort will not disappoint. My Midwestern accent may seem a little strange to your ears. I hope you'll get used to that. But where I come from it is customary to bring a gift when you go to the house of a friend. The first gift I bring you is hanging on the wall back there. I hope you like it. The second gift is one you already possess. That gift is the word of God. They are not my words any more than the cross on the wall is mine. I may have taken the wood and put a saw and a couple of chisels to it, but the cross and what it means is far beyond that. It represents the greatest gift that ever was, that is, and can be. I suppose in that sense it is mine. It is mine as it is yours, for you and I have been given together the gift of the grace of God. All we must do to receive this gift is reach out and embrace it, reach out and receive. It's there. It's hanging there waiting for us. It is our choice whether we take it. I don't know about everyone, but I need it. I need it as I need my life. I need to live in a state of grace because if I don't there's something missing inside. I don't think I'm allowed to live in that state of grace out of any natural innate goodness on my part. Oh no. I'm far too human, far too many flaws, far too many things gone wrong. You talk about feet of clay, well ..." he held one very large foot up to one side of the pulpit so everyone could see, "Let's just say I need to be a little extra careful where I put these boys down, 'cause as big as they are, if I don't the probabilities are pretty high they're going to find something in a pasture a little less than pleasant."

A little chuckle ran across the farmers in the congregation.

"Yes, I have to be careful where I put these clodhoppers because if I don't I'm gonna trip and fall. I'm only human. It's a good thing that gift is there to hold me up. I figure, as far as the Lord is concerned, it's my job to do my earnest best that I can to be worthy of that gift. I know I never fully will be. There's only one man who ever lived on this green earth that was and the folks around killed him for it. And what did that man do in return? Gave us a present. The present of grace, the present of forgiveness for the sin of his death and everything else, the gift of undeserved love. You know that release of tension in your shoulders when you know something you did has been forgiven? Your spouse or your parent has let you move on? There's this little feeling of spring, a little feeling like a brand new flower blooming and you can breathe

543

again. That's a good feeling to have. So our verse today is John, chapter twenty, verse twenty-three, 'Whosoever sins ye forgive, they are forgiven unto them: whosoever sins ye retain, they are retained.' We know what it means. There are times when it is near impossible to forgive someone for what they've done. Some of the toughest are the ones repeated, like the cap on the toothpaste or tracking dirt in the house. But there is a deeper meaning. Forgiveness is not to be extended just to your neighbor or your spouse or your child. It also means we need to forgive ourselves. We all have done things we are ashamed of, in one fashion or another. Whether it was yelling at someone that didn't deserve it, to making a decision that was picking among evils and still feeling guilty about it because it caused pain, or not letting go of something that was over and done with years ago, there are things we have done in our lives that we are and should be ashamed of. There are two keys to opening that door to release the pain in our hearts. The first key is to make a sincere resolution to not do it again. Don't wait for New Year's when you're eating your black eye peas and drinking cider. Do it now. The second key is harder. That key is forgiving yourself. You see, if you are truly repentant and ask him, Jesus will oblige and forgive you. If he forgives you, how can it not be right for you to forgive yourself? When that happens, you can look the world in the eye again. When that happens, you can walk straight and strong. When that happens, all will be right in the eyes and the hands of God. And to that end, let us stand and sing hymn 464, Rock of Ages."

The pews creaked and the sliding shuffle of feet surrounded Jamie as he stood and reached for the hymnal. He tried to sing, but his voice was undependable, a cough stuck in his throat. For once in his short life, a sermon actually applied. The thing was that even with the sermon telling him what he should do, he just couldn't let it go. He knew it was sin to wish someone ill, but even here trying to sing a hymn of forgiveness in the Lord's house, Jamie could not cast off the driving desire to see Eueas Canfield bleed.

Chapter 92

The Trick is Played

Jamie trotted to the side of the road in a stooping run, trailing string behind him. He fed the string to Ned through the branches of the low spreading cedar at the edge of the ditch, then ran around to the back of the cedar and crawled through to where Ned lay hunkered down, string in hand, waiting to bring the coiled snake to life.

They didn't have to wait long.

First they heard the sounds of laughter just a bit too loud, companion to the talk of rough men concerning women. Tongues wagged hard, trying to blow down house-of-cards stories while building their own in the teeth of a hurricane of jeers.

These men were the backbone of the mill. They were hard men with hard hands working from "can't see to can't see." Hard humor helped them along.

Jamie and Ned had not yet been initiated into these mysteries, not that they hadn't tried to listen in. They almost forgot to pull the string, so hard were they trying to pull their eardrums tight to listen. As the men approached the bend in the road they quieted somewhat. They strolled along, gravel quietly crunching underfoot.

Eueas dragged his leg as usual, the leg that kept him from heavy work, the leg that had gotten him his job. He leaned on his wooden stockman's cane, walking apart from the others.

Jamie crouched low, hand on Ned's shoulder. Ned peered through the thick branches, lightly rubbing the string between his fingers. They sat in electric anticipation, afraid to stir a twitching muscle.

The trick worked better than they could have imagined.

When the men were almost on top of the make-believe snake , Jamie squeezed Ned's shoulder. Ned pulled, jerking and tugging like he was playing a fish. When the men saw the twisting curl slide across the road they scattered in a human explosion.

Crazy Charlie yelped and jumped straight up in the air. Snow moved faster than they thought the old man could. Jamie and Ned beat on each other to stop snickering before they saw the wonder that froze the laughter on their lips. Jamie gripped the snake in his hands.

Eueas howled and dashed like a sprinter past the others and came to rest panting at a distance, his cane dropped in the dirt and his limp right along with it.

Snow was the first to notice the cane was no longer in Eueas' hand. His voice split the air.

"Hey Eueas, where's your cane?" Snow stood, eyebrows drawing his head forward, the other hand pointing one bony finger where Eueas' bad leg was now holding him up as straight and as strong as could be.

All heads swiveled at the whip crack of Snow's voice. Their eyes drilled into Eueas, who slowly sank to sit on the ground under the gaze of his no-longer-fooled companions.

"I don' feel so good."

Jamie twisted the snake and felt his mouth almost water at the prospect of Eueas pounded into the dirt.

Snow's hands rested in fists on his hips. He squared off his shoulders and his lip pushed forward to join his eyebrows pointing at the man.

"I'll just bet you 'don'. Humph." His gaze pinned Eueas to the ground. "An I went and told them boys to quit lyin' in front of all everbody. They was tellin' the truth when they said you kicked they dog, didn't they? They been tellin' truth about you the whole time."

Eueas looked at the ground.

"Thought so." Snow spat a stream of tobacco juice that spattered on the dusty earth. "Boy, you ain't worth the dirt you sittin' on."

Marshall plucked Eueas' cane from the ground, hefted it in one massive hand by the iron tip.

Eueas frowned and stared at the ground with half-closed eyes. His lip curled in anger, but his eyes flicked from the dust in front of him to the sticky creak of his cane gripped in Marshall's hand. Jamie recalled Marshall's quiet rage in the engine shed and how Marshall had lost everything, including his wife, to betrayal, to lies.

Ned whispered. "They're remembering."

It was true. Jamie could smell the ugly silent stares of the men standing around Eueas. Each remembered when Eueas had begged off, pleading his leg whenever there was heavy work, particularly if it was dangerous. They remembered the accident and Caleb laid up unable to work, unable to feed his family.

Marshall walked slowly up to Eueas. "You woulda let little Jamie and Caleb die, wouldn't you?" Before anyone could move to stop it the cane in his hand whipped back. Eueas bent his head away, but not fast enough to avoid the cane crack across his ear. Eueas' hat went flying as the wood bit into his ear and ripped open his scalp. Blood gushed from the wound.

Jamie's stomach heaved up to the back of his throat and gagged him.

Eueas rolled over on the ground, eyes wide, his mouth scraped gasps and whimpering cries, and blood streamed down the side of his face. He clawed at the ground, his eyes scanning the dirt like an animal scrambling for a hole to hide. "It won't my fault! It was an accident!"

Marshall nodded slowly, his mouth drawn in a tight grim line across his face. "That's as may be. But you woulda let Caleb and little Jamie die just 'cause you couldn't tell the truth."

The second blow thumped into the back of Eueas' skull and hammered his face into the dirt. Eueas groaned and lifted his head. Blood streamed from his nose and covered his mouth.

Jamie's chest closed until he couldn't breathe.

Ned's whisper was rough. "I'm not sure we should be seeing this. I'm not sure I want to."

Jamie wasn't sure either. A moment before he had wanted to see Eueas bleed more than anything in the world. Now the reality of blood lust hit him. Nowhere in a single eye in the circle of men that surrounded Eueas was there a feather of pity.

Snow frowned down at Eueas, his face hard. "Marshall 'bout to beat you to shit. Bet you so scared you 'bout to throw up. Ain't that right?'

Eueas gasped, wiped the dripping blood with the back of his grimy hand and kept his eyes on the dirt in front of his face.

"Thought so. You don't know what it is to stand up to somebody, do you? Never had to do it 'cause you never had the backbone of a straight man."

Snow spit in the dirt beside Eueas, then looked up and scanned the group of glaring faces. He shook his head. "He ain't worth it, fellas."

It took a long beat for his words to sink in past their anger.

"Right now you got more to lose than he has. Think about Lester, you don't want the law here. Think about it."

One at a time, the faces drifted to Snow, not wanting to hear the voice of reason.

"There's a drink waitin' for all ya'll at my house that's a lot more important than him. Go on, I'll take care of this. Tell the missus to break out the big mason jar."

Marshall hefted the cane, frowned at the blood on the wood, then twirled it in his hand. He looked at Eueas. "Mr. Snow here is a wise man and I thank him most kindly. But let me tell you one thing Mr. Canfield, let me tell you this." He held the cane by the iron foot and shook it in the air like a club. "This here cane is mine now. I know how to use it and I know what you deserve. You remember that."

Snow nodded, slowly. His voice was so soft Jamie could hardly hear it. "Thank you, Mr. Marshall. You are a better man than I." He nodded toward his house up the road, the yellow lamp lights burning in the distant windows. "I expect you need to set a spell. I'll be on directly. Go on now."

Marshall nodded once, then turned his head back down to Eueas. His eyes latched to the man sprawled on the ground until he stepped past, then snapped straight ahead to stare toward the end of the road, shoulders stiff, feet plodding the ground.

One by one, the men filed off, finally leaving Snow and Eueas, two figures stone still, thrown into relief in the darkening dust.

As Snow watched the men walk away, their feet grinding the gravel, he rubbed his chin then tugged the brim of his hat. He pulled smoke fixings out of his overalls pocket. Jamie heard the paper quietly crackle as Snow calmly rolled a cigarette while Eueas sniffed and bled.

Snow's voice was low and quiet and matter-of-fact. "Whether you know or not, you just been given a chance. A chance to live honest and stand up to life like a man. It ain't easy, but there it is." He scratched a match and the flare lit his face as he held the flame to his cigarette. "So, either you come to work tomorrow early, ready to keep your trap shut and work harder than you ever worked before or don't you come back at all. If not, best you leave now while you still got a skin."

Snow spat on the ground, turned his back and walked away in his rolling, bow-legged gait. The fire tip of the cigarette glowed bright then faded as he strode away.

Eueas lifted his head from the ground, rolled to a sitting position, slowly pulled his hat from the ground and slapped it across his knee. He pulled a bandana from his back pocket, wiped the blood from his face, then pressed it to his scalp. He looked toward the receding figures, then back down to the dirt, as if deciding which to embrace.

He slowly got to his hands and knees, then straightened till he was kneeling, bareheaded to the sky. He drew one foot up, placed both hands on one knee and pushed himself to his feet. He looked up the long road then walked, very slowly, after Snow's diminishing form. He sometimes limped slightly, sometimes not, like his body no longer knew what it was like to walk straight and he had to remind it with every step.

Jamie and Ned watched him until he was lost in the growing gray light of the moon shining through pine trees lining the road.

They both knew, grown ups being grown ups, that they would never hear any of this. They would never hear either apology or explanation about Toby or anything else. The only evidence would be Eueas bandaged and walking without a cane, maybe a bit quieter.

But Jamie and Ned knew. And that was enough.

They never told a soul.

Chapter 93
Aftermath Part Deux

As a rule, Grant Garrath did not think it his business when he saw a worker come into the mill the worse for wear. As long as they were sober and able to work, he figured it none of his concern. But when Eueas came in this morning he was different. Very different. His nose was misshapen, he had two black eyes and a bandage wrapped around his head that covered one ear. But the thing that really twisted Grant's head to one side was the fact Eueas was without his cane.

"Morning, Eueas."

"Morning, Mr. Garrath."

Grant looked closely at the bandage, then gazed straight into Eueas' eyes to be certain his pupils were the same size. "What happened to you?"

"Oh, I fell down on the road last night, landed funny. My own fault."

"No cane?"

Eueas nodded once. "It was the fall that done it. Found out I don't need it no more."

Grant saw something that stopped his next question about how he had fallen. Normally Eueas' eyes darted around like they were afraid to light on anything and stay there. Today they were steady. The fear was there, but in the open like a burst blister with raw flesh in open air, naked and calm.

Grant rubbed his chin. "How's the leg? You feel strong enough to help the Viking put up new timbers on the loading platform?"

"Oh yeah."

"All right then." Grant waved Harald Josefson over to them. "Harald? Here's you a helper for the platform."

Harald Josefson was called 'The Viking', not only because he was from Norway. He was tall, bearded, all broad shoulders, and spun the iron pry bar in his hand like a twig. "Eueas, you up to work? I gotta say you don't look you got good feeling in your head."

Eueas pulled his hat down and winced. "Do my best."

Harald nodded. "The first thing we got to do is chop flats in the timbers where they sit on top of the posts, then drill holes. After that ...."

The two walked away toward the sawing shed, all contradiction. Harald was so tall he had to lean over to talk to Eueas. Eueas was so short he had to trot along like a Trojan to keep up with Harald's long strides and tried to keep his hat from falling off.

Grant chewed his lip, thought of the wisdom of not asking too many questions and went back to work.

Jamie saw them coming toward the saw. Snow had grabbed him first thing that morning to grease and adjust engine linkage and that put him in a perfect position to watch. He tried to keep his eyes on his work, but Eueas acted so different it was hard to do.

Harald had taken the previous afternoon off to go see Caleb, so he had not seen Eueas beaten the night before, but he worked him with a will. Harald was a hard worker and took pride on how much he could do in a day so, unbeknownst to him, he did exactly what the other men wanted done, i.e. to work Eueas half to death without any of them actually having to work with him.

Eventually though, serious lifting was required when the timber beams had to be placed on top of the thick vertical piling and Snow called Marshall over to help. A couple of times during this work, Marshall shouldered Eueas to the ground, and finally, when they were moving one of the last into place, let one drop on Eueas' hand.

Jamie felt the impact when the timber hit the ground. Snow left Jamie at the engine at a half run.

Eueas lay in the dirt, his hand pinned beneath the timber. Marshall stood over him with his head cocked to one side, listening. Eueas never cried out, not a whimper, but his face was white, screwed up tight and he breathed hard.

Snow bent down to the timber. "Let's get this thing up."

Marshall didn't move.

Jamie saw Snow walk right to Marshall and stick his chin up. "I said get that thing off him."

Marshall loomed over Snow but the effect that intimidated Jamie even from a distance just rolled right off Snow. The contest of wills ended with Snow repeating himself so softly Jamie could hardly hear.

"I said … get it … off him."

Marshall leaned down and lifted the timber up while Eueas slid his hand out from underneath. As soon as Eueas' hand was clear he dropped it. The timber thudded to the ground.

Eueas sat grasping one hand with the other and held his breath in between deep gasps. "Thank yuh."

"Marshall, why don't you go help out the draggin' crew?" Snow tugged on his hat brim. "They's not getting near enough logs to keep the saw running tomorrow even if we do get this done t'day."

Marshall glared with no sympathy at Eueas, who still held his wrist and his tongue and looked at the ground.

"Marshall." Snow said in a somewhat louder voice.

Marshall lifted his head to Snow with a face like basalt.

Snow met him eye for eye. "I thank you."

Marshall took a deep sniff and gave one slow nod. He turned away and stalked off down the logging road.

Snow turned back toward Eueas.

"You hurt?"

Eueas held his wrist and flexed his fingers. His jaw muscles worked. "It'll do."

Snow looked at Eueas for a moment then frowned a smile. "Let's get this done."

With Snow directing they soon had the timbers in place and Snow set Eueas to drilling and setting drift bolts to secure the timbers to the pilings. Then he walked back to Jamie. Of course Jamie hadn't gotten any greasing done. He'd been too busy watching the drama outside.

"You be careful there. You get grease all over, you gonna have your mama all over me when she gets to washing clothes."

Jamie nodded toward Eueas. "He all right?"

Snow's mouth tightened. "I think so, the ground was pretty soft underneath. But even if he ain't, I don't think he's gonna admit it now."

Jamie didn't know how to ask, but felt he had to know. "He don't have his cane."

One corner of Snow's mouth drew up as he watched Eueas working on the bolts. "No, he don't. And you ain't asked once what might a happened."

Jamie kept his eyes very carefully on the linkage he was cleaning and greasing.

Snow gave a humph. "Let's just say there comes a time in every man's life when he comes across his snake in the grass." Jamie felt Snow's steady gaze burn at him. "Eueas met his. But you wouldn't know anything about that, would you?"

Jamie looked at the ground, wondering how in the world Snow knew and what he knew. His throat closed up. He could not have said anything if his life depended on it.

Then he felt Snow's hand on his shoulder. "Don't fret on it none. The man been done a favor, whether he realizes it or not. Just remember one thing."

Jamie looked up. Snow's eyes were both serious and kind. "Don't ever let on. Some things are just better let be. Understand?"

As Jamie nodded he thought of Sabastian giving the very same advice and tears flushed to his eyes.

Snow pushed his lips up and nodded. "All right, let's get this thing ready to run. We got logs to cut tomorrow and I got to get work out of you whilst I can, while I gotcha."

"Huh? What are you talking about?"

"You don't know? You don't got too much longer to work here. Another week or two maybe and that's it. You and Ned both. Didn't you daddy tell you?"

Jamie shook his head. "Must have slipped his mind."

"That's likely. Engine ain't gonna be same without you."

"Damndest thing happened today." Jamie's father spooned creamed corn onto his plate at the supper table. "Right before quittin' time, Eueas Canfield gave away his week's pay to Caleb."

Jamie almost choked on his beans and looked at Ned. Ned calmly kept his eyes down as he cut his meatloaf.

"What, all of it?" His mother stared at his father. "What's he going to live on for a week?"

"The very thing I asked him. He said he'd get along all right and asked me again just take it to him. I said I would, he said 'thank you' and walked out. Damndest thing I ever saw."

"What in the world? Are we talking about that same Eueas?"

His father nodded. "Only something's happened to that man. Everybody else is happy as a holiday but him and he's the one who has the use of his leg back."

"He can walk now too?"

"That's right. Don't even carry his cane." His father laughed. "It don't' make any sense, but it's kinda like when corn starts to grow better than you thought it would, you don't dig down to the root to find out why cause you don't want to ruin a good thing."

His mother looked over at Jamie with questions in her eyes.

Jamie shrugged. "Don't look at me."

His mother turned back to his father and Jamie breathed an inner sigh. "Is Mr. Frasier going to be all right?"

"Doc said he'll be up and about in a couple of days. Got a mild concussion but he'll be all right. The money from Eueas will tide them over till he can come back." His father shook his head and glanced over at Jamie as he cut the meat on his plate. "I'm just curious as to what happened to the man. It's probably wise to leave well enough alone, but it's just a damn mystery."

Chapter 94
Set Free

"Hey, Jamie."

Jamie wiped grease from his hand with a rag and turned to Ned's voice from the doorway of the engine shed. Ned grinned big. Toby's head appeared down at Ned's knees, panting dripping laughs.

"What?"

"We got a rabbit."

"No joke?"

"The trap is sprung. I didn't get the chance to look close, but something's in there and it doesn't stink like polecat."

Jamie smiled. "Help me clean up and we'll go see."

Two sets of hands and fevered anticipation made cleanup go very quickly. When they returned the wrenches to the cabin, Jamie's father was in deep conversation with Snow and Little Foot, so they didn't wait for anyone to set them free. They set off out the gate at a trot.

As Ned had said, the trap door was shut. Toby sniffed at the box.

"Move over, boy. Let's see what we got." Jamie kneeled by the trap and lifted the small flap of leather over the bit of screen in the window and peered in. Wide black eyes stared back.

They had one. They had an honest-to-god rabbit.

Jamie laughed out loud. "Finally!" He extended his hand and Ned shook it.

"Now what are we supposed to do with it?"

Jamie stopped at the question. He bent and lifted the little flap again. The rabbit was shaking. "Snow told me the best thing to do first is to grab its hind legs and bash its head against a tree to kill it. It's gotta be done fast and real hard so it don't feel but one quick pain. Then you cut its throat to get the blood out of it and then gut it quick as you can. Not so much in the winter when it's cold, but in this heat it's real important or the meat will go bad. You got a knife?"

As Jamie talked what Snow had told him, the less inclined he was to do it. When he looked at Ned he didn't see any real enthusiasm there either.

"Got one Cyrus gave me." Ned's words were quiet. "But it seems like an awful lot of trouble."

"Yeah. Awful lot."

Jamie reached out his hand and rested it on the door of the trap. He looked up at Ned, who nodded and took hold of Toby's collar.

Jamie lifted the door, blocked it up and sat back. Even Toby sat very still. The quivering nose stuck out the doorway, then the head and then with a bound of brown and gray fur, it was gone.

Ned reached over and lowered the door. "Let's go home. Got a date with Elspeth." At the name Toby gave a little woof. Ned reached to pet him. "Don't you run her like you did last time, boy. Had the devil getting her calmed down enough to milk."

Jamie lifted his hand to Ned to be helped up. Ned took it and pulled him up off the ground. "I thought you said her name was Gramma."

Ned shook his head. "When I thought about it, it just didn't seem right. A date with Gramma?" He shrugged. "Yuck. So it's back to Elspeth. Maybe just call her 'Ellie'."

"She just looks more like a Gramma though …."

Jamie and Ned strolled toward home. Toby trotted lazy circles around them through golden beams of evening light that filtered through towering pines.

Chapter 95

Roughshod Dawn

The very next morning Gil Custis jammed the stickshift and ground the gears of his truck. He needed help at the store; the shelves were in chaos because of the back to school trade, though there was never as much of it as he would like. He drove to Garrath's Mill to pick up his one and only son. Amy had not let him hire because, as she said, 'You already have Ned. He'll do a better job of than anyone else. And besides, I don't know about you, but I'd like my son back in my house.' With that she had lifted her head and stepped away, leaving him at the store counter to sputter his way through the next customer.

That had been yesterday and still not another word out of her. His only words to her that morning had been 'I've got some business. Mind the store.'

She had just stood there with crossed arms glancing from his face to his feet and back with raised eyebrows. He was not about to explain himself to her, not now and he was mad enough to think maybe not ever. Yeah. Maybe not ever. The thing that made him the maddest was knowing the damn woman was right. He shifted his grip on the steering wheel and tried to downshift before he hit the dirt road to Grant's mill. Why anyone would want to live and work so far out in the woods was beyond him. Maybe it would be beyond Ned too. Maybe Ned would be more pliable after his little stay in the backwoods.

The gears resisted loudly as they always did when he downshifted. Damn truck. He had taken to calling it 'damn-shifting', but only to himself. Amy didn't take with that kind of language. The damn salesman had told him it was the finest engine and transmission on the market. 'Best made today.' he'd said. Damn the man. These gears ground like a stone crusher ever since he'd had the damn truck, no matter how hard he's shoved on the damn gearshift. Damn.

He turned into the mill yard and pulled to a stop in front of the cabin. He had to admit the place was looking pretty good, pretty busy, pretty prosperous. All the buildings were whitewashed and the sawmill screamed its raucous ring, punctuated by deep explosions of the engine.

He stepped out of the truck and walked in. Grant sat behind his desk working on columns of figures.

"Mornin', Grant."

Grant looked up, leaned back in his wooden swivel chair and dropped his pencil to the desktop. "Hello Gil. Sit down," He motioned to a chair. "What can I do for you? Need lumber? You could've just used the phone."

Gil sat, hands on his knees. "No, nothing like that. I need my boy back. I know it's early, but it's school time at the store."

Grant pushed his glasses up on his forehead. "He's not here right now, Gil. He's out cruising timber, marking trees for me. He's been my tree scout for a little over two weeks now, ever since the old one had to leave."

Gil could think of no response. The idea of Ned doing a man's job in the woods all by himself rattled around in his head and looked for understanding to connect with. "What's a 'tree scout'?"

"The man that records and marks trees for us to cut in the woods. He has to know what wood we need, both size and species and how much of what." Grant picked up his pencil again. "He's become quite a woodsman, Gil. School don't start for a while yet, I was counting on him for at least another week. And that was our arrangement."

Gil shook his head to the side. He did not want to endure another week of silence and cold dinners. "I gotta have him back, Grant." And suddenly the right words came into his head. "I need him."

Gil watched Grant pull a surveyor's plat over, slide his glasses down to his nose, peer at the plat and scratch his head. "It'll take at least the rest of today and tomorrow to finish the area he's marking and it's not something a body can just come in and do when you're in the middle. If you do, timber will get missed. I tell you what," he pushed his glasses back up on his forehead "Let me keep him until the weekend. Come pick him up Sunday afternoon after church. Have dinner with us, you and Amy. If you take him now you'll be leaving me in a helluva spot."

Gil thought about this. It was reasonable and would end the silence at home. Maybe. "All right."

Grant made to bring his glasses back down but stopped. "He does a good job, Gil. He's a good boy. Can I tell you something?"

Gil waited in silent assent.

Grant nodded. "You're right, Gil. It's just like you said. Ned is a little different."

"Yes?"

"Yes. And he's turning into a damn fine man. And at the risk of puttin' my three cents in where it's not wanted, I get the distinct impression he deserves better than he's been getting. And that's all I've gonna say."

Gil felt his head clench like a fist. Amy had told him he wasn't taking care of his own only son. He had just put it down to her bein' an over-protective mamma, but if this man saw something too?

He stood and carefully pushed the chair up to the table. "I'll be picking him up on Sunday. We'll drive straight down to your place after church." He turned and walked out of the office and got in his truck. He cranked it and drove away, jamming gears all the way. He would have cursed his truck again, except this time the voices in his head were so loud they drowned out the grinding.

Chapter 96

The Woodsman

Ned moved quietly, stepping lightly over fallen branches on a carpet of pine needles. The wood scout belt hung about his waist with the heavy thirty-eight revolver at his hip and he carried a clipboard in his hand. He measured a tall pine, filled in the form and slash blazed the tree. As he turned to the next tree he noticed a plastic and brass shotgun shell on the ground. He picked it up and held it to his nose to smell the cordite, then his eyes found tracks and more shells. From clear edges and depth of the print, someone heavy in new boots had been out hunting, probably yesterday and certainly no earlier than the day before. Dog tracks criss-crossed the narrow path, widespread, probably a dog not well trained, maybe still a big puppy. Apparently Mr. Garrath had been right about the hunters who came down from Raleigh. From what Ned could see they were careless, dropped cigar butts all over and, from the number of shells on the ground, couldn't hit the broadside of a barn with a broom handle. He picked up all the shell casings he could find and dropped them into his canvas bag, then listened to the roar of wind tearing through the pines. He lifted his nose to smell the clean pines. He sat with his back against a tree, closed his eyes and listened to birdsong carve accents in the air. He was still sad Cyrus had been forced to leave, but glad to have met him and held a quiet place in his heart where before there had been confused anger. He felt warm and bright and clear inside like sunlight filtering through pine boughs to the forest floor.

In later years he would try to recall this feeling with incomplete success. But at this moment, he was content.

Toby was with him, had been ever since … it felt like forever. Somehow the dog was settled, satisfied. Toby had still kept between Eueas and Ned or Jamie at the mill, but no longer tense, no longer on alert. He just swung along, his usual Toby laughing self. Now he came over, lay down and laid his head on Ned's leg.

A faint odd rustle came to his ears. He did not move, did not turn his head and saw Toby's ears lift out of the corner of his eye. Then his eye caught another movement, slow and graceful, a small doe delicately stepping her way through the woods.

Mr. Garrath had told him and Jamie this was their last day of work for the summer. He would be glad to see his mom again, but wouldn't have minded another couple of weeks at this and fishing. He knew he was a woodsman now, that he would come back. Maybe he'd start hunting, put a little meat on the table. Shouldn't be too hard to save up for a little 22 caliber Savage rifle for birds and varmints. But that was for later. Right now, he sat back with his hand on Toby's head, watched the doe slowly dance on tiptoe out of sight and listened to the wind caress the trees.

Chapter 97
Final Fishing

"Come on, it's time to get up, time's a wastin', the early bird gets the … oomph."

After Jamie pulled the pillow from his face, he slowly shook his head, hand on hips. "You helping Mom out with her 'throw' pillows now?"

Ned groaned. "I have just two things to say to you."

"What's that?"

Ned folded his hands across his stomach and looked at the ceiling. "One: You have the memory of an addle-pated settin' hen."

"How's that?"

"We don't work today."

Jamie fell back on his bed with the pillow on his lap. "I forgot." He screwed up his face and fell sideways. "Damn. And what's the other thing?"

"With all the jokes …."

"They're not jokes, they're adages. Expressions, you know …."

"I don't care what they are, you're startin' to sound like your dad."

Jamie sat up and gripped one corner of his pillow. "Ohh, you done it now."

"Yeah? Exactly what is 'it' that I 'done'?"

"Don't matter." Jamie stood and wound the pillow round and round his head. "This 'it'" and aimed it right for Ned's head.

And the pillow fight was on, thumps and laughs and near-misses. The fight was well on its way to being epic when a truce of distraction was called by his mother's two-tone morning song for breakfast.

Jamie burst into the kitchen and was greeted by the sight of neatly arranged fishing gear laid out on the table. There were two fly rods with associated tackle in a canvas shoulder bag, a cedar wood box of fly tying tools and materials, and a stack of books on fishing, history and philosophy.

"What's all this?"

His mother stirred bacon in the cast iron frying pan. "Sabastian left that for you in his will. Clara dropped them off early this morning."

Jamie felt his throat close. He touched the cork handle of one of the rods. "Why didn't she stay and say hello?"

"She was crying, Jamie."

He didn't trust his voice, so Jamie just nodded.

"Why don't you take it to your room? Get it all straightened out then after breakfast you can go fishing. How does that sound?"

With Ned's help, Jamie carried the gear into his room and laid it all out on his table and across his bed.

Ned stuffed his hands in his pockets. "I only saw him use it a couple of times. What is all this stuff?"

"Well, these are the rods, of course. These little leather bags have the reels in them. That basket thing is called a creel. That's to hold fish. And these boxes," he dug in the canvas bag, "have the flies in them."

"He taught you how to use it?"

"He let me play with it a couple of times, taught me how to tie the knots'n stuff. I actually caught a fish one time. Little pumpkinseed, too small to keep, had to throw it back."

"You'll have to be careful with it."

"Yeah. But I have to use it. He'd be upset if I didn't."

Jamie stared at the water. The rod rested light in his hand. "I didn't want it like this."

Ned looked over at Jamie. "Didn't want what like what?"

"I wanted a fly rod. I wanted to do what Sabastian did." He held the fly attached to the line but made no motion to cast. "I didn't want his. It don't feel right." He pushed the hook of the fly into the cork handle and sat down on the dock.

"Just sit there for a while. Maybe in a little bit it'll be all right after it's had time to settle on you."

Jamie looked over at his friend. Right now, in this light, in this place, Ned looked like a different person. He looked like somebody's grandfather with slow and steady hands. He watched Ned's eyes scan the lake and trees and the sky. Toby curled up halfway in between, but Jamie saw his eyes were on Ned. Funny, in all his hate of Eueas and Sabastian's death, he hadn't noticed Toby had ceased to be his dog. It was another loss, but felt right.

So Jamie listened to the plop of Ned's bobber in the water, listened to Toby pant and tried to keep from crying as he listened to Sabastian's voice in his head and cradled the rod in his hands.

Chapter 98
Letting Go

Jamie sat in church but didn't feel at all holy. He turned again to look where Sabastian had usually sat. The pew was empty, as if everyone left it alone in Sabastian's memory. Then he saw Eueas quietly enter the back of the church, hat in hand.

He elbowed Ned. "Will you look at that?"

"What?"

"That. Eueas, he's sitting in the back."

Ned craned his head around. "Goddamn, he's ... Oww."

"Ned Custis, you wait till your mother hears about you using that kind of language." Jamie's mother hissed like an old mother goose. "And in church yet. You do that again and I'll take you outside and jerk a knot in you. Now you hush like you're some kind of Christian. I just don't know what I'm going to do ...."

"Hannah." Jamie's father rumbled.

Jamie's mother strong-humphed and crossed her arms.

Jamie whispered to Ned as quietly as he could. "Sorry."

Ned shrugged one shoulder.

Jamie snuck one last glance at Eueas. The man sat in the very back, looked at no one and spoke to no one. His eyes were all shades of purple and green and yellow and his nose was still misshapen. Jamie hoped it always would be.

After the service Jamie caught sight of Eueas walking away from the church in the distance. The man still walked a little crosswise, but otherwise seemed to be all right.

567

Jamie's mother came up beside him and laid one hand on his shoulder. "There goes one lonely old man."

"He deserves to be."

"Maybe. But I would remind you there is such a thing as forgiveness."

"Do you believe him, Mom?"

"Completely? I do not know. Do I accept he may be trying to live different? It's possible."

Jamie saw dangerous ground in the next question, but plunged forward anyway. "Why do you think he's doing it?"

"What do you mean?"

Sometimes Jamie thought his mother could be fairly dense if truth be known. "I mean, why do you think he's making the change?"

"It looks like he's been pretty well beaten up."

"That don't change people."

"Don't say don't, Jamie. And you're right, it usually doesn't."

"Then why?"

Jamie's mother thought for a moment. "In my experience, if the change is real it's because they have no choice. In his case, I'd say it's because he's had enough. It's possible he's just tired of fighting, but most probably it's because he simply has nowhere else to go." She patted his shoulder. "Come on, let's go home."

Jamie wasn't entirely sure he understood, but for now he was willing to sit still about it and keep his mouth shut. He would keep Eueas' secret, set his hate aside with his fear and move on.

When Ned jumped up in the back of Gil Custis' pickup for the ride home, Toby jumped right up and sat down beside him.

Ned started to make Toby get down, but Jamie stopped him. "That's all right."

"You sure? He's your dog, ain't he?"

"He's my friend, Ned. He decided to go with you. I wouldn't be much of a friend if I made him stay, now would I?"

Ned looked into Jamie's eyes for a long moment and that moment forged lifetime friendship. "I sure do thank you."

Jamie nodded, wiped his eyes with the back of his hand. "Get goin'. You'll miss supper."

Gil Custis slung Ned's suitcase into the back. He stopped when he saw Toby and looked back at Jamie's father.

Jamie's father extended his hand to Gil to shake hands. "Fine boy you've got there."

Gil coughed as he took the hand. "He is that. Be seeing you." He pulled open the screeching door to his pickup, cranked the engine, ground the gears again and the pickup pulled out. Ned put one arm around Toby and waved with the other hand as the two bounced in the back.

All Jamie could do was just raise his hand.

As the truck rumbled away, looking smaller every minute, obscured by the dust churned up by the double back tires, Jamie could not help wiping his eyes again. As he watched, he heard the sandy crunch of his father's work boots beside him and felt light pressure of his father's hand on his shoulder.

Jamie stood very still, watching the cloud swirl up as the shrinking pickup reached the end of their lane and turned onto the main highway. He thought he could see two heads in the back above the truck sideboards before the truck faded behind trees at the big curve in the road. He could not tell which was which. Then he laughed. "If Mr. Custis got spooked by Ned knowing things, wait till he gets a load of Toby." Jamie grinned. "He's got two of them on his hands now."

"That was a fine thing you just did, Jamie, as fine as I've ever seen. That was the act of a real man. I'm proud of you."

"What?"

"You letting Toby go like that. Boy or man, that has to be the strongest thing I've ever seen done." Jamie felt his father's hand grab and rub the nape of his neck. "It means you know how to treat your friends."

"It's what you taught me, Dad."

"No."

Jamie turned to his father and saw him shake his head. When his father spoke it was in the soft voice he had heard his father use at the mill. "I don't think you got that from us. We've tried to teach you right from wrong all right, but we didn't teach you that. Truth be told, I'm not at all sure that's something that can be taught. Where you got it, a heart that strong, I cannot say. What I can say is I have never been prouder of you and I look forward to knowing you as a man."

Jamie's throat felt like it had an apple lodged in it. He just nodded and rubbed his nose with his sleeve.

His father patted his shoulder again and said in that same soft voice "It's almost suppertime. Come inside when you've a mind to."

Jamie nodded at the dirt and listened to his father's footsteps grind off toward the house. There was no one around as he walked to the base of the red oak on the far side of the yard and sat down on the big root he used for a chicken head chopping block. Odd his father had mentioned pride. He didn't feel very proud. He felt like he'd lost two friends in one fell swoop and there was nothing he could do about it. He watched his own tear puff into the dust between his feet, then wiped his eyes on his sleeve, leaned back against the rough tree trunk and watched the leaves sway and bounce in the breeze above his head. He sat like that for what felt like a very long time. Then Jamie breathed real big one time, yawned, pushed himself to his feet with hands on his knees then walked towards the home of chaos, his father talking about what was in the paper while his mother rattled dishes and Gloria complained, like usual. He eased in through the front screen door and on his way to the kitchen glanced down at the side table in the hall where his father usually dropped the mail. There was one thick envelope in an unfamiliar hand.

His mother called out from the kitchen. "Jamie, there's a letter for you on the table. You see it?"

"Yeah, Mom. Thanks." His voice trailed off as he saw the name on the return address. A star burst in his heart and stole all the air from his chest. It was from Deidre. He sat down on the stairs and opened it. The paper was tissue thin and fragrant with cinnamon. The hand was small, neat, leaned backwards and covered both sides of all the pages.

'My sweet man of the moon, I hope you can forgive me for vanishing. Papa got a line from a friend on a job on the coast building cabins on ships and boats. We had to drive like we were driven by the hounds of <u>Hades</u> (Pa says I'm not supposed to say HELL) to get there before the work dried up. We got here just in time so Pa is working on the boats again, which is what he's meant for. You'd love it here, I think. Great bowers of trees everywhere and it's cool and green in the evening. They're talking about putting me in a school like you, but there's testing to be done first to see what grade I should go in and I hate tests like death ....'

His mother sang out her evening song call to supper. Jamie ran the letter to his room and hid it where Gloria couldn't find it, washed his hands and face and went to supper.

"You ready to eat, son?"

"Yeah, Dad. I'm good." He smiled at his father. "Thanks."

Chapter 99

Tyin' up Strings

or What Some Folks Call The Epilogue

There are those who always wonder about loose ends and there are those who prefer not to know and to think the best of what might come to pass. For the latter folks, read no further, for the future is about to be revealed.

To the great joy of those who knew him well and found out about it, the Right Reverend Cramphorne was arrested for drunk driving. It seems a certain steely-eyed North Carolina State Trooper in starched gray uniform did not particularly appreciate the speed nor the manner of the right reverend's driving and pulled him over for exceeding the posted speed limit. This same trooper also most decidedly did not care for the rampant smell of whiskey when he walked up to the car. Mrs. Cramphorne was also arrested, for interfering with a uniformed officer of the law in the performance of his sworn duty. Seems she informed the officer with her habitual sensitivity of manner that the right reverend was a complete tee-totaler, that the smell of whiskey upon his noble person was the result of an awful sinner who had splashed it there and that she thought the trooper should be ashamed for abusing her Adonis. During this episode the Right Reverend contributed his usual charm. This not helping the cause, he and the missus soon found themselves in the midst of a golden opportunity to convert the heathen while incarcerated in the depths of the Silerville drunk tank. At the time of this writing they have been allowed their one phone call, that made to her brother. It remains to be seen how long her brother will allow them to continue their missionary opportunity.

Cyrus Conner, aka John Wanderwood, is now a respected holy man among his people. Seems the fellas that started the trouble by selling white lightning to Wanderwood's tribe died laughing while under the influence of massive samples of their own poison, so the case had to be dropped. John is now a free man and walking his true path.

Eueas Canfield, aka Lucas Cane, finally came to understand what end he deserved. He is at present doing his level best not to deserve it any longer. As of yet he has not fallen off the wagon, as it were, but he does have a long row to hoe and only time will tell.

Dancin' Charlie and the boys at the Whispering Waters Fish and Hunt Club are doing about the same. Their latest endeavor was to walk to the mountains. This epic journey had the same result as the Great Beach Walk.

Tom Parsons is getting along pretty well. He and his missus are settling down to the life of a quiet country preacher, though Old Man Mason still keeps the Elders' meetings pretty lively and the pending new addition to Tom's family is about to change his life in ways he never dreamed.

Ned and Toby are getting along famously, with Toby creating enough chaos in the hardware store to keep Ned's father on his toes. In so doing Toby often takes the attention of customers off of Ned, so Mr. Custis' business has no reason not to thrive on that account. If it does not thrive the way Mr. Custis wants it to, he will have to find another scapegoat besides his own only son.

Finally, Jamie and Deidre are still writing. While Jamie knows he keeps every one of her letters, written in her neat cursive hand containing little magical trinkets, what he does not know might scare him. Deidre not only keeps all his letters, but sleeps with them too, slid carefully into her pillowcase every night. It helps her sleep. Her father Seamus, on the other hand, has been up every night since he found out about it, because he does not know what to think. He remembers the determination of her mother. There is certainly something about our young southern boy that ripples her right down to her toes. And after having felt her tremble in the misty evening twilight, Jamie will never be the same. So who knows? Magic crackles between them and with a little magic, most anything can happen. Lord knows, distance and time together are usually the death of young love, but there have been notable exceptions and so our young lovers sail on in the confident hope of a miracle.